Accidental Friends

Accidental Friends

Susan Josephs

Bink Books
Bedazzled Ink Publishing Company • Fairfield, California

978-1-960373-14-4 paperback

Cover Design
by
Sapling
Studio

Bink Books
a division of
Bedazzled Ink Publishing Company
Fairfield, California
http://www.bedazzledink.com

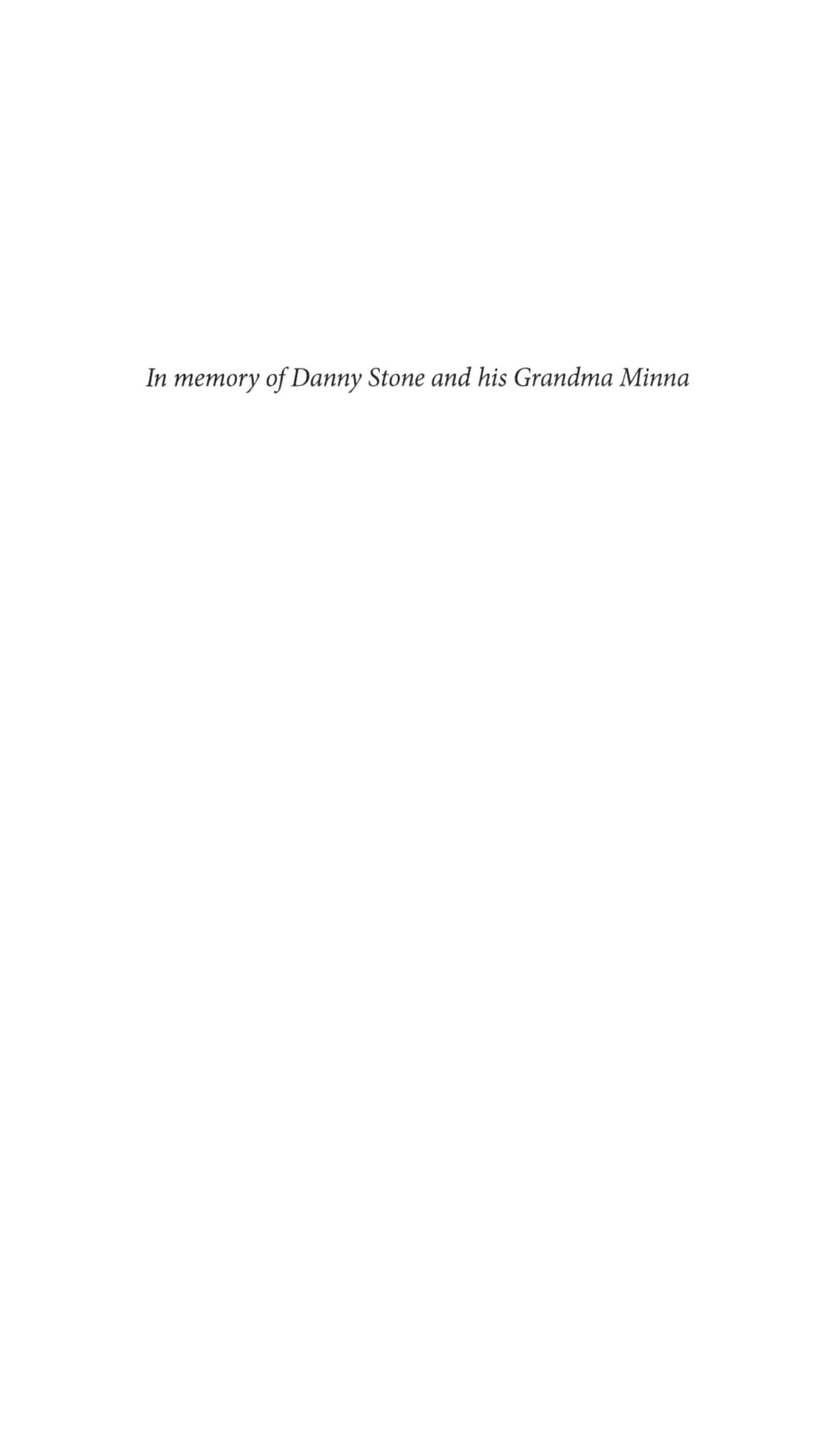

In memory of Danny Stone and his Grandma Minna

PART ONE

One

THERE'S ROSE, SITTING alone in the last row of wooden synagogue pews. She wears the same navy blue suit that she wore to her husband's funeral three days before but with a fresh white blouse. She struggles to sit as upright as possible on the slippery pew and adjusts her bifocals which were knocked askew during the process of fitting her walker into the narrow space in front of the seat next to her. At the very least, she tells herself, she can look presentable. Even axe murderers dress up for their day in court. Rose of course is no axe murderer but this doesn't stop her from feeling like one.

Rose tries to listen to the rabbi, now in the midst of a lovely eulogy. Rose knows from lovely eulogies, having heard one after another in recent years. Unofficially, she's an expert in West Los Angeles Jewish funerals. Also, she has heard this rabbi speak before. His best funeral, in her opinion, had been Vivian Goldenblatt's, when he made rhapsodic pronouncements not just about dear Vivian but an entire generation of European Jewry. *We're losing our bubbes and our zaides, the ones who changed their names at Ellis Island and those who fled the horrors of the Holocaust. One by one, they depart for other worlds, leaving a void that cannot be filled.*

She has never heard this rabbi speak about someone so young. Jeff Wasserman was only thirty-seven years old and boy oh boy did he sound like a wonderful person. A social worker who helped hundreds of people in trouble with drugs, money, mentally disturbed family members, you name it. People in need could call him at all hours of the night because he never turned off his cellular phone. He was someone who always thought about others and devoted himself to his family, friends, and fiancée.

The rabbi pauses to consult his notes and in the several second span of his silence, sobbing sounds erupt in the synagogue. Rose cringes but persists in scanning the synagogue for more information. What a lovely synagogue, she thinks. Cavernous ceilings, an imitation marble floor, stained glass reproductions of the Chagall windows, fresh white paint everywhere, boxes of pink tissue on the windowsills for the allergic and emotional. Rose always has this opinion about the synagogues. They're always lovely but this doesn't mean she'll frequent them other than for prayers three times a year and death.

She spots the person sobbing. It's a woman somewhere in her sixties who must be the boy's mother. Someone thirty-seven years old is clearly a man but thinking of him as a boy allows Rose to feel even worse. And is that the boy's sister comforting her mother? And the man next to the mother? Surely, that must be the father. What a nice looking family.

Rose looks down at the floor and confirms that her hands are shaking. *A criminal with shaking hands, feh.* It's the smallest of voices in Rose's head that expresses dissent. She looks again in the direction of the boy's family, willing them to see her, to understand why she's here and, if they so choose, to punish her. Only then does she notice the woman sitting in the row behind them, her singularity framed by two empty seats.

The rabbi continues his eulogy and as he's speaking, the singular woman turns her head toward the back of the synagogue, granting Rose a full view of her face. Who else could that be but the fiancée? She looks young, more like a girl than a woman. She's pretty, with thick dark hair pulled into a bun, pale skin, and large eyes. Also, something about her seems familiar but Rose dismisses this, as the faces of the young seem to increasingly remind her of people she used to know.

The singular woman, who Rose now thinks of as "the girl," suddenly looks in her direction. Rose's heart starts to beat very fast and she immediately re-directs her focus to the rabbi. She's not ready for this but what else is new?

When the service ends, the rabbi provides basic directions to the cemetery for those who do not have those GPS devices in their cars or installed on those newfangled phones. Rose begins the laborious process of standing up and negotiating her body out of the synagogue. Place hands firmly on walker. Plant feet on the floor and visualize the trunk of a tree. Rise like the sun. Back out in the manner of a rusty and ancient automobile before inching sideways and remembering the days you used to jeté offstage, your splits 180 degrees of perfection. Pay your respects and tell them how sorry you are. Do not expect them to forgive you. Rose knows that such internal directives are hit or miss. Today, for example, everything hurts and her whole body makes creaking noises as she stands.

Upon exiting the synagogue, Rose sees the boy's family huddled in front of a black car that idles curbside and how her fellow funeral attendees trickle toward them in haphazard configurations to offer condolences. Rose watches how the family receives the slow-moving stream of people, some practiced at this; others grasping for words that do not materialize. As always, Rose detects movement patterns: how the boy's father merely nods at each expression of condolence; how the boy's mother grasps the hands of each condolence-giver; how the boy's sister keeps her hand glued to her mother's shoulder. *I'm terribly sorry for your loss.* She practices the line in her head, trying to muster up the nerve. But then what? *My husband didn't mean to kill anyone? If you need to blame someone, blame me?* Rose feels the inadequacy of language bearing down on her spine like a crushing weight. And yet, she forces herself to inch toward the grieving family, who no doubt will be getting into that black car at any moment. She doesn't yet know how she will explain who she is, only that she must.

As Rose gets closer to the family, she spots the girl at the top of the synagogue's steps that lead to the street. The girl lingers there, motionless, and strikes Rose yet again with her singularity. Rose's eyes start to water, as if exposed to a smoking, burning object. Why did this girl also sit alone at this boy's funeral?

"Excuse me?" Rose calls out to the girl while trying to summon the best possible memories of Morry but this tactic fails, as he only reminds her of the wrong words.

Rose? I can't find my keys.

The girl maneuvers down the synagogue steps in a halting, labored gait, as if she's a toddler still learning how to walk. She does not appear to have heard Rose.

"Excuse me." Rose tries again though she fears her voice will go nowhere as usual. The nicotine-stained and grief-soaked sound of her voice, even more than her memory lapses and limited mobility, reinforce her fear of winding up like the ancient and discarded objects she sometimes finds in a burial pile deep inside one of her closets. Many of her dear friends wound up exactly this way, slumped into wheelchairs, their heads lolling off to one side or the other. For proof that they existed, a person had to look elsewhere.

Rose clears her throat and tries again. "Excuse me miss." Better, she thought of her vocal performance. Or rather: not bad for someone who's ninety-three with weak lungs, arthritis in her knees, a double hip replacement, severe osteoporosis, and high blood pressure. "Excuse me."

At last, the girl looks in her direction. Rose knows she's not doing her blood pressure any favors as she meets the girl by the bottom of the synagogue steps. The girl smells like some kind of floral soap and strands of escaped hair from her bun now frame her face. Though she's terrified of this girl, Rose cannot help but feel a kinship with her. She too used to wear her hair in a bun, though of the kind that involved a rigorous laboring to tame every single strand into submission. A ballerina trying to pay the rent in her day couldn't afford to do otherwise.

"I . . ." Rose looks up at the girl and tries to glimpse the person behind the loss. But the girl's sadness swirls around her like a swath of kinetic and opaque fabric.

"Have we met before?" The girl smiles and extends her hand. "I'm Nina. Nina Romaine."

They shake hands and the sensation of the girl's warm and sweaty palm against her dry cold one almost brings tears to Rose's eyes. The tropics versus Siberia, she thinks. Perhaps this is a huge mistake.

Rose tries to introduce herself. She says, "I very much wanted to meet you," but then her hands start to shake.

Rose? Where are my keys?

The girl looks and waves in the direction of the boy's family. "I'm sorry but I have to go. Will I see you at the cemetery?"

What do you need them for? Jewish Family Service has a wonderful ride share program. We can sign up.

Rose shakes her head.

"Oh. Are you coming back to Frances's house afterward?"

Rose shakes her head again and grips her walker with as much strength as she can muster. If only this girl could extract the confession from her heart and perform other God-like maneuvers that on most days have no place in her belief system.

"I would like to speak with you at a more convenient time."

Oy Rose. Who uses the word "convenient" at a funeral?

But the girl only stares at her with confusion, or maybe, curiosity. This gives Rose the courage to finally say, "I'm terribly sorry for your loss."

ROSE SAT ON her favorite boardwalk bench, the one nearest to the police substation. She still loved this bench for its ocean view and proximity to the abstract sculpture that crowned a small grassy hill and marked the epicenter of Venice Beach. And though she harbored new and alarming opinions about sitting so close to law enforcement, Rose believed she had the best chance of spotting the girl from this vantage point. After all, a person had to be practical when conducting a stakeout.

Was it acceptable to feed birds when conducting a stakeout? Rose had no idea. She had never staked out anyone before nor had she bothered to consult experts on the subject. But she knew she had more time to kill before the girl's class ended so she opened her Ziploc bag of breadcrumbs.

For the record: Rose had navigated most of her old age inspired by intact memories of her younger self, who viewed white-haired women tending to various avian populations with a mixture of pity and detachment. But then came the day she felt compelled to leave the house after another pointless argument with Morry about making a doctor's appointment. On her way out the door, she had grabbed the half-eaten loaf of stale challah from her kitchen counter and made an impulse decision to visit the birds of the Venice canals. Only that day, the ache in her knees prevented her from managing the half-mile walk and so she had settled for feeding select chutzpahdik seagulls on the boardwalk. The ducks, egrets, and herons of the canals had been surviving just fine without her so surely they would continue on with their days.

Since then, Rose consistently looked forward to her exclusively boardwalk dealings with the seagulls, pigeons, and occasional sparrow here and there. It cheered her up to imagine Italian counterparts similarly afflicted with osteoporosis and the ghost problem common to the pronounced elderly industriously at work in the original Venice with this exact subset of bird population but of course with more pigeons than seagulls. Her procedure, honed from two years of trial and error, was basic yet effective. She only offered breadcrumbs and when she fed them, she tried to prevent the stronger birds from bullying the weaker ones. It often became important that she do some shooing.

"Shoo." Rose rattled her walker at two large gulls who had ganged up on a small, dark pigeon. The gulls hopped a few steps away from the breadcrumbs before returning seconds later to feast on remains and torment the same small pigeon. Rose sighed. She didn't like bullies.

Rose ran her hand through her mostly empty Ziploc bag and extracted the few remaining crumbs, which she then scattered on the ground. At least nine birds took notice. This comforted Rose, though she had never imagined her life reducing itself to this: her, communing with urban birds while she stared at the ocean awash with nostalgia. To think she was the last of the newcomers from Europe that settled around the boardwalk after the war. That she actually used to be a young person watching the older Jews from a distance. It was she who used to speed past them on her way to rehearsals or to teach her classes as they sat on the benches in front of the old hotels, all of them no longer in existence. All day they sat there, wetting their fingers with their tongues to better flip the pages of their books and newspapers, arguing about Neo-Nazis, Communists, the PLO, and Republicans, playing chess or pinochle, eating sunflower seeds, and mostly, keeping to themselves.

Then came a period of approximately an entire decade when Rose felt as if she attended a funeral almost every day. She and Morry had certainly saved a lot of money at the supermarket from all the noshing, obligatory and otherwise, on shiva food. Quite frankly, they had bagels and lox coming out of their ears. But more importantly, Rose valued these occasions for the sole reason that some of them could still gather, if only to mourn. She personally enjoyed belonging to civilization this way and relished opportunities to dress up in her dark suits and ruin gratuitous eye makeup jobs from all the expressions of sorrow. As they milled around the shiva buffet, she and the remaining Venice Beach first generation alter cockers would reminisce not only about the passing of dear Vivian or Hyman or Myra, but of an entire generation of European Jewry. Collectively, they would shake their heads over the fading great grandparents with Alzheimer's spending their final days in publicly funded nursing homes and the still vibrant Holocaust survivors felled suddenly by heart attacks or strokes while in the midst of speaking engagements at elementary schools and synagogue ribbon cutting ceremonies. Maybe in Heaven everyone still speaks Yiddish, they would say. What of it?

On the other hand, Rose really had no business feeling like the last Jew on earth, considering the senior center on Ozone Avenue continued to open its doors and attracted a fair number of second generation Jewish elderly. Years had simply passed since Rose enjoyed a proper conversation with anyone in Yiddish.

Her dear friend Lillian Rabinowitz, for example, couldn't speak a word. For years, she and Lillian ate lunch together and practiced keeping their minds sharp by trying to invent new complaints about the food. Once, during a routine lament about the collective loss of their taste buds, Rose had reminisced about the rich and salty flavor of her mother's gribbenes, only Lillian could not relate. She was eleven years younger than Rose, a native of Queens, New York, and knew nothing about the treat of chicken fat on Friday afternoons in a Byelorussian town. Which meant that Rose stood alone in a tiny kitchen with a wood burning oven, watching her mother break up a piece of challah into thirds and on each piece, smearing a bit of chicken fat. Her two sisters always reminded her of the wild neighborhood dogs foraging for edible bits of garbage the way they devoured their share of the gribbenes. Even then, Rose had a different approach to food, or rather, to life. She would hold the oily, creamy chicken fat in her mouth and let it melt on her tongue. For one second, maybe two, she believed she literally tasted the story her mother loved to tell about the World to Come, when all the Jews would be safe from murderers, alive and well for infinity in golden and peaceful Jerusalem.

"Shoo." Enough was enough. Rose waved her arms at the hovering gulls and let them know in no uncertain terms that the early bird dinner special was over. She had never enjoyed the immediate aftermath of excess reverie and thinking of Lillian only made her feel even more nauseous. How she had yearned for Lillian's opinion when she decided to exile herself from the Center.

Rose grabbed her walker handles to stand up for purposes of circulation and that's precisely when she saw the girl on the concrete area near the police substation. The girl wore black yoga pants, carried a beach towel, and appeared to be saying goodbye to a man and a woman. Were those her students? She watched the girl continue on alone to the grassy area directly in front of her, where she proceeded to remove her shoes. Rose could not believe that she had gotten this exactly right on her third attempt.

After asking the girl at the boy's funeral if they might speak at a more convenient time, the girl had reached into her purse and produced a flyer with her telephone number. Beach Yoga, six-week session, taught by Nina Romaine. Tuesdays at four. Ignore the yoga information, the girl had told her, unless she happened to be interested. To which Rose had thought: *Does she not see that I can barely stand?* This knowledge of the girl's profession, however, had slightly altered the state of Rose's terror and she had every intention of phoning the girl to make an appointment. But after a week of staring at the telephone in her kitchen, she decided to try and waylay the girl in person. Clearly, she needed a more aggressive nudging toward the acts of confession and restitution.

The first time she tried this stakeout business, Rose had learned that the beach yoga class happened on the sand. This meant that she would have to be especially strategic about waylaying the girl because she had respectfully given up any and all sand navigation activities since using a walker. The second time, she learned that while the beach yoga class met by the police substation, not all of the students returned in this direction afterward. That time, the girl must have also exited the beach from a different access point.

But now, this stroke of fortune. *Say something!* Only Rose couldn't. She lowered herself back onto the bench and thought of her husband.

Rose? I can't find my keys.

Fortunately, the girl appeared to be preoccupied with her hamstrings. This turned out to be a complete blessing since Rose hadn't mind-danced in at least two months and she certainly missed it, even though she currently felt unworthy of its stress relieving benefits.

Right leg forward and lunge. Straighten right leg and stretch. Straighten and bend, straighten and bend. Place your right hand on the ground and raise your left arm to the sky. Twist. Her mind could perform the girl's movements to perfection. Rose had discovered this vicarious ability when she was seventy-one, a few weeks after she stopped teaching and dancing for good. While watching the San Francisco Ballet perform the *Nutcracker* on PBS, her mind began to follow the movements of the dancers in a way that placed her onstage with them, no matter that her body remained rooted to her chair. This led to the discovery that her mind could still execute the choreography that she performed in a 1951 production of *Swan Lake* and her favorite across-the-floor combination she used to teach her most advanced students. And on those occasions when mind-dancing caused her to feel a little too sad and stuck in the past, she would remember the wonderful, also-on-PBS documentary she had the great fortune of catching, where a famous dancer from the Ballet Russe de Monte Carlo divulged that his mind behaved in this exact same way. Dancers never stop dancing, he said and something in the way he struggled to sit upright in his wheelchair made Rose believe him.

But then the girl stopped stretching. She reached for her sneakers and Rose tried to grasp onto the now-or-never nature of this opportunity. "Excuse me."

Only the girl, caught up in the task of lacing her shoes, didn't seem to hear her.

"Excuse me." Rose waved her arms and in the process, freed undetected specks of breadcrumbs that had stuck to her sweater. The gulls immediately returned and frenzied by the sudden windfall, pecked away like there was no tomorrow. Rose kept waving until the girl finally looked in her direction. Rose did not have the eyesight to read the expression on the girl's face and so she did not know if the girl remembered her. But then the girl started walking toward her.

I made a terrible mistake. Rose practiced the line in her head and tried not to succumb to the despair of owing this girl something she did not have the power to give.

"Hi. You were at . . . the funeral?" The girl suddenly stood over her, having scattered the birds in the process. Rose knew she couldn't have been very tall, but everyone looked like a giant to her these days. In her prime, she had been five foot two and couldn't for the life of her pinpoint the moment she became four foot ten.

"Yes. I found you through your yoga advertisement."

"Oh." The girl paused. "Right. I gave you a flyer. I'm sorry, how did you . . . are you a relative?"

Rose opened her mouth to offer clarification but no words emerged and so it became suddenly and urgently important that this girl not think her senile. Rose knew from personal experience that once someone thought you were senile, it became almost impossible to reverse the tide of opinion. "I wanted to talk with you," she managed to say.

The girl smiled. "Do you live around here?"

Rose grabbed onto the question like a life preserver and pointed down the boardwalk, in the direction of the former Waldorf Hotel on Westminster Avenue. She explained she had lived on the third floor of that building for over thirty years.

"You're Jewish." The girl made it clear that she wasn't asking a question.

Rose nodded. "So are you."

The girl smiled and touched her hair.

Rose said, "A lot of Jewish people used to live around here."

"They still do."

"No. The old ones have died out. This used to be like a little Miami Beach."

"Really?" The girl looked interested and Rose did her absolute best to refrain from talking her poor ear off. This was hardly the time or place to start reminiscing about the dates she used to have on the Ocean Park Pier or the kosher bakery on the boardwalk that sold challah not quite how her mother used to make it but very tasty all the same. So many things this girl probably didn't know about the past and who was she to enlighten her?

Rose tried to proceed with the conversation in a lucid fashion. She asked the girl about her yoga teaching and explained she was a former dance teacher and that being ninety-three in no way diminished her love for movement of any kind. And then the girl said, "I used to be a dancer also." And then Rose said, "Is that so?" And then they marveled at this particular coincidence a little longer than what might be called conventional.

And then the girl said, "I'm sorry, I didn't get your name . . ."

"My name is Rose, Rose Perchik. My husband . . ." Rose paused, trying to breathe.

Rose? Where are my keys?

"Your husband?" The girl looked genuinely puzzled and at first this caused Rose a great deal of irritation. She had to talk herself out of the irritation: *What's with the irritation, Rose? Expecting people right and left to read your mind just like that?*

"I'm not a relative of the family. I came because . . ." Rose started to feel terrible, like she might vomit or faint.

Let them stay lost. It's a sign.

"Oh." The girl sat down on the bench. "I think I understand. You're . . . ?"

Rose looked at the girl and her luminous dark brown eyes, wide with nothing more than compassion. "My husband. My husband passed away recently."

The girl grabbed her hand. "I know. I'm very sorry for your loss. That must have been . . . I mean, thank you for coming to Jeff's funeral."

Rose shook her head. She had so much to say to this girl who had no business behaving in this merciful fashion.

"Would you like to grab a cup of tea?" The girl held onto her hand as she waited for an answer.

"Maybe another time, dear." Rose withdrew her hand from the girl's grasp. "But it was nice talking to you." She felt the truth of the words and how they slowed down the beating of her heart. She smiled at the girl and considered a new possibility; that maybe, the confession could wait.

Two

THERE'S NINA, SITTING alone in the second row of wooden synagogue pews and directly behind Jeff's mother, father, and sister. She's wearing black, even though she knows that Jews don't necessarily wear this color to their funerals. She tries to maintain a tall spine, not because she's a yoga teacher with a solid Iyengar background, but because she googled "dealing with crushing grief" last night and stumbled upon an article by a cheery cognitive behavioral therapist who suggested "acting the opposite." She's thinking that maybe she has made a mistake, to sit by herself. But as she stares at the backs of the heads of Jeff's family members, she cannot help but feel the smallest of reprieves.

What exactly do they know?

It's this particular question that guided Nina's decision to sit behind them, though to be fair, Frances had spotted her when she walked into the synagogue and pointed with the limpest of index fingers to the remaining empty seat in her family's pew.

She knows that Jeff was close to Frances, his sister, and on cordial yet distant terms with his parents, whom he always referred to by their first names, Eleanor and Ben. They had this in common, growing up with parents who wanted to be called by their first names. Frances had been the one to call her about the accident and had only asked if she was still out of town. In the relaying of necessary terrible facts and funeral details, Jeff's sister had otherwise given no indication of knowing anything.

If they knew, you wouldn't have been invited. You would have been cast out of the synagogue, branded with some contemporary yet distinctly Jewish version of a scarlet letter. But you want them to know, don't you? That way, you can feel something.

Nina bows her head and focuses on the fake marble synagogue floor. It has not escaped her awareness that she once visited this very West Los Angeles synagogue with the cavernous ceilings and stained glass reproductions of the Chagall Windows on a Yom Kippur more than three years ago. Then, she had been an extremely recent transplant to Los Angeles and unaware that a person named Jeff Wasserman would soon materialize in her yoga class and quickly distinguish himself as a male student of flexible hips and consistently audible Ujjayi breath. She had come to this synagogue still actively mourning the loss of her Bubbe Essie, missing New York, and haunted by the vow she had made about Laz. The onset of grief had been swift and torrential when the cantor began to chant the traditional Kol Nidre prayer. Please don't cry, she had told herself, feeling the tears pooling at the corners of her eyes and threatening to dampen the synagogue floor.

But that was then. Now, Nina feels nothing but a faint buzzing in her fingers and toes as she struggles to recall what she has read about the various stages of grief. *Numbness. Denial. Stage One. I woke up and it was like getting hit by a Mack Truck so I ingested copious amounts of Xanax and Vicodin and finally understood why someone could accidentally overdose on heroin.* She's familiar with the clichés but cannot summon them with precision.

Nina tries to focus on the rabbi's eulogy. Jeff Wasserman: loyal son, dedicated brother, talented social worker, engaged to be married. Nina senses the rabbi works off some hastily scrawled yet heartfelt list of golden attributes submitted by Jeff's parents and/or sister but she can't fully hear him because the word "tomorrow" won't stop echo-whispering in her ear. The word reverberates throughout her body and bulges with subtext. Tomorrow, as in: I can't face you today. Tomorrow, as in: there's still time.

Nina swivels her head away from the front of the room, seeking the briefest of respites from the family that sits in front of her. And in the very back of the synagogue, she sees an old woman. She is tiny, with an entire pew to herself. She has snow-white hair, thick glasses, and is impeccably dressed in a navy blue suit. The woman appears to be fidgeting in her seat yet also seems intently focused on the rabbi, her lips slightly moving as he continues with his eulogy. Nina pays close attention to the woman's lips and remembers the way her Bubbe Essie used to read the newspaper. And so, for the briefest of seconds, she forgets where she is.

NINA SAT ON a storage box in Serena's office, waiting for the new yoga studio manager to finish her phone conversation. It was her first day back teaching at Cat/Cow Yoga and she had arrived twenty minutes early before her scheduled class at the request of Serena, who kept smiling at her and mouthing "sorry" as she talked. Nina guessed from the multiple times she said, "I see what you're saying" and "no problem" and "of course" that she dealt with a superior from corporate headquarters.

Corporate Fucking Headquarters. Everything else in your life is new and not necessarily improved so why not this also? Nina felt a tightening sensation in her chest as she considered the irrevocable shift in the vibe of her workplace. A year ago, when the former owner of Cat/Cow sold his business to a New York City-based mind-body-wellness conglomerate with branches all over the country, she had braced herself for the inevitable change. Instead, months went by where she taught her classes like she always had during the last three years of her employment at this studio, with the sparsest of interference from management. Then came the accident, when she had canceled all of her teaching commitments for two months, with the exception of two private clients and her beach yoga class.

Today, however, was The Day. When she walked into the studio's entrance, new front desk people greeted her, wearing identical gray T-shirts that matched the new carpet. The three Buddha statues and a curvy, abstract, aquamarine sculpture titled "Pranayama," by a local Venice artist, no longer adorned the lobby, having been replaced by racks of expensive yoga pants in colors ranging from sleek black to vibrant hues of scarlet and violet and tank tops emblazoned with the conglomerate's infinity sign logo. Commerce had definitely superseded art in defining the official lobby décor and Nina wondered what Serena planned to do with the office formerly inhabited by a woman named Jane, who held herbal tea-fueled meetings with her employees on soft, peach-colored cushions.

Serena finally clicked off her call and apologized to Nina for both the wait and the mess of the current office environs. "I'll have a couple of chairs in here soon," she promised and pulled up another storage box so she could ostensibly sit at Nina's level and butter her up with friendly direct eye contact before relaying news that Nina most likely did not want to hear.

"First of all, I just want to say . . . on behalf of everyone here . . . how sorry we all are for your loss. I hope you received our card." Serena paused, wearing the expression that Nina now recognized in many people who didn't know her well but had knowledge of her circumstances. These were people with good intentions but awkward delivery—stiff hand gestures, ominous pauses, telling her she'll feel better with time—which often prompted Nina to try and comfort them.

"Thank you. And yes, I did, thanks." Nina made a half-hearted attempt to regard her new boss with compassion, optimism, and non-judgment. Only she couldn't squelch her opinion that Serena looked straight out of Central Casting, with her pink highlights, sparkling purple nose ring, a small tattoo of the infinity sign on her upper left bicep, and a yoga pants and tank top outfit that clearly originated from the new racks in the renovated lobby.

Nina forced herself to smile at Serena. "It's good to be back." That much, she meant, didn't she? Because how much longer could she wake up past noon and debate whether this was the day that she resume showering on a regular basis? Since Jeff's funeral, she had barely managed to move into a new apartment and aside from buying a new futon, had not furnished or decorated her new home. This meant she woke up every morning surrounded by boxes, bare walls, and ample floor space. She and Frances had cleaned out the apartment where she had lived with Jeff and she could only bring herself to save anything to do with the kitchen: the Ikea table and chairs, the dishes, the pots and pans, and other assorted cookware. These objects, she hoped, would connect her to more bearable memories of her life with Jeff, than say, the furniture in the bedroom. Also, she had done most of the cooking during their relationship.

"So . . . I am so sorry to have to review all this with you on your first day back but . . . I got to do my job, right?" Serena scrunched up her face and shrugged, her body language a clear variation on don't-shoot-the-messenger. "Anyway, I thought it was best to talk to you now about the changes in studio policy and what we're asking everyone to do so we can all thrive and keep up our numbers. This country may be in a recession but people still need yoga, right?"

Nina sat up straighter on the storage box and tried to relax the reflexive tightening of her shoulders. Eleven years ago, when she took her first ever yoga class, she could not hook her fingers behind her back to do gomukhasana and had felt a recognizable kind of shame when the teacher brought her a strap. Dancers shouldn't need straps, she remembered thinking, but the teacher, having dealt with the bruised egos specific to dancers during yoga practice, had said this: Some of us are born with certain shoulders or it's where we habitually store our stress. Either way, there's nothing to judge. The words of this yoga teacher seared themselves into Nina's memory and two years later, she could get into the pose without a strap. Since then, whenever she thought about the difficulty of personal evolution, she would remind herself of the first time she could connect her fingers behind her back.

"Well, I haven't been here in two months so it will probably take a few classes before all my students come back," she said to Serena, trying to sound objective as opposed to defensive. Should she remind this woman that prior to her leave of absence, she taught six classes a week at Cat/Cow and averaged fifteen-to-twenty students per class? Should she mention her other professional commitments, such as teaching yoga to at-risk and low-income youth in after-school programs or her healthy roster of loyal private clients? She had considered herself lucky, having secured most of this employment shortly after relocating to Los Angeles and couldn't remember the last time she needed to sell herself to a prospective employer.

Serena nodded with what Nina considered to be a suspicious amount of vigor and launched into a lecture on the importance of personal brand building on social media now that it was 2008 and the world was in the middle of the biggest revolution since the television or the car or . . . Serena had paused there, unsuccessful in her efforts to piece together a coherent history of technology and pivotal inventions. Several times, Nina had to tell herself to relax her shoulders as Serena suggested she create a separate professional Facebook page. "Also, some of our teachers are really loving Twitter. Personally, I think Twitter's been a major game changer for people who are serious about personal brand building. You might want to check it out."

Shit. You're an evangelist. Since moving to LA three years ago, Nina had witnessed an astonishing number of friends and acquaintances transform into no-questions-asked religious fundamentalists who worshipped all things social media and online interactivity. With these people, it felt pointless to express any criticism of these technologies because they would just call her a Luddite and dismiss her as a now un-cool person out of touch with the zeitgeist. And fuck it, maybe she was a Luddite. She had yet to purchase one of those supposedly fabulous iPhones and she had reluctantly signed up for Facebook about eight months ago, where a friend request from Laz had awaited her. She had not friended him, an action that allowed her to feel a false sense of virtuousness, at least until he had sent her that email.

It's only an email. It still made her face flush hot with shame, this monstrosity of a lie.

Nina tried to focus. She nodded and smiled at Serena and told her that she would consider her suggestions as she worked on rebuilding her class following. This seemed to appease Serena, who smiled back. "I'm really looking forward to working with you Nina and I can't wait to take your class soon, I heard it's great."

Nina got up from the storage box, remembering an email from Serena about how she would be taking every teacher's class, not as a formal evaluation or anything but simply to get a better sense of everyone's style, which would then be communicated back to corporate. "Nice meeting you," she forced herself to say.

Serena ushered her out of her office and excused herself to make another phone call. She shut the door and Nina had about ten minutes until the start of her level 2/3 vinyasa flow class. She decided to visit the bathroom though she did not need to pee and locked herself in a stall, where she took several deep breaths. All this training she had as a teacher and student of yoga and yet, at this moment, she had trouble with her breath. Even in this stall, she could feel the outside world encroaching and she remembered the last class she taught before the accident, where she had to tell a student to put away her cell phone. The student had been texting right up until the beginning of class and then had placed her phone right in front of her yoga mat. But this had provoked Nina far less than what had come next: that although the student did as told, she explained to Nina, in that kind of annoyed tone indicating you once thought the person who just wronged you was cool, that she was expecting a super important message. As long as she silenced her phone, what was the harm in keeping it next to her?

Inhale. Exhale. The world is changing whether you like it or not.

Nina sat in the stall for another two minutes trying to breathe. She willed her mind to empty itself of all thoughts and judgments and that's when she remembered Rose and their conversation on the boardwalk. She had promised to call Rose and follow up on her "rain check" offer for a cup of tea. Only she hadn't, as it had both frightened and exhausted her to contemplate their possible discussion topics.

But the truth was this: Since the accident, Nina had felt like she really couldn't talk to anyone. To present the whole picture to someone in some grand gesture of unburdening seemed absolutely out of the question. And what was the whole picture anyway?

Nina exited the bathroom stall, washed her hands, and made a decision: she would call Rose. At least, there would be no explaining of recent circumstances with each other or no having to ease the discomfort of others as they attempted their well-meaning expression of condolences. Perhaps, they could even communicate something meaningful to each other. Or, at the very least, they could have lunch.

"HE SOUNDED LIKE such a lovely young man." Rose said this about a half an hour into their lunch at the Fig Tree Café, after precisely six bites of a grilled mozzarella and tomato sandwich.

Nina nodded and took another bite of her veggie burger. She had not meant to count the number of bites Rose took from her sandwich but she had been trying to stall the moment where they felt compelled to start talking about THEM.

"I always respected social workers," Rose said. "They do so much for people even though their pay is terrible."

"Jeff was good at his job," Nina managed to say. "What did your husband do?"

"He was a professor of art history. He taught at several local colleges."

Nina waited for Rose to elaborate. From the beginning, she had felt soothed by the sound of Rose's craggy vocal chords that still retained a slight Eastern European accent and hinted at a cigarette smoking past. Her Bubbe Essie had spoken with a similar Yiddish inflection.

"Dear. I need to tell you something."

"Sure. Do you want more coffee?" Nina pointed at their waiter, last sighted about a half hour ago. Rose nodded and Nina signaled the waiter for drink refills: lemonade for her and decaf for Rose. *Shouldn't we be doing this over whiskey? Can you drink whiskey with lunch when you're ninety-three?*

The waiter left to procure the requested beverage refills and Rose cleared her throat. "The accident. It was all my fault."

"Oh. I don't . . ." Nina froze and looked down at her plate. *I know how you feel,* she wanted to say.

"It's true, dear, and I'm so sorry. Please don't hate my husband."

"Of course I don't hate your husband. It was an accident." Nina prayed that Rose wouldn't start to cry. Since Jeff's passing, she had discovered that watching other people cry no longer did the job of triggering copycat, cathartic behavior. These days, the sight of other people crying only reminded her of her own inner numbness.

But Rose only stared at her half-eaten sandwich.

Nina said, "You weren't in the car."

"It was still my fault."

The waiter arrived to refill their drinks and Nina watched Rose take tiny, incremental sips of coffee. It did puncture her numbness ever so slightly to recognize another person in the throes of guilt. "It's not your fault, even if it feels like it."

Rose shook her head and spoke in half-finished sentences. "Dear, I . . . I'm very sorry that . . . You must miss him very much."

Nina could only nod. She could barely remember herself as a person who had no trouble crying in public, like at the movies or other people's funerals. A few days ago, she had finally begun to cry in the privacy of her new apartment. This exclusively took place in her bathroom, the only room with a door that locked. It didn't matter that she now lived alone. Locking the bathroom door gave her permission to slump against the bathtub and lower her head toward her chest. And if the tears didn't come, she would put her hands on her eyes and press hard.

"I'm sorry, dear. Forgive me for saying anything."

"It's okay. It's hard, isn't it? Missing someone all the time?"

"Very much so. But you know what comforts me? I like to think about how we first met."

Nina nodded. She understood Rose, even if she could not currently relate. She attempted to eat a few more bites of her lunch and Rose did the same. They talked about the pros and cons of living in Venice and Nina found herself enjoying Rose's company. What was it about this woman that made her feel so at home? She could definitely rule out any physical resemblance to her grandmothers, one who passed away when Nina was twelve and the other, three years ago. Those grandmothers had been more amply endowed and Nina could still grasp onto a childhood sensation of them embracing her with soft, fleshy arms and cushiony breasts. Both had dyed their hair in various shades of brown and red up until finding themselves in the hospital, one, wheezing with severe pneumonia and cognizant that she might be living out her final moments, and the other, felled by a stroke, not so much. She had retained fond if distant memories of Grandma Sylvia, who died when she was in the seventh grade. But Bubbe Essie—short for Esther—still loomed in the front of her consciousness. There she remained, a vibrant, almost tangible force, i.e. Nina could still taste the cloyingly sweet butterscotch flavor of the candies her grandmother used to slip her in shul. Even now, she associated the sucking of hard candy with her parents' efforts to expose her to traditional Jewish experiences by dropping her off at her grandparents' house to spend the Sabbath. How lucky she had been, to have moved back to Los Angeles eight months before Bubbe Essie's death and to have eaten multiple plates of cantaloupe and blueberries with her grandmother while playing innumerable rounds of kaluki.

As they talked, Nina learned that Rose had lived a far more secular existence than either of her grandmothers and seemed neutral on the subject of card games.

But when Rose asked her questions, she felt the same compulsion that she always associated with Bubbe Essie, where she tried to present her best possible self, as if the practice of fake-it-until-you-make-it could actually permeate her innermost core and eradicate all the lesser selves. Every time she visited Bubbe Essie in her final years, they'd play a couple rounds of kaluki and then her grandmother would proclaim, "Tell me about your life." So Nina would, each time becoming an editor par excellence, only serving up the choicest bits from her flawed, all-too-human existence.

They talked for two hours that day at the Fig Tree Café. When the waiter brought the check, Nina said, "It's on me."

"Absolutely not," Rose said. "You must let me buy you lunch."

Beginnings, Nina thought. Beginnings were always beautiful.

NEVER DATE ONE of your students. So Nina reminds herself on a Wednesday evening in 2005. She's been teaching at Cat/Cow Yoga for six months now and has applied the self-imposed policy with the same sort of exactitude that she had in all the studios where she taught in New York.

Nonetheless, there he stands before her, this new student with curly dirty-blond hair and crinkly hazel eyes. She guesses he's about her age, give or take a year or two and yes, she had already given him some extracurricular, distinctly non-yoga-class-related thought more than once since he first showed up to take her class some five weeks ago. He has attended her class every Wednesday and wow, does he have notably flexible hips for a man. This is a man who loves to do double pigeon and half lotus. And like her, his Achilles heel can be found squarely in his shoulders. Sometimes, after class, she has given him further suggestions for relaxing bodily tension. Have you tried alternate nostril breathing or legs up against a wall or child's pose with arms outstretched for an indefinite period of time? Those are great poses to do at home. Good to know, he would always say and his smile of thanks seemed to last a second or two longer than what she deemed an appropriate student-teacher interaction.

"Great job tonight," she tells him on this particular evening, as she's disconnecting her iPod from the studio's speaker system. Tonight, she had felt a special kinship with her playlist, which featured a mash-up of tunes by Thievery Corporation, Fleetwood Mac, Roxy Music, the world fusion virtuoso Natacha Atlas, and her new favorite, the Gypsy Punk band Gogol Bordello. As a yoga teacher who has done her fair share of practicing without music, Nina believes in the power of a good tune to inform the practice. Over the years, she has cultivated a secret pride in her playlists, which reflect both her eclectic musical tastes and her aversion to playing "yoga music," i.e. an hour and a half of non-stop kirtan chants or predictable, Putomaya-esque world music compilations for The Yoga Studio.

"Thanks," he says. "Thanks to you, I think I'm finally getting kounin . . ."

"Koundinyasana B. That's what we did tonight." She finds his attempt at Sanskrit endearing and does her best to sound friendly and peer-like as opposed to pedantic and lofty.

"Yeah. That's my favorite arm balance."

"It's a very satisfying pose when you get it." *You and me and koundinyasana B. Jeff and Nina sitting in a tree.* Nina knows she's skating on thin ice when she feels these compulsions to rhyme.

"So I was wondering . . ." Jeff pauses. To Nina, he suddenly appears slightly on edge. As a yoga teacher, this troubles her, considering he just spent ninety minutes trying to unwind. But as someone who hasn't been on a date since she moved to Los Angeles eight months ago, she finds herself paying close and giddy attention to her student's shift in energy.

"Can you have a cocktail if you're a yoga teacher?" He blushes ever so slightly as he asks the question, which more or less clinches Nina's answer.

"Every yoga teacher is different. Some only drink herbal tea. Others lead wine-chocolate-vinyasa flow workshops."

"And what kind of yoga teacher are you?"

"I've been known to have a drink or two."

She smiles. He grins. She smiles again. Poof goes a rule she supposedly lived by for the last seven years. He takes out his cell phone to get her number and she reminds him that cell phone use of any kind in the yoga studio is frowned upon. They laugh and she feels giddy with lawlessness. Who knew that rule-breaking at her age could be this much fun? She gives him her number and he promises to call, but first, he wants to know what she's doing tonight.

They meet hours later at a Venice restaurant with a late night happy hour. They collectively swill six cocktails and talk about their lives. *You lived in New York? Me too! You studied acting before you became a social worker? I was a dancer before I became a yoga teacher!* In the euphoric midst of processing these rapid-fire discoveries, Nina experiences several seconds of remembering that Laz also moved to New York to become an actor. But this does not give her pause, not when the man now sitting in front of her feels so fresh and indicative of her personal evolution. *You're a vegetarian, Reform Jew with Buddhist/secular humanist inclinations? I'm a quasi-vege-pesce-tarian, culturally affiliated, High Holiday Jew with Buddhist/secular humanist inclinations! It fits! It basically fits!*

As she sips her raspberry mojitos, Nina feels the high that comes from recognizing another person's specifics. Tonight feels like the first time that she has summed herself up like this, no matter that she has done so innumerable times in countless venues and over a kaleidoscopic array of colorful cocktails. Tonight feels like the first time she actually means it, when she says things, like: Me too. Or: I know exactly what you mean.

Finally, it's about one-thirty in the morning and their server drops off the check, a gentle reminder that the remaining restaurant staff needs to go home. They leave the bar and she waits for him to kiss her. Only he refrains from the act until they find themselves standing in front of her car and he asks her if she's sufficiently sober to drive herself home. Afterward, he asks, "Can we do this again?"

"Will you still come to class?"

"Yes."

"Well then yes."

She drives home, suffused by an unfamiliar calmness that commingles with the expected nervy sensation in the pit of her stomach that normally prevents her from sleep after such rarified encounters. The calmness speaks: *You are home. You can rest. Aum Shanti Shanti. Peace, peace, peace.*

FOR THE RECORD, here's what Nina loved about Jeff: He didn't just give money to homeless people; he bought them sandwiches and talked to them but also knew when to walk away. Dogs patrolling their yards almost never barked at him when he passed by. He helped his sister Frances through a bad break up and drove all over the city with her until she found a new apartment she could afford on her own. He overtipped at restaurants. He rarely talked about his clients and when he did, he never slipped up and mentioned them by name. He loved to drive on PCH, past Malibu and into Ventura County, stopping frequently to admire the juxtaposition of mountains and ocean. He always kept tea tree oil in a spray bottle and used it regularly to refresh his yoga mat. He asked more questions than he gave answers and never went on and on about himself. He liked to hold doors open for her, always prefacing the action with an "I know this is sexist but . . ." He struggled mightily against inciting competitions of righteousness between them. He did, didn't he? He sincerely tried his best to withhold judgment, even when he couldn't stop himself from deeming her guilty for behavior more selfish than his own. He loved sharing hot fudge sundaes and bottles of French, Italian, and Spanish wine. He'd forge on with sex until she came, no matter what. And when he finally said, "I love you," she believed him.

Three

THERE'S ROSE, SITTING next to Morry Perchik at a dinner party for thirteen thrown by mutual friends living in Silver Lake. She's recently divorced, almost fifty, and relieved to be of an age where people no longer eye her belly and glance at their watches, as if their mere telling of the time could do what the doctors could not. He's a tall, thin man with thick, prematurely white hair, hunched shoulders, and horn-rimmed glasses that frame piercing blue eyes. *With eyes like that, a person has to be some kind of smart.*

Rose's initial assessment of the man proves to be absolutely correct. Also, he looks directly at her when they talk and seems to chew over his words with the same care he accords his food. He appears to be more of an open book and less a man of mystery, which for Rose, equals an enormous breath of fresh air.

So there they sit side by side. The art history professor with a special love for Chaim Soutine and Amedeo Modigliani and the aging dance teacher with malfunctioning hips but still perfect turnout, coincidentally living in the same neighborhood, isn't that something? Their friends do some mild nudging, peppering the dinner conversation with words full of supposed wink-wink properties. *Jewish. Secular. Democrats. Labor Zionists. Public television. The arts.* With greasy index fingers, they draw diagrams in the air, which indicate how Rose and Morry inhabit different points on the same circle. This, however, turns out to be superfluous, as they ascertain things about the other over the Chicken Kiev without too much verbal hoopla. *You're a divorcee with no children? I'm a divorcee with no children. You love the ocean? I love the ocean. Ditto for sunshine and mild weather. Looking for that suitable person for right now but also for the Golden Years. What does Golden mean exactly? Your guess is as good as mine. Regular card games, maybe? Charity work, certainly, and perhaps an herb and flower garden—FACTBD, future arthritic conditions to be determined. Maybe a cruise here and there or a trip to one of those elder hostels that cheerfully advertise bird-watching expeditions, gentle swimming pool calisthenics, and the resurrection of dances from our youth.*

All this, they manage to say without really saying. Rose simply stares into the piercing blue eyes of this fellow Venetian and gathers the kind of information found in those personal ads she could never bring herself to need in the aftermath of Richard's betrayals. So when Morry hands her a spare paper napkin during the serving of dessert with an invitation to dinner scrawled across it, she blushes and nods her assent.

They have their first date four days later at an Italian restaurant in their neighborhood. Rose wipes tomato sauce from the corners of her mouth and remembers the way her first husband had always looked over her shoulder whenever they sat across from each other at a restaurant. She doesn't know what to make of a man who can publicly maintain eye contact with her for more than five minutes and so she starts traveling elsewhere.

"Are you okay?" Morry's fingers alight on her elbow ever so briefly, but it does the trick. She snaps out of her reverie and accepts a second date.

She appreciates that he waits until the fourth date to ask why she has no children. When she says she couldn't, he places his hand on top of hers and confesses it was the same for his wife but that's not why he divorced her. For them, it was a blessing they didn't, he says. The subject of blessings seems to flood Morry with a recognizable melancholy and so it's Rose's turn to tap him on the elbow. She wants him to know that she understands him perfectly. She considers asking for the story of his divorce but then decides to wait until he requests the specifics of Richard. But all Morry does is order dessert, an ice cream sundae with two spoons.

She wears a lavender dress and a pink rose in her hair for her second wedding. They marry in the lobby of the Moondance Motel. It is a bright pink art deco structure, the kind that once used to proliferate along the Venice Boardwalk and which perishes by the wrecking ball in 1971. An old, white-bearded rabbi with a dwindling beachside congregation officiates. Forty people attend the wedding, mostly friends. Their families are scattered, aging, and mostly deceased, but if anyone notes this, Rose and Morry can't hear them. They can barely hear the rabbi marrying them since the City of Los Angeles has chosen their wedding day to start dismantling the remaining Venice oil derricks, the last of which explodes by accident in 1974. So much clanging and banging and mild explosions accompany Morry's efforts to break the glass! After four failed attempts, he manages and everyone considers this a perfectly respectable omen. When Rose feeds him the first bite of wedding cake, he swallows it in one gulp, smiles, and asks for more. They dance the hora before switching to the waltz and two-step and as Rose tears the bottom hem of her dress, Morry whispers, "I never want this night to end."

Years later and Rose understands the following: her husband never likes to leave a good party. Always, it's she who must drag him home while their party hosts enthusiastically wave goodbye while of course telling them to come back soon. This husband of hers continually seeks out the infinite in the most temporal of moments and furthermore, makes a mean glass of orange juice. He's an expert at squeezing an orange out of every last drop of juice until none exists and then he convinces himself that he can extract just a little more. Sometimes, he's right. But sometimes, Rose wonders whether her husband simply has a hard time with letting things go.

AFTER THEIR INAUGURAL meal at the Fig Tree Café, a weekly lunch pattern had developed between Rose and the girl. For the record, Rose tried to stop thinking of Nina as "the girl" once she discovered that her potential new friend was thirty-six years old. But after several fruitless attempts, she figured this politically objectionable compulsion harmed no one, as long as she kept it to herself.

The pattern depended on the girl's yoga schedule, but the girl always met Rose at the entrance to her building and they generally patronized the Fig Tree Café because it hands down had the best selection of healthy and vegetarian sandwiches and salads on the boardwalk. This was fine by Rose because the girl was an almost vegetarian and, for the most part, she believed in vegetables. Of course Rose also appreciated a juicy steak and sometimes visited the multitude of concession stands across the street from her apartment, which served up a conglomeration of high fat and sodium delights including falafel, malai kofta, pad Thai, and a vegetarian pizza slice with a top layer of grease so viscous that it qualified to be charged as a separate food item. But what was the harm in letting the girl think she lived so long because of a healthy diet?

At these lunches, the botched confession always lingered on the tip of Rose's tongue. *Maybe the next time.* So Rose would think each time she steered the conversation to safe and pleasant topics, such as the weather. *It's sunny again in Los Angeles, how about that?* Or how they both used to dance for the stage. *I once auditioned for Mr. Balanchine and didn't get the part, which was no surprise since I was too short to be his kind of ballerina. At any rate, I never went in for his kind of neo-classicism.* Always, they fought over the payment of the bill and Rose allowed the girl to win forty percent of the time. Sometimes, supermarket errands followed these lunches, which generally consisted of the girl driving Rose to the 99 Cent Store or to the fancy Ralph's in Marina Del Rey. They never went to the Ralph's on Lincoln and California, though Rose sometimes wondered whether it would do them any greater good to visit the scene of the accident. But since she never asked the girl to drive her anywhere, always waiting for the girl to offer first before accepting help, the subject never came up.

When they parted ways from these outings, Rose always included with her goodbye an "I understand if you're too busy next week," but the girl always shooed these words away. Sometimes, Rose employed additional methods in the quest to give the girl an out. *You should spend time with people your own age. I'm afraid I won't be so energetic today.* Only the girl never took the bait. After some weeks of rigorous testing and evaluation, Rose felt obligated to conclude that maybe, just maybe, the girl wanted to be her friend for no other reason than friendship.

At her age, Rose had come to value the priceless nature of an honest-to-God friend, such as the esteemed Lillian Rabinowitz. This meant she had to work hard at avoiding becoming anyone's charity project and quite frankly, she had good reason to harbor overarching suspicions about friendships with young people. Take that vivacious, well-groomed group of youngsters who used to offer singing and Israeli folk dance programs at the Center every Sunday. They would march into the Center with more energy and good cheer in their individual pinky fingers than the Center people harbored as a collective body. These young people would first target those whose hearing aids still worked, encouraging them to sing along to old favorites like "Oyfn Pripetchok" and newfangled tunes set to bits and pieces of classic Jewish prayers. Next, they would get to work on the people who could still stand, herding them into circles and teaching them basic steps like the Yemenite. Afterward, they helped serve the coffee and cake and many of them tried to make conversation beyond the hellos and how are yous. They asked questions of sunshine. *Isn't it a beautiful day? Wasn't the singing great?* They could ask questions all afternoon and receive nothing in return but blank stares and the suggestion of drool from a frozen corner of mouth and still; they never stopped smiling.

Rose had to hand it to those young people because most of the Center members adored them, especially the ones with absolutely nothing left upstairs. But even the remaining Einsteins among them found something to appreciate in the sight of those youthful, pretty, and smiling faces. Only Rose always had difficulty conversing with them, despite their exemplary intentions. If anything, she preferred the ones who seemed prone to depression, and she had learned to spot the depressed souls lurking under layers of false cheer, forced enthusiasm, and perfectly applied lipstick. If only she had the ear of powerful gerontologists, because she could have told them a thing or two about plying the elderly with reasons to live. Such as: Let us help someone else out for a change. Don't give us a healthy, adorable kitten to lower our blood pressure and raise our serotonin levels. Give us a three-legged elderly cat or a teenager with suicidal thoughts or a woman who lost her fiancé in an accident that could have been prevented. Maybe then, we'll acquire the healthy kind of amnesia, where we forget who we are supposed to be at the age we are now.

And then just like that, the young people stopped visiting on a formal basis. No more Sunday afternoon singing and dancing due to budget cuts, which never made sense to Rose because those young people volunteered their time, but that's what the Center people were told. In any case, Rose only had strong memories about the loss of this program because it coincided with the second major Adele Mandelbaum incident. The Mandelbaum woman topped the list of reasons Rose currently had for not setting foot in the Center since she became a widow. The mere thought of that woman's gloating face shriveled any and all reserves of courage that might have allowed Rose to walk into the Center in the aftermath of her husband's death with her head held high.

IT COULD HAVE continued like this: Rose meeting the girl for lunch just so she could strike up safe and pleasant conversation topics. But then came the day that began like any other. Rose woke up, washed her face, and missed her husband the way she always did. She brushed her teeth and tried to cheer herself up by thinking of her impending appointment with the girl. Was this lunch date number four or five? Rose had already lost count. At any rate, she resolved to eat a light breakfast. She opened her kitchen cabinet, stared at her box of All Bran, and thought about how her husband reviled the cereal, preferring Raisin Bran or better yet, a fresh prune. Later, as she got dressed, she stood in front of her bedroom closet and stroked the left sleeve of her husband's light green sport jacket. Morry had loved this jacket because the color reminded him of how the ocean looks in a certain kind of hazy, late afternoon sunshine.

But then something unusual occurred to Rose: her knees didn't ache. She felt well enough to walk outside with only her cane, a risk she had not taken since Morry's death. And so she decided to go downstairs thirty minutes before the girl's scheduled arrival at her apartment building's entrance. She would take in a little additional exercise and convince her agnostic self to thank God for sparing her so far from Alzheimer's, dementia in general, cancer, pacemakers, dialysis, oxygen tanks, nursing homes, falling down the stairs, absolute blindness, acute incontinence, and, if her joie de vivre held up, fatal car accidents.

Rose left her apartment in a special occasion dark blue dress, a powdered nose, and magenta lips. She took the elevator down to the lobby and realized she had forgotten to pick up her mail yesterday. Before Morry's death, Rose would never have neglected her mail. But that was before the trickle of multi-colored condolence cards, which commingled as if brazen strangers to an uninvited party with the sterile white business envelopes still bearing Morry's name on them. *Nu Rose? Did you expect the Angel of Death to arrange for his mail to be forwarded to the appropriate address?* So Rose would think when she opened the envelopes intended for Morry, overwhelmed by the prospect of calling the utility companies and everyone else to inform them that things in her household have changed.

In the lobby, Rose caned over to the mailboxes and saw that she had indeed received mail yesterday. She decided to give the envelopes a quick perusal and open everything later, after her appointment with the girl. But then she spotted the large, square pink envelope, which stood out amidst its monochromatically white and business-like brethren. Rose extracted it for further inspection, glanced at the return address, and froze.

Adele Mandelbaum had sent her a condolence card.

Rose stared at the card, as if its contents contained a particularly incriminating police report or legal summons. And why wouldn't it? Had she not been expecting such news to arrive in her mailbox, even though the police had already made their report and concluded their findings as a "tragic accident?"

We both know it's not his eyes.

She could feel the residual hiss of Adele's words deep inside her ear as she succumbed to opening the card. *Sending you our deepest condolences.* A border of fat pink roses decorated the card's message, expressed in an old-fashioned cursive-style script. Under the message, Adele had printed her name in black block letters. Otherwise, the inside of the card remained blank.

Rose re-stuffed the card into its oversized pink envelope and stuck it back in her mailbox. Who on earth was the "our" in this card? Adele had been widowed more than twenty-five years. Had she taken it upon herself to express the sentiments of everyone at the Center? Of course this was something that Adele would do. The chutzpah this woman had when it came to believing that her finger personally rested on the collective pulse of elderly Venice Jewry and society at large. But why would Adele even send her a card and to have waited to do so more than three months after Morry's funeral?

As if Rose had to ask herself such questions. The white blank space in the card contained a clear message for her, no decoding efforts necessary. *I have your number Rose. I know what the police have ignored.*

Rose gripped her cane. So help her God—if God existed—she would enjoy this day while her knees held up. She forced herself to walk outside and took incremental steps. She managed to pass her building, the organic coffee shop, the juice bar that sold vegan ice cream and other green desserts, and the Sunny Surfwear shop that specialized in joke T-shirts, postcards of topless women, beach-themed paperweights, leopard patterned bikinis, Hawaiian print everything, and "I love Venice Beach" coffee mugs. Finally, she stopped for a breath at the intersection of her street with the boardwalk.

For a Thursday morning in March, the boardwalk appeared unusually pregnant with both regulars and outsiders. The homeless men and women who slept overnight on the benches and grassy embankments had already dispersed, ceding the terrain to the pre-sunset denizens. They walked, jogged, skated, biked, and postured past Mostly Invisible Rose, all variations on decades-old themes: gawking tourists, eccentric locals, fitness-oriented locals, strolling lovers from more inland neighborhoods who paid at least ten dollars, sometimes twenty dollars to park their cars at oceanfront lots, flamboyant street performers, and tenacious hawkers of tarot card readings, purple crystals, talking animal wind-up toys, homemade music recordings, cheap sunglasses, gossamer dresses made in India, temporary tattoos, toe rings, water pipes, Rastafarian rainbow hats, and T-shirts emblazoned with timeless sentiments that Rose had always considered unspeakable. Ever since the roller skaters started flocking to Venice in the 1970s, she had witnessed this nonstop parade of teeming life forms, including costumed dogs, painted parrots, and trained iguanas, all of which exuded an electric and unified spirit that used to fill her with a world conquering energy. Not that she ever wanted to conquer the world. She simply believed she had it in her to do something special; to leave the world something more than a couple of plaques with her name on it, one on a ballet studio wall in West Los Angeles and one in front of a tree in an Israeli forest to be precise.

But that was then. Now, Rose paused at the end of her street and reminded herself as always to be careful. Because here on the boardwalk, she could be felled at any given moment by someone reckless on their newfangled roller skates. *Blades, Rose. They're called rollerblades now.* One of her dear friends, in fact, Bertha Rosenbloom, may she rest in peace, broke her hip from a collision with a teenage bicyclist. When the accident occurred, the bicyclist blamed Bertha "for being in the way" and told the police that old people do not belong on the boardwalk.

As Rose remembered the unfortunate Bertha, she noticed the group of young boys sitting on the narrow stretch of grassy lawn that bisected the boardwalk from the bike path. She had seen these boys before, with their skateboards and pierced eyebrows and overall slovenly approach to fashion. Why on earth did their jeans have to reveal ninety percent of their underwear? For the life of her, Rose could not understand this particular fashion trend and how beloved it seemed to be among all the male adolescents of Greater Venice. How to account for this sartorial unification of the white boys, the Black boys, the Latinos, and Asians; these groups that otherwise seemed frequently entrenched in tribal, war-like affiliations? What did it mean? That people were essentially the same? Or simply vulnerable to farkakte suggestions from clothing companies that profited by trafficking in the notion that everyone was the same? Such questions could easily give Rose a headache and yet she persisted in asking them.

For what Rose? Proof that you, personally, still have something upstairs? Proof Shmoof.

The boys occupied the lawn with the fronts of their skateboards pointed missile-like toward the boardwalk. Surrounded by this suggestion of weaponry, they smoked cigarettes and hard-of-hearing Rose had no trouble making out some of their profanity-laced conversation. *I wouldn't fuck that bitch. And: Suck my dick. And: Your momma's a fat-assed whore.*

Rose sighed, unsure of her next move. Several times, she had observed these boys in motion and taken careful note of their aggressive and reckless approach to skating, where they careened down congested sections of the boardwalk, seemingly intent on terrorizing unsuspecting pedestrians. Something in these boys' angry, bristling body language reminded her of the antisemitic gangs that used to roam the boardwalk and bully members of the Center community.

Rose decided to back up several steps, in the direction of the still shuttered Indian food stand that advertised samosas for a dollar. She had no proof that these boys were in training to become the future Nazis of America but still. Years of experience told her to be careful.

She watched one of the boys stand up and stretch. He was tall and lanky, with dark, greasy hair that fell to his shoulders and obscured most of his forehead. He wore a dirty white T-shirt emblazoned with a black skull and cross bones and a pair of cutoff jeans that slid far below his waist. He radiated a general dirty fingernail and bad breath demeanor that wouldn't have passed muster with the Nazis. However, Rose could not help but think that he would have made an excellent crusading Christian and in general, a perfect fit for the Middle Ages.

There used to be a bona fide gang of antisemitic, vilde chaya types, back when the Center would sell out every day for lunch and people spilled outside from the confines of the building, lingering in the afternoon sunshine and perpetually full of conversation. For every group of old Jews that used to congregate on the benches along the boardwalk discussing the latest news from Israel, a group of teenage boys slouched nearby. They loved to lurk by this stretch of boardwalk just across from the Center, where there was a low wall separating the pavement from a small parking lot that led directly onto the beach. They favored those black combat boots and wore T-shirts with swastikas. Most had a knack for repeatedly festooning the wall with spray painted words either nonsensical or legibly profane. Sometimes, the boys sprayed in broad daylight, forcing the old Jews to fold up their newspapers and chess games and evacuate to safer benches. Or they would chain smoke cigarettes, flicking their ashes deliberately toward those who remained. *Dirty old Jews.* Most of them didn't have much of a repertoire when it came to the hurling of antisemitic epithets but here and there, you'd find one with an education who knew how to use "kike" to perfection in any given sentence. Occasionally, a boy would follow an old Jew home in the time-honored manner of a well-fed house cat stalking a fly. Muggings were rare, mostly because the old Jews lived on modest incomes and had nothing of value for them to steal, but occasionally they happened.

Rose watched the boy bump fists with the other boys. She admired the way he jumped on his board then a second later, jumped off and picked it up with one hand in a single seamless motion. A person could be the worst kind of criminal but if he moved well, Dance Teacher Rose could feel her heart soften ever so slightly in admiration. But then the boy suddenly seemed to be looking directly at her. Did he see her or was he simply interested in purchasing samosas once the Indian food stand opened for business?

Supply and demand. Rose averted her gaze from the boy and reminded herself that one didn't exactly bump into mass gatherings of antisemitic teenagers on the boardwalk these days. After all, when the gazelles no longer graze by the pond, the lions have to go elsewhere. Even the young man who handed out those "Free Palestine" bumper stickers near the Sidewalk Café always made a special point to tell Rose he distinguished between American Jews like herself and the racist policies of the Nazi Zionist State. But what a shame her family couldn't have stayed in Europe, he liked to tell her. That would have solved everything.

A black and white blur of motion suddenly whizzed past Rose and grazed her shoulder, causing her to lose her balance. She stumbled and as her cane clattered to the ground, she used her left hand to brace herself against the wall of the Indian food stand.

A close call. Rose felt an aching, throbbing sensation in her left wrist as she leaned against the wall. She had certainly witnessed the disastrous consequences of falling among her osteoporotic peers. How poor Bertha Rosenbloom had suffered after breaking her hip. Or what about other friends from the Center, who would suddenly be absent for months, then return with newly replaced hips or shoulders or knees? "I fell," they would say, no other explanation necessary.

Rose didn't know how she would manage to reclaim her cane. The cane only lay a few inches away but the prospect of her trying to bend down and retrieve it; this was an ocean to cross. And then the boy suddenly loomed before her. He held his skateboard vertically, which made Rose think of rifles and pitchforks. "Lady, you need to get out of the way."

Rose looked up at the boy and noticed the explosion of pink acne on the left side of his reddened face. The color of his skin reminded her of the Mandelbaum woman's similarly pinkish condolence card and this allowed her to be angry. "You need to watch where you're going."

The boy stared at her and his lips curled into a sneer. *Go ahead young man, give it all you've got. You want to tell me that the Jews control the media, Hollywood, and Wall Street, or that they hired the pilots who flew the planes into the World Trade Center? Or that the Holocaust was invented as an excuse to oppress the Palestinians? Feh. You're going to have to be more sophisticated than that if you want to impress me, young man.*

So many things Rose wished she could say to this boy, who could flatten her with his skateboard in seconds so that she could go join the party with Bertha Rosenbloom and all the other deceased people she used to know, may they rest in peace. A memory suddenly surfaced of her strolling the boardwalk with Bertha and her dear friend Lillian Rabinowitz and how a passing boy in those combat boots had hissed at them: *Jews.*

But the boy's sneer only transformed into open-mouthed surprise. "I need to what?" He asked this question in a tone that seemed much more dumfounded than hostile.

"My cane." Rose felt her hands start to tremble as she pointed to the ground. "Can you please help me?"

The boy advanced several steps in her direction, until he stood so close to her that she could have bitten him on the nose had she stood a foot taller. Rose closed her eyes and prepared for the worst.

Nu Rose? Why not now? Who said you have to wait until you're so farmisht that you wouldn't know from the Angel of Death if he bit you in the ass?

Such questions. Where did they come from? And who was the voice? It had to be someone else's voice because never in her life would she embrace such language. This was the voice of a man with a superficial grasp of Yiddish and flamboyant, vulgar theatricality. *Bit you in the ass?* The voice reminded her of someone from television, some foul-mouthed success story who thought you could master Yiddish by bagels and lox osmosis.

Rose opened her eyes and observed how the boy now held up his skateboard like a shield, as if sufficient barriers did not already exist between them. He studied Rose's face with a wary and puzzled expression. "Damn," he said. "You're old."

Rose suddenly felt the weakness in her knees. The weakness had been there all along, hadn't it? She leaned against the wall of the samosa stand, her expectations of this day completely shattered. Had she become one of those people who believe the entire world is antisemitic, not just anything European or Arab or certain Christmas nativity scenes or that subset of the American Left that so many Jews find appealing until they don't because of Israel? Because she had been wrong about this boy, who didn't need to associate her with the Jewish people in order to treat her as a non-person. She stared at her cane, so close yet so far, and felt heat rising in her face. She knew she needed to sit down immediately.

Only she didn't.

Nu Rose? Why not now? Sure, a mensch tracht und gott lacht but an opportunity is an opportunity. Think of the hushed reverent tones of your funeral guests. They will misconstrue all this for some kind of elderly abuse and say how you did not die in vain, unlike some other people.

Again, this voice and who was he to tell her that man plans and God laughs? For ninety-three years, Rose had led a life devoid of such auditory hallucinations, not to mention UFO sightings, visits with dead people, and in general, Burning Bush moments where she could credit a life change to a supernatural occurrence. She was not about to succumb at this stage in the game to a new type of reality. No, she would not stand for it.

"What's going on here?" The man who ran the organic coffee shop now stood next to her, having safely retrieved her cane. He held it out to her and told the boy to leave the street or he would call the police.

"What the fuck? I wasn't doing anything." The boy expressed additional profane words of protest, prompting Rose to lean heavily on her cane and expel a single "oy."

The coffee shop man produced his cell phone from his pocket and it was unclear to Rose as to whether he actually planned to call the police. Because what could the police possibly do? *He called me old, officer. Well, ma'am, I'm afraid he might be right. Oh and while we're here, we want to ask you some more questions about your husband.*

The boy laughed at the sight of the coffee shop man's cell phone and raised his skateboard over his head. In one seamless motion, he dropped the board and jumped upon it as it clattered to the ground. Rose and the coffee shop man watched him glide down the street at a moderate speed, his board leaving faint and tiny tire tracks in the asphalt. She then spoke with the coffee shop man for several more minutes, assuring him she did not need medical attention. And then the girl showed up, an uncharacteristic twelve minutes late for their appointment.

"Are you all right?" The girl rushed to her side and grabbed her free hand. She gripped Rose's hand with a strength that was familiar to Rose yet forever lost in the dance studios where she used to rehearse and teach. With her other hand, the girl pointed in the direction of the boy, now rapidly receding down Rose's street. "Was that kid bothering you?"

Rose shook her head as the coffee shop man expressed a different opinion. He had seen that boy and his friends with canisters of spray paint, tagging boardwalk properties after sunset. From the vantage point of his coffee shop doorway, it looked to him like the boy had purposely collided with Rose.

"That's disgusting. Maybe we should go to the police?" The girl pointed in the direction of the beachfront station next to the sculpture.

Again, Rose shook her head. She was fine and she didn't want the police involved. The man offered them free coffee and when they both declined, returned to his store.

The girl relaxed her grip on Rose's hand. "Are you sure you're all right?"

"Of course I'm all right." Rose smiled at her, thinking of how from the get-go, they had established themselves as quite the pair of liars. *How are you? Great. And you? Also great. Wonderful. Let's have lunch.* "Should we have lunch?"

But the girl just stood there, her face a mask of anxiety and grief. Rose could see a blue vein pulsating on the left side of her forehead.

"It's not right," the girl said. "People like that."

"Well, I'm not entirely helpless." Even Rose could hear how her delivery sounded less than convincing. She dreaded the return to her apartment lobby, where she would have to re-confront the evidence sent by a bona fide enemy.

"Of course, it's just . . ."

Rose saw the tears brimming in the girl's eyes and felt a new kind of powerlessness. Since their first meeting, neither one of them had shed a single tear. Now everything was about to change and she wasn't ready.

"I've lived here for forty years and everything is really the same," she finally said. "When I was younger, I had to be careful because I was Jewish. Now, it's because of my age."

The girl opened then closed her mouth.

Rose spotted the trace of a smile and asked, "What's so funny?"

"I was about to say that 'you're not so old.' But that would be lying, wouldn't it?"

With a newfound respect, Rose smiled back at the girl who then slightly changed the subject. She told Rose about a certain photograph at the Yad Vashem museum in Jerusalem, of two Nazis pulling the ear locks of a stooped and white bearded Jew. She remembered this photo above all the other images in the museum and it had instilled her with a lifelong hatred of bullies. Then she confessed that she had seen Rose with the boy from a distance but didn't sense the danger until she grew closer. "And now I feel terrible."

"It's perfectly all right, dear," Rose said, who struggled to remember her own visit to the Yad Vashem museum. Had that particular photograph been there in 1973? Rose couldn't remember, though other photographs remained forever seared in her mind. But how nice that she and the girl had both visited Israel and this very important Holocaust museum. Wasn't that something, that both of them could be so profoundly influenced by photography? "Of course you would have helped me."

"No," the girl said. "I'm always too late. I want to do the right thing but that doesn't seem to mean anything. I get . . . paralyzed."

The girl covered her eyes with her hand and released an enormous sigh. Rose did her best not to interrupt as the girl pressed her forehead against the wall of the Indian food stall. She prepared for the sounds of someone else's grief but the girl remained silent. So many things she wished to tell this girl. *I know you will never see him again across from you in his usual chair at the dinner table or when you open your eyes in the morning or at the airport, meeting you after a long trip. You have no idea how terrible I feel, that you lost him. Shah, maidele. Shah.* Rose wished she could comfort the girl in the way her mother used to calm her on those nights she woke up screaming, still trapped in the remnants of a bad dream. Her mother would stroke her hair, kiss her forehead, and promise that everyone she loved was safe. And afterward, her older sister would sing her to sleep. *Shlof zhe yidele. Shlof.* Sleep little Jew. Sleep. Her older sister had a beautiful voice. She could have had a career in the theater had she left for America with Rose. Only she had stayed behind with their parents.

Rose stared at the girl and wondered whether it did any good, to press one's forehead against a wall. *Go on, Rose. Tell her about the last time you spoke to the police. Mrs. Perchik? There's been an accident.* They never did say what was in the bag of groceries. Milk? Cheese? Broccoli? Cereal? Eggs? The police had meant well in their gentle yet firm steering of the conversation but Rose still yearned to know the details of the groceries, those final ingredients of a young man's life, their colors and textures smashed and smeared together: abstract art on a windshield that otherwise remained intact. They didn't have to tell her over at Ray's body shop what got cleaned and fixed and excised so that the car could look like new. Keep the car, Rose had told that Mr. Ray. I'm certainly not going to drive it.

Rose reached out and touched the girl on her shoulder. "Maybe I know something about how you feel. And you should also know that I . . ."

Rose paused, unable to locate additional words of comfort. How could it be that after all these occasions of exposure to death she was still afraid, just like she had been as a young girl waking up from nightmares about Romans plundering Jerusalem, Cossacks on their horses, the Ukrainians living next door, and other murderers of the Jews both past and present? *Remember me, Rose? Thought you'd never see me again.* The fear had the face of an old and unpredictable friend, the type Rose preferred to love from a distance.

But then the girl removed her forehead from the wall and resumed her upright posture that Rose had not stopped admiring from the moment she had met her. "You're very kind," she said.

And then it felt like hours to Rose, how they continued to stare at each other without saying a word.

Four

NINA STARED AT her ringing cell phone and tried to quell the deeply familiar and historically shameful physiological consequences: the rapidly beating heart, the flushed face, the clamminess in her palms, and sweating of her armpits. *Really? After everything? You're going to let him melt you down in the beans, rice, soup, and packaged macaroni dinners aisle at your favorite Marina Del Rey Ralph's?*

For Nina, this was a most unfortunate realization; that she still *reacted* to the unmistakable 917 phone number flashing on the screen, blinking and winking at her to pick up. His name did not appear on the screen because she had deleted his contact information after the accident but clearly, this latest effort at purging had failed. If only he had emerged in her life during a later stage of cell phone ownership, when her brain had thoroughly jettisoned the practice of phone number memorization. He had started using a cell phone years before she finally caved and signed up for a plan and he had never changed his number. And so she could travel back in time to all the moments when she called this number from her landline, readying herself for the jolting sensation in her stomach that would hit her the moment she heard his voice.

"Neeee-naaaahhh." Laz loved pronouncing her name this way, as if he had spent his entire life consumed by a fetish for vowel elongation. *Neeee-naaaahhh.* Like slow cooking a roast in the oven.

"Is everything all right?" Rose now stood next to her, having returned from her slow yet steady expedition down the aisle in search of low-sodium tomato soup. She had declined Nina's assistance for this part of the shopping trip, explaining that she still felt like an actual human being as long as she could roam the aisles of a grocery store.

"Yes. Sorry." Nina stared at the missed call notification on her phone. She could never predict what Laz would do when she refused to take his calls. Sometimes, he left elaborate voice mails; other times, terse texts. Occasionally, he wouldn't leave any message, and she could only guess as to when he would contact her again. But he always got back in touch, a phenomenon better known as One of Nina's Central Problems of Adulthood.

"Dear. You look like you've seen a ghost." Rose gestured to her shopping cart, which contained the desired tomato soup, and suggested they move onto the cereal aisle.

Nina opted for partial honesty. "It's someone I don't really want to talk to."

Rose nodded somberly. "I know about such people."

As they made their way to the cereal aisle, Rose told her about a phone call she recently received from the daughter of a close friend, who wasn't well. The daughter had pleaded with Rose to speak with her mother, who on a good day, maintained that she would rather die than move out of her apartment into a nursing home. The daughter had wanted Rose to convince her mother that "assisted living" wasn't so bad.

"I let her know I was the wrong person for the job," Rose said, as she selected a package of Kellogg's Raisin Bran.

Nina stifled the impulse to encourage Rose to buy organic cereal. "I'm sorry about your friend."

Rose shrugged and changed the subject. "Sometimes I still think I'm doing the shopping for both of us. Morry loved to cook. It helped relax him."

Nina nodded. She always learned something new about Rose whenever they grocery shopped. Inside supermarkets, she could see how Rose harbored a fierce pride in her independence and she had learned to be strategic with her language. *It's no trouble at all. It's definitely not out of my way. I was going there anyway. Didn't you say you were out of avocados?* She had also discovered that Rose shared her Bubbe Essie's affinity for meticulous, tactile inspections of fresh produce and a passion for coupons but not her grandmother's gift for cooking. Rose also happily consumed genetically modified corn, did not fear pesticides, and interpreted most price differences between organic and non-organic foods as a personal insult.

Jeff, on the other hand, used to accompany her to the grocery store filled with facts about the latest article, health study, and/or purported superfood. Goji berries. Chia seeds. Turmeric. She had enjoyed shopping with Jeff, the two of them perusing the aisles in search of ingredients for recipes she found in the *Vegetarian Times*. Back at home, she did most of the cooking. During the week, she had her go-to, under-an-hour recipes: a mélange of stir-fries, braised vegetable dishes, and pastas with fresh sauces. On the weekends, she experimented with more challenging dinners, where she created vegan versions of Coq Au Vin or chicken piccata with tempeh and seitan. Sometimes, she yearned to cook fish for herself, but Jeff, a strict vegetarian, always became viscerally upset by the smell.

For the most part, Jeff had appreciated her cooking. She would be stirring and seasoning at the stove, and he would pour her a glass of wine and tell her that he couldn't wait to eat. Then, they would sit at their wooden Ikea kitchen table and review the good and bad of their respective days. Jeff always preferred to focus on the good, even if the bad demanded a little processing for purposes of mental health. "I don't think it serves us to dwell in excess negativity," he would say in his social worker's voice with a pointed glance at Nina, who wanted to vent for more than thirty seconds about one of her high-maintenance private clients or relay a near perilous traffic incident involving extraordinary amounts of road rage. But then he would thank her for a delicious dinner and Nina would try to forgive him.

She almost always forgave him, until the night she couldn't.

"I'm ready to check out, dear." Rose nodded in the direction of the cashiers. "Is that all you're buying?" She gestured to Nina's shopping cart, which contained five bananas, three apples, a hunk of cheddar cheese, a container of hummus, two packages of chamomile tea, and five bags of organic corn chips.

"I think so." Nina looked at her shopping cart and realized that she hadn't cooked a single meal since the accident. "Usually, I love to . . ." She considered telling Rose about the copious amounts of cooking she used to do but couldn't find the words. The words had become colors, a river of bright yellow morphing into a pool of molasses black.

"Dear, it's none of my business but maybe you should eat more?"

Nina smiled. As she assured Rose that she still ate plenty, her cell phone beeped.

Just tell me if you're okay.

It was only a text message.

Cue the rapid beating of Nina's Pavlovian heart.

HEY NINA, I'M in LA and of course thought of you. Any chance of getting together? Yours, Laz

There's Nina, telling herself it's only an email. It's approximately four months before the accident and she's sitting in the living room with her laptop in the apartment that she shares with Jeff. She has just removed said laptop off her lap and placed it on the coffee table, where she regards it with a new level of distrust, as if it's some unidentified object on the subway in New York or a bus in Israel. On her living room couch, she re-arranges into a cross-legged position and waits for her heart rate to return to normal. *Five, four, three, two . . .* Nina counts down, as she does when afflicted by anxiety or insomnia but at the moment, the technique doesn't work. Instead, her feet fall asleep and she attempts a different kind of math. How long has it been since he's contacted her? It's a word problem requiring only a modicum of memory and in seconds, she has the answer: almost two and a half years ago, when he called to not-so-casually ask how LA was treating her.

"Do you need help in there?" Nina calls out to Jeff, who's in the midst of scrubbing dishes and cleaning the kitchen.

No answer from Jeff. Nina hears the water from the faucet and assumes he hasn't heard her. In their world of strict justice and equitability, she doesn't need to ask him if he needs help. Tonight, she had been the one to cook dinner, a virtuous broccoli and tofu stir-fry to counter the excess of their Tempranillo and artisanal cheese-fueled Saturday night at a Santa Monica wine bar. When she cooks, he washes dishes and scrubs down the kitchen, end of story. Early on in their cohabitation, they had discovered that they organically excelled when it came to household divisions of labor. She cooks. He cleans the kitchen. She pays the grocery bills; he pays all utilities. They split the rent and pay for their apartment to be cleaned every two weeks, even though their respective yoga teacher and social worker salaries do not allow for a surplus of luxury goods and services. Both Nina and Jeff, however, do not see their use of a cleaning service as a luxury. Rather, they believe in the wisdom of placing the messiest of household tasks into the hands of objective, third party strangers.

Nina stares at her dust-encrusted computer screen and notes how it makes the email seem ancient, as if uncovered by an archeological dig. A relic, she thinks, but not the kind that deserves to be dusted off and displayed on her coffee table.

Delete, delete, delete. And empty your trash!

Only she can't.

Nina closes her laptop and flees the living room for the kitchen, where she finds Jeff diligently Swiffering dinner crumbs off the floor. She watches him clean and tries to sink herself back into the deep familiarity of this Sunday night routine. She watches Jeff crumple the dirty Swiffer cloth into a ball, which he tosses into the trash with perfect aim. Then, he returns to the sink to scrub out the wok she had used for tonight's stir-fry. She stares at his back, feeling herself swell with the habitual, insatiable need.

Save me. Or at least, distract me.

If she answers the call of the need, then he will inevitably succumb to their now entrenched pattern. She knows this and yet she tiptoes over to the sink and stands behind Jeff. She puts her arms around his waist. "Hey."

"Hang on." Jeff holds up the now spotless pan and places it on the drainer. "Let me finish."

On some other evening, Nina might have found another method for curbing the insatiability of her need. She might have stood on her head for two minutes or tried to scrawl out her emotions in her journal. She still believes in private, analogue journals even though most people she knows have traded this coping method for public, online emoting. On some other evening, she might have purposely recalled recent and arduous conversations that she had conducted with Jeff about their differing emotional needs. She needs verbal and physical affirmation; he doesn't, blah, blah, blah. On some other evening, she might have reminded herself that she will be marrying him with open eyes, armed with the belief that they had mutually accepted what each found difficult about the other.

Instead, Nina nibbles on Jeff's left earlobe and whispers, "You know I'm hot for any man who does the dishes."

"Yeah, yeah." Jeff remains facing the sink as he reaches from behind with his wet hands to remove Nina's dry hands off his waist.

Nina feels the familiar stab of rejection but decides to ignore it. She starts rubbing his back and says, "It's true."

This time, Jeff turns around so that he's facing her. He sighs and says, "I know. Your father never did the dishes so the opposite is a turn-on."

You want to go the pseudo psychoanalytic route? Fine, I'll play. Nina opts to smile at him. "That's right. I used to date guys like my father and now I don't."

"So the question is, have you evolved or are you still rebelling?"

"Rebelling from what?"

"You tell me."

I need you. Right here, right now. I need to be reminded of all the ways that I love you. So please, no hiding in your shell Mr. Hermit Crab. Not tonight.

Nina wishes she could reveal herself this way to Jeff. She wishes that he would stop playing the toying psychoanalyst, which then prompted her to refute him or play shrink to his shrink. They had developed a certain shtick two years into their relationship, which only served to obscure what they didn't have the guts to address.

"I'll help you finish cleaning." She re-wraps herself around Jeff, determined to ignore the way his body immediately stiffens at her touch.

"Nina." She hears it in his voice, that tone he reserves for clients and colleagues that call his cell at three in the morning under the auspices of an emergency and keep him on the phone for two hours. "Please."

"I just wanted a hug." She releases him and moves to slouch against their refrigerator, knocking off the magnet attached to their analogue—her idea— list of emergency phone numbers. She watches Jeff catch the piece of paper as it flutters to the floor and devises a test. If he reconsiders these last couple of minutes and moves in to hug her, then she will tell him about the email.

She watches Jeff refasten the emergency number list to the fridge. He smacks the magnet, as if that will permanently fix the problem.

"Is that really so hard? Hugging?" She hears her voice, small and mousy, and she's filled with self-loathing. She hates the fact that once again, she's with a man who makes her beg.

Jeff grabs her left shoulder and squeezes twice. "There."

"Jeff."

"What? You asked for a hug, I gave you a hug."

She clenches her jaw and folds her arms over her chest.

Jeff sighs and squeezes her right shoulder. "I'm sorry but I can't have this discussion right now. I'm exhausted and I still need to take a shower."

"You do that."

"Nina—"

"I was going to tell you something."

He folds his arms across his chest as he waits for her to speak and a well-traversed trail opens between the point A of her and the point B of him, littered with highly developed yet mostly unspoken sentiments. Such as: *I hate it when you make me feel this needy.* And: *I get it, you know. I know your mother forced you to hug and kiss her when you were a little boy and now you distrust affection when it's solicited from you. I know everyone wants a piece of you at work so when you come home, you can't respond to someone else's emotional needs unless you're feeling "authentic" about it.*

And: *I know I shouldn't be testing you right now but there's also my stuff in this equation. What you said about my father earlier and how I reacted? Yeah that. You got one type of parents and I got another, not that they're really to blame because that would be reductive, not to mention a shitty abdication of personal responsibility, right? Anyway, I would tell you that I'm sorry but I'm just not up to it.*

And: *I thought I accepted the way you show love but maybe I don't.*

Nina stares at her fiancé and swallows the whole, hot mess of everything she thinks and feels. In her mind, she visualizes the words of the email she has yet to delete. She says, "Forget it. Go take a shower."

Five minutes later: Nina returns to her cross-legged position on the living room couch. She hears Jeff turn on the shower and the whooshing sounds of flowing water create the illusion of privacy. She reads the email twice more, feeling ripped apart by a sensation of weakness. She knows the drill. If she doesn't act soon, she will become paralyzed by the fear that he will never contact her again. Because as long as he persists in reaching out, she's reminded of how she used to feel about him and the resulting sensation, God help her, still makes her grateful to be alive.

Why am I not surprised to hear from you? Sure, let's meet. Nina

She finally writes this message and hits the send button after seven other failed attempts. Oh well, she thinks. So she didn't write the message of her good intentions: *Hey Laz, All is well on my end. I wish you a great stay in LA and all the best in your life –Nina.* She had really wanted to wish him "all the best," hadn't she? On matters of downgrading people from sizzling intimates to vague and sterile acquaintances, she can't think of a better boundary-building phrase.

She hears the bathroom door open and slams her laptop shut. She tries to soak up the sounds of Jeff switching on the lamp in the bedroom and opening drawers. She hears the creak of their bedsprings and stares at her hands. They haven't stopped shaking since she clicked "send."

From the bedroom, Jeff yells, "You want to watch a movie?"

"Sure."

Tell him.

But she can't. The familiar light-headed sensation has kicked in and she has successfully transported herself to a candlelit bar full of strangers, awaiting his arrival.

"You okay?" Jeff now looms over her. He's wearing ancient gray sweatpants and a Bugs Bunny T-shirt. For Jeff, Bugs Bunny still ranks as his all-time favorite cartoon because of its pioneering appeal to both children and adults. They have this in common, staying faithful to the television shows that they loved, no matter how much they had faded from the zeitgeist.

Nina watches Jeff comb his hair and feels scattered drops of water drizzle her face. She knows that Jeff harbors a large, not-so-secret amount of pride for his thick, curly hair, which distinguishes him from most of his male friends, who contend with some form of hair loss. She tries to focus on this fact about her fiancé, as it makes him more human.

"Yeah, I'll be fine."

She watches Jeff considering her words, knowing there's a seconds-long debate raging through his head: To engage or disengage, that is the question.

Jeff sighs. "I'm sorry about before, okay?" He cuffs her on the leg.

"Yeah. Okay." Or rather, maybe it would have been okay had he not cuffed her on the leg.

Jeff sighs again. "You're still mad, aren't you?"

"We don't have to get into this right now. I know you're tired."

"Okay. Why don't you pick what we watch?"

She stares at his Bugs Bunny T-shirt and decides they should bring out the box set of *Sex in the City* that he had given her for her thirty-fifth birthday. She had loved him for this; buying her all the seasons of a TV show that he mocked, until he started watching it with her. Now, she knows that he enjoys the lives of Carrie, Samantha, Miranda, and Charlotte more than he cares to admit.

She chooses an episode with care, avoiding season three, when Carrie and Big have an affair. On the couch, she makes room for Jeff and he doesn't cringe when she snuggles against him, her thighs smashing into his thighs. Together, they watch Carrie leave her apartment in her customary pair of Manolo Blahniks. Nina has always empathized with Carrie, for whom all roads lead back to Mr. Big. She doesn't even bother to convince herself that writing back doesn't necessarily equal a dark bar. She knows that she will soon be there, waiting for him.

NINA FOUND A rare parking spot right in front of her apartment building. When she got out of the car to retrieve her groceries from the trunk, one of the feral cats scuttled across her building's front yard and zoomed over the wall that separated it from the adjacent property. Nina appreciated the flash of orange. So far, she thought of these cats by their colors: orange, black, splotchy gray, splotchy brown. One day, she sensed she would name them, however their relationship might evolve. But so far, since moving into this building and discovering their colony, she simply admired them for their stealth, speed, and grace. These cats did not require yoga classes to make peace with their spines. They also kept her company, even though they could be skittish and prone to panicked flight, especially if she tried to approach them while they foraged through the garbage cans at the back of her building.

We're all homeless, even though we all live here.

It still didn't register that she lived somewhere else, no matter that almost four months had passed since the accident. Nina opened the door to the apartment bearing her lone grocery bag and surveyed her living room and kitchen area as if for the first time. She put her groceries away and resisted the impulse to pour herself a glass of wine and open her laptop to mindlessly google the rest of the afternoon away. She had no more classes to teach today and she could not bear the thought of going out into the world again. Had Laz not texted her, perhaps she might have felt differently about the world. Perhaps, she would have suggested to Rose that they see a movie. Or maybe, she would have invited Rose over for dinner after helping her put her groceries away. It would be nice to cook for someone again, wouldn't it?

Nina decided to sit on the floor in the middle of her living room, which only contained a beige futon couch and a small purple beanbag. She had not yet purchased a non-futon couch or new coffee table or love seat or other chairs or hung up any art on the walls. At the moment, her living space evoked the vibe of a vacant college dorm room.

She re-arranged herself into a cross-legged position and tried to recall what she knew of Jewish mourning rituals. Three years ago, she had spent a week at her mother's house to sit shiva for Bubbe Essie. Sandra, however, had always displayed an indifference to Jewish tradition and this hadn't changed when she divorced Nina's father when Nina was twenty-two. Nina had been the one to do a little research and insist that they cover the mirrors in the house and sit on low stools when greeting visitors. Surely, Bubbe Essie would want them to perform these traditions, in addition to ensuring that their visitors could munch on bagels and lox to their hearts' content. Sandra had said yes to the mirrors and bagels but no to the stools.

Her mother had experienced some difficulty with the sitting part of sitting shiva. Sandra kept getting up to deliver used dishes to the sink or to purposely open the unlocked door for those who came to pay their respects. "I'm sorry," she had said to Nina on the last day of shiva. "I didn't always act like a mother when you were growing up."

"What do you mean?" Nina of course knew exactly what her mother meant.

"Your father and I . . ." Her mother had closed her eyes and sighed. "We made some mistakes."

You're choosing to apologize now? When I'm not allowed to be mad at you because you're in mourning? All Nina could say to her mother that day was, "it's okay" and swallow the whole, hot mess of everything she thought and felt on the subject of parental neglect.

Nina bowed her head and closed her eyes. She thought of Jeff sitting in their living room, waiting for her to play another episode of *Sex and the City* and how she allowed all the unsaid things to bubble and boil inside her. What if she had expressed to him what truly lay in her heart that night? What if she told him that when he refuses to hug her, she feels like she's eight years old again, the lone kid still waiting for her mother to pick her up from school or spying on her parents having sex in their kitchen or watching her mother kiss a male neighbor on the lips at one of the parties her parents used to throw when she and her sister were supposed to be asleep. *Nina, go to bed.* How many times had her parents shamed her into getting out of their way? But when her mother tried to apologize for decades of making her feel like a disturbance or worse, an afterthought, she could only say, "It's okay."

But it wasn't okay.

Nina's cell phone beeped and she forced herself to stay seated for another five minutes on her living room floor. She tried to stay angry as she returned to the kitchen to grab her phone.

Can you spare a second to write back?

Please?

Nina?

Neeee-naaaaah.

Her loneliness overruled her anger. It told her to dial the number that remained embedded in the part of her memory that stored the now defunct phone numbers of her childhood home and Bubbe Essie's Westwood apartment. She still knew them by heart, despite the fact that they became disconnected years ago and were no longer in service.

Five

THERE'S ROSE, shopping at the Sunday farmers market in Santa Monica. She's just bought a dozen oranges, primarily for juicing. Morry is with her, having felt each orange prior to purchase. They've been married for twelve years now and living the happiest of symbiotic lives, where there's no need to bring up the past. Sure, a week before their wedding, they had traded pertinent confessions over dinner with the briskness of business travelers rushing through an airport. *Richard was repeatedly unfaithful and finally left me for another woman. You? She drank too much and suffered from money and anger management afflictions. Oh. Should we look at the dessert menu?* But that was then, not to mention end of story.

But now, Rose wrestles with the following question: Should she or shouldn't she tell Morry about the phone call she had received three days ago at the studio? *Hello Rose, I saw that lovely little write-up in the paper about your students preparing for their Nutcracker production and I felt like I had to call. And I must say that photographer took a lovely picture of you. You haven't aged a bit.*

Rose surveys her immediate surroundings, as if it's imminently plausible that her ex-husband will suddenly materialize by one of the produce stands, squeezing peaches or tomatoes like he's milking a cow. A tactile soul, you might call her ex-husband, the type of person who lives for touching all the objects in a museum when the guards aren't looking.

But Richard lives in North Hollywood now, a world away from Santa Monica. This much she knows from their phone call. *But I still get to the West Side occasionally, so, I was wondering . . . I would love to stop by and say hello.*

"Your ex-wife," Rose suddenly says to Morry, who's now in the midst of paying for a loaf of sourdough bread. "Aren't you curious sometimes about her whereabouts?"

"Can't say I am. Do you want to look at those turnips?" Morry picks up the bread and starts walking toward a stall that seems to only specialize in circular produce—turnips, onions, those small round potatoes. Rose understands her husband well enough by now to know he's generally averse to following the threads of out-of-the-blue questions.

"Not yet." Rose grabs her husband's arm, unsure how to fix a conversation that she botched from the get-go.

"Well what then? Lettuce maybe? Rutabagas?"

Rose glances in the direction of the nearby peach stand. "I have something to tell you." She thinks: if she buys any of those peaches, she will imagine her ex-husband squeezing them each time she tries to eat what she has purchased.

"Nu?" Morry looks at her, expectant and slightly irritated. Her husband adores these expeditions to the farmers market and shame on her for disturbing his food shopping rhythms.

"I heard from Richard the other day. He telephoned me at the studio. It was a shock to the system." She doesn't understand this sudden surge of adolescent desire that floods her sixty-two-year-old body as she names her ex-husband.

To counter the sensation, Rose flashes back to the day she and Richard stood in the rabbi's office and he deposited the get into her hands. *You got what you wanted, you bastard.* She had held that freshly signed divorce document and nodded at Richard for effect. As she moved several steps away from him in the prescribed manner, she saw how his lips stretched into the slightest of satisfied smiles.

"Really? You don't say." Morry's voice fills with false geniality and this reminds Rose of how they sometimes behave in the car: one lost person trying to give another lost person directions.

Rose explains: Richard saw the write-up in the *LA Times* metro section about the ballet studio. So he called and they engaged in a particular form of catch-up conversation otherwise known as: My life is great without you, thank you very much. *Life in Venice is still wonderful. How do you like North Hollywood? Don't miss the ocean at all? You don't say. Morry is retired but I'm still teaching. Why yes, I have always loved organizing little girls into Sunday recital appropriate lines and formations best suited for the family photo albums. I love teaching, always have. Why yes, we're very happy, thank you. And you? How nice, that your marriage to someone so much younger gives you energy. And you have a daughter now? You don't say. Well, good thing you're still employed. I'm sure there will always be a need for accountants. Death and taxes, the two constants, right? What was that? Her friends call you "grandpa" behind your back? You don't say.*

In this re-telling, Rose omits the fact that Richard also complimented her. And finally, she gets to the point: her ex-husband wants to pay her a visit.

Morry tightens his grip on the plastic bags he's holding and starts walking over to the strawberry stand without consulting her. She follows him and he says, "Does he want to pay us a visit or just you?"

"He said he wanted to discuss some private matters with me. I said I would check with you."

Correction: What she actually said was: *I don't think that's such a good idea.*

"What sort of private matters?"

"I don't know."

They take slow, measured steps toward the strawberry stand. Once there, the strawberry vendor offers them free samples. The fruit tastes sugary sweet and melts in Rose's mouth. She and Morry glance at each other and agree: two boxes seem like a worthy investment. They have always been able to communicate this way without speaking. Richard, on the other hand, always required an excess of speech and still, she had often failed to express herself.

You haven't aged one bit.

Is she really that much of a fool, so easily seduced by a mere scrap of compliment issued from the mouth of a man who, provided he was still the same old Richard, told the truth about once a year?

"Anything else?" Morry looks at her for further instructions.

"I will tell him to come to the studio if he wants to see me."

She watches Morry pay the strawberry vendor and shift his grip on their purchases. He says, "So you do want to see him?"

"It's not like that." She says this a little too quickly.

She's unable to look at Morry as they leave the market for the parking lot. They get into their car and Morry barrels out of the lot. Rarely does her husband drive so fast.

"Careful," Rose says. "You could have an accident."

"When have I ever had an accident?" With both hands, Morry grips the steering wheel and Rose watches his knuckles turn white. She remembers how quickly she had learned to ascertain Morry's moods by the position of his hands on the steering wheel. One hand: happy. Two hands: angry. A constant shifting between one hand to two hands: sad.

A car cuts in front of them, its driver honking three times for effect. It zooms through an intersection, while Morry brakes at the yellow light hard and sudden.

"Is there anything else you'd like to know?" Rose feels an unfamiliar urgency; that if she doesn't confront Morry right this very second, a type of loss will occur that requires coping mechanisms beyond their collective capability.

"Why would you want to see him again? After what he did to you?"

"I don't have to see him. Not if you don't like it." She doesn't mention suffering the plague of nostalgia-tinged curiosity, of wondering if she would still feel the things she used to feel when she was with him.

Silence from Morry. Rose watches him continue to drive with tremendous caution: both hands on the steering wheel and easily a few miles under the speed limit. She thinks: how dare you. One look into the past does not an adulteress make.

She feels both relieved and tormented by the silence that accompanies the rest of their drive. She cannot find the right words until Morry secures a rare parking spot on Pacific Avenue around the corner from their apartment, which sweetens the air in the car ever so slightly.

"Richard is not a good man," Rose finally says as they stand outside the entrance to their building, fumbling for their respective house keys.

"What does one thing have to do with another?"

"Everything."

She prepares to divulge further details about Richard's betrayals. Morry, after all, doesn't know all the particulars of how her ex-husband, afflicted with the most clichéd shiksa-complex imaginable, had a predilection for entertaining blond, blue-eyed, Scandinavian-looking women in the privacy of their home while she was out teaching little girls how to plié and pirouette. But then she looks at her current husband's face and reconsiders. What lies at the bottom of his heart? Can he conclude that he trusts her, for example, merely by the way she looks at him?

She decides to say nothing further about Richard and allows Morry to be the retriever of the house keys. He unlocks the door to their building and as she walks inside, he puts his hand on her shoulder.

LATER: JUST BEFORE bedtime, they make love and it feels like always. But afterward, Morry says, "We're getting old."

"Not so old."

"Old enough not to recognize myself in the mirror."

"I recognize you just fine."

She sees the fear in his eyes as they kiss goodnight. She does not stop stroking his shoulder until he falls asleep. Then, she lies there with her arms folded over her chest. She touches her shoulders, closes her eyes, and feels the futility of replacing one human being with another. After a while, she opens her eyes and continues to watch Morry sleep.

Careful Rose. Careful of the spaces between people.

TWO WEEKS LATER: In the midst of teaching the final center floor phrase to her Friday afternoon students—glissade, assemblé, pirouette, rinse and repeat—Rose notices a man standing in the hallway of her ballet school, directly in front of Studio C's large window. He wears a dark blue suit and carries a briefcase. He smiles and waves, so she's forced to do more than just glance. Is that Richard?

Her ex-husband appears nearly unchanged. He is shorter than Morry though more powerfully built, his arms and legs muscular from years of weight lifting, running, and swimming. Richard had always taken excellent care of his body and as Rose grew older, continually implored her to do the same. *Do you really get enough exercise from teaching? I remember the first time I saw you perform. You were so beautiful.* And then he would reminisce about their first meeting, how he had waited for her outside the stage door after a performance of *Cinderella*. Love at first sight. Surely, Richard considered himself a lucky man, to have experienced this particular human ritual with a regularity more commonly associated with eating or sleeping.

Rose decides not to acknowledge Richard just yet. Two days after her market expedition with Morry, she had telephoned him and explained that an in-person visit wasn't a good idea but if he had something to say to her, then he should do so over the phone. *I can't say it over the phone but if you ever change your mind, call me.* And here he now stands watching her teach class, in deliberate disobedience of her wishes.

Rose returns her attention to the class, which she purposely ends eight minutes late. After she exits the studio, she continues to ignore him as she makes small talk with several of her students' mothers and tries to evade the usual questions from one particular mother. *Do you think Lisa can play Clara this year? She's been a mouse for three years in a row now and we've always been big supporters of your* Nutcracker *production.* Finally, when the last student and her mother have said goodbye and the dance school's receptionist steps out for a coffee break, Rose approaches Richard, who has seated himself on a chair in the front office with his briefcase opened on his lap. Upon sighting her, he immediately slams the briefcase shut and stands, holding out his arms. Rose manages to bypass his arms but she cannot dodge the soft, moist kiss that he plants on her lower left cheek.

"What are you doing here?"

"I know you told me not to come by but . . . I was in the neighborhood." Her ex-husband, smiles, shrugs, and smiles some more. "Wow. It's been a long time."

She watches her ex-husband perform the not-so-subtle eye sweeping movement of appraising her from head to toe. "I'll say."

Her ex-husband smiles again and this time, he looks directly into her eyes. And there it is: the original electrical current that had existed between them, traveling from her eyes to her shoulders and into her torso and pelvis.

"It's wonderful to see you Rose. I have thought about you over the years." Richard says this looking ever so slightly over her right shoulder. Quickly, she understands that he's distracted by the oversized black and white poster of the ballerina Alicia Markova in a glittering short tutu and perfect arabesque that dominates the wall in front of him. Rose never fails to glean inspiration from Markova, a fellow Jew in the ballet business, and perhaps she should now also thank her for this public service reminder: her ex-husband remains very much a leg man and in possession of a wandering eye.

And yet: this reminder does little to zap the original electrical current from Rose's body.

The secret thrill and shame of it.

She invites him into her office, which doubles as a costume room for the ballet school's semi-annual productions. On the walls hang other enormous black and white and Technicolor posters of Ballet Russes luminaries: Leonide Massine, Frederick Ashton, Alexandra Danilova, and ballerina of all ballerinas,

Anna Pavlova, on pointe with those beautiful arms raised above her head. The posters have been there since the days of her marriage to Richard but she certainly doesn't expect him to remember this since he rarely visited her place of business.

Rose gestures for Richard to sit on her spare metal folding chair placed on the other side of her desk. She asks, "What couldn't you say over the phone?"

He says he wants to show her something. He removes a picture from his wallet and places it on the desk. It's a school photograph of his blond, blue-eyed, seven-year-old daughter. "Never thought I'd be such an old father," he says with the most perfect of self-deprecating chuckles.

Rose starts to say, "Better late than never," but then she stops right there. She glances at Richard, who at least has the manners if not the humility to avert his eyes as she contemplates a history they never shared.

Remember the doctor I visited who finally told me the truth? Rose picks up the photograph and examines the beautiful little girl. *That it was me, not you. Remember what he said? Maybe we could adopt, a nice, reasonably well-off Jewish couple like us. He said other things too, this doctor with consolation prizes coming out of his ears. And when I came home and told you this, what did you say? You said, "I married you for you." You said, "We can still have a wonderful life."*

Richard clears his throat. "I'm sorry it didn't end well with us."

She slides his photograph across her desk. "What's done is done."

He grabs her hand. "I've changed, you know."

She laughs and withdraws her hand. "Well, I've heard that becoming a parent will do that to a person."

He grabs her other hand. "It's true."

She recoils her other hand. "I wouldn't know."

"Rose." He says her name in the softest voice possible without whispering. "When I saw your picture in the newspaper, it surprised me. I didn't think that . . ."

She closes her eyes, figuring it wouldn't hurt for one second, maybe two, to simply sink into the softness of his voice. A finger that doesn't belong to her strokes her left cheek. She feels a hand tilting her chin and lips grazing lips.

Rose?

There's her husband Morry, hovering directly above her. He's wearing a dark blue suit for the occasion and he's promising to always keep both hands on the wheel. *No matter what.* And does she know that he was actually awake on the night she stroked his shoulder for hours? He knows how hard she worked to extinguish the chasm that had opened between them at the farmers market. *You do the best you can Rose. And it's enough.*

Rose opens her eyes and removes Richard's hands from her face. She figures she can at least wash her face at the studio though what she really craves is a scalding hot shower, where her entire body turns pink as she spends an hour scrubbing her skin. She says, "You shouldn't have come."

"Rose . . . please," he says in that same almost-whisper and gives her the smile that used to melt her insides during the first days of their courtship. *I know you. In fact, I know you better than you know yourself.*

"You need to leave." She stands up from her desk and opens the office door.

He sighs and takes his time gathering his briefcase and straightening his tie. He crosses the threshold of her office and pauses. "I just thought . . ."

She slams the door in his face, which lucky her, has the kind of lock that would take an amateur thief at least ten minutes to pick. Against this barricade, she now leans, breathing hard and feeling lost, since she has never slammed the door in anyone's face before. As she hears him walk away, she wants to scream: I FEEL SORRY FOR YOUR WIFE AND SORRIER FOR YOUR DAUGHTER!

Only Rose remains silent. She continues to lean against the door until she hears the bustling sounds of her receptionist, newly returned from her coffee break, and the voices of her early bird students, now stretching in the lobby before the next class. In a minute, she will have no choice but to open her office door. She needs to tell the janitorial assistant to run a mop over Studio C's floor for the next class. She doesn't have time to ruminate over how many times a person needs to say goodbye.

ABOUT THREE WEEKS after the incident with the skateboarder, Rose woke up missing her husband like she always did but also thinking: enough is enough. Wallowing in paralytic misery had never been her forte. Also, she had to prepare for visitors today.

For three weeks, Rose had mostly hibernated, subsisting on canned food and relying on her stash of bargain basement toilet paper, a now five-year-old mistake with its egregiously cardboard overtones that took up space in her coat closet. The briefest of lapses in Rose's long-term history as a convert to Charmin, which she always tried to buy on sale at Ralph's.

With the exception of her weekly social engagement with the girl—no shopping, only lunch—Rose had forsaken outside world activities, preferring to stay in bed until noon so she could torture herself with a revolving door of questions. Did that skateboarder mean her intentional harm or had she simply been in the way? Just like that poor boy had simply been in the way. And would the girl ever be okay? And how would she manage to visit her dear friend Lillian Rabinowitz, recently exiled by her daughter to a facility deep in the San Fernando Valley? And why on earth did Adele Mandelbaum send her that cloyingly pink condolence card? And the question of all questions: Why was she, of all people, not dead yet? Then, she would spend the rest of her day in her nightgown, staring at her television but not really watching it. This of course reminded her of Morry, who had stared at the television this way, albeit for different reasons.

But then Rose had received a phone call. She had answered on the third ring and a voice, which at first sounded like the girl's, asked "is this Rose?" The girl, of course, would not have asked such a question and so Rose had immediately stiffened. These days, she only expected phone calls from the girl, medical and dental receptionists reminding her of various appointments, and telemarketers trying to sell her things she already had: credit cards, health insurance, a place to live in a sunny climate.

The caller then identified herself: Her name was Carla Tannen, daughter of Richard Tannen. Did she have the right Rose? At first, Rose could barely speak due to the onset of an increased heart rate and profound déjà vu. To be contacted out of the blue because of another article in the newspaper? Since when did young people start reading newspapers again? From what Rose understood—from reading newspapers—young people had abandoned this source of information for the Internet, where apparently opinions thrived and facts were an endangered species.

Like father like daughter? Rose would never know unless she met the young woman and so she had acquiesced to the request for a face-to-face visit.

Rose got out of bed. As she got dressed, she pondered her options. She could try to tidy up her apartment and visit the mini-market around the corner to buy the most appropriate-possible refreshments. Cookies? Pretzels? Those mediocre containers of guacamole? Or she could greet them—this Carla said she would be bringing her husband—briefly in her apartment, then suggest eating lunch across the street where they could choose among the multitude of concession stands. Personally, it might do her good to lunch on falafel or a vegetarian pizza slice while sitting in the fresh air amidst boardwalk hubbub, no matter the likely digestive discomfort.

She fixed herself a cup of instant coffee and made a decision: She would wait for Richard's daughter downstairs. Perhaps there would be empty tables outside the organic coffee shop, where they could have their meeting in a more impersonal environment.

Rose finished her coffee, grabbed her walker, and went downstairs with about ninety minutes to spare. That same nice man from the coffee shop waved at her from his usual place behind the cash register. He invited her inside, where he plied her with free coffee—Rose didn't need any more coffee but felt it would be rude not to accept—and asked how she was feeling.

"Getting along all right." Rose then changed the subject by profusely thanking the man for the coffee, though truth be told, she preferred the instant kind. When she drank her daily cup of instant, she would invariably think of Morry, who introduced this specific coffee habit early on in their marriage.

The coffee man told her he had seen that skateboarder again three days ago with two of his friends. They were tagging the side of the Indigenous world music shop around the corner from the Sunny Surfwear with red spray paint.

"One day, they'll get into enough trouble for the cops to do something," he predicted.

Rose nodded, not so much in the mood anymore to think about these potential future Nazis of America. But she appreciated how the coffee man tried to be kind. So she tried to exude an air of generalized joie de vivre as she explained she would now wait for some visitors. The coffee man pointed to the empty outdoor tables. Thanking the man for his hospitality, Rose took her coffee and a copy of the local free Venice newspaper from the stack by the coffee shop's entrance. She seated herself at the cleanest-looking outdoor table, glanced at the front page of the newspaper, and felt her arms erupt with goose pimples. Impossible, she thought. A cruel trick of her failing eyesight. From her coat pocket, she extracted her magnifying glass and read the horrific headline three times.

99 CENT STORE DAYS ARE NUMBERED. WHOLE FOODS MOVING IN.

Rose placed her magnifying glass on top of the newspaper and froze. The visceral meaning of the "last straw" now flooded every part of her body, as if all the mourning of her life now coalesced around the headline in the local Venice newspaper. She and the 99 Cent went way back, at least twenty-five years. Since Morry's death, it had become an even dearer friend, and she tried to shop there as often as she could. But now it was going kaput and she would have to sit shiva, just like she had done for everyone and everything else. Ninety-three years of telling herself: they had their time, as I have mine, and for what? So Whole Foods could move in and charge ten times the price for bananas and vegetarian chicken cutlets? Is this why she continued to live while so many others have died?

For the next hour or so, Rose sat with her newspaper and coffee, not reading and not drinking. About fifteen minutes before the scheduled arrival of her visitors, she saw a man and woman dart into the coffee shop. Five minutes later, they emerged back outside with small coffee cups and seated themselves at the table next to hers.

Was that them? Rose appraised the young couple and their shared blond, blue-eyed, all-American good looks. There was something in the man's facial structure that made Rose think about the fair-haired, light-eyed Jews she knew as a child of White Russia. Such Jews had a much better chance of assimilation and survival. The woman looked more Scandinavian in origin and she wore a purple T-shirt inscribed with the words "Dunder Mifflin."

Could this be? Rose stared at the woman's T-shirt, marveling at the coincidence. She owned the same T-shirt, which she had purchased at the Sunny Surfwear in size medium for use as a housedress. For at least fifteen years, Rose had taken advantage of the boardwalk's abundant beachwear shops, having made the practical discovery that T-shirts in size medium translate perfectly into comfortable and utilitarian calf-length housedresses. She cared little for the words on these T-shirts—she only recently learned that "Dunder Mifflin" came from some television show—only that she should wear no expletives.

Rose put her magnifying glass away, folded up her newspaper, and cleared her throat. "Excuse me. Are you—?"

The woman stood up, grabbed her coffee, and walked over to Rose's table. "Of course! You must be Rose. It's so nice to meet you."

Carla insisted they shake hands and then introduced her husband Jon. Carla spoke in that sunshine tone that made Rose think of the young people who used to visit the Center. Was she one of them? Rose couldn't yet detect the type of soul that lived beneath the cheer and enthusiasm. She did take an immediate liking to the husband, however. Something in his face suggested he was a kind man and once again, she thought of Morry. That had been most important to her, hadn't it? She had loved her husband for his intelligence and lucidity but above all because he was kind.

Good for you, marrying someone who isn't your father. Rose stared at the young woman and her husband, at a loss for further words.

Fortunately, Richard's daughter seemed to have a knack for taking charge of a conversation. "Thank you for agreeing to see us. I can imagine that it must be . . ."

Rose held up her hand. "It's all right."

But Carla persisted. "We're very sorry for your loss."

Rose nodded and forced herself to smile. *Morry was a wonderful man in good health and he'll be sorely missed.* The newspaper reporter had omitted that part of her statement from his article. He had only included what she had to say about her husband possessing a valid California driver's license.

Carla exchanged a glance with her husband. "The strange thing is, I recognized . . . um, Jeff, from his picture. I didn't know him really but I . . ."

Rose nodded in encouragement but Carla merely shook her head. Had she winced at the sound of the boy's name? To think that she had just met another person who knew this boy while he walked the earth. "Did you know he had a fiancée? She and I see each other now. We're . . ." Rose paused. What were she and the girl to each other exactly?

"Would either of you like more coffee?" Rose glanced across the street and noticed that the tamale stand had a new mural painted on its front wall. Under Morry's enthusiastic tutelage, Rose had developed an eye for the street art in her neighborhood. This particular mural featured a baby-faced clown painted pink and white and framed by the caption: *Thanks Mom for making me eat my vegetables.* A gray tabby cat with thick matted fur sauntered past the mural and posed in front of it before darting into the alleyway behind the tamale stand. This made Rose also think of her husband, who derived considerable aesthetic delight from sighting such striking juxtapositions. Morry would have taken a photograph of the cat and mural and then insisted it live in a frame somewhere in their living room.

Carla and her husband politely declined her offer for more coffee. The husband gestured at the vanishing tabby and asked if Rose liked cats. Personally, Rose preferred birds and dogs but she was no despiser of felines. So she shrugged and the husband explained that he rescued stray and wild cats in his spare time and helped find homes for the cats that could live with humans. Rose said, "How nice," hoping she made herself perfectly clear.

Then Rose and the husband looked to Carla. It was her turn but one second of silence turned into another and Rose thought that surely these people did not come here to twiddle their thumbs and make small talk about cats.

"I had wanted to contact you for years," Carla finally said. "And when I saw the article in the newspaper, I . . . I had to get in touch. My dad left my mom when I was ten and I had always thought, that when my mom was still alive, that the two of you could have . . . talked."

"Your mother?" Rose didn't know what else to ask.

"She died two years ago."

"I'm very sorry for your loss."

"Thank you. I also wanted to see you because I'm trying to write about my parents so it's important I understand them as much as possible."

"You are a writer?"

Carla looked to her husband for some cue that Rose could not decipher but nonetheless, she sensed its existence. Did the husband approve of his wife's writing? Again, Rose thought of Morry, who had professed unwavering support for her career as a dance teacher until the day she had retired.

"I write essays and I'm working on a memoir," Carla said.

Rose then glanced at the husband, who immediately said, "Carla is a great writer."

"How nice," Rose said. Had she known that this encounter was to be more of an interview than a conversation, she might have stayed put in her apartment.

Carla smoothed her straight blond hair and succumbed to what seemed like an unconscious habit: stroking her necklace like a treasured pet, first the gold chain, then the purple stone at its center. Carla noticed how Rose watched her. "My dad gave this to me for my bat mitzvah. It's one of the few gifts from him that I still have."

Rose forced herself to smile. She stared at Richard's daughter and saw that her lips still formed words. But she couldn't hear them. She felt that rushing sensation in her ears, as if the ocean waves had taken up residence there.

This is how she remembers her father.

"I thought maybe you could share your memories of my dad. Whatever comes to mind."

Nu Rose? Who will remember you?

She saw how this young woman looked at her; the hope, the need, the insatiable hunger now clearly readable on her face. Suddenly, Rose saw the complete picture.

Go on Rose. Tell her what she thinks she wants to hear, that her father was a real vilde chaya who couldn't stop shtupping all the pretty girls. Tell her about the power he had over you, until one day, he didn't.

Instead, Rose told Carla the story of her father's reunion visit to her ballet school by highlighting certain details and omitting others. "Your father showed me a picture of you and I still remember it well. You looked about seven years old and I thought you were so beautiful."

"Oh." Carla did not appear to be satisfied in the slightest by this tidbit. "So you and my father were on good terms after your divorce?"

Rose shrugged, fully aware that she employed the gesture for performative purposes. "Dear . . . your father and I were a very long time ago. But I can tell you that he was so proud of you. He told me he couldn't believe his luck, to be such an old father."

Nu Rose? What's with this business of calling all young people dear?

Rose didn't know. She only knew that this young woman had a hole in her soul that might or might not be possible to fill. In case she had any second thoughts, she only needed to focus on the necklace around Carla's neck. So Rose decided to say that she was very tired and needed to rest.

"I understand," said Carla, who extracted a business card from her purse. "But if there's anything else you remember and want to share, please call me."

Rose accepted the business card and thought of her original wedding photo, slumbering in a shoebox on the floor of her bedroom closet. Should Richard's daughter be privy to this particular heirloom? She tried to stand, gripping her walker for support, and felt a hand on her elbow. Carla's husband had no intention of allowing her to lose her balance. She thanked the husband for his assistance.

"If you or someone else you know is interested in adopting a cat," he said, "you can call the number on Carla's card."

She nodded, too exhausted and shell-shocked to register any sort of annoyance toward this last-minute sales pitch for pet ownership. "Nice to meet you both." She only lived next door but at the moment, she felt far from home.

She resisted the temptation to look back until she finally completed the more-laborious-than-usual twenty-feet journey from the coffee shop to the front door of her apartment building. As she took out her keys from her coat pocket to unlock the door, she allowed herself a backward glance and saw that Richard's daughter and her husband still sat outside the café. The husband had his arm draped around Carla's shoulder, until she pushed him away. Rose couldn't be certain but it appeared that Carla was crying.

Rose averted her eyes and unlocked the door. She walked inside the building and remembered Jewish holidays from long ago, when she was a child sitting in shul with her mother and two sisters. From their not-so-panoramic position on the balcony, her mother insisted on teaching them to purposely look away from the Kohanim when they stood up in front of the congregation to recite the priestly blessing. Divine fire flowed from the fingers of the priests, her mother told them. Look and be scorched. Shield your eyes and be blessed.

AN HOUR LATER: Rose stood in the middle of her living room, thinking how one brown couch, two gray easy chairs, a coffee table, two bookshelves, six paintings, and eleven framed photographs do not a museum make. Still, she had chosen this room for a personal exhibition of additional and beloved objects that now took up every inch of space on her coffee table and half of the couch. They included: a burgundy leather coat she bought in Israel in 1973; a pair of brass candlesticks she bought at a flea market in 1962 because they reminded her of her mother; her final pair of practice toe shoes, pale pink of course and the back of them black with scuffmarks; a wooden jewelry box that played Beethoven's Ninth Symphony that Morry had given her for her sixtieth birthday; both wedding pictures, one in black and white, the latter in color, and the three photographs from when she was a young girl.

All three of those photographs were formal studio pictures; of her, her parents, and two older sisters; of her and her sisters; and just her, wearing two pale ribbons in her hair. Rose's mother gave her those three photos several hours before she had left their home for good. She had just turned eighteen and was an expert in pretending that her emigration had only to do with escaping the confines of her female Jewish upbringing and pursuing a dance career in America.

"Until we come." Her mother had pressed those photos hard into her hand. It was 1933. Of course, they didn't know then that they would never hug each other again, that their family would split up indefinitely: Rose in Los Angeles, her middle sister in Chicago, her oldest sister and parents lying next to strangers in mass graves.

Rose stared at her possessions and waited for them to dispel the presence of Richard's daughter, who now haunted her apartment. In Rose's mind, she would forever be clutching her gold and purple necklace close to her throat. Had Richard been the one to initially clasp the necklace around his daughter's neck, imbuing it with the eternal spirit of a family heirloom?

That coat which she bought in Tel Aviv: the more she stared at it, the more she remembered. *What do they call that these days? Therapy shopping?* She could still remember her feelings of relief and escape as she and Morry wandered the streets around Dizengoff Center in search of travel mementos. They had spent three prior days in Jerusalem, where they visited the Yad Vashem museum. It had surprised Rose; that she could make her way through this museum without completely breaking down, though she could feel how her mother, father, and oldest sister walked with her, pausing just as she did to examine every single photograph.

But toward the end of her museum visit, she found herself hypnotized by a photograph of three women, each pushing a baby carriage. The women were very thin but their hair had grown back. They wore dresses embroidered with flowers and they all smiled for the camera. They were living in a DP camp but they had already made important contributions toward the continuation of the Jewish people.

Rose could not tear her eyes away from this photograph and its caption, which explained that the DP camps were filled with pregnant women and young families. She didn't know how long she had stood there before Morry tapped her on the shoulder. He had apparently been searching for her all over the museum. Morry had looked at her, initially confused, but she only had to point at the photograph in front of them. They stood there together for what felt like hours, possibly days. And finally, Morry had to say, "Rose? Rose. It's time to go."

So many years later and Rose could still see this photograph of the women and their baby carriages through the portal of her Tel Aviv coat. They stared at her through the decades, reminding her that a Jewish woman's failure to conceive has multiple ramifications. *You have not only failed yourself and your parents, who now lie in unidentified graves. You, Rose Perchik, have not done your part for the survival of the Jewish people.*

Rose felt lightheaded and short of breath and barely made it to the unoccupied part of the couch. She closed her eyes and felt the absence of her children. She heard non-existent knocks at her door, indicating the presence of long-lost and much-hoped for kin. She visualized how she would open the door to familiar faces and how, over glasses of lemon water in her living room, they would find the solution to her continuity.

It took at least an hour for Rose to disengage from her web of fantasy and speculation. And as usual, she did not enjoy the immediate aftermath of excess reverie. *I am alone. There is no one else. My family line ends with me. You must accept this.* She drank these thoughts like strong and bitter coffee, doing her best to wake up.

But later that afternoon, as Rose sat in front of her television not really watching a rerun of *Seinfeld*, she received another unexpected phone call. But it turned out to be the girl, calling weekly as she usually did since they met. How could Rose forget? Only she needed to be sure and so Rose asked twice if it was, indeed, her. Yes, the girl said. Who else could it be? And so Rose remembered what she had forgotten: she wasn't entirely alone.

Six

NINA PAUSED OUTSIDE the Santa Monica cottage-style home of Lindsey Baumgartner and took a moment to silence her buzzing phone and muster up the necessary motivation. Baby showers were not exactly her favorite activities of all time but maybe today could be a useful distraction. For the last three days, Laz had left twice daily voicemails. This morning, he had resorted to text bombing multiple variations of call-me-are-you-okay-I'm worried-about you-so-can-you-just-let-me-know-you're-still-alive?

You know what he's doing. Do not respond. Nina took a deep breath and tried to focus on how Lindsey, one of her colleagues from Cat/Cow and designated host of their mutual friend and colleague Allison Rogers' baby shower, had gone all out with the decorations. Pink balloons festooned the wooden, white-painted fence surrounding Lindsey's property and a "Welcome Friends of Allison!" sign in large pink bubble letters on the front door featured a decorative border of tiny pink rattles. One did not need to be a brain surgeon or rocket scientist to deduce that Allison was having a girl and Nina suspected that Lindsey had somehow gained unilateral control over the scope and direction of Allison's baby shower. Having befriended Allison almost from the moment she moved to LA, Nina knew her as someone who wouldn't deny her little girl opportunities to play with trucks and wear blue clothing. She also knew that Allison hadn't wanted anyone to throw her a baby shower but Lindsey had insisted.

Nina eyed the pink balloons and felt an intense urge to pop every single one of them. She had not foreseen feeling this much resistance. Was it partially because of her Bubbe Essie, who warned Nina weeks before she died to never have a baby shower when the time came because it was extremely goyish to do so? *If you plan for your baby, you risk the ayin hara.* Bubbe Essie's passion for the subject of the evil eye almost rivaled her love for the subject of future grandchildren.

She forced herself to push open Lindsey's unlocked door and reminded herself that she didn't know Lindsey well enough to dislike her. Lindsey had joined the staff of Cat/Cow about a year ago and had quickly become a favorite of their boss Serena. Apparently, Lindsey did care about her class numbers and had happily mastered the art of the compelling blog post and endearing social media update that garnered hundreds of likes and re-tweets.

Nina walked through the small foyer, maintaining a death grip with one hand on the bottle of sparkling cider that she brought to add to the festivities. Earlier this morning, she dutifully bought several onesies in assorted colors off Allison's Target registry and steeled herself for the possibility that this shower would feature games and crafts. She had been to showers in the past where guests had to taste test baby foods and express their best wishes for the baby with construction paper, Elmer's glue, and dried macaroni.

"I don't even want to go," Allison herself had confessed to her only a few hours ago when she called under the auspices of giving Nina an out.

But Nina had insisted: She wanted to celebrate this momentous change in Allison's life. Besides, she was fine. She said the word "fine" three times in the course of their conversation, and Allison had finally capitulated and said it would be great to have Nina there today for moral support.

But then Allison said, "Just because I'm about to become a mommy doesn't mean I can't be here for you."

Nina blew her a virtual kiss and said she had to go, lest her friend suspect her inability to absorb such kind words. God bless well-meaning Allison, who didn't have any nieces or nephews and so didn't know how all-consuming new motherhood could be. But Allison knew how to be a good friend, having answered her phone at eleven-thirty in the evening on that dreadful night when she needed a place to go. Allison had offered up her living room couch, no questions asked, even though Nina wanted to explain the reasons for her semi-self-imposed eviction. And then, when she told Allison what had happened, her friend had merely listened and offered her a cup of chamomile tea. "You can stay here as long as you need to," she said afterward.

She had stayed with Allison for four nights before driving to Las Vegas. (The mere thought of that city still made her flinch.) Allison had also attended the funeral with her husband Mike and the two of them hugging her with their condolences had prompted her sole uncontrollable sobbing episode of that day. Of course Allison would have advised her differently on that night, had they known there would be an accident. Would she not have counseled Nina to race back to her apartment ASAP and at the very least, try to make peace?

"Hi, Nina. So glad you could make it." There stood Lindsey, resplendent in a white dress and pink and white stilettos, bearing a platter of pink and white mini-cupcakes. Nina absorbed this extreme attention to color coordination and tried not to conflate it with Lindsey's social media savvy and perfect relationship with Serena. After the baby shower, she could go home and resent and envy the hell out of Lindsey and then try and tell herself how she could learn from such people once she achieved a different state of mind.

Lindsey air-kissed Nina, apologized she could not hug her due to her occupied hands, and directed her to the living room, where practically the entire female staff from Cat/Cow and a handful of people Nina did not know sat drinking non-alcoholic beverages and nibbling on finger sandwiches and chips and salsa. Nina observed the pile of gifts on the coffee table, which signaled to her that most people didn't have gifts sent directly to Allison's home from her registry and that there would be a gift-opening component to the shower. Poor Allison, who would have to ooh and aah over every gift and validate the gift-giver. But maybe Allison enjoyed that sort of thing. Maybe Nina would too, if only she could escape her current mood.

Nina tried to snap out of it as she said hello to her yoga colleagues, hugged Allison congratulations, and introduced herself to the women she didn't know. She then headed for the kitchen, where she poured herself a glass of sparkling apple cider and helped herself to cucumber and egg salad finger sandwiches. As she headed back to the living room, she nearly bumped into Serena, who greeted her with the huge smile that she normally flashed at her before the start of an awkward conversation about brand building in her office.

"Nina! So good to see you outside the studio," Serena said, giving her a quick one-armed hug.

She gave small talk with Serena her best shot in Lindsey's kitchen. Surely, she could try to see her boss as a fellow human being as opposed to a nemesis who threatened her livelihood. Since she resumed her full-time teaching schedule at Cat/Cow, Serena had requested several more meetings in her office, where she gently yet insistently pointed out the declining numbers of students in her classes. "Now I know it's a hard time for everyone," she would preface, before deflecting any responsibility that the yoga studio might have for promoting its teachers' classes and diverting the subject to Nina's personal lack of self-marketing strategies. "In a recession, everyone has to think outside the box."

"I'm so excited for Allison." Serena refilled her cider glass and pointed to the curried tofu finger sandwiches. "These are amazing. You have to try them."

"Me too. I'm really happy for her." Nina made a point of choosing a tofu sandwich and taking a bite with enthusiasm. Finally, she could comply with one of her boss's suggestions.

"Do you think about having children one day?"

Nina felt her face both freeze and burn. She stared at Serena, who took several seconds to remember a few salient facts about her employee. "Oh . . . sorry." Serena reached out to touch Nina's hand. "I'm—"

"It's okay."

Serena opted for a self-deprecating laugh. "I guess that's a really personal question to be asking anyone."

Nina smiled at Serena, trying to let her off the hook. Of course, if she had really wanted to let Serena off the hook, she could disclose that all sorts of people had no qualms about asking her if she wanted kids. Or, if it was someone she didn't know, the question was: do you have children? This is what people asked a woman in her mid-thirties after she taught a yoga class or stood in line at the grocery store or waited to get a pedicure.

"I have thought about it. A lot."

Nina placed her plate on the kitchen counter and excused herself. Quickly, she found the guest bathroom, locked the door, sat on the toilet, and experienced immediate déjà vu. Right. She had locked herself in the bathroom after her first meeting with Serena and as she struggled to breathe, she remembered Rose.

And now, in a different bathroom, Nina thought of her friend, who never had children. Their shared lack of offspring wasn't something they had discussed, though certainly it had not gone unnoted. Why didn't Rose and her husband have children? Could Nina ask the question without causing harm?

I'm not sure I want to bring more children into this world. There are already so many children in need. But if you really want them, then we'll have to keep talking about it, I guess.

She could still see him lying in bed with a book face down on his chest. She could see the way his brow furrowed and how he put his hand over his eyes, as if this effectively shielded him from the topic of parenthood.

You have to want them too. I can't be the only one who wants them. Maybe some women are like that but I'm not—

Do we have to talk about this now?

This was his go-to refrain for another unresolved topic: his inability to express his love for her in moments when she most needed him to do so.

Nina knew she couldn't stay in this guest bathroom forever. She didn't even need to pee. Still, she decided to make the mistake of checking her phone and there it was: a new voicemail for the collection. Another reminder of how the voice of one man could be so quickly subsumed by the other and how she lacked the tools to stop flashing back. She didn't even know if she had the ability to feel genuine happiness for the lives of others anymore and this terrified her. Why even bother leaving this bathroom if she had become someone she despised? Someone monstrous in their self-involvement; someone who elevated their personal tragedy above everyone and everything else.

She had made the mistake of engaging in several brief phone conversations with Laz since that day she took Rose shopping. The first time she called him, he had answered on the first ring. "Fuck . . . how could you not tell me what happened? I had met a friend in Venice and was thinking about you and then I'm ordering a latte at Abbot's Habit and there's this huge photograph of him by the cashier and well . . . fuck."

She allowed him to express his "deepest" condolences. But when he said that he wanted to see her, she explained that she needed to go and that he shouldn't call again. But of course he did, under the auspices of checking up on her and nothing more. Twice, she had called him back under the auspices of letting him know that she was okay and nothing more. But for the past three days, she had been trying to disrupt this new mode of staying in touch, understanding that their communication patterns hadn't changed at all.

Nina opened the bathroom door, determined to join the other women on the couch. She would sip cider with them and attempt conversation, despite how Jeff and Laz occupied her mind. One man was dead and the other, alive, but both of them still beckoned to her with their respective glasses of wine. *Let's drink to our eternally unfinished business.*

THERE'S NINA, SITTING at the bar around the corner from her apartment, a purposeful five minutes early. It's precisely 4:25 p.m., a couple of hours before Jeff will arrive home from work and at least fifteen to twenty-five minutes before Laz will saunter into this bar. He's always late and why should this time be any different?

Nina orders a glass of Rioja and settles herself into the process of waiting. She has purposely given herself the time to both get into the mood and delude herself into believing she's simply on a fact-finding mission. Fact, as in: Seeing him now will confirm that she has finally moved on with her life.

The friendly female bartender sets the glass of wine in front of her. It's a generous pour and Nina raises her glass in thanks. Since moving in with Jeff, she has cultivated a great appreciation for her neighborhood bar, with its exposed brick walls, black plush banquettes, and dim-at-all-hours lighting. It only serves wine and beer and, at the moment, it's mostly empty except for the bouncer at the door, the lone bartender on duty, a group of twenty-something women in office clothes sprawled out on one of the banquettes near the entrance, and a fifty-ish looking man with a much younger woman. The man and woman sit in the low-ceilinged, cave-shaped room that juts off the main area by the bar counter, like the tip of an archipelago. Nina can't help but watch them, provoked by their overtly father-daughter appearance. They both have blond hair and tanned skin and the woman wears a sparkly red miniskirt which rides so high up her thighs that it assumes the shape of a narrow, lipsticked mouth. The man's hand rests squarely on the woman's upper left thigh and only when he starts nuzzling her ear does Nina avert her eyes.

Since Laz's email, she has indulged in a repeat fantasy about the two of them sitting in that cave-like room, furnished in contrast to the rest of the bar with red velvet banquettes and lit only by a circle of tea lights, artfully arrayed on the vintage black lacquer coffee table in the center of the space. Nina loves this cave-like room, which always seems a few shades darker than the rest of the already dimly lit bar. Once, she had persuaded Jeff to sit with her there. She had bought them a round of drinks and then pressed her legs against his but he deflected the advance by holding his drink between them. Really? He had looked at her, disappointment clearly etched on his face. In this little house of wham-bam-thank-you ma'am? Why did she want to be with him in this cramped, public space that reeked of cheap perfume when they could do whatever they wanted in the privacy of their bedroom?

"It suggests things," she had told him, imagining a hand not her own caressing her thigh.

"Not to me."

She never sat in the little room again, which only increased her longing for it.

When he finally walks into the bar, twenty-one minutes late, she sees immediately that he hasn't changed, i.e. he looks the same kind of good on the outside. Those eyes. That skin. Still thin and without a trace of receding hairline. No lines under his eyes or furrows in his forehead. But she also spots the perseverance of youth in the way he moves toward her, his locomotion suggesting a cross between a swagger and a saunter. He is exactly how she remembers him and so she can pretend that they are still in their twenties.

"Nina." He stands over her, pronouncing her name the way he always did, especially when he wanted something from her. *Neeee-naaaaah*, as if slow-cooking a roast in the oven.

"Hey." She tries to perform her best rendition of a platonic hug: half-standing up from her barstool with one arm bent at the elbow and loosely draped around his neck for about one second.

He kisses her left cheek. "I take it you have a boyfriend."

"We're engaged."

He scans her left ring finger with its lack of engagement ring—she and Jeff had agreed on wedding bands only. He has mastered the gaze of detached inquisitiveness, like a rubbernecking driver passing a bloodless accident on the highway.

"Yeah. We're planning the wedding for next October."

"Wow. Congratulations."

He reaches out to hug her again and this time, she responds with both arms and a few more degrees of force. "Thanks."

She looks at him. He looks at her. She feels the familiar giddy-unsettling-tender-burning feeling in the pit of her stomach. If she really stops to think about it, she first felt this sensation at age ten, the day before her eleventh birthday. That was the first time she didn't want her birthday to happen. At almost eleven, she already knew that it could only go downhill from there, that it was best to stay young forever.

He offers to buy her a drink and she points to her half-full wine glass. He shrugs, buys himself a beer, and makes a toast. "To the happy couple."

"Thanks."

Laz consumes a deep swig of beer, the kind of swig that thanks to TV commercials and pulpy romance novels, Nina associates with burly construction workers letting off steam after a tough day on the job. She cannot ignore the blatant masculinity of the act just as she must acknowledge his ongoing mastery of donning the disguise that fits his needs at any given moment.

She tries not to gulp down her wine as they attempt an ordinary, civil, let's-catch-up-like-old pals conversation. Laz has moved to LA on a "temporary basis" for his acting career. Over the years, he has worked less in theater and more in TV and film so it makes sense for him to be here. Plus, he has a friend with a guesthouse in the Hollywood Hills where he's currently crashing rent-free.

She plays dumb as he discusses the last three years of his life, though surely he must suspect that she has googled him with some degree of frequency. Has he ever googled her and does she care?

Is the sky blue?

"Are you happy?" he asks suddenly and in a markedly more serious tone.

She makes a point of directing her focus to her slightly shaking hands. She can't afford to look him in the eyes at this moment. But then she feels his finger on her chin and she allows him to guide her face back up to his eye level. They look at each other and she knows that he knows.

"How long did you say you're in town for?" This is what passes for her official last question on her fact-finding mission.

"Indefinitely."

"Oh."

So much for facts.

He finishes his beer and puts his hand on top of hers. "I've always rooted for your happiness. I hope you know that," he says in a whisper.

She closes her eyes. She doesn't need to see it, this moment that now unfolds between them.

A WEEK LATER: They have a whole new pattern of persistence and resistance. It begins with him leaving atmospherically themed voicemails about how Los Angeles looks from his friend's guesthouse balcony in the Hollywood Hills or how the lights from the Santa Monica Pier illuminate the ocean and how much better these vistas could be experienced together. "I understand why you're not calling me back but . . ." He always pauses after the "but," at which point she becomes short of breath and suffers from hot and itchy skin. Then she plays his message again, touches herself if she's alone, or if Jeff is asleep, and travels. Fifteen years of memories at her disposal plus refraining from sexual intercourse with him since 2001 equals the multiplication of fantasies that bloom and swirl in her present-day bedroom, leaving her conflicted about imploring the man sleeping next to her to wake up.

Finally, on one such sleepless night at around two in the morning, she calls him back from the relative privacy of her locked bathroom.

"Hey."

"Heyyyyyyy . . ."

"I shouldn't be doing this."

"Meet me."

"I can't."

"You can."

"I'm getting married."

"So you say."

"Well, I am."

"Those things aren't mutually exclusive, you know."

And boom, just like that, she sees a potential answer to her increasingly overwhelming problem. The answer shimmers in front of her, its origins stemming from a recurring conversation initiated by her very own fiancé. It's definitely unconventional and self-serving and possibly harmful but it could also lead to the continuity of everything.

It takes a few more days to muster up the courage to speak with Jeff. But she chooses an evening where she waits for him to come home from work. She opens the front door before he can insert his key into the lock and gets straight to the point. "Hey. We need to talk."

"Okaaaay." Jeff looks tired and, understandably, suspicious. Nina experiences a moment of compassion for him that almost makes her reconsider what she wants to propose. *Just look at the exhaustion on his face from all his trying to save the world in his own way.*

They sit on their couch and Nina tries to start from the beginning. "I didn't tell you something the other week. I heard from Laz."

She registers the initial blank expression on Jeff's face and waits for him to remember.

"Your ex or what did you call him, your—?"

My lover. My fuck buddy. My tormentor. The man who has made me scream the loudest in this lifetime for a variety of reasons. "Yeah. He's in town."

Jeff runs his fingers through his hair and slouches further into the couch. She wants to suggest to him that perhaps, he could at least feign interest in this conversation. This way, she still might change her mind. But he only sighs and asks, "And?"

She tries to make her voice sound as casual as possible. "Well, I'd like to see him and wanted to know if it was okay with you."

Jeff shrugs. "Why wouldn't it be okay?"

"Well, I think I've told you a little bit about him . . . we had a complicated relationship."

"You? In a complicated relationship? Impossible."

She tells him to can the sarcasm. He complies and his slouch becomes slightly less slouchy. She decides to accept his incrementally more upright posture. "I saw him the other week. I didn't tell you."

He looks at her and waits.

"Maybe we should have some drinks," she says.

Over a bottle of wine, she reviews with Jeff the story of Laz, emphasizing certain scenes and deleting other ones.

"Do you still love him?" Jeff asks.

"I don't love him like I love you." The words feel stuck in her mouth, as if coated in the kind of tongue film that results from extreme thirst.

"But you love him?" Jeff speaks in his social worker's voice but instead of finding this infuriating, Nina for once welcomes his detachment, as if it spares them from something they will not be able to manage.

"I still feel something . . . something that was there from the beginning. But I told you, he and I can't be together. It's impossible."

"Why do you think you never got over him?"

"I don't know. Maybe because I lost my virginity to him? Maybe because he and I were always so . . . undefined? He imprinted me somehow . . . I don't know."

"But you think that if you can fuck him one last time and he treats you badly enough, you can be rid of him once and for all?"

"Is that what you think I'm asking you?"

"Isn't it?"

Nina takes a large sip of wine, reminding herself that Jeff's assessment stems less from any mind-reading capabilities and more from iterations of a macro discussion that dot the landscape of their relationship history. It began when Jeff, who rarely discusses his clients' lives, came home from work one evening intent on having a discussion about polyamory. One of his clients was trying to convince his wife to be polyamorous but his wife promised she would divorce him before agreeing to such a "degenerate" lifestyle. It was his client's use of the word "degenerate," he said, that got him thinking about the destructive nature of jealousy and how society conditions everyone from birth to accept the rightness of monogamy in romantic relationships. And that got him thinking, he said, about how it's maybe society's ideas about monogamy and its emphasis on sexual ownership and possessiveness that are actually degenerate and ultimately toxic to human beings.

"And what else did it make you think about?" she had asked.

To which he responded, "Don't you think it sounds brilliant in theory?"

To which she responded, "Sure it does. In theory."

Now, Nina swallows her wine and chooses her words with care. "What prevents me from fucking him is how you might feel afterward."

No answer from Jeff.

"Sure, you can't predict how you'll feel but don't you think there would be some consequences? I know you wish that we could sleep with other people consequence-free but how would that really play out?"

More silence from her fiancé.

"I know we've talked about how the issue with affairs is the deception and dishonesty between people. But don't you think it's still pretty risky, even if we gave each other permission?"

Still more silence from her fiancé.

"I wouldn't stop you from going after something you wanted," Jeff finally says.

"Even if it hurts you? If it hurts me?"

He shrugs. "That's for you to decide."

She winces. "Do you always have to be so aloof about everything?"

He shrugs again. "You know who I am. And if you marry me, that's who I'm going to be."

She whispers, "Why. Are. You. Always. Like. This?"

He knows better than to ask, like what? "Why don't we give this some thought?" he asks instead.

Later, she pretends to sleep while he reads in the living room. When he finally crawls into bed around one in the morning, she continues to play dead while he whispers, "I know I don't say it very often but you have to know I love you. I may not express myself the way you want me to but that doesn't mean . . ."

She wants to answer him after he falters, to steer them both off this dangerous track. But she can't get past the fact that he thinks or at least pretends that she's asleep. So she remains silent and allows her anger to fuel her sleeplessness. Eventually, it's Jeff who falls sleep and there's nothing to do but listen to the sound of his breath.

THE SHOWER COULD have been worse. So Nina thought as she hugged Allison goodbye and semi-jokingly promised that they could still be great friends after she had her baby. Allison then semi-jokingly retorted that she would never say certain things to Nina, such as: You wouldn't understand because you're not a parent. Nina also made a special effort to thank Lindsey for throwing the shower and silently expressed gratitude for the fact that they had played no games, though they did open gifts and at Lindsey's direction, went around the room clockwise to express personal blessings and hopes for Allison and her unborn daughter. To Serena, she said a slightly awkward goodbye. It would always be a little awkward with Serena, she realized, because on an elemental level, they really didn't click as human beings.

Which then made her think yet again of Jeff. Had they really clicked as human beings? Would they really have reconciled had there been no accident? Would they have raised children together, even though both of them suffered from a profound ambivalence?

But at the very least, she had begun to reckon with what was difficult about Jeff, whose best qualities loomed so much larger than anything else since his death. *Only in death are saints born.* Before the accident, it had always irritated her when she read obituaries about famous people that glossed over the dark, complicated parts of their lives. Now, she understood the compulsion to only remember the good.

She left Lindsey's house and checked her phone as she headed for her car: two new missed calls from Laz and a long text about really wanting to see her in person so please, will she reconsider? He'll come to her apartment or meet anywhere she wants so he can tell her something that can only be communicated face to face.

Nina got into her car and as she turned on the ignition, experienced the exhaustively repetitive yet still irresistible sensation of weakness. It would be so easy to meet him again, despite everything that had happened. She could picture it so clearly, meeting him at a bar where they had never met before, where they would seamlessly re-form their universe of two and erase the passage of time. Since the accident, she had been valiantly trying to thwart the onset of the sensation but right now, post-Allison's baby shower, she lacked the necessary will power.

You are not alone. There is someone else you can call. She materialized with perfect timing, the face of her new friend, reminding her that they hadn't yet consummated their weekly phone call, which almost always led to a weekly outing.

She called Rose, who sounded disoriented, as if she had woken from a deep sleep that affected short-term memory.

"Is it really you?" she had asked.

Nina promised that yes, it really was her and when could they see each other again?

Rose proposed lunch in two days. "Dear, thank you so much for calling me today. You have no idea."

Maybe I do. "So how's your day going?" Nina heard the sound of her voice, bright, effort-filled, maybe an octave too high. And yet it was enough, at least for now, to take refuge in the safety of their small talk.

Seven

THERE'S ROSE, SITTING in the passenger seat of their 1986 Buick Century with her hands folded on her lap. She keeps her eyes on the road as Morry drives west on Arizona Avenue with both hands gripping the steering wheel. They've just left Dr. Bernheim's Santa Monica office and are heading to their regular pharmacy on Lincoln Boulevard to fill Morry's prescription for antibiotics. More than anything, Rose wishes she could be the designated driver today but alas, she had allowed her driver's license to lapse just four months ago. Failing eyesight. A fear of driving in the dark. The horror of parallel parking on Pacific Avenue. She's up to her ears in excellent reasons in the event that anyone should ask.

Morry starts coughing and takes one hand off the wheel to cover his mouth. His cough sounds terrible. Full of phlegm, it's an exemplary public service announcement for all the possible toxins that can coagulate in the body of a neglectful host. Rose lets him cough in silence. She's angry that he hasn't seen a doctor in almost two years, shortly after his seventy-ninth birthday to be precise, when he had flat out refused to see his longtime internist for his annual checkup. His official reason: he simply no longer saw the wisdom in taxing Medicare just so some overworked medical professional could X-ray him to high heaven and prescribe him a bunch of pills that made him nauseous. *Believe you me, if I'm sick and you know what kind of sick I'm talking about, you'd know it by now.*

Morry stops coughing and resumes driving with both hands on the steering wheel. "Slow reflexes? I'll show him slow reflexes."

Rose tsk-tsks. When did her husband lose his ability to remember the big picture? *We should all be so lucky to receive such a glowing medical report. Especially at our age.* This is what she does not say to Morry, figuring the words would be wasted. So okay, he has a terrible bronchial infection, which is what finally drove him to Dr. Bernheim, who, after prescribing antibiotics, conducted a thoroughly encouraging physical. He praised the condition of his heart and eyes, specifically noting their lack of cataracts, and Morry let it slip with pride that he passed the vision test for his driver's license on his eightieth birthday with flying colors. But then the doctor tested Morry's reflexes and pronounced them slow. Nothing to worry about; it's just something to watch as a person gets older. Especially when driving. So said the doctor, who then told Morry to return in six months for a blood pressure check.

"You're lucky that's all he said to you." Rose tries to keep her voice light and breezy. "He could have diagnosed a lot worse."

"He wants me to come back for my blood pressure. That's what he says but the next thing you know, he'll be pushing surgery on something and before you know it, he'll decide my whole body is in need of major repair. The same thing happens whenever we take our car in for an oil change. These people will do anything to make an extra buck. What do I need that for?"

"They're trying to keep us alive, that's all. Look what they did for me when I was in the hospital." This is her wild card, the dredging up of her almost dying from pneumonia when she was seventy-five. Morry had lived with her in the hospital during her illness. And for three days, both of them hovered between life and death, with only one of them aware of their condition.

Rose yearns for her husband to at least connect the more obvious dots between her almost dying and his fiery adoption of an all-out medical boycott. But Morry only says, "We got lucky."

"Most doctors are good."

"Baloney. Most doctors take one look at you and make assumptions. All they do is follow formulas and avoid lawsuits."

"They know what they're talking about. What? You don't want to go to the pharmacy now? You want to skip the antibiotics?"

They're now approaching the shopping center with their pharmacy as a matter of fact, but her husband does not look the slightest bit sheepish as he turns into the parking lot. He finds a parking spot right in front of the drugstore.

"He asked me if I have trouble remembering things," he says. "Who doesn't have trouble at our age?"

"Listen," she says. "The next time you get sick. Or if you don't feel like yourself—"

"There was an article in my *National Geographic* last week about these villages in Japan. When a person in one of these villages is ready to die, they say goodbye to their family and go up a mountain."

"For what?"

"They wait."

"Why would they do a thing like that?"

"Because they get to say when they're finished, not some quack doctor. You should read the article."

"I don't want to read the article."

Morry doesn't look at her as he performs the most dismissive of hand waves and turns off the engine. "Now that's the way to do it."

As they walk into the drugstore, Rose remembers the now long ago day at the farmers market when she disclosed to her husband that Richard had contacted her. After that day, she never once heard her husband admit that he was getting old. If anything, Morry became a relentless Pollyanna on the subject of entering the winter of his life, embracing talismans such as the "Age is Just a Number" bumper sticker, which lasted on their car for a good decade. In Rose's opinion, he spent far too much time on the bleachers at Muscle Beach, watching the weightlifters and other young men performing their calisthenics on those metal bars and rings. But who was she to tell her husband how to cope?

As they position themselves at the end of the line for the pharmacy window, Rose thinks about all the Sunday afternoons they have spent on the boardwalk, sitting on the benches and watching the boardwalk entertainers perform for tourists. Morry's favorite performer has always been the man in the white robes and matching turban who patrols the boardwalk on his roller skates while playing mostly incomprehensible compositions on the electric guitar. It all sounds like noise to Rose, who's definitely no expert on Led Zeppelin and Pink Floyd and displays a hundred percent deafness to Mr. Turban's aggressive bastardizations of famous songs. Personally, Rose never saw much charm in Mr. Turban's act, her eye always having been drawn to the legions of tap dancers, acrobats, and now those break dancers with their masterful body contortions and head-spins. Though Rose will never understand the sartorial aesthetic of these performers and their early adoption of those egregiously baggy pants that set the trend for all the other Venice boy populations, she respects their art. But Mr. Turban? Why him? She finally posed this question to Morry one afternoon as they watched the man regale two giggling young women in matching blond pigtails and pink string bikinis.

Morry's response: "The man hasn't changed his act since 1977." He said this with wonderment and pride, as if watching his non-existent grandchild graduate from an excellent university.

Have you changed your act since 1977? "Have you looked in the mirror recently?" Rose blurts this out in anger as they wait in line to fill Morry's prescription and the cruelty of the words produces an immediate regret. Again, she recalls that day in the farmers market. She was what then? Sixty-two? A baby. Fantasizing about her ex-husband while buying strawberries with her current husband. As if she had all the time in the world to live multiple lives without any consequences.

Rose apologizes but her husband ignores her. In silence, they fill the prescription and return to the car. Morry keeps his hands on the wheel and his eyes on the road. She can barely hear him when he finally speaks. "At some point, a life isn't worth living. If I can't tell you when that is, you need to do that for me. Will you do that for me? Rose? Rose?"

She can't look at him, not even when they arrive home safely.

ON THE MONDAY after learning of the 99 Cent Store's prognosis, Rose went outside with her shopping cart rather than her walker and caught the bus to her favorite strip mall of all time located at Rose Avenue and Lincoln Boulevard.

Business as usual. She kept telling herself this falsehood, still unable to accept the numbered days of her beloved store. Why the 99 Cent and not the adjacent drug store or the Laundromat or the combination hamburger, taco, and fish and chips stand? Sure, the Big Lots was also scheduled for demolition to make way for Whole Foods, but who cared about the mediocre discount merchandise at the Big Lots when you could shop at the 99 Cent?

Especially at the 99 Cent, Rose never just shopped willy-nilly. She had procedures and today was no exception. After getting off the bus and surviving the walk from the bus stop to the store's entrance, she stopped to catch her breath. When she felt reasonably full of life to continue the process, she extracted her magnifying glass from her pocketbook and walked inside.

She never knew what she might find. This was the best part. Sometimes, a huge crop of bananas would be lying in one of the produce bins, other times, cucumbers, papayas, watermelons, or avocados. It was a beautiful day in the neighborhood when she could buy ten avocados for ninety-nine cents. At the mini-market on the boardwalk around the corner from her apartment, she could pay up to a dollar-fifty for one avocado.

The shopping commenced: Rose thoroughly enjoyed her sojourn through the packaged and canned food section and decided to catch her breath en route to the fresh tomatoes and apples. She paused in front of the cosmetics and personal hygiene aisle and that's precisely when she spotted Adele Mandelbaum fondling numerous bottles of hand and body lotion with pursed lips.

We both know it's not his eyes. I'd keep him off the streets if I were you.

Rose froze, trapped amidst haunted fragments of hissed warnings. Why had she not foreseen this inevitability? Over the years, she and the Mandelbaum woman had collided in the 99 Cent numerous times. Occasionally, they even found themselves stuck in the same checkout line, where they could either ignore each other or attempt some miserable form of small talk.

Know-it-all. Yenta. And that condolence card! A mensch would sign their name but you, you had to print your name in block letters like an axe murderer. Rose backed up several steps in the direction of the produce section as she appraised Adele and her snobbish attitude toward those bottles of body lotion that she would buy anyway because the price was right. Adele more or less looked the same: she was still a large woman; zaftig and/or voluptuous in her youth the polite ones would say and her gray-blue eyes now matched the color of her hair.

Rose remembered all too well the days when Adele used to make entrances at the Center with blond hair and a face chock full of multi-colored cosmetics. *Well hello Morry. You're looking well.* All those simpering smiles and coy glances as she asked calculated questions about famous artists. *I was just at LACMA to see the Kandinsky exhibit. Didn't you specialize in his paintings?*

In those days, Rose normally didn't mind sharing her husband, considering that men only comprised about thirty-five percent of the Center's membership.

Every time a man passed away, at least five more women stopped dying their hair and going crazy on the eye shadow. Rose could very well understand such reason-to-live motivations for getting dressed up for someone but with the Mandelbaum woman, things had been different from the get-go. Whereas most of the Center women took care to befriend the wife while flirting with the husband, Adele had immediately treated her as a rival. Either she would ignore Rose completely or treat her to a barrage of poorly veiled insults. *Your hair looks nice today Rose. Your hairdresser must be extremely talented.* Or: *I was watching a PBS special on the history of American ballet and I learned so much. Seems to me that the truly talented ballerinas stuck it out in New York to dance.* And then Adele would perform these narrow-eyed, come-hither gazes directed exclusively at her husband. Morry, however, always kept his responses to a bare minimum before excusing himself to go play chess with Harold Zimmerman, the only other chess-playing man at the Center. As if Rose needed another reason to love him.

Rose stared at the Mandelbaum woman, remembering the day Adele abruptly stopped flirting with her husband. Not that this really changed anything. Adele was who she was and right now, Rose could not bear the sight of her.

Lucky, undetected Rose, who watched Adele take slow, laborious steps down the personal hygiene aisle toward the checkout lines. She waited until Adele disappeared from her field of vision before continuing her journey toward the produce. As she felt the tomatoes on sale without interest, her heartbeat refused to slow down. A close call, she kept telling herself.

She selected four tomatoes and five apples and moved onto the frozen foods. Perhaps it wasn't too late for her to learn how to self-medicate with ice cream. All her years as a ballet dancer and teacher and she apparently stood apart from a number of her colleagues because she never once confused food for psychology. This is what Rose had learned from reading the newspaper.

As Rose walked past the freezer with the macaroni and cheese dinners, she felt her feet start to skid and grabbed one of the freezer handles to prevent herself from falling. Clutching the freezer handle, she recalled the collision with the skateboarder. Then and now, she felt this same curious mixture of relief and guilt at having narrowly escaped what could have been a serious injury or even death by accident. *Lucky, lucky, always lucky. Why you?* Try as she might, Rose could not escape what had become her most central question. And so she succumbed to its now predictable seductions, until she realized her difficulty in catching her breath.

Rose felt nauseous and understood she needed fresh air immediately. She tried to take her hand off the freezer handle but nothing happened. She could only see black dots swimming in her field of vision that grew larger and larger, until they formed a complete world.

WHAT A BEAUTIFUL day for a cemetery visit. It feels about seventy-six degrees and it's impossible to spot a single cloud in the sky. And there he is: Jeff Wasserman, forever thirty-seven years of age. A beloved son. A dedicated social worker. Another perfectly engraved gray square plaque raised ever so slightly off the ground. A person she never knew. But she knows him now. She sees him leave his grave so he can drive Morry's 1997 midnight blue Buick Skylark, now in pristine condition. He's taller than her husband and so has to push his seat back a few more notches. No time like the present to befriend the car that killed you.

Hello Rose. You can be my friend too. In Heaven, everyone is friends with everyone, like on that Facebook.

Rose shakes her head in confusion. She's read so many articles about this Facebook in the newspaper but it remains thoroughly incomprehensible to her that she can be friends with everyone on a computer while picnicking in the cemetery. She's eating a cheese sandwich and sipping white wine under a stately oak tree that rests in peace on perfectly mowed grass, so bright green in color that it can easily be confused for Astroturf. Rose takes another bite of her sandwich and concludes that it tastes like grass.

She keeps eating as she watches the girl prostrate herself at the boy's grave, her forehead touching the earth. She's about to tell the girl that Jews only prostrate themselves on the Rosh Hashana and Yom Kippur holidays but stops herself. She's torn between reading the girl's mind and admiring the surrounding flower gardens. Amazing what they've done with cemeteries these days, she cannot help but think of all the finely manicured landscaping. She might as well be vacationing in Florida or closer-to-home suburbs in Orange County.

Only Morry always hated Florida and he arrives to tell her so. He's looking well, not a day over eighty-five and with his white hair still relatively thick on his head. He's wearing a dark blue suit and matching tie and it's unclear as to whether he's attending a wedding or a funeral.

Remember Rose? I wanted to go to Cambodia to see the temples of Angkor Wat. And to India. Remember how I pushed India? For you I prepared all that meticulous research on every alter cocker tour that featured door-to-door service from LAX and included an unlimited supply of Pepto Bismol and antimalarials. By me, I would have been content to wander around like a sadhu. Mr. Turban always reminded me of a sadhu, did you know that? A sadhu on roller skates.

But you, my beautiful Rose-in-bloom, you always preferred to stay home and what could I say because what did I know from leaving Belarus in 1933 for America? But you enjoyed our trips to Israel and Spain, didn't you? Anyway, I now visit the Taj Mahal at least twice a week with my remedial driving teacher.

Rose wants to ask her husband a million questions. For starters, what is his opinion of the Taj Mahal? Does he not agree it is the most spectacular mausoleum in the entire world? Granted, splendid examples of Mughal architecture were never his realm of expertise but surely he must harbor an opinion? And what should she do about all the furniture in their apartment? What about the books and photographs and jewelry boxes and paperweights and empty medicine bottles that eluded death by trashcan for no apparent reason at all? They don't make tombs like they used to, wouldn't you agree? They hadn't thought everything through; that was one of their problems. Morry? Are you there? Alas, he is not. She can't find him anywhere in the cemetery but he did take the time to leave a note: *Make sure the kitchen sink faucet ceases its perennial drip. There shouldn't be any leaking provided the stove remains in the off position.* His Buick Skylark has also vanished. Only the boy and the girl remain. They stand facing each other, so close together that their noses touch. And then they waltz, their bare feet hovering several inches above the earth. The girl's white dress billows around her like a parachute as the boy leads them in fast and perfectly synchronized spinning. Eventually, they will land back in their shtetl. Rose knows this because she has seen this painting before, maybe in something by Chagall.

Am I right? Morry? Are you still somewhere? Rose proceeds to search for her husband, even though she knows it's a lost cause. She looks all over, even within the folds of her favorite lavender dress. But she sees nothing except the ocean. Even the birds have flown somewhere else.

AT FIRST, ROSE didn't understand her decision to lie face down on the wet floor of the 99 Cent. Or why the store manager leaned down to ask whether she was all right. He didn't listen to her at all when he called an ambulance and neither did any of the curious onlookers, who halted their shopping to observe the spectacle of the paramedics lifting her into a stretcher.

It was only several hours later at the hospital, after the doctor determined that she had suffered nothing more than a fainting spell, when Rose began to understand. Unbelievable, the doctor kept saying. A miracle. Here she was, a ninety-three-year-old woman with osteoporosis, who fell on a slick concrete floor and suffered nothing more than six stitches on her chin. This emergency room doctor who claimed to have seen it all kept calling her a nonagenarian wonder of the world, even when Rose tried to explain that she had already been low to the ground clutching a freezer door handle and that furthermore, she had been a dancer who knew how to fall.

This doctor also performed tests on her heart and brain before ruling out a stroke or a seizure or any sort of arrhythmia. He asked questions about her memory and coordination that she must have answered all right to have received nothing more than two tablets of Percocet for the pain in her chin, a diagnosis of fainting, cause unknown, and the directive to stay put on her emergency room bed for at least an hour. And was someone available to take her home? Rose nodded. How fortunate for her that she knew the girl's phone number by heart thanks to her incorporating the reciting of this phone number into her daily memory exercises.

A nurse brought a phone and Rose called the girl, who actually answered that cellular implement of hers on the first ring after the third attempt to reach her and said she would be there within the hour. *A day of miracles, with absolutely everything working out for the best. So go ahead Rose. BE HAPPY. HAVE SOME FUN FOR A CHANGE. DON'T YOU THINK MORRY IS HAVING FUN, WHEREVER HE IS?* Only Rose lay in her hospital bed and realized she would soon go blind if she kept staring at all the whiteness in the room.

So much white. The sheets on her bed. The curtains separating her from other emergency room patients. The ceiling. The clouds in the sky within the painting on the wall calendar to her left. Those funny looking machines right in front of her. Even the contraption now monitoring her heart rate and blood pressure had been painted an eggshell white. Rose closed her eyes, starving for color. Sure, the nurses now wore those blue or green uniforms but it wasn't enough. She could not look at the nurses' uniforms and conjure up the ocean. She would die here if the girl didn't come soon to save her.

Nu Rose? Why not now? Who said you have to wait until you're so farmisht that you wouldn't know from the Angel of Death if he bit you in the ass?

It was that same man from television speaking to her. Maybe, he had learned Yiddish from his grandparents and this had served him well professionally. Surely, she had seen him before in a commercial, stuffing his face on Hebrew National hot dogs or extolling the virtues of some other ethnically resonant product to stereotypical perfection.

Oy gevalt Rose, I'm trying to tell you something! So nu? Do you see them? Your husband? Your best friend? Do you want to wind up like them? That doctor could have asked you a few more questions about your faculties . . .

Rose opened her eyes. For so many people, it ended just like this: lying in a hospital bed connected to a machine but otherwise entirely alone. The last time she occupied a hospital bed, Morry had sat right next to her, holding her hand whenever possible.

The girl arrived within the hour as promised. She wore her yoga clothes and her hair in a disheveled ponytail. She had canceled the rest of her classes today, she told Rose. Whatever she could do to help.

Rose thanked her for coming. She needed to get up from this bed, sign the necessary papers, promise to make the necessary follow-up doctors' appointments, and return to her apartment so she could fall asleep in her own bed and behave in a manner that passed for taking it easy at her age. This was for sure.

Nu Rose? And everything else?

She observed how the girl looked at her but also at how the girl *looked.* There it seeped through the girl's mask of concerned facial expression and upbeat attitude, that unmistakable sadness. It wafted toward Rose like plumes of pungent smoke.

Had she known the girl in any other way? Surely, there was more to both of them and Rose suddenly thought of that frivolous board game someone had donated to the Center; a game that had belonged to a grandchild who had probably grown up and went on to buy more current games to play with his own children. Depending on your roll of the dice, you landed on various squares that told the player to go back to start or go ahead twenty-seven or run around the room like a chicken and score five points. But one square required you to stay put until another player landed there. Only then could the second player roll the dice, allowing both players to move forward together.

Once or twice, Rose played that game with her dear friend Lillian Rabinowitz and several others. Far less intellectually challenging than bridge, they all agreed. Less like fine literature and more like trash television. But it did the trick of passing the time.

Rose grabbed the girl's wrist. "You must miss him terribly."

The girl nodded. And then she said, "But it's complicated."

"The accident," Rose said. "It really was my fault."

"Rose—"

"Please." Rose tried to sit up in bed but felt lightheaded. She allowed the girl to help her lie back down. "Please. I've been meaning to tell you something."

"What if we get out of this hospital first?"

"I swore I would never get into a car with him again. And that morning, I hid his keys. I tried to prevent him . . ."

"It's okay."

"He . . . he found them."

Even now, she could not deliver the complete confession.

But the girl didn't seem to care. She merely asked if Rose felt well enough to get out of bed.

So Rose got out of bed, and the girl helped her leave the hospital, which included the happy retrieval of her shopping cart. She could see how the girl struggled to remain calm as they got into her car and started driving. As they waited in the interminable left turn lane at the intersection of Lincoln and Washington Boulevards, the girl said, "I never got to tell him I was sorry."

"For what dear?"

But the girl didn't answer as she made the left turn onto Washington Boulevard, where she proceeded to honk at one of those oversized SUV vehicles that tried to cut directly in front of them without signaling. The SUV veered back into its lane and its angry driver honked back.

"Sorry," the girl said. "That was a close call."

They haven't thought everything through.

She could only grasp at this fragment from her recent dream. But it did the trick.

It's just like that silly board game no one ever plays anymore.

"I want to talk to you about a proposition." Rose regretted the word "proposition" the second it flew out of her mouth.

But the girl only nodded and kept her eyes on the road.

She doesn't blame you so far. Maybe you don't have to tell her the rest of it.

It began to assume a solid shape, this brief glimmer of a plan, at least the first part. Rose tried to talk the girl through it as they arrived at her apartment and the girl put on her hazard lights because of course there was no parking in front of her building. She kept talking as the girl helped her upstairs and she could see how some words furrowed her brow and how other words soothed her like a mother's touch to her frightened daughter's forehead in the middle of the night. *Shah, maidele. Shah. Everything will be all right.* Already, Rose was learning.

Eight

NINA AND LAZ: A Brief History

August 1991: There's Nina, twenty years old and seven weeks into spending her junior year abroad at Hebrew University in Jerusalem. She has long black hair down to her waist and wears a favorite pair of ripped and faded jeans. Her face bears a recognizably collegiate fullness, which can be traced to lingering baby fat and a steady diet of pita bread, hummus, and chocolate spread. On this particular night, she's drinking with friends at a cheap bar in downtown Jerusalem to celebrate the end of their summer intensive language program and improved proficiency in Hebrew that allows them to bargain for eggplants and cab fares with slightly more credibility.

At the bar, it's two for one Maccabee beer night and Nina has just ordered her third and fourth beer when she sees him walk into the bar. He looks familiar and she vaguely recalls standing behind him in line at the café inside the university's overseas student center. He's tall, rangy, and dark-haired and when he approaches her friends, she notices his shiny olive skin, his large, slightly upturned green eyes, and a small black kippah skewed sideways on the back of his head.

"Everyone, Laz. Laz, everyone," Paul says, the group's sole lapsed Catholic, whom Nina had befriended two years ago in an introductory art history class at UCLA. Since arriving in Israel, Nina has appreciated having a friend from home and she particularly values Paul for his ability to explore Jerusalem through an anthropological and historical lens sans partisan political or religious agenda.

She watches Laz wave hello to the group and park himself on the opposite end of the table from her. She sips her beer and does her best to filter out the ambient noise as she collects some facts. Laz skipped the summer ulpan because he's fluent in Hebrew. He's from New York and goes "to this school in Boston." He slouches when he sits and downs cheap scotch straight up like water. He has a dimple on the left side of his face. Laz is short for Lazer, the name of his great-grandfather. It's his ninth trip to Israel. He's descended from a long line of rabbis and his family donates heaps of money to Jewish schools and synagogues all over the world. He's a political science major but truth be told, he'd pursue a professional acting career if it didn't conflict with his Sabbath observance.

Nina tries not to stare at him when he speaks. She's certainly no expert on Orthodox Jews but she nonetheless concludes that the little black kippah does not belong on his head. His personality seems more Tel Aviv than Jerusalem and this gets confirmed when he tells the group how he studied at a Jerusalem yeshiva before Harvard and would have been kicked out, if not for his parents' philanthropic contributions to the school.

"What did you do?" Finally, Nina asks a question.

He looks at her and smiles. "Everything."

She feels it for the first time, deep in the pit of her stomach. But she doesn't know how to describe it yet, this fluttery sensation that simultaneously makes her feel both weak and alert. She only knows that he's the cause and for this reason, she will remain seated on her plastic bar chair. As long as it takes, she will wait for him.

Four hours later: she's sitting next to him at the now mostly vacated table, where a multitude of glasses, empty beer bottles, and soggy napkins from this evening's revelry form a river of detritus between their carefully positioned elbows. They've already swiftly reviewed childhood and adolescence. *You're from New York? Cool, I'm from Los Angeles. No, I never went to your summer camp or attended events with that youth group. I definitely don't know anyone from Ramaz and why would I know the name of your high school? Sorry, but I suck at Jewish geography. I'm a public school kid who had a classically mediocre Hebrew school education, give or take a few things my parents thought I should experience. What are my other credentials? Well, my grandmother was very religious, but okay . . . sure, I'll admit it, your world is kind of exotic to me. Am I searching? I'm not sure what you mean by that. I mean, I've been trying to figure out what being Jewish means to me personally, is it a religion, a culture, blah, blah, blah. That's partially why I'm here. No, I'm not "one of those." I don't even know what Jerusalem Syndrome is exactly. But yes, I'm looking for more insight. That and wanting to see the world. You strike me as someone who also wants to see the world, am I right?*

"You could say that." He slouches in his seat and smiles at her. "So basically, you're trying to find yourself."

She decides not to be insulted. "Aren't we all?"

He laughs and swigs the rest of his beer. "Do you want to go for a walk?"

Nina looks around the bar and decides to glean inspiration from Paul, who's cuddled up at the opposite end of their wet and littered table with Diana, Nina's across-the-hall neighbor in the Resnick dorms. Diana's also a kosher-keeping Sabbath observer and Nina knows from previous conversations with her that she doesn't believe in dating non-Jews.

"Okay, Harvard Boy."

"You got something against Harvard boys, Miss UCLA?" His knee is now definitely pressed against her thigh and she can feel his breath, hot and alcoholically aromatic, graze the hairs on her bare arms.

"I don't really judge people based on what university they attend."

He grins at her and she tries to stay afloat on her newfound, no doubt alcoholically enhanced brazenness by pointing to the kippah on his head. "I wouldn't have figured you for an Orthodox Jew. I mean, aren't you not even allowed to shake hands with a woman?"

"Nina." *Neeeee-naaaah.* "You've got a lot to learn about the world." He grabs her hand and raises it to his lips.

They say goodbye to a preoccupied Paul and Diana and leave the bar for King George Street. Laz guides them to Gan Ha Pa'amon, a city park with a main path well lit by overhanging wires strung with white Christmas-style lights. He explains, "I thought we could sneak onto the trampolines."

He already gets me! She doesn't tell him that she's been to these trampolines twice during daylight hours where she has paid the five-shekel fee to see if she could still do a back flip. (She could.) She only says, "I used to be a gymnast."

"Is it true what they say about gymnasts?"

She mock-glares at him.

"Let's see if you can climb a fence."

They walk through the park to the trampolines, enclosed within a chain-link fence. She climbs the fence first, after declining Laz's offer for a boost. In seconds, she's performing seat drops. After a minute, she does a back flip. She doesn't consider the gymnastics to be a form of showing off. Rather, she's simply exposing a key aspect of her true self.

Laz jumps on an adjacent trampoline, watching her. She falls on her back after another back flip and suddenly, he's next to her. "You do know what they say about gymnasts." He talks to her as if he's yanking off her clothes. As if he's flinging her onto a bed or against a wall.

"Whatever they say, it's a myth."

He leans over to kiss her and she immediately understands that this boy is an expert in the ways of using just the right amount of tongue. Afterward, he tells her that he's no longer an observant Jew and his family doesn't know.

"So you're in Israel to escape religion? Fascinating."

"Not really. Have you been to Tel Aviv?"

She laughs. "I was right about you."

They kiss. They touch. His hand starts to slide down her pants. She whispers, "I'm a virgin." She's imparting this information far sooner in the process than she normally would.

"I thought you might be." His hand freezes in mid-travel and Nina thinks of airplanes delayed on runways, filled with impatient and restless passengers.

"Why?" She's both flattered and insulted.

He shrugs.

"You're not a virgin," she says.

"That is true."

They remain on that trampoline until sunrise. For at least an hour, her head simply rests against his chest and she's struck by the realization that she desires nothing else from life at this juncture in time. But as the sun comes up, she remembers her visit to a Venice Beach palm reader, two days before she left for Israel. She had consulted the palm reader for the hell of it and was told: *You are at the beginning of a very long process.*

Aren't we all? Nina allows the memory of the palm reader to recede into the present moment, where she's still resting her head on his bare chest. There's a chill in the early morning air but his skin feels hot. She presses herself into it, sucking up as much warmth as she can.

JANUARY 1992: THEY'RE lying on top of a sand dune in the Sinai Desert, snuggled under a blanket that Nina had the foresight to bring for their mid-week, let's-ditch-some-of-our-classes getaway to Dahab. Near them lie the ruins of an ancient Israeli tank. Laz thinks it's from the Arab-Israeli war of 1956 but it's hard to know for sure since all they have for purposes of illumination are a flashlight and the moon. Nina thinks they're maybe a mile or two from the main Dahab strip but at the moment, she doesn't have a firm grasp of distances.

Don't they say you learn so much more about a person once you travel with them? Don't they say that travel can make or break relationships? Nina snuggles closer to Laz, feeling the urge to laugh. No matter what, she believes she will have escaped experiencing a certain rite of passage as a mediocre and uninspired affair.

"What's so funny?" Laz rolls on top of her and kisses her hard on the mouth. She didn't realize she had been laughing.

"Nothing."

"You liked those hookah pipes, didn't you?"

She starts giggling again as she considers their last twenty-four hours: They had taken the night bus from Jerusalem to Eilat, crossed the border at Taba at sunrise, and soon found themselves in the back seat of a 1970-something dirty white Toyota station wagon. The Bedouin taxi driver drove the S-curves of a two-lane highway to a medley of Bob Marley music while sand flew through the car's windows and got trapped in everyone's teeth. Nina, however, didn't mind. As a native Californian, she had always loved the vastness and emptiness of the desert and here in the Sinai, she reveled in seeing nothing but miles of sand, some mountainous landscape in the distance, the occasional tumbleweed, and the infinite, bright blue desert sky. And when they finally got to Dahab after the driver had almost killed them twice—near collision with a pick-up truck; near collision with a herd of goats—she found similar joy in the narrow pot-holed street paralleling the Red Sea that was apparently Dahab's main drag. Their driver cruised past a strip of campsites, thatched-hut hostels, and restaurants with crayoned signs promising "Deelishous Foods for a Cheep, Cheep Prise" and deposited them in front of a semi-circle of huts at the edge of town.

"My friend, he run Star of Sinai. Cheap price, not expensive," their driver had promised, offering them two cigarettes to seal the deal. "Cold showers. No scorpions."

Laz had nodded and grabbed their backpacks out of the taxi. "I'm sold," he said, looking directly at Nina, who tried her best to prevent the onset of a blush.

On the bus to Eilat, Laz had told her that all the accommodation in Dahab was basically the same so it didn't matter where the cab drivers took you. "You're going to love it," he had promised, opening a side compartment in his backpack to pull out a bag of potato chips, and that's when she had spotted the package of Trojans.

After settling in at the Star of Sinai, they took naps, feasted on vegetarian rice mixtures and chocolate banana pancakes, and visited two different thatched-roof cafés to drink sweet tea and smoke apple scented hookah pipes. At the second café, the proprietor offered them a special pipe for special customers. Nina had never smoked hash before and by the time Laz suggested night walking in the desert, she was in the throes of rubbery leg syndrome and could translate thought into articulate speech about fifty-five percent of the time. Laz had been the one to remember the blanket she had packed and guided them back to their hut for it, before heading out into the desert.

And now this: She can't stop laughing and Laz laughs with her.

"If you like this, you'd love shrooms," he says. "Or maybe even acid."

She shrugs and he climbs on top of her. He traces the area around her belly button and she closes her eyes, sensing it would be easier to remain silent. "So what's the worst thing you've ever done?" She keeps her voice light and breezy, in direct opposition to the urgency that lies underneath the haze of her high. She knows exactly what she's willing to sacrifice but does he?

He starts to kiss her again. When they come up for air, she persists. "I want to know."

He laughs. "You want to know that about me already?"

"I want to know everything about you." She could blame this blurting, clumsy admission on the hash but she's cognizant enough to know better.

"Do you now?" He re-arranges them so that his whole body covers hers.

Vaguely, she recalls the refrain of a women's studies professor she had during her first year at UCLA. "Knowledge is power."

"Smart girl."

She stares at him as he reaches down and pulls her sweater over her head.

A minute later: She feels a flash of fear burst through her joie de vivre; it's a bolt of angry lightning streaking across an otherwise clear and placid sky. She experiences her nakedness as something private and unique but also global and urgent, as if illustrious representatives from every single country suddenly left important UN committee meetings to gather in the Sinai Desert for the sole purpose of witnessing what they're about to do.

"I'm . . ."

"I know."

"I guess . . ."

"We don't have to."

"But I want to."

"Yeah?"

"Yeah."

"I'm going to hurt you."

"I know."

He kisses her on the lips before rummaging in his pants pocket. He rips off a condom from his six-pack, which makes Nina think of both beer and bananas. He promises to go slow and she tries to keep her voice light when she tells him he'll probably have no choice.

He starts guiding himself into her and it's like a million paper cuts and finger burns from the stove all at once, ripping her insides apart. She forces herself not to scream. He keeps asking if she's okay and each time, she tells him to keep going. But the pain only intensifies and Nina's insides pulsate as if all her organs have coalesced into one gigantic heart.

It couldn't have been long, two or three minutes at most. Afterward, he whispers, "How are you?"

"Good."

"Then congratulations."

"Congratulations to you too."

They lie there naked, wrapped in each other's arms. Eventually, they put their clothes back on and remain huddled for warmth under the blanket. Nina keeps her eyes open, trying to stay awake for as long as she can.

JUNE 1993: THERE'S Nina, slumped on a tattered and stained faded-red couch in her archetype-of-student-housing apartment. One bedroom, one roommate rarely there due to a boyfriend two blocks away, two twin beds, a shower with a perennially clogged drain, a profoundly un-vacuumed dark blue-turning-black living room carpet, and a fridge full of Diet Coke and Entenmann's Devil's Food Crumb Donuts. She's studying for the final exam of her college career on "Modern Art History: From the French Revolution to the Twentieth Century." At the moment, she only has patience for the dreamscapes of Dali and Rousseau but that probably has less to do with a lack of sleep and more to do with the fact that she's always felt a kinship with the Surrealists.

She's debating getting another Diet Coke from her fridge when there's a knock at the door. The knock sounds especially ominous since she hasn't slept in two days and quite frankly, she wouldn't even want her roommate to see what she looks like at the moment. She's wearing her ripped-in-eight-places jeans and a blue UCLA T-shirt that barely reaches her navel, a casualty of over laundering in cheap washer/driers. Her hair gleams with unwashed glamour; if it were a pan, she could fry an egg on it, no oil necessary.

She groans when she rises from her couch and feels her stomach grumble in protest from all the vats of coffee and cans of Coke she has drunk. At the door, she looks through the peephole and her reaction is immediate.

Dear Nina, I'm beyond flattered by what you wrote but I'm sure I did not mislead you. I told you from the start that I don't do long distance. Of course, if we were in the same city . . .

Only at the end of the letter did he call a spade a spade. *I met someone else.*

"What the fuck are you doing here?" She still feels it deep within her stomach, the burning sensation of betrayal.

"I'm in town for a family bar mitzvah." He drums some faux-African beat on her front door. "Thought I'd say hello."

She glares at the door, her anger building with every breath. *You think you can pound a rhythm on my door and I'm going to shake my ass for you just like that? Mr. I decide to buy myself a djimbe drum my senior year at Harvard and attend drumming circles by the Charles River because I have been to West Africa and am now not just another New York Jew boy but a citizen of the WORLD.*

"Didn't you get my last letter?" She's still proud of her response, despite some overtones of melodrama and immaturity. *Dear Laz, Thanks for finally making me understand that we're actually nothing to each other. So no, I can't just be your friend but maybe one day I'll be happy to hear that you've met someone. Anyway, have a nice life.*

"Yes, I got your letter. That's why I'm here."

"I don't understand."

"I think you do. Are you going to open the door?"

She exhales an enormous sigh. She wants to shower him with expletives and kiss him until she runs out of breath. She wants to kick him out of her life for good and open the door immediately with her arms outstretched. Was this the definition of a broken heart? Nina knows she has no basis for comparison. She only knows that her ex-boyfriend is a genius at finding the loopholes, textual and otherwise, his skills honed from years of Talmud classes at his Judaically correct yet secularly rigorous—fifty-nine percent of its graduating seniors get into Harvard, Yale, and Princeton—Jewish day school. Lying naked in her Jerusalem dorm room bed, he would perform these drunken, post-coital riffs using the traditional, singsong chants and whirlwind thumb motions of Talmud scholars for his own subversive purposes. *From this ev-i-dence that she fu-ucked all the bo-oys in lev-el four ul-pan*—left thumb swooping horizontally toward an upright hitchhiker's position—*we deduce that Re-na Gold-stein*—right thumb pointing south, otherwise known as the universal symbol for this is a shitty movie thanks to Siskel and Ebert—*is a big, fat sl-u-ut!*—both thumbs leveled horizontally and placed under her nose as an olfactory reminder about the activities committed before the lesson in yeshiva-talk.

Laz tried to teach her how to do yeshiva thumbs but she could never perform them with the same stamp of authenticity. And after he broke up with her via his breezy letter, she found herself cringing at the recollection of their bedtime shtick. *I'm just an agnostic. But you, you're a HERETIC.* He had asked her to say this in a breathy, baby doll voice one night as she nibbled her way down his neck. The word "heretic," he had confessed, made him hard.

She takes a deep breath and opens the door. He stands there, tall and slouching in a black leather jacket and with thick and tousled hair. It takes her several seconds to notice he no longer wears a black kippah skewed sideways on his head and she wants to believe that this simplifies him. Simplifying him, she thinks, might make him less attractive.

She glares at him, trying her best to stay angry. "I'm studying for a final and you aren't going to stop me from graduating."

He grins at her. "Nina." *Neeeee-naaaaaah.* "It's good to see you."

She watches the way he looks at her and thinks about Dali's most famous painting, *The Persistence of Memory. Can a person transform another person into a melting clock just by looking at them?*

She forgets to close the door as they start kissing. She hears him kicking the door closed as she rakes her fingers through his hair.

Twenty minutes later: They sit on her couch drinking Diet Coke and discuss their plans for the future. She discloses that she's moving to New York in a week, where she will do absolutely nothing with her art history degree. Rather, she will reclaim her childhood passion for dance and attempt a career as a professional dancer. He reveals that he already moved back to the city two weeks ago and currently resides in his grandmother's three-bedroom apartment on West 87th Street near Columbus Avenue. His grandmother, now living in an upscale, Westchester-based assisted living complex, had wanted to keep her apartment "in the family." And come September, he's starting a two-year program at the William Esper Studio. His family doesn't yet know he's decided to become an actor. They think he's in the city to procure a real job before getting his Ph.D. in something, not to mention a wife. And when they do, he might just have to call himself a starving artist.

"Sounds romantic." Her caustic tone is the shabbiest of fronts; she can feel her hope spilling out all around her. Word for word, she can remember some of their conversations in Jerusalem, how he layered his speech and gestures about the future with implicit messages of inclusion. *You're planning on New York after graduation? Me too.*

"You and me in the same city again. How about that?" He stretches his legs, puts his feet on her coffee table, and traces their initials into her left forearm with his index finger. She can't help but appreciate the symbolism of this invisible tattoo. Somehow, it feels analogous to the renewal of wedding vows, the way that he imprints her now and how for a second, it conjures up the cold, painful, and delicious interlude in the Sinai Desert.

He whispers, "I've missed you."

"What about your letter? All that crap about us wanting different things?"

"People change."

"You don't."

He says nothing.

"So who was she? Or should I say, 'shes'?"

"They don't matter."

"And I do?"

He moves toward her and she's acutely aware that the moment, which she delayed twenty minutes ago, has arrived. She can silently point him to the front door or, if she wants to be dramatic about it, lock herself in the bathroom. Or, she can do what she so desperately wants to do.

And so it plays out in her shabby, collegiate living room: The primeval battle between reason and desire with Plato, Hegel, Kant, Maimonides, Freud, black hatted Jews, fundamentalist Imams, anti-abortion, banner wielding Born-Again Christians, and various judgmental peers weighing in on the sidelines with a cornucopia of dualistic terminology. Indeed, Nina's college education has taught her that absolutely everyone has their own terminology surrounding impulsive and unregulated sexual encounters. The id, (psychology) yetzer hara, (Jewish studies) Satan, (Intro to world religions) Dionysus and the Maenads, (Greek and Roman art). These terms pepper stories and myths with the same message: Hear me young woman, do not give in! This way, we don't have to . . . Fill in the blank with the policing verb of your choice. Judge; ostracize; brainwash; psychoanalyze; honor kill; shame; etc.

He moves closer and she hears the soft yet clear voice of dissent that punctures all the arguments she has encountered during her college education. *You're young, you're unattached. So what if he treated you like shit? He's sorry now, isn't he? You feel how you feel don't you? And what's the alternative? Repression of desire? Why do so many people believe that casual sex is worse than murder anyway? What kind of fucked-up world is that?*

And then, there's another voice. It's a voice neither influenced by her college education nor her desperate need for immediate gratification. *For fuck's sake Nina, when has sex with him ever been casual?*

He's about to kiss her when she says, "I want to show you something."

She leans over him to retrieve the art history textbook that lies on her coffee table. She flips through its pages until she finds the print of Chagall's *The Lovers* that hangs in the Metropolitan Museum of Art. They had already broken up when she first laid eyes on the painting but she thought of him instantly. In the painting, a man embraces a woman who sits on his lap, her body intertwining with his. She wears a blue dress and holds a white rose. His white body blends into the nearby red table. He is of course part angel, part devil. She is frozen forever in the moment just before her lips touch his. They have faces but at the same time are faceless. Outside their window, a red sky looms, as does a Russian village that no longer exists.

"This painting . . ." Her voice refuses to cooperate.

He puts on a show of studying the painting from different distances and angles by first holding the book close to his face and then, after about a minute, further away.

"I think we have the same taste in art," he says.

When he caresses her face, first the right side and then the left, she simply closes her eyes. In this way, she takes a break from remembering the history of absolutely everything.

JANUARY 1994-SEPTEMBER 2001: A pattern emerges several months after Nina says goodbye to her California childhood and freshly divorced parents and moves to New York City. She rents a tiny studio on the Upper West Side, a mere twenty blocks away from Laz's apartment. For $650 a month—a Manhattan bargain even in 1994—she lives in a room with a mini-fridge, multiple Combat traps to keep the roaches at bay, and a pink carpet that sprouts a tan colored fungus if not frequently and thoroughly steam cleaned. Night after night, she never knows what she might find when she returns home after long days of work and classes and auditions. Fungus? Roaches? One of the rats that she has spotted rooting around the garbage cans on the side of her apartment building? And yet, the very thought of her apartment unfailingly causes her to tingle with pleasure. In this vastly complicated and challenging city where she's committed to dancing for the rest of her flexibly mobile life, she literally has a room of her own.

Laz, however, prefers that they get together at his place. "This is a real shithole," he pronounced the first time he set foot in her apartment, a mere five days after she moved in. "How can you live like this?"

"Not all of us can live in a three-bedroom rent controlled palace," she answered, defensive and almost begging him to concede that her studio will look much better once she has decorated its bare, grainy-white walls and bought a bedspread to cover her newly purchased futon.

They see each other frequently during her first few months in the city. Laz introduces her to the joys of affordable Indian cuisine on East 6th Street, the Ramble in Central Park, and the $10 clothing stores that cluster around the World Trade Center. One Sunday afternoon, he suggests that they visit the Met and it's understood that they will go out of their way in that labyrinth of a museum to view Chagall's *The Lovers*. Afterward, they speed walk through Central Park and beeline for his apartment, where they have sex on the oblong kitchen table that Laz's grandparents bought in 1961. She says it then, the sacred, vulnerable words, and he responds by tightening his embrace. She hadn't meant to say it first but oh well. She thinks: it's been two years, why shouldn't she say it? And surely, he will reciprocate.

But something shifts after that encounter. Nina lands a job waitressing at a Mexican restaurant in Midtown based on her status as a native Californian with superior exposure to tacos and burritos compared with her East Coast counterparts. During the day, she goes on auditions and attends multiple dance classes. She reads a lot of books on the subway as she traverses the city for her downtown modern and African dance classes and her uptown ballet, jazz, and hip hop classes. She's determined to be as versatile a dancer as possible and five months after moving to the city, she gets cast in an experimental dance-theater production about reproductive freedom, where she rolls around as an embryo in an egg-like contraption made of white sheets and Styrofoam. It's usually after 11 p.m. by the time she can visit Laz at his apartment, but more frequently, he's been leaving messages on her answering machine telling her he's busy.

One night, she decides to surprise him. She knocks on his door shortly before midnight and he greets her wearing nothing but a towel around his waist. "This isn't a good time," he tells her. "You should have called first." She feels herself blush as she swivels to leave and when he says, "We never said we were exclusive," the sacred, vulnerable words drip out of her memory and take the form of proverbial egg on her face.

Once again, she resolves to cut him off. He stops calling her after several attempts and she embarks on a quest to diversify her sexual/romantic/soul mate preferences. She goes on dates with a South African businessman, a fellow college alumnus who initially seemed much more attractive in New York than in California, and an attorney who preaches the gospel of cocaine before having sex. The attorney does lines on an almost nightly basis but Nina has never been interested in that particular drug. She soon ditches the attorney and has months of decent if not terribly exciting sex with a co-worker from the Mexican restaurant who only wants to talk about his aspiring actor's career.

Men are everywhere in New York City only Nina cannot replace him. So the next time he calls, she agrees to meet him.

Rinse and repeat. Rinse and repeat. For seven years, Nina remains stuck in a shampoo commercial of her own design. He calls her. She agonizes over calling him back. She calls him back. They meet. They have hours of sweaty, acrobatic sex followed by excursions through the city where Nina feels as if they're travelers from another country. Laz may have his flaws but he also possesses a uniquely contagious zest for everything that the city has to offer. With him, the markets in Chinatown with their exotic produce and sharp fish smells remain an endless source of fascination. The cappuccino and biscotti at Veniero's in the East Village taste even better in his presence, and when they walk the Brooklyn Bridge in the middle of the night, she feels a deep love for her adopted city that she didn't realize she had.

One Friday night, on their way downtown to a jazz club, he asks if they can make a pit stop while still on the Upper West Side. They walk over to 79th and West End and stand outside a synagogue in the midst of the Friday night service. Nina has passed by this synagogue countless times but has never been inside.

The doors of the synagogue are wide open. It's a small space, lined with overflowing bookcases and jammed with men and women collectively engaged in loud and raucous singing. *Lecha dodi. Likrat kalah. P'nai Shabbat Nekabelah.* She recognizes this prayer about welcoming the Sabbath Queen, a prayer she learned from attending the day camp Gan Israel the summer she turned eight. Separate dance circles soon form, one for the men and one for the women. Nina absorbs the focus and fervor of the dancers as she watches them. In the pit of her stomach, she begins to feel some kind of deep identification and yearning. Does she not try to do that in her own dancing, to attempt a connection with the divine?

"I miss it, sometimes."

She looks away from the worshippers and refocuses on Laz, whose gaze remains planted on the inside of the synagogue. She sees something in his face that she's never seen before, some mixture of sadness and vulnerability and pain. She knows that he barely speaks to his family these days, that aside from allowing him to live in his grandmother's apartment, they have pretty much cut him off.

She puts her hand on his arm. "Do you want to go inside?"

He looks at her then and smiles and it's maybe the saddest smile she's ever seen on his face. He says, "We're not exactly dressed for Shabbos."

"Well, maybe another time? I'd go with you, if you wanted."

She sees it again, this facial expression hinting at genuine suffering. But he only says, "We need to get downtown."

Before they descend the stairs of the 79th Street subway station, she grabs his arm and pulls him into a hug. She embraces him as hard as she can. *You make me feel so alive.* She doesn't dare tell him this, nor does she expect to hear him say the sacred, vulnerable words. He still has never said them to her but on this particular night, she understands why.

"IT'S COOL THAT it doesn't go away." This, he does finally say to her in a dark bar after they hadn't seen each other for eight months. Later that night, they wander the city and at his instigation, wind up having unprotected sex under a stairwell of a vacant apartment building in the far West Village. She immediately regrets the unprotected sex and when she expresses her fear of getting pregnant, he tells her that he's not cut out to be a father. She then asks if he's ever thought about her seriously in relation to the future and when he doesn't answer, she makes him give her money for the morning-after pill. She tells him that this time, it's over for real. For a few months after that, the subject of sexually transmitted diseases makes her queasy.

Rinse and repeat. Rinse and repeat. The pattern becomes exhausting and sometimes, humiliating, but it's also never boring and she always forgives him, no matter the transgression. Over the years, his transgressions vary. Sometimes, he's met someone else. Sometimes, he's too busy with his acting career to have a serious relationship. Sometimes, he tells her that he'll never get married and have a family, that he's just not that "kind of guy." Sometimes, he tries to persuade her to have sex without a condom, despite what has happened before.

Occasionally, Nina will ask herself: What the fuck do I see in this individual? And truthfully, she cannot articulate her reasons in words. It's the feeling of their encounters that convince her of their specialness. When she walks with him through the city, she's reminded of when she does her best dancing because she has ceded all consciousness to the intuitive powers of her body. She never stops to ask herself what it might feel like if they saw each other every day in a shared dwelling where they split domestic duties. All she knows is how it feels to lay eyes on him after a hiatus.

Once, Nina doesn't see him for two years because of her almost fiancé Alan, an attorney with a summer home in the Catskills who wants to marry her if she agrees to change her last name, transform her dance career into a hobby, and bear him two to four children. Two months after she breaks up with Alan, she runs into Laz at a bar on newly gentrified Avenue C. It's the first time in the history of their relationship that they have serendipitously collided and this fills Nina with hope. They have broken part of the pattern, where he calls and she forgives, so what else might be different as they stand in line for the bar's unisex bathroom, buzzed off five-dollar mojitos and watching each other for cues as they sum up the last two years of their lives?

Her: She has just completed the first of three yoga teacher certification trainings and came to this bar tonight with her friend Lisa, *you remember Lisa, the one who's always despised you because she thinks you treat me and by extension, all women, like shit,* to abort her month-long status as a teetotaler. Now that she's no longer attached to Alan, which made her rigidly pursue a dance career she didn't necessarily want, she understands that what she really wants to do with her life is help other people find joy and transcendence through movement. Yoga, with its emphasis on the breath to achieve personal evolution and healing, really speaks to her.

Him: Life has been awesome and he's currently starring in a new Off-Broadway production of Sam Shepherd's *Fool for Love.*

And then he says, "We've never gone to a rave together."

"We've never done a lot of things together." It surprises her that she manages to say this, considering she normally thinks of the best responses long after the moment for responding has passed.

He grins and explains that a friend of a friend produces rave-like events at this warehouse in Dumbo and there's one tonight. Does she want to go? If she does, he has a little gift for her, something they can experience together.

She makes a flimsy attempt at resistance and tells him she came here tonight to hang out with Lisa. He nods and asks her if she's still an E virgin. "The first time you do E is the best," he says.

She says goodbye to Lisa, who tells her she's making a big mistake but that she can call her when this latest round of Laz-itis is over and she recommits to becoming a healthy, balanced human being. She and Laz take a cab to the Dumbo warehouse and he slips her the pill once they're inside the cavernous space that feels much smaller than its actual size because it's jam-packed with people. In the center of the warehouse, a DJ spins a mix of house, techno, trance, and industrial music from a high and narrow platform lit up with flashing blue and silver neon lights and Nina instantly feels the rhythms pulsating throughout her body. Always and forever, she's a dancer who doesn't require any pharmaceutical encouragement or even better than average electronic dance music to move her body. The walls of the warehouse are kinetic and colorful with video projections of abstract shapes and designs and Nina spots a bartender behind a fluorescent yellow table dispensing intriguingly green cocktails. Laz tells her it's an open bar and those in the know can also ask for sips of Absinthe.

They wander around the warehouse while they wait for the E to kick in. He puts his arm around her and tells her that he missed her; that in fact, he always misses her. She appreciates that he's saying this while still sober. She then suggests they start dancing now but Laz shakes his head. He is definitely the type of dancer who prefers pharmaceutical prompting.

She's dancing by herself when the E kicks in and she feels the difference in her body, how she's able to slide between movements with a liquidity she has never before possessed. Her body knows exactly how it wants to move at any given moment and suddenly, she's spinning repeatedly with her arms outstretched, trying to simulate what she thinks Whirling Dervishes do. Finally, she spirals down to the concrete floor and starts performing a series of over the shoulder rolls; it's a move she's been perfecting in a modern dance class she still takes. A crowd gathers around her and someone yells, "You're a kick-ass dancer!" but she's too preoccupied to acknowledge the praise-giver. She doesn't know how long she's been dancing when Laz joins her on the warehouse floor. He pulls her to her knees and whispers in her ear, "I know you know."

She yells back, "I know what?"

He kisses her just as she starts to dance again and she can feel the E uniting within her body the two activities that make her feel most alive. The sacred, vulnerable words slip off her tongue, smooth as silk, and she feels powerful in her capacity to give. Did he hear her? She doesn't know because a few minutes later, he disappears into the core of the crowd. She continues dancing and it only occurs to her to look for him much later, when she's started to come down. She looks for him everywhere in the cavernous space but she can't find him.

SEPTEMBER 2001: THE pattern experiences a fissure that's surprising in its immediacy yet predictable in its aftermath on the night the towers fall. He calls her while she's at a dive bar with her boyfriend David watching CNN footage on two screens. As she hears the sound of his voice, she immediately thinks about the last time she saw him, when they went to that rave and New York was a city on a different planet.

"I'm just checking to make sure you're okay."

"I am." She stares hard into the TV screen, at the footage of one plane plunging into one tower, then the second into the other. She grips her vodka tonic and glances at her boyfriend who mouths, "Who is that?" She mouths back, "a friend," and feels the lie, heavy and incriminating within her gut. On this night of all nights, she's lying for the first time to her lovely boyfriend who awaits news of the whereabouts of his best friend, who works, correction, worked, at a law firm on the thirtieth floor of Tower One.

She could reciprocate his inquiry but it seems superfluous. Besides, he volunteers his whereabouts: he's working at a makeshift clinic near Ground Zero, running errands for the medical staff assisting the injured. He just called to tell her that he's sorry.

"For what?"

"Everything."

She sucks in her breath as she looks around the crowded bar, where patrons mostly huddle on the stools and tables closest to the TV screens. The talking heads on CNN, she thinks, cannot compete with the clip of one plane slamming into one tower, then the second into the other. She doesn't know yet about tomorrow, when she'll stare at the front page of *The New York Times* and see a photograph of Tower One surrounded by airborne people. She will scrutinize these people and attempt to memorize who wore suits and who wore jeans; whose ties flung up over their heads like nooses and whose shoes fell off.

She figures it can't hurt to ask him about David's friend David Mehlman, otherwise known to them as the other David. She explains that he's the best friend of her boyfriend. "If for some reason you hear anything about him, let me know."

He promises to call if he hears anything, wishes her lots of luck with the new boyfriend, and explains the real reason for his call. When this madness blows over, he wants to meet her for coffee so he can tell her "some things" in person.

She can't ask, "What things?" right in front of her boyfriend, who's been listening to her every word since she mentioned the other David. Instead, she says, "Take care of yourself. Be careful."

"You too. I love you. I always have."

She hangs up, unable to answer her boyfriend, who asks, "Are you okay?" And: "Who was that?" David grabs one of her hands, which now display visible tremors, and the order of his questions adds a dollop of guilt to her state of fury, elation, and grief. *There is no private tragedy here, only a public one.* But she cannot quite believe this.

He calls her again five days later, shortly after she returns home from the other David's funeral. She's sitting cross-legged on the floor unsuccessfully trying to meditate when her cell phone rings. The acrid smoke still blanketing considerable swaths of the city remains trapped in her nostrils and she can't stop thinking about the differences in funerals. She's now attended the funerals of three of her grandparents, events where everyone cried but no one was afraid. At the other David's funeral, mourners sat with downcast eyes and frozen postures while the rabbi did his best to give a personal eulogy interspersed with bits of pointed sermonizing on The Evil which has forever crippled the world as they know it.

She sees the number light up her phone and her heart can't help it, the way it thumps. Her heart dismisses its extremely recent expression of grief at a life-cut-short-funeral and sickness over a horrific national tragedy. Instead, it's a mercurial child with a nascent long-term memory, feeling what it feels and wanting what it wants from one amnesiac moment to the next.

He says, "I'm across the street. But I thought I'd call first. Just in case you moved or something."

All she has to do is keep her front door locked.

"Nina?" *Neeeeee-naaaaahhhhhhh.* "Is your boyfriend there?"

"No."

"No?"

"No."

He asks if she found out what happened to her boyfriend's friend. She tells him about the funeral and he expresses the kind of basic and muted condolences that people usually do when they've never met the deceased person. And then he reverts: "Do you remember what I said to you that night?"

"Yeah."

"It's true."

She opens the door for him, overwhelmed by multiple strains of déjà vu. She looks at him and pretends that one of them is in prison, separated by a wall of glass.

He says, "I have something for you."

From his knapsack, he pulls out a postcard-size print of a painting. It's *The Lovers* by Chagall, the one that hangs in the Metropolitan Museum of Art. "You loved this painting," he says, extending the print toward her.

She takes the print, holding it with two hands as she might a fragile glass object. Is she the recipient of a calculated ploy or a sincere gesture? At the moment, the question doesn't matter. She now knows that it's possible for two people to remember the same thing in the same way.

She says, "I still do."

Later: They're lying naked in her bed and she asks, "What do I see in you?"

He lights a cigarette and says, "You love what you can't tame. You love the way I love you."

She says things like: I'm a terrible person. And: I've never cheated on anyone until now. And: David isn't you. No one is you.

He says: Blame the circumstances. She says: For fuck's sake this isn't wartime Europe circa 1942 in between Blitzkrieg bombings. He says: Things are bad. She says: But not for us. We're not even in Lower Manhattan. And are we being bombed at the moment? Are we living on food rations? Are we hiding out from the Gestapo in some rat-infested basement? Is America the only country in the history of civilization to have ever suffered a terrorist attack? We're all losing perspective and it really pisses me off that . . .

He interrupts. "Leave him."

She says, "I already have." And: "You are the most selfish person I've ever met."

This shuts him up for a few seconds. Then he says, "I want to work it out with you this time."

This time. A new sensation has become palpable in all parts of her body. Her rage finds its epicenter in the space between those two words.

She reaches for her T-shirt on the floor and gets semi-dressed. She thinks of what she's going to have to say to David. She pulls her hair into a tight bun and says, "You need to leave now. And put out that fucking cigarette."

He takes his time getting dressed. Finally, he joins her in the foyer by her front door and says, "If I've learned anything in life, it's to never have regrets."

She laughs a non-laugh. She tries to speak but she can't due to the rage, which seems to have formed an enormous lump in her throat. *What am I going to regret? Watching you wake up one day, back in your little self-inflicted prison and having to hear your always passionate and heartfelt speech about personal freedom mattering more than anything or anyone else? You want to know my greatest wish? To no longer feel anything. Where you're just some guy and the past feels a million miles away and I'd have no trouble inviting you to my wedding.*

She feels him appraising her with what feels like compassion and this only increases her fury. She says, "This isn't love."

As she slams the door in his face, he says, "You were always the one."

JANUARY 2005: SHE breaks down and calls him two weeks before she moves to Los Angeles. "I have some news," she says and suggests they meet in person but in a public place. "I'm intrigued," he says and agrees to meet her two days later after his acting class at the eastside entrance to the West 4th Street subway station. "Perfect," she says, merely noting she needs to be in that neighborhood but does not disclose it's to pick up a final check from a West Village yoga studio.

At the subway station, she spots him first. While they have periodically spoken on the phone, she hasn't seen him in about two years, when she attended the premiere of a new play where he received rave reviews for his performance as a sex and drug addicted con artist forced to take care of his newly discovered six-year-old son. And now he's walking down the street toward her with that loping tall man's gait, as if he was some alpha giraffe leisurely scoping out the trees with the tastiest leaves. It occurs to her that he has always stood out in public spaces, deviating from the behavior of the rest of the New York City animal kingdom by acting as if he has all the time in the world.

Briefly, she considers standing him up. After *everything*, why can't she just board the plane to Los Angeles, end of story?

And then he sees her. "Hey."

"Hey."

They stand there at the subway entrance, their stillness in stark relief to the people rushing around them. Nina envies these people, how they move on to their next destination without a second thought.

He says, "It's great to see you."

She nods.

He says, "I still think about you."

She continues to nod.

"All the time."

She slips into the memory of when she slammed the door in his face. She remembers the rage of that night but can no longer feel it.

She asks, "What have you been up to?" and learns he moved to Fort Greene. He recently completed two indie films and is in the midst of final callbacks for a new Broadway play. But the truth is he's burning out on the New York acting scene. He's thinking of trying to write a screenplay. He confesses he'd move to LA if he didn't hate the place so much.

"I'm moving to LA in two weeks."

He squints at her with suspicion and disbelief, as if she has just told him she's relocating to Saudi Arabia or the moon. And then he lets out a low whistle.

"So that's your big news. Returning to your roots, huh?"

"In a way."

"I'm honored . . . that you called to say goodbye."

"You should be."

He smiles and says he has about two hours so what else can they do besides stand in front of this subway station? Suddenly, it's understood that they will walk toward the East Village, the neighborhood where they spent the most time. They head to Bleeker Street and switch to East 1st once they hit the Bowery and Nina does her best to ritualize this traversal. They've never commemorated anything, she thinks. They never attended each other's bar or bat mitzvahs or birthday parties or had dating anniversaries. They will never have a wedding. Perhaps, one of them will attend the other's funeral, representing that person in the back pew who keeps the sunglasses on at all times. No one will know her and everyone will wonder why she's crying so hard or volunteering to be the first to shovel the dirt over the coffin in the cemetery.

Finally, they stop outside a bar on Avenue A that they used to frequent. Laz offers to buy her a drink there for old time's sake. She considers the proposition, remembering them on the bar's second floor, their bodies squeezed into a bite-sized bit of uninhabited space hidden behind two couches that otherwise rested against the entire length of a wall. The space had reminded her of the kind of secret fort you make as a kid for purposes of plotting your take-over of the world. He thought they could get away with having sex there undetected, despite all the people sitting on the couches. She had disagreed.

She shakes her head. "Not a good idea."

He nods. "Are you seeing anyone?"

She shakes her head.

"So you have a clean slate then. For moving."

They stare at each other and she allows herself to ask if he's seeing anyone. Yes, as a matter of fact, he is. And this time, it could be serious. She's an actress who went to Harvard and graduated three years after he did. They didn't know each other then.

"That was then, this is now." They had both read that book by SE Hinton as children but she doesn't know if he remembers this. In fact, she has no idea just what exactly he remembers.

"She's no you."

"Please."

"It's true."

"Are you going to marry her?"

"I don't know."

"So you're no longer against marriage?"

"I'll always be against marriage."

She forces herself to say "good luck" and tells him she needs to go home and pack. "I hope you figure things out," she says.

And then she says, "I'm glad I called."

"Nina."

He reaches for her and they stand there, locked into a hug where she can barely breathe. She's that marginal person in the back pew of a funeral, feeling an insatiable grief for all the years she never spent in the presence of the deceased.

They let go of each other and he opens his mouth as if to speak, only he doesn't. She nods, as if he has said something. Then, she heads north on Avenue A. It's understood that he will be walking south.

She does not look back. As she walks, her mind recites a mantra.

Never again.

She will remember this oath-like fragment eight months later, when she's attending Yom Kippur services at a West Los Angeles synagogue. She's listening to the cantor chant Kol Nidre and, for the first time, she understands the significance of the prayer. It is a prayer about renouncing vows, often associated with the Spanish Inquisition, when Jews, practicing their religion in secret, understood all too well the implications of getting caught.

In the traditional manner, the cantor chants the prayer three times and Nina mourns her Bubbe Essie, who passed away two months ago. Every other year, she went to shul with Bubbe Essie on Yom Kippur and she had always loved sitting next to her grandmother, who wore a white summer coat over her dress with two pockets: one stuffed with tissues and the other with the beloved butterscotch candies, smuggled into the synagogue just in case anyone fainted from fasting. Bubbe Essie always cried during Kol Nidre and afterward, she would explain Poland to her granddaughter. In Poland, everyone dressed up in their best clothes to go to shul on Yom Kippur. This, she would whisper while the cantor moved on with the evening service. In Poland, Kol Nidre was the time when everyone— men, women, and children old enough to understand—filled each and every synagogue with the sounds of weeping.

After the cantor finishes the third round of reciting the prayer, Nina bows her head and listens to the complete silence of the synagogue. She squints hard and stares at the floor as she tries to quell the pooling of tears in the corners of her eyes.

Times have changed.

So Nina thinks.

Nine

"I'LL BE ALL right, dear. You should go home. They do terrible things to cars not parked in the right places."

"I can stay. If you want." Nina sat on a white wicker chair near Rose's bed, wishing she didn't have to go anywhere.

"That's all right, dear. I kept you long enough."

Nina debated how to answer. She couldn't tell if her friend truly wanted her to leave. Rose had already declined her offer to cook dinner and really, how many times could she re-arrange Rose's usual medications and newly acquired Percocet into a neat, horizontal line on her nightstand? The ER doctor had said that Rose was fine, that she simply needed rest, but Nina still wanted to help and to hell with her car, now parked illegally in front of Rose's building for some forty-five minutes. She hadn't yet heard the sounds of cops or tow trucks so why couldn't she stay?

She would do anything, anything at all, so that she didn't have to go home and be alone with herself. "Are you sure I can't get anything else for you?"

"I'm going to try and sleep now. Just lock the door behind you when you leave."

Nina nodded and stood up. "Promise you'll call if you need anything." She tried not to sound disappointed.

"I'm fine, dear." Rose reached out and patted Nina's elbow.

Nina could only see Rose's head and hands protruding from the blue comforter and matching covers of her bed but somehow, this made Rose seem less fragile. After all, these were the parts of her that still worked. It certainly had not escaped Nina's attention that Rose gesticulated frequently with her hands while speaking and this made her wonder about the kind of dancer her friend had been.

"Do you have any videos of you dancing?" she blurted out. "I would love to see them."

Rose suddenly seemed slightly more alert. She attempted to sit up a little straighter before sinking back into her pillow. She seemed lost in thought before she shook her head. "That was a long time ago."

Rose closed her eyes and Nina chastised herself. Clearly, her friend was in no mood to answer questions about her past. But as she exited the bedroom, Rose said in an almost-whisper, "I can still dance in my mind."

She watched Rose close her eyes and succumb to the ephemeral charms of a drug-induced slumber. An image suddenly flashed before her, of the two of them dancing together: the former ballet dancer and ex modern dancer engaged in some form of intergenerational duet of slow-motion movements and simple gestures that could be practiced as opposed to performed. They shared this in common, a love for an art form that transcended professional ambitions. Did she not still dance in her living room, fusing free-form movement with yoga poses, so that her mind could switch off and she could feel a temporary yet clear absence of pain?

Nina left Rose's apartment, taking care to lock the door behind her. At the very least, she could help her friend stay safe.

AN HOUR LATER: Nina sat on the steps leading to her front door, engaged in a stare-down with the orange tabby kitten that she had un-originally named Garfield about a week ago. The kitten had a white nose and white paws and a shameless, fearless stare, though he still hadn't allowed Nina to get within petting distance. A few minutes ago, she had spotted him through her living room window and found herself transfixed by the way he strutted along the wall that bordered her apartment building from a group of 1970s bungalow-style cottages that still dotted sections of Venice. Was Garfield consciously communicating to the other cats that he was cool and/or not to be messed with or was that simply the way he loved to move? So she could further indulge in anthropomorphizing, Nina had decided to step outside and observe Garfield more closely but the kitten had froze the second she opened her door. Now, he eyeballed her, his posture stiff and upright and his tail wrapped around his legs, and she stared back, sensing she was days away from buying large bags of kibble and becoming a stereotype in the eyes of many. So far, she had counted six feral felines who lived in and around her apartment complex, including a beautiful black cat with green eyes and a Diva-esque personality. She had already named that cat Angelina Jolie and called her Angie for short.

Please don't leave that wall. Nina did her best to communicate her emotional needs to the orange kitten but unfortunately, he wouldn't listen. He allowed Nina to win the stare-down and jumped off the wall into the adjacent yard.

Nina stood up, stretched, and considered driving somewhere, to a mall, to the movies, somewhere neutral and escapist. She needed to be careful with this business of using other people and animals to stave off a particular kind of loneliness she could not assuage. But it had only gotten worse since Allison's shower two weeks ago, this visceral itch to call him under the auspices of simply hearing his voice but knowing in her guts that she would succumb to his request for face-to-face interaction. The only way to resist fate was to cut off communication entirely, she had firmly told herself two weeks ago.

But now, Nina stared at the kitten-less wall, suddenly awash with alarm by a new thought: There might come a day in the very near future when Rose would return to the hospital only she wouldn't be able to call for help. She would instead hear from a nurse, telling her that Rose had listed her as the emergency contact number and that she didn't know who else to call.

Earlier, she had tried to squelch her anxiety when Rose said she had a "proposition" for her after they left the hospital. *Dear, I have some things that you might like for your new apartment. Maybe you will take them off my hands?* She had felt guilty that she couldn't immediately say yes. But to accept Rose's household items felt like a departure from how they currently knew each other and more reminiscent of the way her Bubbe Essie in her final years always had a gift ready whenever she visited. "I don't need this anymore," she would say to Nina, bearing a handmade knitted afghan or ancient bottle of perfume or glass vase with visible watermarks from decades of housing flowers. *But you're still alive.* This, Nina always wanted to say to her grandmother.

It's risky, isn't it? Making friends with someone who wants to start giving you her things? But then again, anyone that you've ever cared about can die at any time.

And that's when she couldn't stand it for a second longer. The itchiness became overwhelming as she grabbed her phone and called him.

"Hi."

"Nina." *Neeeeee-naaahhh.*

Pause.

"I'm happy you called."

She didn't directly ask him to come over. She simply said she had finally decided to call him back.

"When can I see you?"

She said, "I'm not really in the habit of going to bars these days."

He said, "I'll come over. You moved, right? When are you free?"

She paused and for the briefest of seconds, considered what it might feel like to hang up the phone and do nothing but sit on her living room floor and commune with her loneliness. *Remember how you could see him in Vegas? Remember how you strained to drive the speed limit on the 15, telling yourself that it did no good to break the law. And then you got off the 10 and called him. And called again. And again. Only he wasn't there.*

She swallowed hard. "I'm free right now."

THERE'S NINA, STUMBLING into her kitchen on a Tuesday morning in dire need of coffee and wondering how she will teach her three yoga classes and two private clients today based on last night's four hours of sleep. Jeff sits at their kitchen table, a half-filled coffee cup in front of him. Nina sees immediately that he's in some kind of anticipatory watch-and-wait mode and so she looks around her kitchen for clues. It takes her about five seconds to spot Jeff's "list of terms," which he has tacked to the refrigerator door with a Pepto Bismol-pink magnet that expresses a truncated Goethe quote in plump bubble letters: "He is the happiest . . . who finds peace in his home."

It takes her another half minute or so to read Jeff's list, which has been blatantly modeled after the Ten Commandments.

"Are you serious?" Nina scrutinizes the face of her fiancé, understanding for the first time that he would have made an excellent clown. How has she not noticed this before, his knack for spotting the humor in the saddest of situations?

Jeff answers in his social worker's voice. "I had two cancellations from clients yesterday so I decided to be productive with my spare time. Go ahead, read it again, and make sure you catch the nuances."

"The Ten Commandments are not exactly nuanced." But she reads the list again with her arms folded over her chest.

My List of Terms, by Jeff Wasserman, LCSW:

I am your primary romantic partner. There is no other.

Thou shall not create other romantic partners. Thou must only take care of business with the pre-existing romantic partner.

Thou shall have five chances to take care of business with said pre-existing romantic partner.

Thou shall not have unprotected sex.

Thou shall not bear false witness when asked about any of the five sanctioned encounters.

Thou shall work toward breaking as opposed to furthering the emotional bond with the pre-existing romantic partner.

Thou shall allow the primary romantic partner to take a secondary partner for reasons of quid pro quo and if he does so then thou shall accord to him a similar set of rules that he must approve in advance.

Thou shall immediately cease and desist with the encounters should the primary romantic partner have second thoughts.

Thou shall not scheme over additional encounters with the pre-existing romantic partner if planning to remain with the primary romantic partner. Once the five encounters are over, thou must choose one way or the other.

Thou shall allow the primary romantic partner to supervise any of the encounters.

"Are you sure about that one? Exactly how many cans of worms do we want to open here?" She asks this after exceeding Jeff's expectations by reading the list three times.

"Did Moses ask God to re-think a commandment or two?" It's Jeff's turn to fold his arms across his chest. He squints at her, as if she too is a list of rules to decipher.

"There's still time to forget the whole thing."

"But then all my hard work would go to waste." He points to the list. "You got to admit, it's clever."

Nina appraises the smirking expression on Jeff's face and for the briefest of seconds, tries to remember everything he has ever said to her when he thinks and/or pretends she's asleep.

But then Jeff says, "It's good to have rules and regulations during troubled times, don't you think?"

She narrows her eyes at Jeff and nods. *Game on.*

SANCTIONED ENCOUNTER #1: Nina insists on meeting in the Venice bar of their California reunion. If he agrees to brave cross-town traffic and experience the viscous crawl of the 10, 110, and 101 in time for happy hour specials, then she has one more reason to update him on her personal circumstances.

Laz arrives fifteen minutes late and insists on buying the first round of drinks. She leads him to the cave-like room and they sit side by side with their thighs pressed together. Before she even takes a first sip of her Malbec, he squeezes her hand and whispers, "I'm so glad you called."

She puts her drink on the candlelit table in front of her and grabs the photocopy of Jeff's Ten Commandments from her purse. "There's been some developments."

He takes the list, grabs a candle, and reads while she watches him, trying to see him through the eyes of others. She's aware, for example, that a fair number of her friends past and present do not quite understand why she finds this man eternally irresistible. "He's sexy but that's not everything," they might say or occasionally throw her an "I guess I see what you mean." And she can only paw at their objective, third-party detachment like a lost dog scratching at the door, begging entrance to a safer world.

He hands the list back to her. "Wow. Well . . . I'm not sure what I find more interesting . . . you asking him permission or him granting it."

"What? Are you worried it won't be as thrilling, now that it's out in the open?" She tries to keep her voice light but she can't quite disguise a certain bubbling anger that has much more to do with their past than anything expressed in the present. Honestly, how exactly had she expected him to react?

"Nina." He puts his hand on her thigh.

"The last time," she says. "When we said goodbye in New York. I thought that was really it."

"Me too."

"We weren't supposed to get back in touch."

"I know."

"I can't believe I asked Jeff for this."

"I know."

"Here's the thing Laz. What do you not know?"

He smiles and grabs her wrist, which he then brings to his lips. "The future."

LATER: SHE ARRIVES home around three in the morning, feeling distinctly unqualified to open her front door. These rules do not cover everything, she thinks. For example, what should the etiquette be regarding crawling into bed with your fiancé less than an hour after having sex with your ex-who-knows-what-the-fuck-to-call-him? What is supposed to happen now? Will she wake him up from a sound sleep so he can greet her like a 1950s housewife with all the energetic cheer he can muster? *Hi honey! How was your day fucking the one you no longer want to love so that you and I can live the 2007 version of happily-ever-after?*

She forces herself to unlock the door and decides to sit in the lotus position on her living room floor. She will sit there until she no longer smells Laz's mixed scent of sweat, sandalwood soap, and red wine, and her mind stops replaying the moment in the bar when he leaned over and kissed her on the mouth. He kissed and she kissed back and they forgot and she raked her nails through his hair and history repeated.

She takes a few deep breaths to clear her mind and presses her fingertips together in the Hakini Mudra to unite the hemispheres of her left and right brain. After a decade of practicing and teaching yoga, she knows how to use her breath in service of halting the onrush of aggressive and repetitive thoughts. Only now, her breath proves ineffective in purging his scent that remains trapped in her nostrils, causing her memory to interfere with the process. It truly befuddles her, that she has this ability to guide hundreds of people toward mind-body balance, proper alignment, and self-acceptance on a cellular level while she personally has failed to ascend the path of HEALTHY LIVING. All these years and she has continued to keep him close. He's that bottle of booze in the trunk of her car, the special occasion joint at the back of the freezer, the dildo in her nightstand that serves as a portal to . . .

In vain, Nina tries to empty her mind. But the yoga won't help her tonight and suddenly, she finds herself praying to God.

Please Hashem, help me, even though I don't deserve it and have no business asking.

She can't remember the last time she prayed this way, or more specifically, when she had last associated the concept of divinity with the Hebrew name for God that she had learned the summer she was eight years old. That year, her non-religious parents, somewhat guilted by their own parents into agreeing that Jewish children deserved to be exposed to Judaism, had the bright idea to enroll her in the Chabad-Lubavitch day camp Gan Israel. And so she had spent the summer with other children from a wide range of Jewish backgrounds, where they went to Disneyland and Universal Studios but also learned how to braid challah—a job she did poorly—and sing catchy tunes inspired by Chabad's teachings on Messianic Judaism. *We want Moshiach now! We want Moshiach now! We want Moshiach now! We don't want to wait!* She would line up with the other members of her group for the end-of-day, camp-wide sing-a-longs where they chanted this at the top of their lungs. But the song that she loved best had only to do with God. *Hashem is here, Hashem is there, Hashem is truly everywhere.* It had comforted her as a child of agnostic parents, of parents who sometimes forgot to pick her up after school or gymnastics practice, to believe that God was wherever you needed God to be.

Nina decides to chant the Sanskrit prayer she regularly teaches in her classes. *Loka, samasata, suhkino, bahvantu.* May all living beings be free of suffering. This was a prayer that anyone could recite, regardless of religious background or aversion to more intensely liturgical Sanskrit chants. This is the prayer that first spoke to her in her early days as a yoga student. *You too deserve to be free of suffering.* This had comforted her in the same existential way as the Hashem song.

Afterward, she rises from the living room floor and takes a long hot shower. She takes extra special care in brushing her teeth. Then, she opens her bedroom door and slides into her side of the bed. From his deep and heavy breathing, Jeff appears to be asleep. He lies there with the covers bunched fortress-like around him and she decides to remain cover-less, not wanting to disturb him.

"Hey." Jeff pushes a hefty share of the covers onto her.

"Thanks. Sorry to wake you."

"It's okay."

They lie there on their backs, close together but not touching. She thinks about the early days of their relationship, when they cuddled for hours after sex. She didn't know then that the cuddling had been an extra effort for Jeff, who loved sex but preferred to sleep alone. She hadn't understood just how often Jeff had been making an effort to be someone else. But now she understands that it exhausts him, this business of maintaining intimacy with another human being. She can imagine him confiding this to another social worker and how that person would feel nothing but empathy for his condition.

She whispers, "Are you okay?"

"I don't know. Are you?"

"I don't know either."

He touches her hand. "Didn't you just take a hot shower? Your hand is cold."

His hand on her hand: it feels as if a wild bird or some other feral creature perches there, poised to flee if she performs the slightest of movements. So she wills herself into stillness and feels the tears start to pool in her eyes. "That feels good," she finally says.

"I'm glad."

Pause. And then: "The list. You didn't include a rule for what should happen if I want to bail in the middle."

"Do you want out?"

Which out are you referring to? She says, "This doesn't feel right."

"How do you think it was supposed to feel?"

"I was pissed at you. You went from 'let's give this some thought' to making this list without explaining to me how you got there."

"Yeah, well . . . I did give it some thought. A lot of thought actually and . . ."

"Yeah?"

Jeff won't look at her as he starts his retreat to the far end of his side of the bed.

"I decided I wasn't going to stand in the way of anything and you wanted permission so . . . I gave it to you."

She tries to make him look at her and fails. "Well, maybe you should have stood in the way."

He whispers, "This is on you."

"You wrote the fucking list."

"Which you didn't have to take seriously."

"How many times did I ask you if you were serious?"

Silence.

"Hello? So what should I take seriously?"

Silence. Then more silence.

Finally, she asks, "Do you want me to want out?"

"I want you to do what's best for you."

"How can I know that if you don't . . ." She feels the familiar anger, bubbling through the exhaustion wrought by the circularity of their conversation. "It isn't only on me, you know. You need to fucking speak up or else . . ."

"I need sleep. We can talk about this tomorrow."

"We need to talk about it now."

No response.

"Jeff?"

A few minutes later: She watches him sleep, trying to see the person who asked her out for a drink three years ago at the end of her yoga class. She can still see him, despite everything. But maybe that was part of their problem; that she had affixed him and their beautiful beginning to the part of her brain responsible for envisioning the future.

TWO DAYS BEFORE Sanctioned Encounter #4: She comes home at almost nine in the evening after a session with one of her private clients and finds Jeff drinking a beer in the living room. "I want to watch," he says. "Invite him over."

"No." She lets her yoga mat and bag fall to the ground and resists the temptation to also succumb to gravity. Right now, she wants nothing more than sleep. The Jeff she loves has always noticed her exhaustion, she thinks. That Jeff would postpone his agenda until she felt more rested.

"You agreed that if I wanted to watch, then I could watch. The Tenth Commandment." Jeff holds up his beer and toasts the air.

"You really think that's going to do something for you?"

"That's the hope."

She hears it then, a definitive shift in his tone. She says, "I don't know how many times I need to tell you that we can just stop the whole thing."

"I mean it though." Jeff puts his beer on the coffee table and rakes his fingers through his hair—his best quality, his hair. "What if watching you with him turns me on and it's . . . something we both get into?"

"That kind of thing has never interested me." If Nina has learned anything from Sanctioned Encounters #1-3, it's that she's a one-man-at-a-time-kind-of-woman and that it's sufficient cognitive dissonance to leave one man's bed for another in the span of a single night.

She feels Jeff appraising her from his corner on the couch. Does he notice it now, her exhaustion? Or what about her fear that they will not be able to recover from any of it? "I want to know if it's something I can do. Do you think you can do this for me? Help me see?"

She stares back at him and believes he's completely serious. He continues speaking in a soft voice. "Because what if it isn't temporary, you and him? Do we break up or do we . . . find another way?"

She's terrified to ask him exactly what he might be suggesting. She thinks about the night she spent with Laz during Sanctioned Encounter #3, which began like Sanctioned Encounters #1 and #2: at a candlelit bar with a killer wine list and nooks and alcoves where people can disappear. But the third time they met under these circumstances, she had agreed to spend the entire night with him at his Hollywood Hills guesthouse abode. The sex that night had been rough and mutually aggressive and afterward, they lay side by side on the disheveled bed and Laz had asked, "Does Jeff tell you you're beautiful?"

"What makes you ask that?"

"Because I'm gathering he doesn't."

With her finger, she traced the perimeter of his chest. "Actions are more important than words, don't you think?"

"He's not the guy for you."

She poked him hard in the area around his heart. "You really need to stop getting in touch with me. It's kind of ruining my life."

He nibbled on her left ear before whispering, "I still love you."

She could only shake her head, thoroughly disoriented. Where was she anyway, exactly? *Jerusalem, New York, Los Angeles, ten years ago, six weeks ago, five minutes ago, another dark bar and rumpled bed and pack of condoms and broken promises and threat of another destroyed relationship looming, looming, looming.*

                    Susan Josephs

It was official, though. She had broken Jeff's commandment regarding the breaking versus the furthering of the emotional bond.

And now, Nina can only stare at her fiancé and concede the failure of their project. Nothing, she thinks, is actually out in the open.

"Nina? I should tell you something."

Jeff's social worker's voice has again been replaced by this new soft and hesitant tone. She waits for him to tell her the thing that has the power to transform his voice this way. When he doesn't, she says, "It's okay, you can tell me."

But he shakes his head. "Forget it. Just do this for me. If you want, think of it as a favor."

SANCTIONED ENCOUNTER #4: The doorbell rings and Jeff asks in his best British butler's voice, "Shall I get that madam?"

She can't help but wince at the word "madam." Jeff has been a British butler since this morning and in this persona, she cannot detect even a shard of the man who had asked her for a favor.

"I'll say it one more time. Fuck the Tenth Commandment."

"My dear girl. We must finish what we start. Such is the mark of a solid and moral character."

She glares at him and decides to ignore the various calls to action that her highest self wants to express. She will not, for example, throw on a large sweatshirt to cover her red, cleavage-baring tank top. And she will not take her fiancé's face in her hands so as to force him to look at her, to really look at her, so that they can more clearly envision what might be lost.

The doorbell rings again and Nina adjusts the straps of her tank top. She makes a point of walking purposefully to the kitchen to open a first bottle of wine. "Fine," she tells Jeff. "You want to be the butler? Be the butler. Get the door."

FIFTEEN MINUTES LATER: In the living room, they sit in a configuration that reminds Nina of a job interview. She and Jeff sit next to each other on the couch with enough distance between them to suggest a distinctly non-sexual, strictly businesslike relationship while Laz perches on the love seat opposite them, his posture indicative of an open and enthusiastic candidate. For the last fifteen minutes, she has engaged in non-stop guzzling of Tempranillo while Jeff and Laz attempt get-to-know-you-small-talk chit chat. *How's LA treating you as an actor? Much better than I thought. Nina tells me you're a social worker? That's right. I do a mix of case management and individual therapy. Cool, sounds rewarding. It is.*

Nina listens to them, struck by their similar viewpoints and affinities as they discuss the never-ending crisis in Darfur, the dictatorship in Myanmar, global warming, the economy, the ever escalating price of gas, and the great, Black hope embodied by presidential candidate Barack Obama. She consumes about a half bottle of Tempranillo as they compare stress reduction techniques: yoga versus running versus surfing versus adopting a pet. Briefly, they talk about Burning Man and how Laz, now that he has relocated to the West Coast, wants to check out the annual festival and do they know people who have been there?

See? You guys can be friends. So let's call the whole thing off.

But then Jeff picks up the bottle of Tempranillo, tops off their glasses, and says, "Okay then, might as well get started."

"What did you have in mind . . . exactly?" She looks at Jeff, who's staring at Laz with an expression she cannot read.

Jeff shrugs. "I don't know, show me your greatest hits. You guys have a long history, right?" Jeff's tone places clear quotation marks around "history" and it's suddenly crystal clear to Nina that her fiancé has no idea what he wants from any of this.

She eyeballs Laz, who yawns and stretches like a housecat waking up from a luxurious nap. "Well, I'm up for anything. Whatever you guys decide is cool with me. Just remember that this sort of thing can only enhance relationships if it's done in the right frame of mind."

She can't help but laugh. "Yes, that's exactly why you've agreed to come over tonight, to help us enhance our relationship."

"Manners, Nina. He's our guest." Jeff resumes speaking in his British butler's voice.

"It's all right." Laz waves his hand, a royal figure pardoning his subjects. "This is new territory for all of us. But you know me." He pauses and smiles at Nina. "I'm all about new experiences."

For the briefest of seconds, Nina has the unprecedented thought that in order to free herself from one of them, she might have to destroy the bonds with both. For the most fleeting of moments, she sits there, looking at one man, then the other, and, grasping with a strong sense of déjà vu, the necessity of an imposed loneliness.

Jeff says, "Go sit on his lap and make out with him. We'll go from there."

She does as she's told. She's sheepish and tentative at first but as she kisses Laz, she understands that she wants Jeff to watch. *Do you see how he is with me? Take a fucking lesson.* She's full of anger and need and buoyed by ancient familial grievances based on not feeling seen as she allows Laz to grab her breasts and take off her shirt. She unbuckles his jeans, pulls down his underpants, and knows that this is no performance. With Laz, she is always a dancer, never an actress, wedded to Martha Graham's belief that the body never lies. And so she actually manages to forget about Jeff until she hears her bedroom door slam. The slam alerts her to the fact that it's colder in the living room, now that she's completely naked.

She disentangles from Laz on the loveseat and retrieves her clothes. She hands Laz his shirt and he says, "So much for experiments."

They get dressed and she tells Laz that he better leave. He nods but as they stand at her front door, he reaches out to stroke her cheek. He whispers, "Leave him."

She whispers back. "And then what?"

"Run away with me. For real."

"And then what?"

"We'll stop running. We'll figure it out."

"Like we've ever figured it out before."

"That was my fault. You've been nothing but—"

"Stop." She opens her front door and points toward the great outdoors. He puts up his hands in the classic surrender position and says goodbye but tells her to call him when she's ready.

It takes her about ten more minutes to gather the courage to knock on her own bedroom door. Knock, knock. No answer. Rinse and repeat. She finally opens the door to the sight of Jeff lying face down on the bed, an open book beside him. She sits on the edge of her side of the bed with her legs tightly pressed together, her hands folded in her lap, and her head bowed. She can, at the very least, look the part of a penitent. She says, "How could you have known how you'd feel?"

Silence.

"Please? Can we talk?"

Silence.

"I'll . . . move out if you want. Tonight even."

Silence.

"Okay." She stands up, walks over to her closet, finds her duffel bag, and starts packing. Just the necessities, she tells herself, as she rummages through her drawers for T-shirts and clean underwear. She grabs her yoga mat and decides that crying in front of him is out of the question. The mutual use of manipulative tactics, intentionally or not, has to stop. Instead, she says, "I know I've behaved badly here but you didn't have to push it so hard."

Suddenly, he stands in front of her. She drops her yoga mat as he grabs her hard by the shoulders. *So this is what it takes for you to be physically intimate with me on a non-sexual basis.* She freezes, waiting for his next move.

He releases her with what feels like the slightest of shoves, certainly nothing that can be proved in a court of law. He glares at her with a clenched jaw and she desperately wants to shove him back. They had never touched each other in conflict before and until now, she never imagined herself in possession of such urges.

But then she watches his face crumple and sag. "I tried," he says. "I fucking tried."

"You just pushed me."

"You don't understand. I really tried."

She can still feel his hands on her shoulders, his nails digging into her flesh.

"You still love him."

She refuses to even look at him but after several seconds, she realizes that he's crying. It occurs to her that she has never really witnessed him cry before. And then she thinks of the list she has on her computer of different caterers, florists, DJs, and photographers. They had already booked the wedding venue, a spacious multi-purpose room in Temescal Canyon's Gateway Park.

She says, "Yes. But I love you too."

She reaches out to touch his arm but he flinches even before she makes contact. He says, "What does that even mean?"

"Jeff. Look at me."

But he won't.

They're silent for maybe a minute but to Nina, it feels like an hour. Then Jeff says, "You don't have to go right now. I'll sleep on the couch and we can figure things out in the morning."

Her fiancé has done his best to compose himself but she can still see shards of the hurt and vulnerability that comprised his previously crumpled face. She has to try one more time while this smallest of windows still exists.

"Can't we at least try to forgive each other?"

Why is Jeff laughing this harsh, guttural laugh?

"What have I done wrong? Do you even know?"

She's confused by his questions. "Well, it almost always takes two to—"

"But why should I tell you? You never told me how all this time you were pining for him while making me feel like whatever I do isn't enough."

He walks toward the bedroom door and she grabs his arm. "What are you talking about?"

He wrests his arm away from her. "I'd say you have lousy taste in men. But then I'd be dissing myself."

She feels her face start to burn. "Laz may be fucked-up but he's not cold and self-righteous. He doesn't hold people to impossible standards."

He just stares at her. Then he says, "I can't do this right now."

She watches Jeff escape to the living room and decides to leave as soon as possible. She dashes off an SOS text to her friend Allison asking if she can crash on her couch and finishes packing in ten minutes while the fight rages on in her mind. *This is not all my fault, asshole. You're a fucking social worker and you don't know shit about taking personal responsibility. Yeah, maybe I always had feelings for him but you checked out of our relationship long before I got his email.*

On her way out the door, she pauses in the living room. Jeff now lies on the couch with his eyes closed, a man turned metaphorical ostrich-in-the-sand. She stands over him and devises a final test, which she acknowledges is fucked-up on her part but oh well. At least now she has an enhanced understanding of how much easier it is to fuck up if you keep practicing.

She waits exactly five minutes for him to open his eyes. If he passes her test, then she will stay.

Five minutes later: she shuts the door as quietly as she can, taking care to lock it.

A WEEK LATER: *VEGAS, baby. Vegaaaaaaas.*

With a small duffel bag, Nina stands outside Allison's house and directly in front of the driver's side of Laz's green PT Cruiser rental. Already, she has her doubts about the two of them employing the most escapist of all clichés. Even Allison, someone famous for never judging anyone for anything had asked, "Are you sure you're up for a trip like that?"

She waits for Laz to roll down his window. "Yes ma'am?"

"I'm not sure about this."

He reaches out to stroke her cheek. "I have reservations at Mandalay Bay. A suite at The Hotel. And tickets to Cirque. To the water show."

"O."

"Right." He grins and opens the car door on the passenger side.

She gets into the car. "You realize that Vegas is a family-friendly place now. It's not what it used to be."

He says, "Neither are we" and in his otherwise jocular tone, she can detect the slightest of somber notes. She wonders if he too possesses a growing collection of gray hairs that he does his best to conceal from public view. How much longer can they keep running away like this? How much longer will they spend their energy on trying to repeat history, as if as long as they do so, they can escape the passage of time and never grow old?

She says, "Let's go before I change my mind."

BY THE TIME they get to Barstow, everything seems like a good idea. They switch places at the wheel and she drives over eighty-five miles an hour to keep up with the left lane traffic. She blasts "The Doors Greatest Hits" CD, which competes with the whoosh-whoosh sounds of the wind serenading them through her slightly cracked open window. She loves driving in the desert, either on the 10 or the 15, where the wind often forces her to keep both hands on the wheel so the car won't list from side to side. In such conditions, she has no choice but to focus on nothing except the rules of the road. It feels similar to the effects of a rigorous yoga practice, which allow her to ultimately lie in shavasana with an empty mind. Only here, her eyes remain wide open and tuned into the desert landscape of relentless blue sky and spiky Joshua trees on the side of the road, their wayward limbs suggestive of the human body.

She fast forwards to the last song on the CD and starts singing. "This is the end. My only friend, the end."

She puts her hand on Laz's thigh.

"My only friend, the end."

He lifts up her hand and brushes it against his lips.

"The End" happens to be her all-time favorite Doors song and when she listens to the instrumental section of the song in reverential silence, she senses that Laz feels the same way.

Three hours later: She can't help but think of Jeff as they check into The Hotel, where Laz has requested a non-smoking room for her sake even though he smokes. Jeff has always hated Las Vegas. The Jeff that she knows has other ideas about weekend getaway fun, such as meandering up Highway 1 to Big Sur or wine tasting in the Santa Ynez Valley, where they can stay in modest bed and breakfasts and watch sunsets whenever possible. In strange beds, they would cuddle for warmth, sometimes having sex and sometimes just reading books. Regardless, she had been content. In those strange beds, she would sleep well, secure in the belief that what they had was enough.

She and Laz take the elevator to the twenty-second floor and enter a suite with a king size bed, a separate living room/office area, and a bathroom with abundant grooming products and a tub that can easily hold four people. Mirrors are everywhere and huge windows afford views of Las Vegas Boulevard, distant mountains, and part of The Hotel's exterior, with its nighttime façade of neon yellow lines of light that vertically traverse the building and dissect it into multiple and enormous black rectangles.

They place their luggage on opposite sides of the bed and it occurs to her that they have never escaped the world in quite this way before, via a plush hotel room located within a city originally designed for their evergreen shade of yearning. She looks at Laz and absorbs his smile, enormous and wicked. She asks, "What do you want to do first?"

This is, of course, the most rhetorical of all questions that she could possibly ask.

Afterward, they migrate downstairs to the casino, where she watches him play craps. They drink multiple cocktails heavy on the ice cubes proffered by scantily clad casino cocktail waitresses and she cheers every single one of Laz's lucky numbers. Seven. Eleven. Seven again! He's definitely on a winning streak and in this she tries her best to see personal vindication. They leave the craps table with him three hundred dollars ahead and return to their room. They order a bottle of champagne and get undressed. She's prepared to have sex all night but then Laz extracts a cigarette from his pack of Dunhills after downing his second glass of champagne.

Put out that fucking cigarette. It takes her a few seconds but eventually she remembers: Had she not told him that all those years ago, fueled by her own and everyone else's post 9/11 epiphanies to live life as fully and consciously and ethically as you possibly could?

She takes a deep breath. "What are you doing?"

"I'm taking this out to the balcony."

"You're not supposed to do that."

"We're not supposed to do a lot of things."

"Is that supposed to make me feel better?"

He grins and then appears to take his own deep breath. "I think we should move in together."

So he finally says it. Is that why he needs to smoke right now?

"You think you're ready for that?"

"Yeah, I think I am."

"Okay. So we move in together. And then what?"

"We live. One day at a time."

She can't answer him.

"I knew you were going to leave him."

She still can't answer him.

"What's up Nina?"

"I can't be careless with you anymore."

"What do you mean?"

"I mean, maybe we're getting a little too old for this shit."

"Hey . . ."

She brushes off his attempted hug. *This is a guy who has no problem hugging. Shouldn't you be grateful?* She tells him she needs to take a shower and when he offers to soap her back, she thinks about all the times during the last fifteen years when she woke up in the middle of the night in deep and sudden mourning for her vanishing youth. It had always bewildered her, these feelings of loss that distorted her perception of time. Overwhelmed by some sadness she couldn't quite name, she would try and envision possible futures for a life worth living. Only she couldn't if it didn't in some way include him.

"I'm sorry," she tells him. "I need some space right now."

SHE GETS HIS text message over breakfast while sitting in the hotel's soothing, almost library-like The Café restaurant. In between bites of a vegetable omelet, she feels the vibration of her cell phone, ensconced in the purse on her lap.

Let's talk? Not working today. Let me know.

She looks at Laz across the table. For one second, maybe two, she sees him as he exists in the present moment.

Laz asks, "Something important?"

She puts her fork down. "I have to go."

He calls out to her as she speed-walks through the lobby, headed for the elevator and the twenty-second floor. She has just finished packing up her toiletries when he walks into the room. He wants to know if he can drive her somewhere. When she shakes her head, he says, "You're the last person I'd ever imagine turning down Cirque Du Soleil," and once again, she can hear the slightly somber notes punctuating his otherwise jocular tone.

She can't help but smile as she thinks about the first time they met. "Do you remember when we snuck onto the trampolines in Gan Ha Pa'amon?"

He smiles. "Yeah. I actually do."

She zips her duffel bag shut and walks to the door. "Do you remember what you said?"

He smiles again. "I think I probably said a lot of things."

"You made this comment about gymnasts and I told you that whatever you thought you knew about gymnasts was a myth. Do you remember this?"

"Vaguely."

She opens the door. "I was always a sucker for a good myth."

He neither answers nor follows as she shuts the door.

She takes a cab from The Hotel to a car rental place off the Strip. There, a bright and shiny customer service woman hands her the keys to a dark blue, boat-like Chevy Impala and tells her how lucky she was to have nabbed the last car available and on such short notice. Before she gets into the car, she calls Jeff at their apartment. No answer. She calls his cell and leaves a message. She wants to talk and can they do it in person? She can be at their apartment later today.

When she stops at the Starbucks in Barstow, she tries the apartment and his cell phone again. No answer. She starts to wonder why he took the day off. Maybe he's hiking or taking a long walk on the beach? And somewhere between Barstow and Victorville, she feels a small yet unmistakable surge of hope. She decides to drive directly to their apartment and if he isn't home, she'll sit on the stoop and wait for him. She'll wait and wait, as long as it takes. Surely, he hasn't changed his mind.

But when she at long last exits the 10 at 4th Street in Santa Monica, her hope has been replaced by fear. What if he regretted texting her? She can't bear the possibility of him slamming the door in her face. So she pulls over after crossing the intersection of 4th and Rose and calls him again. She tries him at home and on his cell. She even calls his work number, though he said he wasn't working. Finally, she winds up driving to Allison's apartment, where she spends the rest of the day trying to get in touch, her fear growing incrementally each time she does this.

Please forgive me. At least that.

She gets the call three days later at nine in the morning from Jeff's sister Frances. The cops had contacted Frances since her number had appeared at the top of Jeff's cell phone call log. Frances wanted to know if she had returned from her vacation. Nina doesn't have time to digest the fact that Jeff had decided in the last week to lie to his sister. She can hear the numbness in Frances's voice as she relays the news of the accident, about how Jeff had been walking back to his car in the Ralph's parking lot at Lincoln and California and how the old man had apparently confused the accelerator for the brake. Or just hadn't seen him. Or maybe a combination of the two. And then Jeff's sister gets to the point: He was dead by the time the paramedics arrived. The funeral is tomorrow.

LAZ ARRIVED AT her apartment about an hour after she called him. He stood at the entrance to her front door, one hand clutching a supersize bottle of Grey Goose vodka, and she watched him stare at her with that recognizable wariness that people accord to the grieving. But he was also Laz, who couldn't help but grin at her the way he had always grinned at her.

"What's with the cats?" With his free hand, he pointed at the wall upon which Garfield and Angie crouched, ready to disappear into the neighboring yard should the interloper human move one millimeter into their safety zone. Nina appreciated the way they eyeballed him. Perhaps, they sensed that Laz was more of a dog person, not that he would ever take on the responsibility of a pet.

"They're my guard cats." She studied his face and tried to see what she had glimpsed in Las Vegas. She could still tell him to leave and watch him saunter back to his car, knowing she finally behaved in a manner that reflected where she actually was on the timeline.

Instead, he asked if he could hug her and she found herself unable to prevent her head from resting on his chest. She couldn't let go of him, not even when he asked if he could come inside.

He didn't make a move right away; after all, she was still in mourning. They sat for at least an hour on her beige futon couch and drank vodka tonics. He asked how she was coping and she told him the truth: not well. Had she been coping better, she informed him, he wouldn't be sitting next to her right now. He then semi-jokingly played the part of the insulted guest but she detected something else in his act, something grasping and urgent.

"This . . . doesn't feel right . . . especially after . . ." She could hear the lack of conviction in her voice. And then she stared at him through the lens of three vodka tonics and an avalanche of memories.

"It doesn't?" He looked at her and brushed a strand of hair away from her face.

She did not regain her clarity of vision until he lay on top of her after performing the multi-tasking feat of simultaneously removing her pants and his shirt. He had thrown her jeans to the floor and she suddenly saw him exactly the way he was at that moment in time, bare-chested and hungry, with his independence and ego sharply etched around his body, forming a shield only visible to her.

"No." She said it first as a whisper.

She could feel his full weight on her as he whispered back, "You know you want to."

"No." She said it again, slightly louder.

He touched her between her legs and this time, she saw him through the prism of a funeral for a life cut short. She sat there in the second row of synagogue pews watching a mother sobbing for her lost son. She would always be too late in her attempt to rent a car and drive back to Los Angeles.

"I mean it." This time, she didn't whisper.

He said nothing as he continued to touch her and she realized that she had told him "no" multiple times throughout their history when she had really meant "yes." Had she not personally set up this moment, after fifteen years of toying with the fine lines separating love and violence? The leitmotif of: you know you want to, so . . .

Why would he think that anything was different?

She tried to make "no" mean "no." She said, "Stop. Please stop."

Did he not hear her? Did he pretend not to hear her? Has any self-serving medical researcher done a study on the pursuit of sex causing temporary deafness in human males? All Nina knew for sure was this: She forced herself to look at him as she lay pinned beneath him. He lowered himself into her and she recognized the fear in his eyes. There it shimmered in the black of his pupils: their mutual desperation to continue living after they died and unwilling to accept that they wouldn't. The blueprint for their love.

Just before her brain started to feel as frozen and paralyzed as her body, she had a final vague thought: They were not using a condom and he had never asked her since materializing in LA if she was on the pill.

Afterward, she couldn't move or speak. He lay next to her and asked politely if he could smoke. She said nothing, which he decided to interpret as acquiescence. So, he smoked and she continued to lie naked on her living room floor. They had rolled off the couch during the brief period when she had tried to physically resist him.

"Why?" This, she finally asked.

"Why what?" He answered from her kitchen, where he found a water glass to substitute for an ashtray.

"For someone who has no interest in being a father . . ." She closed her eyes, subsumed by a multitude of small, wriggling sensations in the general vicinity of where she believed his sperm was currently swimming.

"What?" He returned to the living room, holding the water glass containing the now extinguished cigarette.

"I meant it. When I said stop."

She pulled on her shirt as he returned to lie down next to her. He started to stroke her hair. "When did you say stop?"

"Before." She removed his hands from her hair and stood up to retrieve her jeans.

"You did?"

"Yeah. Multiple times."

She waited for him to respond. For the first time since meeting him, she had no ideal scenario in her head for how things should play out.

"Oh. I don't think I . . . I didn't hear you."

"You . . . you . . ." She tried to say what he did. When she couldn't, she buttoned the top button of her jeans and fled to the bathroom, the only room in her apartment with a lock. She leaned against the bathtub, brought her knees toward her chest, wrapped her arms around her legs, and zoned into the black cracks of space between the whiteness of the door and the beige color of the doorframe. The black cracks formed a perfect square outline of unprotected territory and she considered the tactics of sealing this perimeter with cotton balls or masking tape. Only there was no tape in the bathroom and cotton balls seemed way too painstaking. The lock would have to suffice.

She sat there in silence as he called out to her and knocked on the bathroom door. She didn't say a word, even when he finally said, "I'm sorry if . . ."

She continued to sit there long after she heard the front door click shut and her legs went numb. She sat there and she waited.

PART TWO

Ten

ROSE FELT READY when the girl knocked on the door at precisely three in the afternoon. Officially, she had invited the girl over for nothing more than a cup of tea. But the plan was twofold: tea first; the unveiling of the proposition's particulars second. As for the outcome, Rose found herself on the optimistic side. Surely, the girl had warmed up to her proposition since the day she had driven her home from the hospital. A terrible place, that hospital, but on the other hand, the experience had helped her decide.

Rose opened the door. The girl wore a lovely red sundress and appeared to be all smiles and good cheer but as usual, Rose knew a mask when she saw one. Also, the girl's eyes seemed slightly red and swollen.

"I've missed you," the girl said.

"I'm glad to see you, dear." Rose ushered the girl into her apartment. *Stick to the plan Rose. The girl's eyes are her business.* She proceeded to offer the girl a choice between herbal strawberry tea from a box purchased on sale for seventy-nine cents at the 99 Cent Store and orange juice from that fancy Marina Del Rey Ralph's, part of a two for one special. Rose always bought the kind with the calcium, so at the very least, she figured she could make a contribution to the girl's bone health. But the girl wanted the tea and Rose was certainly in no position to lecture her about osteoporosis. So Rose put on the kettle and the girl insisted on monitoring the water and serving the tea. Rose acquiesced to sitting on the couch, though she could not help but notice the trembling of the girl's hands as they retrieved the two sky blue porcelain mugs from the cupboard above the sink.

"How are you getting along these days?" A fair question, considering Rose hadn't seen her for at least two weeks. It wasn't like the girl to skip a week. And now this business of the girl's swollen eyes and shaking hands.

"Okay. Everything's fine." The girl's smile was large and suspicious. "How are you?"

Rose decided to change the subject. "Dear, are you still feeding those cats?"

"I am," the girl said. "It's only been three weeks since I started doing it but I'm starting to think of them as my children. Or something."

"That's lovely, dear." Rose proceeded to immediately reconsider this assessment.

The girl then shared details about these cats with the kind of pride and enthusiasm that reminded Rose of every single Center acquaintance in the possession of grandchildren. And so she did her best to feign interest in the black cat with beautiful green eyes that the girl named after the movie star who kept adopting all those children. The girl explained how this cat paced the wall in her yard with mincing steps, as if it wore borderline-unmanageable high heels. There were also three orange tabbies, two of them kittens and one of them full-grown, plus two cats with yellow eyes and mottled fur that the girl insisted resembled Jackson Pollock paintings at the height of the artist's career.

Jackson Pollock. Even now, any mention of this artist forced her to travel back to that terrible day. *You once wrote a terrific article on Jackson Pollock for Art in America.* She could still remember every word of what she said to Morry and how her agnostic self had prayed for results. Please God, who may or may not exist, that she should safely return her husband's biography to him so that he might reclaim ownership of his soul.

"Rose? Are you okay?"

"Morry was an expert on Jackson Pollock. He would have appreciated your metaphor."

Is that so? She could still hear how her husband asked this question when she would tell him something essential about himself. He would ask this question as if attempting to insert a bookmark into a book in the hopes of finding his place at a later time.

"Ah." The girl nodded and continued to monitor the rattling and hissing of the teakettle. "They're everywhere, aren't they? That's why I like feeding the cats. It's something new . . ."

Nu Rose? Would it kill you to try harder to be a friend? Even if you could do without all this feline-related enthusiasm? And then Rose remembered: the business card in her purse. "You know, dear, this young lady came to visit me the other day with her husband and he does something for cats that live on the streets, I think. Maybe you should call them?"

"Oh. How do you, uh, know these people?"

"They seemed very nice. I have their business card." Rose hoped this explanation would suffice, as they had more important things to do today than talk about Richard.

"Okay." The girl looked understandably suspicious. "Sure, I'll take it. Why not?"

"You never know what might help."

"Right. Thanks."

The teakettle started whistling and the girl quickly turned off the stove. She moved further into the kitchen so that Rose couldn't see her from where she sat on the couch. Rose heard a thumping, then a sliding noise, as if the girl wound up slumped against her refrigerator after a collision with the appliance. Should she express concern?

Rose thought of the girl alone in her apartment, surrounded by large, unwieldy bags of cat food, the kind she always saw on sale and stacked on the bottom shelves at Ralph's. Did she really think of those animals as her children?

"Do you want children? You still can. You're still young."

The girl didn't answer. After a few minutes, she returned to the living room with the teacups. "Careful, it's hot."

"I couldn't have any children."

The girl took a first sip of tea and seemed to have trouble swallowing. Rose decided to keep talking. "Sometimes, I still think about what kind of mother I might have made. Maybe I would have been a good one. Who knows?"

"There was another man."

"What was that?" Rose watched the girl turn the same shade of red as her lovely sundress.

"Another man. In my life. Someone I've known for many years. Jeff knew about him and that's only . . . part of it."

"Oh." Rose took a vigorous sip of tea and burned her tongue. So far, this visit had not gone at all as planned.

She waited for the girl to say more. But the girl only blew on her tea and her cheeks remained flushed. Maybe she should make some concerted effort to express solidarity? What if she told the girl about her marriage to Richard and what he used to do in their bedroom while she taught little girls how to plié, pirouette, and cultivate stage presence? You must first envision yourself as if you've mastered the movement and the mastery will follow, she used to tell them. A positive attitude goes a long way. Chin up. Shoulders down. Arms like wings. Do this and you will be loved.

"I'm sorry . . . is it okay if I use your bathroom?"

"Of course, dear."

The girl stood up and fled the living room.

The trepidation that flooded Rose as she awaited the girl's return! What was this business about another man? In vain, she searched her mind for beige-colored conversation topics but could not locate anything appropriate. Rather, Rose suddenly found herself wondering if they should finally bite the bullet and go shopping at the Ralph's on Lincoln and California. Maybe, they could do something memorial-like in the parking lot. Something sufficiently non-denominational and involving scented candles and kind words.

You could do something else in that parking lot, bubbeleh.

Rose's heart started to race. The Man from Television hadn't spoken to her since the day of her hospitalization. But here he was, pandering to his audience with his superfluous Yiddish, and she could maybe detect a pattern in his comings and goings.

Several minutes later, the girl emerged from the bathroom with newly red and swollen eyes and Rose opened her mouth to make the announcement that, truth be told, she had been preparing for since the day she met Richard's daughter.

Only the girl spoke first. "I'm sorry but . . . I'm having kind of a rough day today. Maybe I should go? I'll come back and visit when I'm better company."

Rose closed her eyes and saw Morry yet again on that terrible day, when they could no longer pretend to be the people they once were. She would not make this mistake again and so she forced herself to persist. "Dear, I have some things for you in the bedroom."

TODAY IS THE day she must say something. So Rose resolves on the fourth morning of the iteration in their morning schedule. As she finishes the breakfast dishes and contemplates a stroll on the boardwalk before repairing to the Center for cards and a hot lunch, she turns away from the sink and toward the living room. Morry's still there, sitting on the couch and staring at a silent and blank-screened television. In front of him on the coffee table rests the television remote. To his right, her magnifying glass lies unused next to sections of today's paper. Morry claims he doesn't need a magnifying glass to read a newspaper but sometimes, Rose catches him squinting. *Big deal. What's a little far sightedness when you can still pass your driver's vision test with flying colors?* If she's to be fair, Rose can see her husband's point. He's eighty-five years old and still in the possession of a perfectly legal driver's license.

Rose, however, knows better than anyone that the DMV is not God, creator and protector of the universe. A driver's license can only test so much whereas she will have to do the rest. And so she wipes her hands on a faded and stained dishcloth and leaves the kitchen for the living room.

She carefully organizes the scattered newspaper sections and places them in a neat pile on the coffee table. Then, she sits next to her husband and waits for him to notice her. Only Morry continues to stare at the blank television screen.

Rose looks up and into her husband's blue eyes. Aside from a pronounced blood vessel in his left eye, everything appears as it should. "What's the matter? Why don't you watch something?"

"What was it that I taught?" Morry keeps his eyes focused on the television. Rose has never seen such unwavering commitment to a blank screen.

"You don't know what you taught?"

"I know that I taught. I can't remember what." He's raised his voice ever so slightly.

"Art history."

"Is that right?"

"You specialized in the late nineteenth and early twentieth centuries. Van Gogh. Braque. De Koonig. Picasso. Modigliani. You preferred them to the medievals."

"Is that so?"

She watches her husband's eyes cloud and mist, as if generating such precipitation could wash away his growing collection of cobwebs.

"You were a professor. You taught at three different universities. You had office hours. You once wrote a terrific article on Jackson Pollock for *Art in America*." She's shouting now, as if he's deaf, and she silently curses herself for falling into this obvious trap.

"Is that so?"

"I'm sorry," she says. "I don't mean to scream."

She's about to bring up the matter of visiting the doctor but her husband suddenly stands up, knocking her magnifying glass to the floor in the process. "It's too much." This is all he says before retiring to their bedroom and slamming the door.

Rose picks up her magnifying glass and examines it for cracks. She flicks a white speck off the lens and tries to figure out how many times in the past five years she has watched her husband make snow in their apartment. Truly, this is an excellent question. He has it down to a science, her husband, i.e. the perfect recipe for snow in Los Angeles. Take an appointment reminder card sent in the mail by a responsible and organized medical receptionist. These cards are always white. Grab the card and hold it high above your head for maximum effect. Tear into bite-sized pieces, suitable for feeding the birds if birds ate paper—which many would sadly enough—and watch them succumb to gravity. A perfect complement to the winter of one's life.

Her magnifying glass has survived the fall and Rose decides to use it for reading the newspaper. Not a bad way to pass the time and right now, this is precisely what Rose craves, no matter how much further she may travel into the future.

ROSE LEANED AGAINST the wall next to her nightstand while the girl took a good hard look at everything she had placed on the bed. The leather coat she bought on her trip to Israel in 1973. A pair of brass candlesticks she purchased at a New York City flea market in 1962 because they reminded her of her mother. Her final pair of practice toe shoes, pale pink of course and the back of them black with scuffmarks. A wooden jewelry box with ornate carvings of nymphs and other Greco-Roman female types bearing platters of grapes that played Beethoven's Ninth Symphony bought by Morry with a sense of humor for her sixtieth birthday. The jewelry in the jewelry box, which included her two diamond engagement rings. A selection of photographs: some dated with black ink and others completely mysterious. (Who was that smiling couple in formal wear standing next to Rose outside the Wilshire Ebell Theatre in 1940-something and why on earth was she wearing a sequined, dark colored tutu number that caused her to bear a marked resemblance to that jocular fish character with the sunglasses she used to see on all those cans of tuna?) A multi-colored pile of tablecloths and placemats, the fabrics only slightly faded. Copies of a life insurance policy and some other papers she never paid much attention to while Morry was still alive and well. These papers she wouldn't give away just yet. Along with the photographs, she had merely wanted to display them for the sake of presenting the big picture.

The girl looked, looked away, looked, looked away, and looked some more and Rose couldn't put her finger on the type of sadness that this repetition seemed to produce. Was the girl sad for her? For herself? For that poor boy? For this other man?

Why did you ask if she wanted children? That you of all people should ask such a question to another childless woman.

The girl's perusal stretched far beyond the confines of what Rose considered a reasonable amount of time. Still, she waited for the girl to make the next move but the silence between them only grew thicker.

"Maybe you can pretend you're at one of those nice yard sales. Except you don't have to buy anything."

"Oh Rose . . . I don't think I can . . ."

"Sure you can. You told me just the other day that your apartment is empty."

A few rounds ensued of the girl saying, "But you're still alive" and Rose responding, "That's the point." Then Rose almost told the girl about the day she sat on her couch with her beloved possessions and forced herself to admit that she was entirely alone. Anything to help the girl understand her wish for her most storied possessions to land in a safe home before she died. Her brass candlesticks, for example, which reminded her of her mother. Her mother, who made the best challah she ever tasted and was buried in a mass grave full of strangers.

But on the other hand, why should Rose expect that the girl would swoop up the mementos of her life one, two, three, and adopt them into her own? Why should any of it mean anything to her? Was it not the case that so many people, after uncovering the mirrors at the cessation of the shiva, simply gut the house for the money, the life insurance policies, and the diamond rings while bagging the rest of it for the garbage dump?

"Oh," Rose said. "Maybe you can sell some of it then."

The girl cleared a space on Rose's bed and perched carefully between the leather coat and a stack of photographs. "I'm just overwhelmed right now. I mean, you're being very . . . generous."

Generous? "Dear. It's like this. I have no children. I wanted them but it wasn't in the cards. Anyway, when I die, the landlord will close up my apartment.

Maybe, if he's the thrifty sort, which he isn't, he will hold a yard sale. Otherwise, he will buy a package of plastic garbage bags and throw everything away. Morry and I never talked about this part, though he was a very organized man and planned ahead for the both of us. You should know that there's a plot waiting for me right next to him over at the Mount Sinai and there's instructions for a funeral home and what our bank should do with any remaining money so nothing to worry about there but—"

What was that sound that had escaped the girl? Was that a cough or a cry?

"Are you all right, dear?"

Silence.

"Is everything okay?"

The girl shook her head. "I'm sorry but I don't think I can do this. I should probably go."

"Please." Rose put a hand on the girl's shoulder. "Tell me what's the matter."

She kept her hand on the girl's shoulder as the girl took a few deep breaths. Then the girl suggested that Rose sit. So Rose sat and observed how the girl tried not to cry. The excess blinking, the audible breathing, the redness seeping into her cheeks.

"I'm sorry but I can't talk about it," the girl finally said. "Not today."

"It's okay, dear." Rose sighed and prepared to surrender.

Only the girl didn't go. She asked Rose whether she had any living family, any nieces or cousins, for example. Rose thought carefully before explaining she had a niece who lived in Chicago and was nearing seventy. Her sister and her sister's husband, may they both rest in peace, had willed this niece everything but the kitchen sink. Additionally, her niece maybe called her once every two years and happened to be married to a voracious real estate developer who brushed his teeth less frequently than he bought and bulldozed properties. Rose never knew exactly how much zest a person could harbor for pillaging the earth until she met this niece's husband but anyway.

Rose's point: her niece was not the correct person for the job. "I know it's something of a large favor but maybe there's some things you might enjoy."

The girl: It's not a favor, it's an honor. It's just . . .

Rose: I know we're not related and you have your own parents to think of—

The girl: It's not that. It's . . .

It continued for a while, this elliptical beating around the bush, until Rose couldn't stand to be in the same room with either one of them. So she picked up the leather jacket and thrust it into the girl's lap. "Take it, just take it. There's no one else."

"No," the girl said. "That's not true."

Rose pushed the candlesticks and the jewelry box in the direction of the girl's lap. "It's perfectly all right, dear. There simply comes a point in a person's life when they look around and realize that everyone else is gone."

The girl laughed a nervous laugh and adjusted the contents on her lap. "I'll take the coat. It's beautiful."

"And everything else?"

Silence.

"Please. I really have no one else to ask."

"Okay."

"You promise?" Rose knew how she pushed her luck but what could she do? She had no choice. Or rather, she did.

"I promise."

Rose looked the girl carefully in the eyes and after some degree of research, decided to trust her once and for all. So she stood up and shuffled over to her closet, in search of any and all available shopping bags.

Eleven

HE KNOWS WHAT he did.
Does he know what he did?
He knows, that's why he hasn't called.
Why the fuck hasn't he called, after what he did?
After what he did, why would you want him to call?

Fifty minutes into her Tuesday 10:30 a.m. 2/3 vinyasa flow class, Nina succumbed to an onslaught of the circular, repetitive, and intrusive thoughts as she handed two blocks to Flo, one of her regulars. For fifty minutes, her class had been a refuge as she guided her students into preparing for the mother of all ego-reckoning poses, hanumanasana. Nina loved teaching splits pose, as it challenged both the experienced and novice yogi. For those with inflexible hamstrings, the pose often required props and an acceptance of personal limitations. For the former dancers with gorgeous external rotation, the pose demanded a retooling of alignment, which usually led to the humble discovery that you couldn't go as far into the pose when you had to rein in your hips. Every time Nina taught this pose, at least one student in the class would start to glare at her.

"This is a pose that brings up anger and judgment, which gives us an opportunity to practice compassion for ourselves," she told the class, as she helped Flo place her hands on the blocks to achieve maximum leverage.

Compassion. She should not have used that word.

Nina tried to banish the thoughts as she scanned the class to see if anyone else needed assistance with the pose. She caught one of her students, a forty-something man who occasionally dropped into her classes, staring at her with his face curled up into a telltale scowl. Yep, there was always at least one student. Nina opened her mouth to make a joke about not hating the yoga teacher but something in the man's expression made her think of the way Jeff used to glare at her during class. This only happened whenever she taught one of her warrior three sequences, which she liked to introduce toward the end of class, when everyone was already fatigued from her riffs on warrior one and two, extended side angle pose, and half moon. But Jeff could hold warrior three for ten breaths. He would persist despite his misery, especially if she was watching him.

Nina blinked hard and gave her class two more minutes to work through hanumanasana. Best not to adjust anyone right now, she thought, since who knows what kind of energy she'd be transferring to her students. Instead, she simply walked the room, trying not to panic about this new development in her life as a yoga teacher. After the accident, she somehow possessed the ability to temporarily leave her grief-soaked thoughts and feelings outside the yoga studio while she taught her classes. But that was then.

"Time for handstands. Please move your mats to the wall." She could do this, move onto handstands, then backbends, then finishing poses, and she would definitely make time for the class to have a full five minutes in shavasana. Then, they would recite a simple mantra. Perhaps the concise yet powerful lokah samastah sukhino bhavantu, may all living beings be free of suffering. Lately, she had been silently adding the Shema prayer to this mantra, splicing ancient Hebrew with Sanskrit. *Lokah. Shema. Samasta. Yisrael. Sukhino. Adonai. Bhavantu. Echad.* Her students didn't need to know how she currently searched for God in every possible place, despite how disingenuous that felt.

One of her students remained in the center of the room. He looked about her age and his thick, dirty blond hair reminded her of Jeff, while his playful energy made her think of Laz. She watched him kick up into a handstand, which he held for at least ten impressive seconds, and she realized that she had avoided paying him any attention since the beginning of class.

What could she possibly say to him if he were to call? *Don't you know that no means no? Did you not take any women's studies classes in college, asshole? You were probably too busy hooking up and missed the lectures on consent and sexual violence.* It brought her no comfort to imagine the perfect telephonic unleashing of her angriest, most acidic self, even when she envisioned a response where he spoke words of spectacular repentance.

Nina averted her gaze from the inversion expert and zeroed in on a student practicing handstands with bent elbows and an arched back. For the next half hour, she had a responsibility to this student and all the others who paid good money to take her class. And then she could go home and commune with Rose's possessions, which now lived in a Diaspora otherwise known as her living room. She would sit in her living room, stare at these material remnants of someone else's life, and try and remind herself that she could not live like this forever.

After the class, Nina had to remind herself to smile at her students who took the time to thank her. "That was awesome," Flo said, who waited until the other students had left the room to tell her how much she needed a reminder about having compassion for herself after the morning she experienced.

Nina gave Flo a "your welcome" hug, turned on the studio's air conditioner, and rolled up her yoga mat. In the past, it had always deeply inspired her anytime a student thanked her for a great class when she personally was having a bad day. Even after the accident, she could derive comfort from this confirmation that she still contributed to the healing of other human beings. But now, she could only feel the hollowness of her "your welcome" echoing deep within her chest. It was on that part of her body where she still felt the heaviness of his body and how his weight had pinned her to the couch until they had both fallen off. He kept doing it even then and all she could do was focus on a throbbing pain in her thigh that had erupted through all the frozenness.

TEN MINUTES LATER: "Hi, Nina. Do you have a minute?"
She had just left the ladies' room after changing into her street clothes when Serena summoned her from the entrance to her now fully furnished office. She fake-smiled at Serena and took a seat opposite her on a swivel office chair covered in some kind of eco-friendly black mesh fabric. Serena folded her hands on her wooden, walnut-stained desk that oozed stellar office feng shui—one laptop, one stack of papers, one photograph of Serena and her boyfriend in front of ancient ruins, perhaps Machu Picchu, and another photograph of Serena doing a headstand on the beach with her legs in eagle pose—and made a point of clearing her throat. "I hate having to be the bearer of bad news so I'll just get to the point. I have to cut your Monday and Wednesday evening classes."

Nina nodded, confused by this surge of relief that seemed to effectively slow down her heartbeat. She had been dreading this moment ever since she resumed teaching classes at Cat/Cow. Really, she had simply been marking time from the moment she met Serena to when her boss would finally tire of her ineffectual promises to learn how to be a marketing whiz. Because, let's face it, she was never going to be a marketing whiz, no matter what was happening in her personal life or in whatever watershed technological and economic era where she found herself an unwitting denizen.

"You can keep your Tuesday, Thursday, and Sunday classes for now," Serena continued in a soft, low tone; what Nina surmised to be her tough-boss voice. "But there are other teachers at the studio who are putting in the work to keep their numbers up and those are the teachers I need to reward. Monday and Wednesday at six is prime time."

"But . . . are they good teachers?" She tried to match Serena's soft, low tone.

"What do you mean?" Serena looked genuinely confused.

"Teaching and self-promotion . . . those are two very different skills."

"And both are necessary for succeeding in the yoga world." Serena now looked distinctly less confused as she flashed Nina a brisk and efficient smile. Surely, Serena would now spend the next few minutes trying to get her employee to admit that she was simply self-sabotaging her career with this Luddite resistance to working on her personal brand and improving her social media IQ. The future was clear and inevitable and Nina could either join it or drown in her self-created Luddite Sea.

The Luddite Sea, that sounds kind of nice. Nina pictured a placid, bright blue body of water dotted with rafts and small boats that resembled her memories of the Sea of Galilee. To this place, people could pilgrimage with their laptops and smart phones and the Sea would swallow up any technology fed to it, black hole-style, without any harm done to the environment. Afterward, you could sit on cushioned lounge chairs reading old magazines, sipping vintage cocktails with dangerous yet tasty maraschino cherries, and remembering who you were before you started searching for yourself online.

"Nina?"

She didn't want to leave the Luddite Sea. She couldn't remember the last time her mind offered her refuge in such a relaxing venue.

"Nina?"

"I don't know if I can work here anymore."

"You're a great yoga teacher. We want you to stay but—"

"How would you know if I'm a great yoga teacher? You've still never taken my class. All you care about are your precious numbers."

Serena merely stared at her as she grabbed her bag and yoga mat and headed for the lobby. But while putting on her shoes, she felt a tap on her shoulder. There stood Serena, blocking her exit. "This isn't personal," she said. "I live with my boyfriend and I can't imagine what you're going through . . . but . . . I have a studio to run so . . ."

"It's always personal." The words escaped her before she could understand what she meant.

With shaky legs, Nina walked to her car and managed to drive herself home. As she opened the door to her apartment, she hoped that one of the cats would materialize to greet her but no such luck. Wine, she thought, even though it was only one in the afternoon. Why not drink the day away? Tomorrow, she was supposed to meet Rose for lunch but depending on how she felt, she might need to cancel.

Thinking of Rose compelled Nina to detour to her couch en route to the wine. The couch directly faced the wall where she had lined up all of Rose's possessions, which remained in their temporary dwellings in plastic bags from Ralph's and the 99 Cent Store, boxes from extinct shoe stores, and the relatively more commodious and glamorous storage receptacles—both bag and box—from defunct department stores like Bullock's, Mervyn's, and Robinsons-May. This still comforted her, to host someone else's material history, as if she had a permanent houseguest camping out on her floor; someone who always clamored for coffee or glasses of wine, which led to luxurious conversations and satisfying distractions from the rest of her life.

Maybe today was the day to finally sift through the bags and boxes and try to figure out a process of incorporation. What should she do, for example, with those brass candlesticks? Did they belong on her Ikea kitchen table? Or should she stick them in a drawer and only take them out on Friday nights? She had not grown up in a family that regularly lit the Sabbath candles but she had always admired the ritual. During her year in Israel, Laz had taught her that lighting the

Sabbath candles was an opportunity to practice gratitude, that when you said the blessing, you were not asking for favors but rather thanking God for what you already had.

Serves you right, letting him into your apartment.

She had already done this multiple times, willing herself to do something with this de facto inheritance before deciding to let it all lie against her living room wall for one more day. But now, Nina eyed the burgundy-colored leather coat that remained draped over the couch ever since the day she came home with Rose's possessions. She had lacked the energy to even hide the coat in her closet, which would have helped her feel righteous in her default opposition to leather products.

Nina grabbed the coat and even though her apartment was warm, wrapped herself in its leathery confines as tightly as she could. The coat extended just past her knees. It possessed an aged, burnished quality while the soft silk lining had only one small tear near the right sleeve. Two large black buttons on the front were missing, easily replaced.

She closed her eyes and tried to envision a Rose who was thirty-five years younger than her current age, with dark and thicker hair, a more upright posture, and fingers and toes prune-like only after lengthy soaks in the bathtub. Why did younger Rose buy this coat on a trip to Israel in 1973? Was she sick and tired of all the vendors who eyeballed her American tourist appearance and pushed her toward the expected trinkets and schlock art? Those tinselly wall hangings of the Western Wall, tin menorahs, paintings of white-bearded rabbis hunched over enormous books, huge silver earrings, prints of the Chagall Windows, T-shirts that say "Drink Coca Cola" in Hebrew? Was she walking down some bustling Tel Aviv street full of sidewalk cafes and shops, saw this jacket on a mannequin in the display window of an upscale clothing store, and fell in love? How often had she worn it and how old does a person have to be before they stop wearing a burgundy leather jacket? When does one transition into old lady clothes? The floral housedresses and polyester pants with elastic waistbands and blouses with too many ruffles and high necklines?

Nina took off Rose's coat and re-draped it over her couch. She stood up and decided to clean her bathroom. If she still craved wine after that task, then she would allow herself to open a bottle. Rose's possessions, however, would have to stay put for one more day. Perhaps it was their presence in her living room that allowed her to sit on her couch and feel safe, despite what had recently transpired on that piece of furniture.

A WEEK LATER: Nina's landlord called. Was it true that she was feeding stray cats on his property? Because one of his other tenants who will remain nameless—of course Nina knew who it was, her next-door neighbor and his girlfriend who fake-smiled at her whenever she visited—had called to complain. Said tenant didn't appreciate the cat shit recently spotted on the front lawn and noted that his visitors (his girlfriend) were extremely allergic to cats.

Do I ever complain about how loud they are when they have sex? Nina tried to compose herself as her landlord awaited her response. On principle, she despised people who chose behind-the-back tactics in lieu of direct communication.

"The cats were living here when I moved in," she told her landlord. "I'm just helping them not die of starvation."

She prepared for a battle only her landlord surprised her. He owned other properties populated by other tenants who fed stray cats. "It's a real problem in Venice," he said, and told her the legend of how these felines came to colonize their neighborhood. "They say that people used to dump their unwanted cats in Venice because it's one of the only neighborhoods in LA that doesn't have a raging coyote problem. So now we have an out-of-control cat problem."

"Well, I'm sorry if it's bothering people but I really just want to help." As she said this, Nina looked outside her window and saw Garfield butt-sniffing one of the Jackson Pollock cats, whom she now called Splotchy One and Splotchy Two. Splotchy One had darker gray splotches than Splotchy Two, plus a black spot on her otherwise all-white nose. Nina suspected that Splotchy One was Garfield's mother since those two cats seemed to pal around together. Now, she watched Splotchy One groom Garfield with what looked like gentle and loving tongue strokes but Nina knew what was coming. And, sure enough, she watched Splotchy One, without any apparent provocation, thwack the kitten with a well-placed paw. Garfield thwacked back and the cats zoomed off beyond her range of vision.

You never know when the shit is going to hit the fan. It's all in how you deal with it. Take a lesson from your new friend Garfield.

And that's when Nina remembered the cat rescue business card that Rose had pressed into her hand that day as a final parting gift to take with all the other gifts. That day, she had thrown the card into her purse without even glancing at its details.

Nina rummaged through her purse as her landlord talked about his own pets—he had a ten-year-old Lab and a twenty-six-year-old parrot—and then suggested that she contact the Los Angeles chapter of the National Stray Cat Society. As long as Nina remained diligent about cat shit removal and the building didn't develop a flea problem, then he didn't see why she couldn't pursue these outdoor friendships. Nina promised that whatever she decided to do, she wouldn't let "things get out of control."

After hanging up with her landlord, Nina kept rummaging through her purse until she found the business card buried under various receipts that she had yet to document for tax purposes. The card confused her as it only read: "Carla

Tannen: Writer/Blogger/Independent Thinker" and included a phone number, email address, and website. It said nothing about cat rescue and Nina found it somewhat pretentious that someone would advertise "independent thinker" on a business card. *Don't we all fancy ourselves independent thinkers?*

Nina googled the LA chapter of the National Stray Cat Society and learned all about TNR—Trap, Neuter, Return. She could do her part in preventing the proliferation of the Venice feral cat population by capturing her homeless brood in special traps. The LA chapter had several cat trap depots scattered throughout the city that loaned out traps and provided onsite cat-trapping advice. Then, once she trapped these cats, she could transport them to a West LA vet who performed discount spay/neuter surgery for stray/feral cats. After fixing the cats and assisting with their recovery, she could set them free, secure in the knowledge that she had saved future feline lives by preventing their existence.

Nina stared at the phone number and email address for the West LA cat trap depot and compared it with the business card. Yep, Carla Tannen had the same contact information. How did Rose know this person?

Nina decided to call rather than email. A woman picked up on the second ring and Nina asked if this was the West LA cat trap depot. "Shit," the woman said. "They were supposed to fix the number on their website."

"Oh, I'm sorry, I guess I have—"

The woman cut her off. "No, no. My husband's number is supposed to be on the website. I keep getting calls for him. Are you interested in borrowing traps?"

"Uh . . . yeah." Nina could hear a businesslike impatience in the woman's voice.

"You can call my husband's cell for the info. Sorry, but he's the one you need to deal with." The woman then gave out her husband's number and hung up.

Well, you weren't exactly encouraging. Still, Nina could not help but feel intrigued. She dialed the woman's husband's number and got voice mail. A distinctly male voice directed her to press "one" for information on trapping feral cats. She could either stop by next Tuesday between two and five in the afternoon or make an appointment. In exchange for a fifty-dollar deposit fee, she could borrow traps and receive detailed instructions in how to use them.

Nina hung up, feeling more encouraged by the voice mail. She would definitely pay this cat trap depot a visit and focus on how good it felt to be genuinely interested in matters that existed outside her impenetrable Wall of Grief. Because it had only gotten worse, this feeling of monstrous self-involvement each time she left the house to teach yoga, supposedly in service of helping other beings. *Stop making it all about you, for fuck's sake. Like you're the only one on the planet that has suffered and been the cause of suffering. You know people like that and you can't stand them.* She would remind herself of this when the flashbacks started to descend and she couldn't stand to be anywhere near her living room couch. But inevitably, she could not prevent their descent. She could only continue in her attempts to get out of the house and hope for something different.

SHE ARRIVED AT the cat trap depot a few minutes after four on the specified Tuesday. The depot was a modest one-story home in Palms, a block away from an Indonesian restaurant that she and Jeff used to frequent. The house had an unlocked brown wooden gate and Nina pushed it open to the sight of a brown shed situated at the back of a large grassy yard dotted with rose bushes and two palm trees and various other flora producing plants that she had seen in other people's yards but never bothered to learn what they were called. She tried to sharpen her powers of observation as she looked around the yard and saw two black cats lounging on the grass near one of the palm trees. She took a few steps toward them and they immediately scuttled away in the direction of the shed. Feral or stray? Thanks to Google, Nina had learned about the differences between these two cat populations. In a nutshell, strays could be adopted and re-domesticated. Ferals, not so much.

"Can I help you?"

She jumped and turned around. "Oh . . . hi."

He was a man who looked mid-thirties. Of medium-height, he was thin yet muscular with blond hair, green eyes, light skin, and a straight nose. Each of his biceps bore a tattoo of a single red flame and he wore faded, ripped jeans and a plain white T-shirt.

The man smiled and extended his hand. "I'm sorry if I scared you. I'm Jon."

She shook his hand. His grip was warm and firm and induced the kind of déjà vu that left her feeling perplexed and inappropriate.

"I'm Nina. I had called and left a message."

"Right. You want to borrow traps."

She followed Jon to the shed at the back of the yard and inquired about the provenance of the two black cats, one of which now chased the other up one of the palm trees.

"Former strays. Currently indoor/outdoor cats after a three-week fostering, re-socialization intensive."

She nodded, appreciative that Jon spoke to her like an insider.

Jon unlocked the door to the shed and beckoned her inside to a sight of wall-to- wall small metal cages, enormous bags of cat food and litter, and a few scattered garden tools.

"Wow," she said. She had no choice but to stand close to him in the crowded shed and this made her anxious for a variety of reasons.

"Yeah. The city subsidizes the traps. The rest is on my dime."

She tried to focus on what she had come here to do. She reiterated to Jon that she wanted at least four traps and he reminded her about the fifty-dollar deposit and that personal checks with her home address were acceptable.

Jon moved past her to retrieve the traps and brushed her shoulder. The sensation, both surprising yet familiar, caused her to time-travel and she found herself back on her bathroom floor, zoning in on the crack at the bottom of the door. She heard the knock and the calling of her name and then sentences of supplication splintering into unusable fragments.

Is this how it's going to be, every time you can't help but feel something good?

"Are you okay?" Jon stood in front of her, four traps balanced in his arms.

"Yeah, I think I just need some air."

They went back outside, where she felt slightly less dizzy. *Whatever Nina, it happens, energy between people.* She wanted to ask him if he was an artist or a healer. Something about him that she couldn't yet articulate suggested this to her and generally, she read people this way with great accuracy. She could survey a room of yoga students, stripped of their professional and personal uniforms and rendered externally homogenous by Lycra stretch pants and tank tops decorated with Sanskrit slogans and ohm symbols. In seconds, she could correctly identify the screenwriters from the lawyers; the actors from the doctors; the unemployed from the prosperous; the sufferers from the tormentors; the superficially peaceful from the truly at ease.

She tried to pay close attention while Jon gave her a cat trap tutorial under one of the palm trees. He explained the necessity of becoming a cold, heartless bitch by withholding at least three feedings so that the cats would be sufficiently starving to jump into a trap. "And I know our website recommends canned mackerel but I vote for sardines in tomato sauce. They go ape shit for that. And make sure the food is at the back of the trap. Also, after you nab one, don't forget to cover the trap with a towel or something. They will appreciate that. Cats have a lot of dignity so it's all about saving face."

She nodded. "I can understand that. I wouldn't want the whole world to see me trapped in a cage."

He smiled. "That's good. Successful cat trappers have empathy."

"It sounds tough, though. This whole process."

As Jon launched into what Nina supposed was a standard cat-trapping empowerment speech about the process sounding harder than the reality, his front gate creaked open and in stepped a tall, blond woman carrying a yoga mat. To Nina, she looked definitively Scandinavian, with blue eyes, high cheekbones, and a small yet perfectly straight nose. And why did she visit Rose? She certainly did not look like a relative, genetically speaking.

"Hi, I'm Carla." The woman stuck out her hand and gave Nina a broad smile. She too, had a firm handshake and exuded an effortful cheer and enthusiasm that Nina recognized in some of her yoga students.

"Yes, I'm Nina. I had called you and you referred me to your husband."

"Right. Sorry if I was a bit abrupt, I had a lot going on that day."

She watched Carla give Jon a look when she said "a lot going on." And she noted the shift in Jon's energy, from relaxed to wary.

"That's okay. Jon was very helpful." Nina gestured to the traps that now lay at her feet.

"Some cats sucked you in, huh? They do that, you know." Carla fiddled with a necklace around her throat and Nina could not help but admire its slender gold chain and small purple stone. "I got sucked in first, but then I got really busy with other stuff so now Jon is the main cat rescuer of our household."

Nina looked at Jon, who wore the kind of pained expression that people did when they wanted to openly disagree with something but instead kept their mouths shut. Did these people have a recent fight? Maybe she should collect the traps and say goodbye?

Only she couldn't. Rose had referred her to them with good intentions. Also, she had left her apartment for reasons unrelated to making a living or performing survival-related errands. So she pointed to Carla's yoga mat. "Where do you practice?"

They talked about yoga for at least ten minutes. Nina disclosed that she was a yoga teacher and Carla detailed her experiences with practicing at five different West LA yoga studios. Carla had never practiced at Cat/Cow but told Nina that one of her friends had a membership there. "She told me she's not so happy with the place, now that the studio's gone corporate."

"They're trying to keep up with the times, I guess." Nina could hear the edginess in her voice. It still stung, the loss of her evening classes. She thought of Serena then, who somehow reminded her of Carla.

"Anyway," she forced herself to continue. "I should tell you that I found you guys not only through the Stray Cat Society but through my friend."

"Cool," Jon said. "Did your friend borrow our traps?"

"No. You came to visit her. Her name is Rose Perchik."

Carla at first looked confused, then surprised. "Oh . . . how do you know Rose?"

No one had ever asked Nina this particular question before and she stared at Carla, suddenly feeling nauseous and light-headed. *Oh, you know. From around the neighborhood. Venice is really a small town, where people just can't help but bump into each other . . .*

"Her husband was in a car accident with my fiancé." This was finally her answer, unadorned and fact-based; something she could deliver to two people who didn't know her and would process the information accordingly.

But now Carla's eyes dawned with some kind of recognition. "Oh my God, I know who you are," she said.

She felt a slight and gentle tap on her shoulder. "I'm sorry," Jon said.

She nodded. She could see that for some reason, he was genuinely sorry, and this put her more at ease.

"Rose was my dad's ex-wife," Carla said.

"Rose was married . . . before?"

Carla smiled what Nina could only describe as a bitter smile. "My dad is a long story. How much time do you have?"

Twelve

THE TELEPHONE RANG just as Rose sat down at her kitchen table with a fresh cup of instant coffee so she could finish her preparations for unveiling Proposition Number Two. Was that the girl calling again to cancel their now not-so-weekly engagement? Last week, she had telephoned last minute before their scheduled lunch to say that she had been pressed into emergency service as a substitute for a yoga teacher afflicted with food poisoning so could they reschedule? What could she say except "of course, dear?" Who was she to stand in the way of the girl's livelihood? But then there was the week before, when the girl had canceled because she wasn't feeling well.

Rose picked up the phone on the third ring and steeled herself for another round of disappointment.

"Hi, Rose? This is Carla . . . Richard's daughter. How are you?"

"Oh, yes." Rose paused, equal parts relieved and suspicious. "I'm fine, thank you."

Carla proceeded to speak quickly and Rose struggled to keep up. Something about the girl visiting her and her husband for help with the girl's stray cats. Something about hearing that she may need help with errands?

"I get along all right, thank you." Poof went Rose's relief while her suspicion deepened. Had the girl actually told this Carla that she needed help?

Only that wasn't the worst part. Richard's daughter wanted her to know that she had some free time on her hands and would be delighted to drive her to the grocery store, the doctor, the pharmacy, the post office, you name it. Rose listened to this sales pitch, her anger and confusion building by the millisecond. Sure, she needed help, lots of it to be precise, but over her dead body would she acquiesce to becoming someone's official charity project. The chutzpah of the girl to pawn her off on someone else, as if she was!

"And, well, I also thought that . . . maybe we could get to know each other better. I would really like that."

"I see." Rose wracked her brain for a suitable explanation. It made her nauseous to consider that a) the girl could be capable of such chutzpah and b) maybe the girl did not view their relationship as one of mutual exchange. And then she remembered: This Carla had seemed most interested in memories about her father that day when they met for coffee.

Nu Rose? Maybe you should feel a little bit sorry for her?

"Maybe I could drop by sometime next week?"

Rose tried to be polite. She thanked Richard's daughter for calling and said she would take her number. She didn't have her number anymore, she explained, because she gave the business card to the girl. "And thank you for your kind offer but everything I need is right in the neighborhood," she added for extra emphasis. "I get along all right without a car."

"I'm glad to hear it." Only Richard's daughter didn't sound so glad.

Rose took Richard's daughter's phone number and said goodbye without promising to call. Had this Carla expected her to be starving for any and all offers of help, to perhaps resemble one of the overjoyed models on the brochures for Meals on Wheels and other Jewish Family Service programs that promised to improve the lives of their elderly clients?

After hanging up, Rose needed to catch her breath, as if she had been walking or in the good old days, dancing. It was a rigorous workout at her age, she realized, to try and stay angry.

Rose took a sip of her now cold coffee and tried to calm down. She needed to hear the girl's side of the story before passing judgment, did she not? And then maybe she would persist with Proposition Number Two and ask the girl to accompany her to the Center on the tastiest possible lunch day so that she would maximize her chances of bumping into Adele Mandelbaum and maybe put some affairs in order. Perhaps the girl could still provide the necessary moral support for this most dreaded and foolhardy of tasks.

THERE'S ROSE, SITTING on a metal folding chair at one of the Center's long, rectangular tables. Directly across from her sits Morry while her dear friend Lillian Rabinowitz sits next to her on the left. The chair to her right is unoccupied. They have just endured the conclusion of "Mental Fitness with Rosemary" and happily await the serving of lunch—baked chicken, mashed potatoes, peas, fruit cocktail. In truth, Rosemary has none of the comedic skills possessed by Patricia, the former mental fitness instructor, and so it's not as fun for any of them to remember their favorite song on the radio when they were sixteen or what they liked to eat for dinner in 1948, the year Israel declared its independence.

"Look what the cat brought in." Her dear friend Lillian Rabinowitz points a newly manicured pink fingernail in the direction of the front entrance. Adele Mandelbaum stands there with a brand new cane, fashionably late, and surveying the scene as if perched on a royal balcony high above a crowd of subjects. She's wearing a light blue dress with matching low-heeled pumps. Her blond hair appears freshly dyed and her face is a rainbow-colored mask of cheap cosmetics. Dressed to kill; what else is new? So thinks Rose, who has reasons coming out of her ears for why she surveys the empty seat to her right with dread.

"She's coming," hisses Lillian. "Get ready."

After glancing at Morry, who's staring into space and oblivious to the impending crisis, Rose gets ready. Personally, she feels all right today, with just enough energy to deflect any insults the Mandelbaum woman might hurl her way. Now if only Morry will cooperate.

Adele canes over to their table and gestures to the chair now occupied by her purse. The resulting question is of course terrible.

"Is this seat taken?"

"Guess it has your name on it," Morry says this with a smile and a wink.

A wink? Rose can't believe it. Her husband has never been one for winking, not at pretty women or adorable children or even, at the world. Rose performs reluctance as she moves her purse off the seat. How she longs for the days when Morry excused himself from the lunch table to go play chess with Harold Zimmerman, may he rest in peace.

The nice ladies from the kitchen start to wheel out the large stainless steel carts filled to the brim with their hot lunches as Adele makes herself comfortable. She hooks her cane to the back of the chair and lowers herself into the seat, grunt by grunt, sigh by sigh. Her dress spills out over the edges of the seat, making contact with Rose's legs, fortunately covered up by a pair of dark blue, fake-silk pants. Adele tells Morry he's looking well, ignores Lillian and Rose, and launches into a tirade about an absolutely revolting play she attended the night before. Naked actors that looked about their age rolling around onstage like children in a sandbox. Is this what people should do with their twenty-five dollars earmarked for supporting the arts, senior citizens' discounts notwithstanding?

"What if the naked people were young and beautiful? Would it be all right then?" Rose feels compelled to say something, though it's always a mistake to initiate any and all communication with the Mandelbaum woman.

One of the kitchen ladies begins to serve their table as Adele appraises Rose with an exaggerated wrinkling of her nose. "You are missing the point," she says.

What is the point? Rose does not have the opportunity to ask because the chicken has been served and the subject changed by Morry, who pats Adele on her hand just as she picks up her fork and says, "It's very nice to see you today."

Adele takes a bite of chicken and beams with pleasure. "Morry Perchik, you're making my day," she coos upon swallowing.

Rose and Lillian now exchange glances of concern. This is something else, this unprecedented display of disloyalty; some new development in the grand unraveling of her beloved husband.

Morry moves the food around on his plate with his fork without eating any of it. He's humming a tune that Rose does not recognize and smiles at Adele. "Do you remember this? It's our song."

"Is that so?" Adele giggles and reaches out to pat Morry's hand.

"You wouldn't dance with me. You only drank champagne." Morry abruptly drops his fork into the middle of his still full plate.

"Now, now, what party was this?" Adele still smiles at her husband but Rose knows what's coming.

"Morry." Rose reaches across the table and places a hand on her husband's forearm. *Look at me.* This, she does not dare say out loud.

But now her husband won't look at anyone. He's staring into space again and addresses the air in a loud voice. "Why wouldn't you dance with me? You were never in the mood."

Rose joins her husband in staring into space. She's too mortified to even look Lillian in the eye. She hears Adele ask: "What are you talking about?" She hears her husband reply: "Rose is a much better dancer than you."

In the end, it's Adele who excuses herself to use the bathroom. On her way out of her chair, she whispers to Rose, "Check his medications first. My husband had a problem once, he . . ." Adele stops right there and seems almost embarrassed before shaking her head with the familiar doom-and-gloom judgment.

"Were you talking about Ruth?" Rose waits to ask about Morry's first wife until Adele has disappeared into the bathroom. "That was Adele sitting across from you."

She sees it, miracle of miracles, in her husband's eyes. The glimmer of recognition. *You're back.* Of course, her elation cannot last, not while she watches Morry understand what just transpired. She sees the shame and fear on her husband's face and wishes she could cover him up, like the mourners do with their mirrors when they sit shiva. Because right now, her husband does not need to stare at himself.

Rose reaches again across the table for her husband's hand. She whispers, "Look at me."

And miracle of miracles, he does.

"WHY DON'T WE go to that newfangled ice cream parlor instead? Have you tried it yet?"

They sat in the girl's car, which illegally idled in front of Rose's apartment building. Rose watched the girl look absolutely confused by this suggestion.

"Oh," the girl said. "Do you mean the Pinkberry on Abbot Kinney? Are you sure you don't want to eat a proper lunch?"

"I wouldn't mind trying it."

"It's yogurt, not ice cream. And it's tart. People usually add toppings."

Rose shrugged. "You only live once."

The girl pursed her lips and started to explain how she had recently signed some petition circulated by the organization KeepVeniceLocal to boycott this yogurt shop and keep all chain businesses off Abbot Kinney. But then she paused in mid-explanation and shrugged. "Why not? It's good to shake things up sometimes."

To a point, dear. To a point. Rose tried to prepare her remarks during the mostly silent seven-minute journey to the yogurt store, a perfectly cheerful place in Rose's opinion with its shiny, white walls and neon green and pink counter. This Pinkberry had replaced a seedy liquor store popular with those skateboarders and other vagrant-like individuals and so Rose did not despise it, the way she knew she would revile the Whole Foods establishment, still scheduled to usurp the 99 Cent.

Rose insisted on paying for the two large vanilla yogurts with banana, mango, and chocolate chip toppings. They found an empty, shiny-white table and Rose argued that she could manage the process of sitting without assistance. The girl acquiesced and Rose struggled to lower herself, vertebrae by vertebrae, body part by body part, onto the shiny-white seat, while gripping her walker for leverage. Meanwhile, the girl stood within touching distance, ready to act at a moment's notice. They had occupied these roles now multiple times and each time, Rose wished that the girl could have seen her in her prime; that from one friend to another, she could present something more expansive than the usual diminished picture.

After seating herself, Rose needed some time to recover from the effort. She watched the girl taste the yogurt as she tried to slow down her breathing and almost canceled her remarks. The girl looked happy eating that yogurt and how many times since their first meeting had she witnessed such a thing?

They spent a few minutes eating in silence until the girl asked, "Do you like it?"

Rose shrugged. "It's not bad. So I understand you met Richard's daughter."

The girl looked mystified and it took Rose several seconds to remember: She had not explained Richard to the girl when she handed over the business card.

The girl, however and as usual, displayed the presence of brains. "Oh, you mean Carla."

"She telephoned this morning and wanted to know if she could drive me places."

"Did she?" Now the girl seemed even more confused but Rose could not ascertain the presence of a mask. "I went over to her house to pick up some cat traps. She and her husband are very nice people. She told me that you were married to her father. I didn't know you were married before."

Rose gave the curtest of nods and pushed aside her half-eaten yogurt. "This is too much for me. Do you want to take this home?"

Nina shook her head. "We don't have to talk about it."

Rose stared at the girl, understanding that at the moment, she didn't want to talk about anything. "Dear. I have to ask you something. Did you tell her I needed help with my errands?"

She pretended to eat another bite of yogurt as she waited for the girl's response. How disappointing, that this unburdening of her suspicion brought no relief. And, quite frankly, this yogurt was neither here nor there.

"I told Carla and her husband that you and I became friends and that we often go shopping together. That's all I said."

"Is it too much for you, taking me shopping? I always told you not to trouble yourself." Oy, thought Rose. Maybe she could cut through the pride in her voice with a butcher knife. Maybe. Maybe she needed an even sharper knife. And yet, she couldn't help it, how the pride seeped out through every pore of her body, reminding her that despite everything, she still had her presence of mind. At least for today.

The girl put her hand on Rose's elbow. "It has never been any trouble," she said in a firm, clear voice. "Maybe Carla misunderstood something I said but I never told her I thought you needed help with anything."

"Yes, dear, but . . ." The time had come to unearth one of the unsaid things, hurl it at the girl like a baseball to a window, and hope for the best. "You don't seem like yourself lately, ever since the day I gave you my things."

The girl removed her hand from Rose's elbow and exhaled an audible sigh. "You're right. I've been having a tough time lately."

Rose waited for the girl to elaborate, unsure how to fill the silence between them. She believed what the girl said about Richard's daughter but at the same time, she didn't feel ready to ask the girl for assistance with the Mandelbaum woman.

"I'm sorry to hear that, dear."

And then Rose waited some more.

But the girl changed the subject. "I meant to tell you, remember that awful skateboarder? I saw him getting arrested the other day on the boardwalk, right by the senior center. These two cops had him and some other boy in handcuffs. About time, huh?"

"Is that so?" Rose winced to hear herself ask the question her husband had asked countless times during the so-called winter of his life. Only she was not yet her husband, as she could still remember with a ferocious clarity how that boy stood so close to her before pronouncing her "old."

"I thought you'd be pleased to hear it."

"Of course, dear. The streets will hopefully be a little safer."

"I still think we should have told the police about what he did to you."

Rose shrugged. "I was all right that day so there was no point." *Except that was the day the Man from Television started speaking to you.* How to tell this girl that she faced bigger battles? "Did he hurt someone from the Center?"

"I don't know. But the place was packed. It's great, how close that is to you."

The girl, however and as usual, was no dummy.

"Yes. I used to walk over there." The time had arrived and Rose still wasn't ready.

"You told me you used to go there almost every day. But that was a while ago, wasn't it?"

Rose closed her eyes. She needed this girl's help, no matter how much pride still seeped through her pores. "Dear," she heard herself say. "I have something of a favor to ask."

Thirteen

NINA HAD TO park her car maybe a quarter mile away from the party on a narrow and winding Hollywood Hills street, where only parking on one side was permitted. But now, mission accomplished. After battling an hour of Saturday night traffic, most notably the bottleneck at the intersection of the 110 and 101, she was free to grab the bottle of wine that survived the journey on her passenger seat and finally exit her vehicle.

Only Nina stalled. She studied her reflection in her car's rearview mirror and applied a touch more lipstick. She turned up the lapels of Rose's leather coat, which she wore over a short black skirt and short-sleeved purple blouse. She checked her newly purchased smart phone for email. And then she resorted to breathing exercises. Maybe it was too soon, her thinking that she could attend a party filled with strangers and maybe, just maybe, have some fun.

Remember those days, when you had fun? That euphoria you would get when you took a dance class or finished a two-hour yoga practice or drove solo on PCH to Malibu for the hell of it with open windows, happy to be alive? That was you also.

She had been invited to this party by Carla, who described it as technically a mixer for people with a general interest in attending Burning Man and a specific interest in joining a camp that Carla helped run. What sort of camp, Nina had asked but Carla would only tell her that this camp was an offshoot of a much larger Burning Man camp called "Boundless Hearts" and Nina should just "come and check out the vibe."

She had spoken to Jon and Carla for about two hours on the day she picked up the traps, which continued to lie dormant in her living room in an aesthetically mismatched co-existence with Rose's possessions. She had sat in Jon and Carla's kitchen, which had the same blond-wood Ikea kitchen table that existed in her own apartment. At this table, they drank Trader Joe's green tea and Carla explained that her father had left Rose to marry her mother, and then left her mother for someone else when she was ten.

"My dad was a serial adulterer." Carla said this in a matter-of-fact-I've-processed-the-shit-out-of-this-in-therapy voice. "He had a knack for seducing women who liked the older man thing and I understand now as an adult that the part of adultery my dad liked best were all the lies he got to tell my mother. I resolved that my own marriage would never be this way."

At that juncture in the conversation, Nina had watched Carla and Jon exchange what she supposed were meaningful glances. Then, Carla resumed telling Nina about how she had tracked down Rose hoping to learn more about her father, but had instead emerged from their encounter disappointed.

"It was like come on, we both know what kind of man he was but she wouldn't bite," Carla said. "She only told me that he once came to visit her and that he showed her a picture of me. She told me I was a beautiful child."

Carla then excused herself from the table, promising she'd "be right back." Alone with Jon, Nina could only stare at him from across the table and remember what she had felt standing close to him in the shed.

Jon said, "I think it's really nice that you became friends with this woman, with Rose."

"Rose is a really cool person." Nina could hear the edge in her voice, as if she was reacting to thousands of well-meaning people telling her she was doing some good in the world by befriending an older woman; as if an older woman and a younger woman could never bridge their generational divide to become authentic friends.

But Jon had nodded, as if he perfectly understood the edge in Nina's voice. Then Carla returned to join them and the conversation became gradually lighter. They spoke a bit more about Nina's friendship with Rose—Carla had seemed especially interested in the details of the friendship, hadn't she?—then changed the subject back to yoga, which led to a conversation about dance, which led to a conversation about the ecstatic dance workshops that Carla had done at Burning Man, which led to a general conversation about Burning Man and how Carla and Jon had been four times and prepared to go again this year. And then Carla had extended the invitation to the upcoming party, along with the mysterious suggestion to read her blog beforehand.

Only Nina hadn't read Carla's blog. Now, as she got out of her car, she grabbed the wine and replayed the final exchange that she had with Jon, who had walked her out of his kitchen and helped her fit three traps into her trunk and one in her back seat. She thanked him and he said, "If you have any questions or anything, you can give me a call. He had stood there by the car door on the driver's side, looking as if he wanted to say more. And then he said, "You should probably read my wife's blog."

"I should?"

"It's about polyamory. As is camp 'Boundless Hearts.'"

"Oh." It took her a moment to recall her discussions with Jeff about the subject and she felt dizzy from the effort.

You sitting on Laz's lap while Jeff watched.

"Yeah. There are a lot of misconceptions about polyamory and my wife is very passionate about educating people who think that being poly is about cheating or kinky sex or an excuse to be a perv or whatever. She's all about fighting the stigma around it."

"So you guys—"

"Yeah. And so are a lot of the people coming to the party. Not everyone but a lot. I don't know why Carla was being so mysterious about it but . . . well, maybe I do."

"What do you mean?"

"Sorry, I just think you have a right to know what you're getting into before you show up to something."

"Thanks. I'll think about it."

He waited for her to pull away from the curb before disappearing behind his wooden gate with a goodbye wave. She waved back, already determined to do something that scared her.

Yep, still scared. So Nina thought as she walked down the street to the party held in a cream-colored, Ranch-style house with a garage that had been decorated with off-season, multi-colored Christmas lights. She could hear the hum of multiple conversations punctuated by bursts of laughter as she climbed the driveway. She pushed open the front door just as a petite dark-haired woman in a black, sparkly cocktail dress dimmed the lights in the living room.

"Welcome." The woman smiled at Nina and beckoned her inside. "I'm Lola."

Nina introduced herself, stepped into the living room, and observed the sea of people. They milled about the space, perched on the edges of couches and chairs, brandished an assortment of beverages, and wore an enormous variety of clothing: more black cocktail dresses, multi-colored vintage evening gowns, expensive jeans, not-so-expensive jeans, sequined tank tops, ripped T-shirts, shorts, and sweatpants. Two women wore only bikinis and one man wore a tuxedo and top hat.

Lola identified herself as the party's hostess, pointed the way to the kitchen, and told Nina to help herself to the food and booze. "Oh, and are you a virgin?"

"Excuse me?"

"Sorry. A Burning Man virgin. I'm guessing you are." Lola's bubbly and ethereal laugh somehow made Nina feel more at ease.

"That would be true."

"I'm asking everyone I don't know if they are. I'm happy to answer any questions you have. I'm assuming you're interested in going to Burning Man this year?"

"I'm thinking about it." The words popped out of Nina's mouth. She hadn't been thinking about it but somehow, the words felt true.

"Cool! You should go."

Nina smiled at Lola, who excused herself to go hug a man in a penguin costume.

She kept telling herself this was a party like any other party as she made her way to the kitchen, a spacious room with gleaming appliances and a shiny black granite island bearing bottles of wine, vodka, scotch, mixers, and platters of Mediterranean hors d'oeuvres: grape leaves, mini spinach pies, crackers slathered with baba ganoush and topped with feta cheese.

Nina poured herself a glass of white wine; her standard party-with-strangers drink of her thirties, ever since she realized just how much red wine, particularly of the Spanish and Italian varieties, could stain her teeth. Jeff had been the one to point out how her mouth turned purple with too much Tempranillo about three months after they started dating and she had thanked him for the information in the way she would thank any well-meaning friend who detected the spinach caught between the teeth or suggested that she blow her nose. And then she had wondered: why hadn't Laz ever told her about her purple teeth? They had drunk red wine together in countless bars and different cities and he never said a word all those times he leaned over to kiss her stained mouth.

"Hey . . . you made it."

Jon stood at the entrance to the kitchen holding a glass of fizzy, clear liquid. He wore those same faded, ripped jeans from the day she met him and a long-sleeved T-shirt that concealed his flame tattoos. His shirt made Nina think of the year she lived in Israel, when she had to wear long skirts and sleeves that covered the elbow if she wanted to visit holy sites. That year, she had wondered if these mandates in the Old City or in the ultra-Orthodox neighborhoods of Jerusalem for the daughters of Israel to dress modestly really achieved their intended effect. Did it not make everyone even more prone to sexual distraction, this covering up of flesh that defiantly continued to exist under the fabric?

"Yeah, I made it." Nina raised her glass of wine and took her first sip.

"Cool. I'm happy to introduce you to people."

"Maybe in a bit."

He asked if she had made any progress with the cat trapping and reiterated his offer to help when she admitted to still feeling overwhelmed. They engaged in a bit of small talk and she found out that in addition to his animal rescue efforts, he worked as a lighting and sound designer for a variety of theaters and freelanced as a film editor. For fun, he played with fire. He got together with a group of fire performers every week at Dockweiler, the only beach in town that allows the building of fires. He knew how to both eat and juggle fire and last year, he performed with thousands of fellow fire dancers at Burning Man.

"Is Carla a fire dancer too?"

Jon shook his head. "At Burning Man, Carla and I tend to have different interests."

"Oh."

They each sipped their drinks. Nina waited for him to speak but he just kept looking at her. "Is that why you have those tattoos?" she decided to ask him. "Because you're a fire dancer?"

He smiled. "That's one reason."

She smiled back. "I never had an interest in getting a tattoo. Maybe it's because I'm Jewish. I guess I grew up thinking that Jews didn't voluntarily get tattoos."

"I'm Jewish too."

"Really? I wouldn't have guessed." His Jewishness genuinely surprised her. Perhaps she had gotten cocky over the years, assuming she could spot the Jews in any given room just as she could intuit the careers of her yoga students. But still, she should not have been tripped up by his tattoos, or for that matter, the polyamory.

"In fact, Carla and I go to this really cool alternative Friday night service in your neighborhood."

"Really?"

"Yeah. This rabbi has services sometimes on the beach and sometimes in this wine bar. She's very cool, the rabbi. She always has . . . relevant things to say."

And then Jon inched closer to her, which surprisingly made her feel less exposed. "I know that we don't know each other very well and this is going to sound kind of weird, but, when we met, I could tell that you had been through . . . something."

"Oh." She paused, torn between conflicting conversational impulses. She could say too much or nothing at all and either way, she doubted she could express what she currently felt.

"Yeah, I guess I wanted you to know that—"

A group of people suddenly flooded into the kitchen and spilled out toward the counter with the beverages, forcing Nina, then Jon, to back up toward the refrigerator. And then Carla strode into the room flanked by a tall man and even taller woman wearing matching red spandex unitards. "Hey you two. This is Wilson and Vanita. They're going to do this performance on the balcony in about an hour."

Carla looked at Nina and smiled. "You guys having fun?"

"We are." Jon answered his wife in the driest of tones, which led to the tiniest of light bulbs popping up in Nina's brain.

Are you flattered? The Nina before the accident would be flattered.

Nina picked up her glass from where she had placed it on the island and took a hearty gulp of wine. Wilson and Vanita had commandeered the conversation, but she didn't feel like getting to know them at the moment, though they apparently led fascinating careers as performance artists with gigs and commissions all over the country.

She excused herself, making a point of asking the location of the nearest bathroom. Carla pointed toward the living room and said there was a bathroom at the other end, at the edge of the hallway leading to a guest bedroom and Lola's office. She left the group, feeling both relieved and agitated, and wandered back into the living room, where the ongoing roar of collective chatter, punctuated by volleys of laughter, somehow made her think of the Pat Benatar song "Love is a Battlefield," which then made her think about war zones both global and personal, which then compelled her to touch her left thigh which still bore traces of bruises that she incurred from falling off the couch that night with Laz still inside her. Good lord. Would she ever start behaving again like these other people, who seemed to be fully present party guests as they enjoyed their evening, their interactions with others remaining exactly that?

Someone turned up the music and Nina felt the thud, thud, thud of the electronic beats vibrating and rippling around her heart. "All right people!" Lola shouted, who grabbed the arm of another woman.

Nina watched them dance. She recognized the speed of their hip gyrations and the frenetic pace of their limbs; the flinging arms and the gliding, stomping legs. Circumstantial evidence pointed to everyone's favorite party drug or some close cousin and on some other night, Nina would have experienced a vicarious high from watching these dancers before deciding to join them.

Nina exited the living room, discovered the bathroom, and continued down the hallway. She passed what she supposed was Lola's office, noticed a door to a room that seemed purposely closed, and stopped in front of a candlelit bedroom with a half-open door. On top of the bed, there appeared to be four people in various stages of undress lying together in different angles, so that their limbs and heads and other body parts intersected with one another. Sculpturally, the scene caught Nina's eye. At first, these people seemed frozen in some kind of tableau, but Nina kept staring and realized that the human sculpture was definitely moving; that the man kissing a woman's upper thigh was being suckled in the neck by another woman whose bare breasts were being fondled by another man.

"Do you want to join us?" The woman whose thigh had just been kissed beckoned to Nina with a well-manicured index finger. Nina noticed the woman's bright red hair and thought of Jon's tattoos, each one an elegant, single flame.

You sitting on Laz's lap while Jeff watched.

She smiled a "no thank you" at the woman and walked backwards a few steps, unable to take her eyes off the group. This time, she would watch. She was no longer eight years old, stumbling uninvited into the living room during one of her parents' parties and wondering why her mother was kissing their neighbor on the lips. *We were just being friendly honey. Adults are like that.* For years, her parents had thrown those parties but something changed when Nina was in high school. In the years leading to their divorce, her parents almost never entertained at home and went out separately with increasing frequency.

Nina turned her back on the group when she realized her breath had become shallow and labored. She needed air and then she would flee to the self-contained environment of her car and drive back to Venice, the more traffic on the 101, the better, as far as she was concerned, because she didn't really want to go home either. There had been expectations, she realized, or rather, a singular hope that she could lose herself in the rhythm of a party where no one knew her. No one here knew of her past and so would not regard her with sympathy or pity or project yearnings, fears, and insecurities about their own lives onto her. In this place, judgment for the lives of others didn't seem to exist and everyone could do as they pleased. So why couldn't she?

She took a few steps down the hallway, in the direction of the living room and front door. She would thank Lola for her hospitality, note a rapidly developing migraine, and make her exit. Surely Lola could convey this information to Carla and Jon.

But there stood Carla just in front of the room with the closed door. "I was looking for you. I thought we could talk."

"Here?" Nina gestured behind her to the room with the moving human sculpture. "There's some . . . activity over there."

"That's what we call an R-rated cuddle puddle." Carla spoke in a light, breezy tone.

"Is that what you call it?"

"Actually, those people are all in a committed relationship with each other, though they are also open to others. So maybe I'd call it a structured, R-rated cuddle puddle."

"Ah."

She watched Carla attempt intense direct eye contact, as if they were participants partnering for a warm-up in an acting or communication skills workshop. Then Carla said, "I want you to know that you have my blessing."

"Your blessing?" She didn't really need to ask for clarification.

"To get to know my husband. To date him even, if that's where it's leading. I suppose I should have explained all this to you before I invited you here but I thought it might be better if my husband talked to you about it first. And then I saw you guys talking in the kitchen and I mean, I'm not trying to play matchmaker or anything but you guys seemed—"

"Look, I can't . . . date your husband and it's not because of your . . . lifestyle."

She paused and winced. *Lifestyle. Now that's a word with some slippery and judgmental connotations.* "It's just . . . I think it's too soon for me to date anyone right now."

And she felt what she had so briefly grasped on the night she sat on Laz's lap while Jeff watched: the necessity of an imposed loneliness.

She tried to listen as Carla explained her marriage; how she and Jon took on what they called "secondaries" and did so with each other's full permission and commitment to transparency. "I knew you were Jon's type from the moment I met you. And Jon just told me that you're Jewish, which is always a plus for him. And yes, it did throw me when you told me that you knew Rose and I understood who you were but, I don't know . . . I mean, yes, I totally get what it means to be in mourning. But I also know that sometimes you don't realize that you're ready to move forward unless you actually just do it."

She tried to protect herself while Carla searched her face for clues to her opinions. Instinctively, she grabbed the lapels of Rose's coat—she would always think of it as Rose's coat, wouldn't she?—and wrapped the garment tightly around her. *A leather shield, so that no unauthorized individuals will be able to read your soul.*

And then she remembered her other agenda for the evening: "Listen, I saw Rose recently and she told me you called her and, well . . . I was wondering what exactly you said to her . . . because . . ."

She struggled for the right words while Carla waited, a model of patience and some other virtue that Nina couldn't quite grasp. "Rose thought I told you that she needed help and, uh . . . I don't think I said that."

"Oh." Carla tossed her hair to one side and put her hand on Nina's shoulder. "I was actually trying to help you."

"I don't understand."

"That day you came to our house, well, no offense but you seemed pretty stressed out. And when you were telling me how involved you've become in Rose's life, I just thought you could use some help. Rose doesn't have any family to help her out, right?"

Nina backed up two steps so that Carla could no longer touch her shoulder. "Rose is not a burden to me, if that's what you're trying to say. She's also super independent."

Carla nodded with enthusiasm, as if she had predicted how Nina would respond with perfect accuracy. "Of course she's not a burden to you. And yes, when I spoke to her on the phone, she basically told me she didn't need any help. But she might a year from now, or sooner. I mean, have you thought about that, what that might mean when Rose will need more help?"

"Why are you so interested in Rose?" Nina heard herself sounding sharper and more defensive than she intended. But Carla had struck a nerve. Since Laz's visit, she had not been the greatest friend to Rose. She would call Rose, thinking she might be able to tell her everything but instead, she only wound up canceling their plans. *If you knew the truth about me, you wouldn't want to be my friend.* She had allowed the thought to corrupt their carefully established routine, to seduce her into believing that it would be a mistake to try and be a friend to others if she could not be a friend to herself.

Carla's expression shifted from beatific to pained. "I didn't grow up with grandparents," she finally said. "And now I no longer have any parents. When I read that article about Rose, I don't know, I felt this . . . pull, like . . . she was the closest thing I had in Los Angeles to a living relative so I had to get to know her. Yes, I am working on a memoir and I thought that Rose could tell me things about my dad. But it's more than that. I've never really had older people like her in my life and I guess I wanted . . ."

Carla paused, prompting Nina to stare at a bright red abstract print on the wall. Was that a Mark Rothko? Nina struggled to retrieve her increasingly distant art history education. She heard sniffling noises as she studied the print and it occurred to her that Carla was an incredibly lonely person, even though her life seemed full of people.

Nina took her eyes off the print and saw that Carla looked both sad and hopeful. "Look, I'm sure you have good intentions here and we can talk more about Rose some other time but I think I need to go now. Thank you so much for inviting me here and I'm sorry but—"

"There's something else I need to tell you. When I read the article about Rose's husband, there was some information that tripped me out. The article had listed your fiancé's name and included a photo and . . . I recognized him."

She stared at Carla and wrapped the coat even more tightly around her. Vaguely, she thought that some former version of herself would have made things easier for the other person.

"There was a guy that came to a couple of our Burner, poly mixer events. I had noticed him the first time he showed up and I met him the second time he came. He introduced himself as Jeff and he told me he was a social worker. We got to talking and he told me that he had been interested in 'our scene' for a while but didn't know how to tell his partner. I didn't get into it too deeply with him but . . . he definitely seemed like he was searching for something."

Don't you think it's brilliant in theory? She could finally hear it, Jeff's voice trapped in her mind, the hope mixed in with the joke.

"I'm sorry but I really have to go. We can talk about this another time."

She didn't turn around while Carla called after her. She walked quickly down the hallway, into the living room, and out the front door. She could hear her quick, sharp exhales that accompanied her flight down the street and into her car. She pulled out of her parking spot with care and drove with caution down the dark, winding Hollywood Hills road. She turned on the radio to KCRW, which played something pulsing and electronic, just like the music in Lola's house. As she headed to the freeway, she bypassed two coyotes crossing the street and thought about the people in the bedroom. Whatever they had been expressing, love or lust or something in-between, they looked as if they had nothing to hide. Is that what had triggered her so, their absence of shame and their appearance of having no other agenda except to enjoy each other in their present moment?

Have you ever loved or lusted in that way? Without testing, without deception, without manipulation, without wanting him to be something he isn't?

Nina drove the rest of the way home, unable to either process what Carla had told her or exile the people in the bedroom from her mind. Those people, in their various states of undress, continued to beckon her in their direction. They seemed to present themselves as her teachers but of what make and model, she did not yet know.

Fourteen

ROSE WAS HAVING second thoughts as she stood outside the Center's Ozone Avenue entrance on a cloudy Wednesday shortly before noon. The girl stood next to her, ogling the *Chagall in Venice Beach* mural, which covered about three quarters worth of the Center's exterior walls. Rose found the girl's ogling to be slightly embarrassing, as it reminded her of one of those goggly-eyed tourists from Mississippi or North Dakota or some other place where they've never seen a Jew before.

Rose said, "Okay. Are you ready to go in there?"

"Are you ready?" The girl kept her eyes on the mural. "You said you wanted to be here in time for lunch."

Yes, yes, Rose knew what she said. She remembered almost word for word the telephone conversation from three days ago, when she swallowed her developing concerns and confirmed their appointment to go to the Center this Wednesday, i.e. on a Salmon Day. Wednesday was by far the most desirable day to visit the Center, she had explained. Tuesdays meant some sort of dangerous beef stew and shame on the Center for serving it to senior citizens with delicate arteries. Thursdays were simply negligible: dried out turkey legs with potatoes and carrots cooked to such a pulp that they no longer could be legally recognized as vegetables. But Wednesdays: now those days were something else. Someone in that kitchen knew how to cook a piece of salmon, not too rare and not too overcooked. Plus, the salmon came with decently prepared potato latkes and some creamed spinach.

"She would never miss a Salmon Day."

The girl nodded like someone who had mastered the crash course on the Mandelbaum woman. "Right. So let's do it."

Did she or did she not trust the girl? Rose still didn't know as she and the girl stalled, united in paralysis though clearly for different reasons because it appeared that the girl could not get enough of the mural.

They took a few more minutes to examine the mural in its entirety: at the fiddler perched on the roof of a wooden shtetl house; at the winged fish playing the violin with a human hand; at the man embracing the woman as he gazes into the distance filled with abundant California fruits and a large cat; at the muscular roller skater with blond, shoulder-length hair and angel's wings gliding past a robed family of four floating into the starry sky; at the bearded man with the Torah scroll surrounded by flames.

"The artist had the right idea," the girl said. "Chagall belongs in Venice. He was my favorite artist when I was younger."

Rose nodded. It occurred to her then to try and examine the mural through the girl's eyes and the effort embarrassed her. The flying menorah, the enormous dreidl, the floating Jews juxtaposed with the Santa Monica Pier. What would Chagall think of this knockoff? Rose wondered. She was no art critic but in her opinion, the artist had created an eye-catching spectacle. Even Morry always had reasonably pleasant things to say about it. After all, centuries of Jewish history reduced to a few cartoons on a building by the beach in Venice, California was better than nothing. And for every group of non-Jewish tourists who saw the mural and thought: there go those funny-looking Jews again floating into the air, no wonder why the world still hates them, a lone Jewish roller skater would emerge from the crowd to catch his breath and study the Center's exterior. The mural would of course remind him of his grandparents and of a bygone world that, in a few more years, would cease to exist in the memories of the living.

"I heard from Richard's daughter again, excuse me . . . Carla. She wants to meet me for coffee." It was Rose's turn to keep her eyes on the mural.

"Oh. That's nice. Are you going to meet her?"

"I told her I was very busy these days."

"Okay. She seems nice though. Did she tell you we spoke recently?" The girl looked as if she wanted to say more on the subject.

Rose nodded and decided she did not want to say more on the subject. She knew enough now about Richard's daughter and her bright-as-sunshine voice to firmly associate her with those young people who used to visit the Center every Sunday. She had always been partial to the depressed souls that she detected beneath those questions of sunshine so why not Richard's daughter? *Because she's Richard's daughter?*

Rose peeled her eyes off the mural and watched two women she did not recognize walk through the Center's entrance. "You know something? Let's have lunch at the Fig Tree today." She tried to sound blasé about the whole business, as if to say: here, there, lunch is lunch.

The girl looked at her with narrowed eyes and folded arms. "I canceled on a very reliable yoga client today. And we can go to the Fig Tree any day of the week. What about the salmon?"

Rose pooh-poohed the salmon, even though it broke her heart to do so. She whispered, "I can't do it."

"Is this woman that bad?"

Rose could only stare at the girl, struggling to remember the last time she felt this type of powerlessness. *Nu Rose? How about when the police told you the facts of the accident? How the boy had died of a broken neck and that some of his groceries had collided with the windshield. How Morry suffered a heart attack by the time the paramedics arrived and had passed away in the ambulance en route to the hospital.*

Should she tell the girl about the number of sleepless nights endured since the accident, when she drifted far into half-dreamed scenarios where a righteous, angry mob descended upon her with shaking fists, demanding she answer for her crimes? In every single scenario, Rose found herself pleading with the mob. *What would you have done in my position?* Then she would hold the car keys as high as possible over her head before tossing them into the voracious crowd, which, upon closer inspection, was essentially a sea of exhausted fists, deaf ears, and grimaces baring teeth in various stages of disrepair. And then she would try to tell them, even though no one could hear her, that the keys to the kingdom belong to everyone, until one day, they don't.

"It's not so much what they think about me. It's what they say about him. That's why I have to go in there. For him."

"I understand," the girl whispered. "But he was what, ninety-five? Maybe he shouldn't have been . . . didn't you tell me that you wouldn't get into a car with him?"

Rose shook her head and looked at the ground.

"I don't blame you for what happened. Why should they?"

Rose kept her eyes on the ground. She could not afford to cry or succumb to the temptation of sinking to the ground, beating her chest, and letting the God of the Jews in the mural make it all better. *Shah, maidele. Shah.* Her mother used to stroke her forehead, murmuring those words as an amulet against terror and despair. Only where was her mother now?

"Morry was a good man. He never wanted to hurt anyone."

The girl nodded and offered her elbow. "You need to say this to that woman."

"ARE YOU SURE?" Rose asks her husband as they begin the slow process of getting into their car. Every day, she asks this question even though she knows the answer.

"Sure, I'm sure." Courteous as usual, Morry opens the passenger door for her.

They fasten their seatbelts so they can continue their now long-running charade: Rose will get dropped off at the Center by her husband, who has lost interest in lunching on Ozone Avenue and prefers to sit in a nearby café on Main Street surrounded by ambitious reading materials. Meanwhile, Rose continues to patronize the Center for the Wednesday salmon specials, games of gin and bridge, and for the company of loyal friends such as the esteemed Lillian Rabinowitz.

Morry makes the right turn onto Ozone Avenue and pulls up right in front of the Center's entrance. He promises to pick her up by two and she reminds him to buy a sandwich at the café for his lunch. She gives him a goodbye kiss on the cheek and feels their recent spate of domestic tranquility warming her skin like a blanket as she gets out of the car. She hasn't noticed as many memory lapses or stumblings into other black holes since the episode with the Mandelbaum woman. And just two weeks ago, he celebrated his eighty-eighth birthday with the renewal of his driver's license.

As she gets out of the car, Rose sees the Mandelbaum woman walking on the boardwalk from the direction of Santa Monica with Sylvia Weinreb. On a scale of human excellence, Rose thinks that Sylvia is neither here nor there but she never had a problem with her aside from the company she keeps. Best not to acknowledge either one of them, however, even though they all head for the entrance and could all possibly wind up trying to jam through the door at the same time. A cold peace had settled between her and Adele in recent months, bolstered by Rose's joint policies of Ignore and Avoid. Why ruin a good thing?

Rose beats Adele and Sylvia to the entrance and just as she's gone inside, she hears a dramatic screeching of brakes, followed by a short yet explosive scream. Various Center members with functional ear drums and/or hearing aids look in her direction but none get up to investigate. Rose quickly scans the room for Ms. Diana, the Center's director, but she's not there.

Rose forces herself to go back outside. Adele and Sylvia are huddled against the wall, partially obscuring the image of the blond and winged roller skater. Morry has just gotten out of the car with the engine still running. The car is now perpendicular to the building and Rose surmises that Morry had been in the midst of making one of those three point turns in order to make the right turn back onto Speedway.

Morry speaks first. "Are you all right?"

"You almost killed us!" Adele glares at Rose as she says this. "Where were your eyes?"

"What happened?" Rose walks over to Morry and puts a hand on his shoulder. She notices that her husband's hands are trembling.

"I was backing up, that's all." Rose can hear the conviction in her husband's voice, which clashes with the fear in his eyes.

"He almost ran us over, that's all." Adele continues to glare at Rose.

"We're okay. No harm done," says Sylvia, prompting Rose to feel guilty about her prior assessments of the woman.

"All's well that ends well," says Rose a little too quickly.

"I apologize," says Morry. "I should have been more careful."

Sylvia acknowledges this apology with a slight nod while Adele maintains what Rose surmises to be her most ferocious scowl. Morry returns to the car and Rose follows him. She stands by the driver's door as he gets back inside. She whispers, "I'm going to have to stay here now."

Morry nods. "I'm sorry."

Rose backs away from the car and in the loudest voice she can muster says, "Drive carefully!"

Sylvia has already gone inside but Adele waits for her as she makes her way yet again to the Center's entrance. They eye each other for what feels like a very long time until Rose makes the mistake of speaking first.

"I'm sorry you had a scare. He's usually an excellent driver. The DMV just renewed his license. His eyes are fine." It had surprised Rose that day, that brief episode of grace; that it was Adele who had excused herself to use the bathroom while she and Morry sorted out the past from the present.

Adele launches into a round of tsk-tsking noises. "We both know it's not his eyes," she says in a voice unctuous with what Rose knows to be the worst kind of unearned righteousness. "You need to keep him off the streets. Because if you don't, it's a crime and I'll report him to the DMV myself."

Adele makes a point of letting the Center's front door slam shut as she goes inside. Rose decides to give herself exactly two minutes to recover before following Adele. She knows what's coming next: the rumors about her husband; pointed discussions about the prevention of automotive catastrophe amongst the elderly; her imparting selective information to the right people to combat the scourge of gossip.

This is war. So knows Rose. She takes a deep breath and pushes down on the door handle.

IT BOTH COMFORTED and deflated Rose to see the Center looking exactly like its usual self. The main room, impervious to sunlight, hadn't received any makeovers since her last visit. It was all there: the white-tiled floor, fluorescent lighting, the small stage crowned by a large Israeli flag, the wall-to-wall decoration of members' artwork, and photographs of Jerusalem architecture and the beaches of Tel Aviv. Denise the cashier, whose bifocals did nothing for her vision, still occupied the gray card table and matching folding chair just inside the entrance. Three ownerless wheelchairs, their wheels rusty from disuse and neglect, remained in their ancient habitat in the corner of the main room closest to the kitchen. All else was in order: the long folding tables and metal chairs, the metal bookcases stuffed with both yellowed, tattered tomes by long dead authors and recently donated contemporary fiction and biographies, the bulletin boards full of information about doctors, social workers, holistic healthcare practitioners, geriatric yoga instructors, assisted living facilities, hospice programs, dentists specializing in dentures, and hairdressers specializing in illusion.

So many things Rose remembered as she looked around the Center. A place for friends and also, for enemies. For people somewhere in between, who turned their backs on her when it became clear she had no photographs to pull from her wallet like the rest of them. Even the ones whose children lived a million miles away and never came to visit considered themselves superior. *Poor Rose. She wouldn't understand.* They made such sentiments implicit in the trading of their pictures and complete neglect of all other conversation topics, with the exception maybe of the latest tragedy in Israel and assorted Center gossip. Who was fighting with whom, who was making eyes at whom? Who was too old and decrepit for this and that?

Sometimes, she and Morry ate lunch in the place without conversing with anyone. Granted, her Morry loved to argue the situation in Israel as much as the next person. But for her highly educated husband, there was conversation and then there was *conversation.* There was the conversation with the person who occasionally read the newspaper and voted for presidents based on whether or not they believed Israel should give a little something to the Palestinians in the name of world peace, otherwise known to them as appeasing the world. And there was the conversation with the person who knew every historical and political complication by heart and could quote everyone: the past presidents of the United States, Winston Churchill, Theodore Herzl, Z. Jabotinsky, Golda Meir, I.B. Singer, Anwar Sadat, Aaron Appelfeld, Amos Oz, Ecclesiastes, and everyone else under the sun.

Sometimes, Morry would suggest that they stay home and talk amongst themselves. Those were, quite often, the best days of all. Just him and her, sitting on their living room couch with glasses of lemon water between them. They would talk, talk, and then talk some more, each enlightening the other on their respective fields of expertise. It was during those sessions that Rose felt at her most grateful for who they were and nothing more, no matter that they had no grandchildren living next door.

"Two lunches please." Rose smiled at Denise, a woman maybe fifteen years her junior and one of the Center's most committed volunteers. Rose had always respected Denise, who may have been almost blind but possessed a particularly acute pair of eyes on the back of her head. Indeed, this Denise knew how to run a lunchroom better than anyone. Over the years, Rose had marveled at her knack for pinpointing the exact moment when someone tried to claim an extra meal without paying for it.

Denise took Rose's $2.50—lunch was $1.25 a person, what most Center members proudly referred to as the "best deal in town"—and gave a brusque nod. "Hello Rose. It's been a long time. You're looking well."

Rose squeezed the girl's elbow. "This is Nina." She almost added, a good friend, but instead allowed herself to imagine that she had brought in her long-lost granddaughter for all at the Center to witness.

"I was so sorry to hear about Morry. We all were."

Rose nodded her thanks and waited the usual several seconds or so for Denise to say something else. If she had learned anything at all in her ninety-three years, it was that people often needed to express an additional few words on the subject of death and bereavement. But Denise was not such a person. She simply waved them on with best wishes for a decent lunch.

Rose explained to the girl that they now went straight up to the kitchen window to retrieve their food. It used to be that everyone sat and received table service but budget cuts had reduced the labor pool in the kitchen. Those too frail to perform self-service, however, did receive assistance, which meant that this business of picking up your own plate had become a mark of pride. They collected such marks at the Center, so as to highlight them in conversation in the manner of younger people who boast of their careers or home ownership or any mountain climbing, jungle safari-type achievements. Other marks of pride included living in your own apartment and the ability to still drive the streets of Los Angeles.

They retrieved their lunches and only after they seated themselves at a mostly empty table did Rose venture to see who was there and where. No friends, as far as the eye could see, but no enemies either. In fact, the Center didn't seem too busy today and those in attendance were, for the most part, mere acquaintances.

But then the door to the ladies' room opened and out hobbled Adele Mandelbaum. Rose immediately felt her whole body stiffen. She dropped her fork and whispered, "That's her."

The girl put down her fork and Rose pointed toward the ladies' room, where they watched Adele retrieve the walker that she had placed as close as possible to the bathroom door. Rose had secretly—if grudgingly—always admired Adele's knack for never shrinking in the presence of assistive walking devices. The Mandelbaum woman somehow controlled her walker in a way that made her ankles seem less elephantine, her shoulders less stooped and in general, her entire body less endangered.

It didn't take long for Adele to notice them, though it took awhile for her to advance across the room, exactly as Rose expected: unsmiling, steely eyed, and militaristic in her mission. Finally, the Mandelbaum woman loomed over them, overwhelming in both sight and scent. Did the woman take baths in cheap lilac perfume?

"Hello Rose." Adele, one of the Center's leading crusaders against the wasting of food, eyed Rose's half-eaten salmon with equal parts suspicion and lust.

"Adele." Rose performed the most formal of nods. Had she been wearing a hat, she would have barely tipped it and nothing more. Anything to prevent Adele from knowing how her heart pounded and skin prickled, as if grazed over by the lips of ghosts.

"I'm sorry I missed the funeral. I was very sick that day. Did you get my card?"

"Yes I did. That was very kind." Rose cleared her throat a few times for added effect. They both knew that she had used the wrong adjective to describe Adele's condolence card.

"May I?" Adele gestured to the empty seat next to the girl. And who are you?"

"Nina. I'm a friend." The girl extended her hand but Adele, busy with the transition from standing to sitting, ignored the gesture.

Rose felt both sad and relieved to hear the girl tell the simple truth.

"How nice," Adele said, pointedly addressing the girl. "Do you live around here?"

The girl nodded and one question led to another. To be fair, Rose learned new and admirable tidbits about the girl's life thanks to Adele's efforts. She didn't know, for example, that the girl recently lost a few of her regular public classes but she still sometimes led as many as fifteen classes a week due to substitute teaching. And she was happy to hear that her private clients paid her well. What a great subject to linger over! Rose opened her mouth to start praising the girl's work ethic. But she was too late.

"So," Adele said. "Are you married?"

"No," the girl said.

"Oh." Adele nodded conspiratorially. "Divorced then."

"No."

"Oh. So no children?"

"No children." The girl paused, looking as if she wanted to say something else. "That reminds me," she said to Rose. "You know those cats I'm feeding? Well, one of them has started to—"

Adele interrupted with a little show of tongue clucking and hand wringing and Rose steeled herself for the next maneuver. "I might know some nice young men for you, through my grandchildren. How old are you?"

Rose held her breath and watched the girl hesitate. She was no dummy, that girl. "I'm thirty-six."

Adele tsk-tsked. "Well, if you want to have children, then don't you think you better get started immediately?"

The girl blushed. "Yes. It's true. I don't have much time."

Rose forced herself to make eye contact with Adele. "She has plenty of time."

"No, she doesn't," Adele said. "At this point it could be a matter of luck for her. Or she could turn out like you."

"I should only be so lucky." The girl's voice trembled.

Adele looked at the girl, then at Rose, then back at the girl, and tsk-tsked again. "What's the problem? Are you not meeting any men? At your age, you can't afford to be so picky."

Man plans and God laughs. Rose sighed. It was time for damage control. "If you don't mind, we'd like to finish eating our lunch in peace."

Adele pursed her lips into a scrunched up and miserly little smile. "One more thing, Rose. You didn't by chance catch the article in the *Times* the other day? About the law they want to pass to make sure that people over seventy take the extra driving and vision tests? After those awful murders in Santa Monica, it's about time people did something, don't you think? Surely you followed that terrible story? It was all over the news. How that man just plunged into the farmers market, hitting all those people buying vegetables. Terrible. Just terrible.

Did you know they found him guilty, even though he's ninety-one and uses a wheelchair and—"

The girl stood up and pushed her chair toward the table with excess force. "Rose lost her husband. Don't you think that's enough?"

"You think she's special?" Adele's breath started to sound heavy and labored. "Everyone in this place, we're all in the same boat. So no, I don't think she's special. Not only that, she was supposed to be responsible for—"

"He was a good man." Rose could hear the begging, pleading tone of her voice.

"Sure he was. Until he lost his marbles. Just like your friend Lillian."

Rose froze. Lillian had trouble with her name the last time she telephoned. She kept saying, "it's Rose," and Lillian had kept saying, "who?"

"I pity you Rose, I really do. But it doesn't excuse how you failed to—"

"You know why Rose is special? Because she's also had a lot of death in her life and she's still a nice person. If you'll excuse me."

They watched the girl walk fast and straight across the room toward the bathroom like a perfectly lobbed arrow and it struck Rose how almost no one at the Center ever moved like that. "It wasn't you that Morry ran over." Rose took great care to maintain the how's-the-weather tone of her voice. "It was her fiancé." Rose took one look at Adele's widened eyes and lips so pursed you almost couldn't see them and knew with great certainty that she had to start the evacuation process without the girl's assistance. Fortunately, her cane was hooked just so on the back of her folding chair.

"Why would she . . . ?" Rose couldn't make out Adele's last words as she made her way toward the entrance. She stopped to catch her breath every few seconds but resisted the temptation to look back.

Safely at the entrance, Rose waited for the girl. This didn't take very long, as no one likes to spend all day in the Center's ladies' room unless it's absolutely necessary. Rose noticed that the girl had not even bothered to dry her hands after washing them.

They didn't speak for several blocks as they inched their way down the boardwalk in the direction of Rose's apartment. It had been Rose's idea, to walk to the Center today with only her cane and the girl's hand on her elbow for support so as to mentally prepare herself through physical exertion. As a dancer, she had always warmed up before a performance, hadn't she? But she hadn't anticipated the hardship of walking home and how exhausted she might feel each time she took a single step.

The girl finally broke their silence. "You were brave to face her."

"People like her." Rose couldn't finish the thought.

"They make it worse."

"I'm sorry, dear. For what she said to you."

"It's okay. Who's Lillian?"

"A dear friend. I think I told you once about her daughter. Lillian is now in a home."

"I'm sorry to hear that."

They had paused in front of one of the more upscale clothing establishments on the boardwalk, a store that sold cocktail dresses with only mildly offensive lengths and blouses and skirts for possible office wear. Rose noticed how the girl clenched her jaw and blinked excessively as they looked at one another. "Dear. Please. Tell me what's been bothering you."

"That niece you have in Chicago, do you ever think to call her?"

"Not so much." Rose could feel her heart start to race.

"But she's family, isn't she? A blood relative?"

"Yes, but we're not very close. I told you that." Rose could hear her voice crack on the "that" and felt a slight trembling in her legs. Would she be able to manage the rest of the walk home?

"Well, what about Carla? She's sort of related to you and I know she wants to get to know you better. Maybe you should give her a chance." The girl took a deep breath and Rose could see how she struggled to collect her thoughts. "I guess I'm asking if . . . is there anyone else that you could rely on for . . . things? Because right now, I'm . . ."

"I understand." Rose backed up several steps so that the girl could no longer touch her elbow. "I'm sorry if I have been a burden to you."

"No, that's not what I'm saying." The girl looked as if she might burst into tears. "I'm only trying to make sure that you have other people in your life that you can call if for some reason I can't—"

"You don't have to keep explaining." Rose looked at the ground, at a complete loss for what to say or do. Home was still several long blocks away. *Nu Rose? To think you haven't even told her the most important part.*

But then Rose had to ask, "Is it because of Morry? Because of what he did?"

The girl shook her head. "I promise you, it's not that. Whatever you think you did, no one is to blame."

"That's not exactly true."

"What do you mean?"

Tell her. Now that there's nothing left to lose.

Rose gripped her cane with both hands and noticed that the trembling in her legs had gotten more pronounced. "I'm very tired right now. I better get home." She had to stop herself from using the word "dear" as she spoke.

"Okay." The girl advanced so she could offer her elbow in the manner that had grown customary between them.

Rose took one risky backwards step. "I'll be all right from here."

The girl froze, her elbow still within distance for Rose to grasp. "Please? Can I walk you home?"

Rose could see the concern and hurt commingling on the girl's face. Who was this girl to her really, that she should feel this betrayed? Plus she knew that it was absolutely foolish to decline walking-home assistance when her legs trembled like this.

But at the moment, she couldn't afford to make any more concessions to her age.

"I'm sorry." Rose turned her back on the girl and resumed her journey down the boardwalk. It didn't take the brains of a genius to surmise that the girl trailed behind her from a safe yet approachable distance, ready to assist if necessary. But Rose determined not to look back. She needed to focus on taking one arthritic step forward, then another, without colliding into others. *Make it home alive.* Only for what? So she could come up with a new plan? Should she stop trying to shoo away the Man from Television and his terrible Yiddish? Or maybe visit the library and try to view that self-help section from a less farkakte angle? *How to die with dignity when you have no one in ten easy steps.*

Oy, thought Rose to all of it.

Without ever once looking back, Rose walked home, convinced that she would spend her remaining days alone, until someone called her landlord about the smell.

Fifteen

NINA WALKED INTO the Townhouse and ordered an extra strong Moscow Mule at the bar before peering into the room with the red-tinged chandelier lighting, shiny black leather booths, low ceilings, walls tricked out with foliage-themed wallpaper, and sepia photographs of bartenders wearing bowler hats and bow ties. Immediately, she spotted Carla in animated conversation with a blond woman and dark-haired man. That must be them: Jasmine and Asher, who had kindly agreed to speak with Nina and in her neck-of-the-woods no less, though apparently the couple resided in nearby Santa Monica and lived for excuses to hang out at their favorite bar and nearly one hundred-year-old Venice historic landmark.

Nina stood there sipping her cocktail until Carla noticed her and waved. "Hey!" Carla flashed an enormous smile as she made the introductions. "Nina, meet Jasmine and Asher. Jasmine and Asher, meet Nina."

You love this sort of thing, don't you? Nina shook hands with Jasmine and Asher and took a seat next to Carla. "I have some people for you to meet." Carla had called with this information two weeks after Lola's party. After explaining Jasmine and Asher, she had asked, "Is it okay if I come too?"

Nina thought about it for a few seconds before saying "sure, why not?" Did it really matter if Carla had ulterior motives? And now, she realized that the sight of Carla felt somewhat calming. Of all the entities present at this little conclave, Carla was the most known.

Carla held up her cocktail and clinked glasses with Nina. "Cheers. How's our friend Rose these days?"

"She's fine." Nina took a hearty gulp of her Moscow Mule. She couldn't help herself, resenting Carla for describing Rose as a "friend."

"I think she may meet me for coffee soon. Each time I call she's a little friendlier."

"That's nice." Did Carla hear the sharpness in her voice? Nina kept drinking, listening to Carla relay her last conversation with Rose and trying to suppress her hostility, which she already knew was a cover for a much more difficult emotion. Since the day she went with Rose to the senior center, she repeatedly found herself without any apparent triggers struck by the deepest kind of shame; the kind born from undeserved relief. Her thoughts felt terrible yet true: that someone else could do for Rose the things that would inevitably need to get done, things she would have to do one day for her mother or father or who knows, a spouse. Did she really need the practice right now, at a time when she could barely be there for herself?

"Have you seen Rose recently?"

Nina shook her head. "How's your husband?"

"He says hi. He wanted me to tell you that you need to return the cat traps in another two weeks."

Nina nodded, feeling her face flush. Thank goodness for dark bars.

She smiled at Jasmine and Asher, who smiled back at her with the kind of wary anxiety that reminded her of the way she regarded certain homeless people in her neighborhood or basically anyone exuding the type of unpredictability that could cause all kinds of trouble. They were a striking couple: Jasmine had long blond hair, pale skin, and the long thin arms of a ballerina. Asher had a more olive complexion and while Nina couldn't make out the exact color of his eyes, she noticed their upturned shape and thought of Laz. He had texted her two days ago with his usual breeziness. *How are you? Would love to see you soon.* His message had activated an old and familiar anger that could not be placated by deep breaths and therapeutic movement. She could only pace her apartment with clenched fists and tell herself that one day, she would feel ready to face him.

"We're so sorry for your loss." Asher reached out across the table to touch her on the forearm.

"Thank you." She picked up her glass with both hands and held it close to her chest. She knew that Asher meant no harm but she didn't want him to touch her anywhere.

"So . . ." Carla cleared her throat. "I had explained to Nina that you guys met Jeff at one of our events. It was the one at that club on Cahuenga, right?"

Asher and Jasmine nodded. Yes, they had been sitting on a couch in one of the club's lounges and noticed the guy looking uncomfortable on the armchair across from them. They struck up a conversation to be friendly and wound up hitting it off.

"I'm also a social worker and therapist," Jasmine said, and pointed at Asher. "And they got into a discussion about being vegetarian. We were chatting for at least an hour. And then . . ." She glanced at Carla.

"You should tell her everything," Carla said.

Nina took two gulps of her extra strong cocktail. "It's okay. Whatever you have to say, I want to hear it."

Jasmine and Asher exchanged another glance. "Like I said, we were really hitting it off and then Jeff started asking us questions about our relationship. Were we polyamorous and what did that mean for us? I told him that Asher and I date other people, but for us, a healthy relationship means that we're each other's primaries. I remember explaining to him that it's not always like that and in some poly arrangements there are no primaries or secondaries. Anyway, then we told him that we're also open to threesomes."

Of course you did. A tiny light bulb switched on in Nina's brain while Jasmine paused to drink.

"So, then we talked about that for a while and then . . . we told him that it turns us both on to watch each other get off with someone else. And Jeff was . . . . really interested in that."

"When was this, this . . . party?"

"Last summer. Maybe August?"

It took Nina a second to do the math. Jeff had presented her with his Ten Commandments last August.

"Anyway, we all kept drinking and talking and we could tell that Jeff was attracted to me. So, I said, 'do you want to kiss me? Because you can, as long as you're cool with Asher watching.' And then we were making out . . . for a while."

Nina could only stare at Jasmine and fixate on her blond-haired prettiness.

"I'm sorry if I'm making you uncomfortable." Jasmine looked genuinely concerned.

"It's okay." Nina took a deep breath. She did feel uncomfortable but she also wanted to know everything.

"Well . . . we were only kissing and then I felt his hand on my breast and I asked him if he wanted to come to our house. He said yes, but maybe a second after that, he pulled away. He said he was a horrible person for doing this, that he had a fiancée but that they were having problems. He didn't want to say what kind of problems at first, so we just bought him another drink and sat with him while he calmed down. He was really upset by what he did and kept apologizing to us for not mentioning he had a fiancée. And then he told us that he knew his fiancée was in love with another man and that's why he started coming to our meet-ups. He wanted to know if he had it in him to share the woman he loved with someone else. Because he didn't think he could but he wanted to at least try."

"It seemed like he really cared about your relationship. You could tell by the way he talked about you," Asher said.

"Yeah," Jasmine said. "It seemed like he was really trying to figure some stuff out. But allowing someone you love to love others . . . sharing them that way . . . speaking from experience . . . some people can and some people can't."

"Actually, I would say most people can't," Carla said, her voice edgy and slightly acidic. "Our society and our conditioning from the time we're children make it almost impossible. Though the irony is as children, we're taught to share, aren't we?"

Jasmine and Asher exchanged yet another meaningful glance and Nina could only nod at them, unable to process any of it. She both knew and didn't know the man in their story but really, was that anything new?

She waited for Jasmine and Asher to say something else. But they didn't, so Carla offered to buy them all a round of drinks. Nina stood up to let her out of the booth. It surprised her, to feel nothing at the moment but gratitude.

"Thank you," she whispered.

Carla smiled. "Knowledge is power."

Nina could only finish her drink, seized by a profound déjà vu.

TWO WEEKS LATER: Nina woke up on a Sunday morning, no longer able to ignore the daily reprimands of the dormant cat traps in her living room. *What are we here for anyway? Just so you can transfer that tarnished brass dancing bear menorah and fading R.B. Kitaj print and torn-up ballet slippers and yellowed photographs of (distant?) Israeli relatives posing in front of the Tel Aviv Sheraton from there to us? We're in the cat business lady. We trap cats.*

And those cats had grown tamer. Garfield and Angie now rubbed against her legs on a regular basis and she had actually scratched the notoriously recalcitrant Splotchy Two behind the ears. Garfield now paid her daily visits inside her apartment, where he sniffed the edges of his potential future dens of terror with a bland curiosity before moving onto the inspection of other items of furniture and assorted, unidentified crumbs on the floor. Once, Garfield had even spent the night and woke her up at five in the morning with a well-placed claw on her nose. She could have trapped the cat then without the assistance of the canned sardines in tomato sauce. Only she didn't.

Nina drank a cup of coffee and called Jon for help. He sounded happy to hear from her. "Those traps are due back so I was actually going to check up on you."

She confessed that she didn't have the heart to trap the cats though she knew it was for their own good and explained that Angie and Garfield in particular had become semi-domesticated. Jon listened carefully to her dilemma, asked a few questions in a calm, professional, family doctor-type voice, and suggested that for the time being, she focus on fixing the two tamer cats. If she could pick them up and place them in cat carriers, she could take them to the vet in house cat fashion, which would probably put her more psychologically at ease. He could lend her two carriers and accompany her to the vet, if she wanted.

"That's very kind of you but I don't want to be a bother." She pictured him in Lola's kitchen, in his long-sleeved T-shirt that covered his tattoos.

"It's no trouble," Jon said. "Happy to provide moral support."

They spent the next several minutes concocting a comprehensive strategy to her cat problem. Afterward, she thanked him again.

"My pleasure," he said. "I'm really just here to help. When you get the appointment with the vet, let me know."

She didn't know what to say, though she sensed that his kindness came from the most genuine of places. Jeff used to excel at this shade of kindness, always willing to help people he barely knew with tasks that overwhelmed them. What would Jeff think of her now, the aspiring Mother Teresa of the feral cats? Would he say: My, how you've changed. Or: I would expect nothing less.

It was one of the worst parts, this not knowing what Jeff felt about them during his last moments. It ranked up there with the knowledge of Jeff not knowing he was in fact living his last moments. And what had sparked him to text her that day? Was that before he went to Ralph's? Or had he been thinking about her inside that grocery store, perhaps passing by her favorite boxes of cereal or the Skinny Cow ice cream sandwiches, and thinking: Nina loves those. How is she doing? Maybe I should get in touch.

He could have told her that he was going to those parties. He could have told her that he had kissed another woman. They never shared that potentially watershed moment where she could have told him just how much she understood. In the end, they had been nothing more than partners in a botched trade. A test for a test.

"Nina, you there?" Jon's voice sounded loud and clear, as if addressing a crowd of the hearing impaired.

"Okay," she said. "Let's do this."

THREE DAYS LATER, Jon called her at exactly seven-thirty in the morning to inform her he was across the street, waiting in his car. "You've got some kitties on your stoop. The clock is ticking."

"Thanks," she said. "For being on time."

"I'm always on time," he said. "It's one of those things people find out about me sooner or later."

Nina smiled. Anytime she experienced another person's punctuality, she inevitably thought about all the occasions she waited for Laz to show up. Jeff, on the other hand, had always been scrupulously punctual but Nina now understood that there were other ways in which one human being waited for another human being to show up.

She took a deep breath and opened her front door.

THEY BARELY SPOKE during the twenty-minute drive to the vet, their silence and what Nina still refused to label as sexual tension both subsumed by the almost non-stop wailing of the cats. Nina couldn't believe that she had managed the dirty deed, whisking Angie, then Garfield, into the carriers. When they arrived at the vet, Jon sat with the still wailing cats while she filled out the forms. The woman at the front desk asked if she also wanted all the shots, the checking for worms, and the flea control. Nina said yes to everything immediately. Nothing was too good for her babies.

Well, if you want to have children, then don't you think you better get started immediately?

It still floated in her brain, this not-so-innocent question. She had succumbed to an almost vertiginous sensation of powerlessness after that woman from Rose's senior center had asked It. *Oh Rose, I see exactly what you mean about this Adele person!* She had tried to express this several times to Rose during their now quick and awkward phone conversations. Rose was always polite to her, but removed and formal and too busy now to meet for lunch. She would hang up after these conversations, guilt-ridden but clearly not guilt-ridden enough to overcome her failure to explain herself. She would resort instead to addressing the Adele in her mind. *Well Adele, that's a great question because the truth is I don't know if I want to have children, though I would like to parent some cats and, if you must know, I still haven't gotten my period yet from an unwanted sexual encounter with a man who keeps calling and texting me, as if nothing has happened.*

"Ma'am? We need your signature."

Nina forced herself to finish with the forms. Then a vet tech came out and Jon handed over the carriers. The vet tech said they'd call when the cats were ready for pick-up.

She could feel the silence between them growing heavier and more awkward as they left the clinic and returned to his car. But walking next to him still produced the same giddy sensation that she could not ignore. She determined to avoid any accidental hand brushing or other physical contact. *And do we talk about how your wife wants us to hit it off?* After Jasmine and Asher had left the bar that night, she and Carla had lingered there for another hour, their conversation centered on the pros and cons of polyamory and laced with the not-so-subtle refrain: He's a good man, you should consider it when you're ready to move on, and fuck what mainstream society might think.

"Do you want to get some coffee?" Jon turned on the ignition and started backing out of the parking lot. "Something non-Starbucks, perhaps?"

"Non-Starbucks sounds great."

He took her to a fiercely independent coffee shop a few blocks away, the kind of establishment that displayed the artwork of neighborhood residents, had a bulletin board jam-packed with yoga studio schedules, fliers for multi-media, avant-garde theater productions, and holistic health care treatments, and where people still read print newspapers and felt no shame in lingering over them for hours. They both ordered medium lattes and she insisted on paying. Jon allowed the small effort at reciprocation to transpire with minimal protest and thanked her when she paid the cashier. They found a table by one of the windows that faced the street and she quickly steered the conversation back to the cats. Jon thought she had a shot at fully socializing Garfield. He suggested that instead of releasing the cat outside after he recovered from surgery, she could keep him inside. He recommended that she put a tarp on her floor and cover her furniture. "Prepare for accidents," he warned.

"What if they don't forgive me?" she asked.

"They'll be pissed off at first but they'll forgive you. Cats are like people."

"Right. Time heals all wounds."

Jon just stared at her and she knew that he had heard the edge in her voice.

She tried to revert back to their carefully cultivated vibe of two acquaintances with a shared mission of animal rescue. "Anyway, I really am grateful for your help with all this. I guess there was no way I was going to manage it on my own."

"Well . . . I'm glad you reached out."

They sipped their coffee in silence and Nina tried to put her thoughts in order.

I like you but I'm not going to date you and what's really up with you and your wife and I could really use a new friend right now because the person I was hanging out with the most these days seems to be profoundly pissed off at me and I don't blame her.

"So . . . " Nina tried to say something, anything to break the silence.

"Do you remember what we were talking about at the party, before we got interrupted?"

"Ummm . . . something about Jews and tattoos?"

"Right." Jon smiled for a second before turning completely serious. "I had told you I could tell that you were having a hard time and I think that's because I'm having a hard time myself."

"Oh. I'm sorry."

"Yeah. Look, Carla told me what she said to you at Lola's party and the other night you met up with her and that's all true but . . . let's just say she and I are starting to evolve in different directions."

"Oh."

"Yeah. Carla's been in a lot of pain these last few years and not only because her mom died. I think she might still be processing stuff about her dad, who died before I met her. Carla always described him as being a major douchebag when it came to women. When we first started dating, she gave me this whole spiel about why monogamy doesn't work and how she was never going to have the relationship of lies and fucked-up game playing that her parents had. She was very clear about all this, it was like a philosophy for her, or a religion. We had an open relationship from the beginning and at first, I was like, 'bring it on.' That's what I'm supposed to think, right? Because I'm a guy."

Don't you think it sounds brilliant in theory?

"I think I know what you mean," she said.

"Don't get me wrong, I don't think monogamy is a natural state for most humans and I've appreciated the freedom I have in my marriage, but I've also learned I'm not cut out for juggling more than one intimate relationship at a time. It takes a lot of time and energy to do things right and these past few years I've been . . . exhausted."

"Your wife seems to think it's worth it."

"Yeah . . . you two talked all about it I heard."

"I asked some questions."

Jon smiled. "One thing I know about Carla is that she'll never agree to a monogamous relationship. Which means I have some thinking to do. Also . . . I don't think she told you all of it."

Nina shrugged and waited.

"She's in love with someone else and while she insists he's strictly secondary material, she's been spending more time with him than how we usually do things and . . . well, that's why she wants us to hit it off, to . . . level the playing field. It makes her uncomfortable that I'm currently not with anyone else."

"Ahhh."

"She means well Carla, she always has. It's just . . ."

Nina tried to give Jon all the space he needed to not finish his thought.

An hour proceeded to fly by as they sat nursing their coffees, waiting for the vet's office to call. After Jon confessed his deep unhappiness with the current state of his marriage, Nina told him that she and Jeff were dealing with serious intimacy issues in the months before his death, which got complicated when someone from her past moved to town. She spoke about her relationship with Rose, how their friendship had been a blessing but had recently grown more complicated. Other things she kept to herself, such as her preoccupation with his tattoos or how she didn't fully trust Carla's ongoing overtures toward Rose or how it took forever for the greenish-black bruises that she incurred on her left thigh on the night she fell off her couch to fade completely.

"I guess you never met Jeff at those parties?" she asked, or rather, confirmed.

Jon shook his head. "He never told you about any of it, did he?"

"No. I assume that Carla told you what Jasmine and Asher had to say?"

"She did."

Nina stared at Jon, struck by how comfortable she felt around him, despite the simultaneous giddy-nervy-burning sensation in the pit of her stomach. Had she not felt this way with Jeff at the beginning? "Morally, it always felt like Jeff had the upper hand. He was that type. I guess he knew that about himself and didn't want either one of us to think otherwise."

He grabbed her hand and gave it a brief squeeze and she tried not to read anything into the gesture except for the intended kindness.

"It's been hard since he died, to remember everything about him. I mean, all of what . . . happened."

He gave her hand another brief squeeze and she felt the familiar heat flush her face. "I'm going through this thing." Again, she heard herself expelling words that she had no intention of expressing. "Where I want to cry whenever someone is nice to me."

"Like you don't deserve people being nice to you?"

She shrugged.

He grabbed her hand again and she felt the warmth of his skin and the strength of his grip. "That's bullshit."

She felt nothing but relief at the interruption of her ringing phone. It was the vet's office: the cats were out of surgery. She could pick them up in another half hour. She hung up, relayed the information to Jon, and they sat there in silence with their two empty coffee cups between them until she remembered what she had wanted to ask him at the party before they got interrupted. "So why do you love Burning Man so much?"

He told her that he had discovered just about every important personal truth at the festival, including his realization that he had been unhappy in his marriage. In fact, at Burning Man last year, he had written Carla a practice goodbye letter and placed it in the temple. He explained that this temple gets built every year at the festival and it's a place where people can leave all the sentiments and attachments they want to discard. And then, on the last day of the festival, there is a temple burning ceremony and it's the opposite of watching the Man Burn. When the Man Burns, everyone's yelling and screaming and tripping and dancing to the beats of hundreds of drummers or to the EDM that the DJs are spinning from the art cars. It's an utter cacophony of sound. But when the temple burns, everyone is sitting in complete silence.

"It's a kind of collective goodbye, where everyone around you is letting go of someone or something. I know some people think Burning Man is just some hedonistic sex and drug fest and maybe for some people it is. And sure, maybe it's losing some of its edge, or getting more commercial or whatever. But for me, it's always a kind of . . . pilgrimage." Jon paused, his smile small and internal.

She nodded and told him about these experiences she'd been having teaching her yoga classes, how these Hebrew prayers she had learned as a child have resurfaced in her mind whenever she starts chanting Sanskrit mantras. "I feel like a part of myself is sending me a message but I don't know what to make of it."

She tried not to blush as Jon studied her face in silence.

"You know that rabbi I mentioned to you at the party?" he finally asked. "In her services, she incorporates a lot of Eastern teachings and practices and I know she does these one-on-one-consultations with people. I can put you in touch if you're interested."

She nodded and promised to think about it. Since Jeff's passing, she had developed a resistance to forms of therapy other than yoga. Only once, a few days after the incident with Laz, had she attempted to research therapists who took her insurance but the effort had left her exhausted and angry. *Why am I the one that fucking has to pay for therapy?*

"Clearly, I need some help," she said.

Jon smiled. "Join the fucking club."

Sixteen

ROSE COULDN'T BELIEVE it. Was that him, skating in circles around a beleaguered trio of Amazonian blond women, all clad in white sneakers and matching running shorts, toting enormous shopping bags and sporting tiny cameras strapped to their wrists?

Rose had spotted the skateboarder from a block away as she sat on a bench across the street from the 19th Street tennis courts, directly in front of the Argentine empanada shop. Since her vision wasn't what it used to be, she squinted and squinted some more just to be sure. Hadn't the girl said something about the police arresting him? Go figure. Clearly, the boy was not in prison.

She heard the boy yelling at the women as she watched him glide toward her. He traveled in S-curves and wove through the boardwalk traffic like a lone predatory fish darting in and out of other unsuspecting schools. He seemed to move in sync with the ping-pong rhythms of lobbed tennis balls but that might have simply been an outgrowth of Rose's penchant for seeing choreography absolutely everywhere and in the most undeserving of moments.

As hard as she could, Rose gripped the handles of her walker and raised herself to standing just as the boy neared the empanada stand. He wore a red hooded sweatshirt and baggy black jeans and cast an enormous shadow on the pavement in front of him.

Rose closed her eyes to better prepare for this Angel of Death, who did not resemble any of the illustrations in that Maxwell House Passover Haggadah. Morry had never cared for this Haggadah but you could get them for free at the supermarket and so that's what they used for their Passover Seders. In this Haggadah, the Angel of Death looked exactly how you might expect: a skull for a face, black robes for clothing, a scythe for a weapon, and God's name on his tongue just in case anyone had the nerve to check his credentials. This Angel of Death loomed large inside Rose, mocking each and every one of her efforts to defy him.

Rose opened her eyes. The boy stood directly in front of her, with one foot on the ground and the other on his skateboard. He stared at her for what felt like a very long time and she forced herself to look up and directly into his eyes. They were light blue and quite pretty. Sky eyes. Ocean eyes. Nazi eyes. How to look into them? Rose didn't know, except to keep looking.

"You," the boy finally said, shaking his head.

Rose nodded and remained both standing and ready.

Only the boy made a lunging motion and brought his grounded foot back on his skateboard. In seconds, he existed a block away from Rose but in the other direction. Rose watched him become a red dot in the distance, a quivering bloodspot on an otherwise perfect egg.

It's harder than it looks bubbeleh.

So, what do you suggest I do? Now this was a first, Rose asking the Man from Television for help even though she knew he didn't work that way. And when he didn't answer, she resolved to do what she had thus far resisted.

FIFTEEN MINUTES LATER: Rose stood in front of Tarot and Dream Interpretation by Lucinda and eyeballed the middle-aged woman with long, straight black hair and enormous pink-rimmed, heart-shaped sunglasses with purple lenses. This woman, presumably Lucinda, sat at a card table under a pink and green striped umbrella. She smiled at Rose and beckoned her to sit in her spare pink and green striped beach chair.

"I've seen you before."

"Have you?" Rose hesitated. Was she supposed to shop for a Tarot Card Lady with the same rigor that she applied to selecting cucumbers and apples or searching for clothes that not only fit but flattered?

"I'm always people watching when I'm not working. I used to see you with this lovely gentleman. Is he your husband?"

Rose stared at this Lucinda person, so far unimpressed. Was it not this woman's job to know such things? Rose really didn't know anything about tarot card ladies, only that they had been beckoning to her for years and she, in turn, had been fending them off.

"He passed."

"Oh," Lucinda said. "I'm so sorry."

Rose sighed. "I've never done this before."

Lucinda beckoned to her beach chair. "Maybe I can help."

Rose took a deep breath and began the process of sitting down.

"It's pay what you can afford." Lucinda took off her sunglasses and her dark brown eyes reminded Rose of the girl. With two glossy black fingernails, she tapped on her deck of tarot cards like a novice trying to play the piano.

Rose offered ten dollars for a half hour and Lucinda nodded, noting she believed in senior citizens' discounts. She proceeded to shuffle and lay out the cards on the table and Rose took out her magnifying glass for a closer inspection. Such pictures of strange and gorgeous people! Wizard types in flowing white and silver robes; regal queens dressed in royal purples and blues; armored horsemen carrying ancient and undecipherable flags. The figures reminded Rose of the illustrations in the book of fairy tales she had as a child. It was the only secular book her mother allowed them to keep in the house. How she used to read that book over and over and from cover to cover.

Meanwhile, Lucinda kept nodding and muttering unintelligible sounds that, to Rose, sounded less like a big mystery and more like indigestion. Lucinda finally mumbled something about a cross and immediately, Rose got nervous. What did she need a cross for? Intimidated by her ignorance of the etiquette, she refrained from asking Lucinda for clarification. After all, did she interrupt the rabbi in the middle of his Rosh Hashanah sermon to let him know she didn't understand a single thing he'd been talking about for the last forty-five minutes?

"The empress card." Lucinda pointed to a card with a beautiful, golden-haired woman wearing a sparkling white crown. "You have led a long life."

Poof went Rose's intimidation.

But then Lucinda said, "The cards say that you never had children. And right now, you are not at peace. You miss your husband very much. You also have unfinished business that you must complete before it's too late."

Rose's heart started to race as Lucinda pointed to the card with the armored horseman holding up the strange flag. This was the death card, she explained and again, Rose wanted to tell this Lucinda that she had not paid her ten dollars just so she could state the obvious. Was this woman good at her job or not?

And then Lucinda said, "The death card doesn't have to mean death. It can signify re-birth or undergoing some kind of significant transformation. Let me ask you something. Have you done anything recently that led you to have regret?"

"Yes." Rose experienced a sudden and vicious yearning for her husband. Morry knew what was true about them both without having to consult anyone. If she could speak to him now, what would he tell her to do about the girl? *Did you see what I did that day, the way I walked off in a huff, so consumed by the kind of pride that blinds? Who does that remind you of?*

"Yes," Rose said. "I committed a crime. Do you know this?"

Rose held her breath while Lucinda put back on her enormous sunglasses and pondered the question. "The cards don't say anything about a crime."

Rose shook her head. "My husband killed someone driving. He died too. I let him get in the car."

Lucinda gathered up the cards and made a big show of shuffling the deck. "He was going to get in the car anyway, wasn't he?"

"You're not reading your cards."

Lucinda stopped shuffling the deck and put her hand on Rose's forearm. "I'm very sorry for your loss."

"I wish I could talk to him," Rose heard herself say. "I want to know if he knew what he was doing."

Lucinda kept her hand on Rose's forearm. "This might sound funny, considering what I do for a living, but don't believe people who say they can talk to the dead. If I were you, I'd focus on—"

Rose held up her hand to interrupt. She already heard what she needed to hear: she was running out of time.

FIRST THINGS FIRST: Rose chose to return to the Center on a Friday since that was the other day Adele never missed if she could help it. In the old days, when the Center had elaborate Oneg Shabbat services, Adele loved to be the star of the show. If the Center director told her to give it a rest and let someone else light the candles for a change, then Adele would insist on singing a song or reciting a poem. The Mandelbaum woman even loved the Friday food—a piece of boiled or roast chicken, usually dark meat, served with mashed potatoes and green beans, very little flavor to any of it. But to be fair, Rose's dear friend Lillian Rabinowitz had also lived for the Friday lunch as the food reminded her of her childhood in Queens. Personally, Rose felt fortunate that her childhood did not take place in Queens, though it certainly would have been safer. Because even now, she could still taste the food her mother used to make for Shabbes. Her favorite was a stew with chicken, potatoes, and carrots. Her mother baked her own challah and the smell of it cooling on the counter on a Friday morning would trap itself in her nostrils for the entire day. What Rose remembered most about her mother was the gentle slope of her back as she leaned into the kitchen stove, stirring one pot and tasting from another.

She arrived precisely at noon and as usual, Denise held court at the cashier's card table. She took Rose's $1.25 and whispered, "The other day. I heard the whole thing. A pox on her mother's grave."

Rose merely nodded, as she had nothing against Adele's mother. But on the other hand, maybe Adele's mother wasn't so innocent.

She retrieved her lunch from the new lady at the kitchen window and spotted Adele lunching with three other women. Rose knew them as acquaintances, nothing more. She found a place to sit on the opposite side of the room from them and noted the Center wasn't very busy for a Friday. She longed for the company of her dear friend Lillian, who had been especially unwell these past weeks. Rose had called Lillian's daughter a few days ago to see if she might pay Lillian a visit but her daughter didn't think that was a good idea. "I'll let you know when she's better," she told Rose, who didn't believe her.

Rose didn't know the four women sitting at her table. They were new to the Center, yet another generation of seniors born and bred in America, who had never set foot in Eastern Europe but enthusiastically embraced the "Intro to Yiddish" classes occasionally offered and identified with the building's mural more than she ever would. They nodded hello to Rose and resumed their conversation.

The chicken tasted as expected, neither Rose's worst culinary nightmare nor anything even remotely resembling her mother's cooking. She ate maybe half the plate, before wiping her lips with care and deciding on a straightforward and frontal strategy. Let the Mandelbaum woman see her coming.

As Rose advanced, she saw how Adele talked incessantly to her friends while tracking her progress across the room with the precision of a hawk. The acuteness of Adele's eyes had not diminished with age and now it put Rose face to face with her lack of umbilical relations. The incident with the girl had forced her to accept that she had no one to protect her at the end of her life, no one to assist her in the making of final decisions because it was their birthright. Was that why she had lived so long? But what about the people she knew who wound up in the homes with nothing to show for it except photographs of their absent children gracing their otherwise medication-cluttered nightstands?

Rose looked at Adele looking at her and thought of all the times the woman bragged about her three children and seven grandchildren. Did they ever come to visit her? A clearer source of misery you couldn't pinpoint when trying to figure out the whys and wherefores of a woman like Adele Mandelbaum.

Nu Rose? The girl still wants to visit you. She still calls, even though you're mad at her.

Finally, Rose arrived at Adele's table. Leaning extra hard on her walker for support, she proceeded to say something other than she had intended. "My friend was a guest of the Center. You did not make her feel welcome."

With her mouth still full of food, Adele pointed at Rose and started to choke. After one of her friends patted her on the back, she managed to swallow some water. The other two friends did their best to avoid eye contact with Rose. After several rounds of coughing and gasping, Adele cleared her throat. "I was merely being friendly. Poor thing, to be single at her age."

"What do you know from people her age?" *Or articles in the newspaper about senior drivers? Or how for forty-two years, Morry gave generously to charity and read and wrote like a scholar even after he retired and presented me with a dozen roses on every wedding anniversary and took me to our favorite fish restaurant every year on my birthday?* Standing in front of the enemy, Rose realized how completely bereft she was of any serious strategy.

"My children were much younger than her when they started giving me grandchildren." Adele took special care to enunciate the word "grandchildren" and the effort caused flecks of saliva to dribble down the corners of her mouth.

"That's very nice. I'm sure they come to visit you often."

"All the time." Adele's lips, still in their perpetual smirk, nonetheless wilted ever so slightly.

"A shame you've never brought them here for everyone to meet." The feeling of the upper hand! Rose felt drunk with power.

"You should have had his license revoked when you had the chance, Rose. It must eat away at you that you didn't." Adele's grimace conveyed the usual gloom-and-doom judgment, but her voice contained an exhaustion that Rose recognized.

"You didn't really know us." Rose felt heat in her face and remembered: She had not come here to remind Adele about the absence of her children.

"Morry was a nice man but you always thought you were better than everyone. A real intellectual," Adele said. "But everyone's the same in the end and you could have gotten help. Why didn't you?"

"The last thing he wanted was to hurt anyone." Rose's voice started to crack. She desperately needed a sip of water.

"What does that have to do with it?" Adele folded her arms and pursed her lips.

"Were you really going to report him to the DMV?"

Adele sighed. "My husband had the same disease. I put him in a home when I couldn't watch him anymore. I wasn't there when he died, which is a terrible thing, but at least he didn't hurt anyone."

Rose couldn't speak. But she remembered: It had surprised her that day, that brief episode of grace; that it was Adele who had excused herself to use the bathroom while she and Morry sorted out the past from the present.

Finally, Rose said, "Lillian Rabinowitz is in a home now."

Adele nodded. "I heard."

"His mind was good that day. I tested him before he left the house and—"

"It doesn't matter now what you did or didn't do. It is absolutely terrible what happened to that young man."

"Yes. It is." Rose forced herself to stare at Adele, who kept shaking her head, and Adele's friends, who mimicked their leader's movements. Finally, Rose had assembled the most perfect tribunal for the trial of her not-so-subconscious craving. But instead of falling to her knees or some other capitulation to the wrath of their judgment, she caught a final glimpse of an earlier period, when their relationships mattered so much because they had the horizon of an ocean. How much time did they all have left to gather like this? How nice for them, that they still had the energy to expend in insult and condemnation but what of it?

"I never thought I was better. Sometimes you can't belong when you don't have children. Anyway, I hope you will remember how much you enjoyed speaking with Morry and you should also know . . . you should know how sorry I am for how it all turned out."

Adele kept calling her name as Rose navigated her walker toward the entrance. She felt as if she walked on sand and resisted the temptation to look behind her, so as to register her footprints. The sensation of a last visit. Rose finally understood. It felt almost exactly like the evening when she told Morry that she would never get into a car with him again, as long as he persisted in remaining the driver.

"CAREFUL," ROSE SAYS as Morry brakes at the stop sign hard and sudden. "You could have an accident."

"When have I ever had an accident?" With both hands, Morry grips the steering wheel and Rose watches his knuckles turn white.

Rose grips the door handle and wishes they were still sitting in that warm lecture hall at Santa Monica College, where they heard an old colleague of Morry's read an excerpt from his new biography on Chaim Soutine. The colleague answered questions, signed books, and took a moment to shake Morry's hand and reminisce about the good old days. Wine and cheese were served and Rose made sure that Morry only ate cheese. Now they're driving down 4th instead of Main because 4th happens to be one of the safest streets they know thanks to the stop signs at every block between Pico and Westminster.

It's about eight in the evening, a cloudy night in June, where it's impossible to see the stars and the sky is the color of washed-out cotton candy. Rose weighs the pros and cons of telling Morry to turn on his brights. Pro: Morry will see better. Con: Other drivers will not. Meanwhile, Morry fails to heed the next stop sign and their car rolls through the intersection. Rose feels like they're in the middle of a factory, looping forever on a conveyer belt.

"Every block has a stop sign." Rose tries to speak in her most casual yet helpful voice.

Morry takes a hand off the wheel and waves it dismissively at Rose. "No one's perfect."

Rose sighs. She feels an urgency that used to be unfamiliar: that if she doesn't do something different right this very second, a type of loss will occur that requires coping mechanisms beyond their collective capability.

"Morry?" She starts and stops just as she spots a four-legged and furry creature dart in front of their car. Most likely it is a cat, less possibly an opossum, and unlikely a raccoon. She can't make out the particulars of the animal, with the exception of its proximity to danger.

"Look out!"

Morry looks and swerves. Rose braces her hand against the dashboard and ducks. She hears the screeching of brakes, smells the burning of rubber, and feels the impact of one car hitting another. The cracking, crunching noise of the collision provides a minor jolt to the spine but nothing more. It is only a parked car after all, resting curbside at the little park adjacent to this southbound stretch of 4th.

The car behind them honks and passes as Morry remains frozen at the wheel. Rose gathers up what's left of the part of herself that used to reign in a classroom chock full of unruly, reluctant ballerinas—those beginner classes where mothers forced their daughters to at least try and appreciate the privileges lost to them in their own childhoods—and starts issuing directives. Turn left and park alongside that stretch of uninhabited curb. Get out of the car and check it for damage. Walk to the car we hit and check it for damage. Examine the large dents and paint scratches on its driver's side and consider yourself lucky. Leave a note that both pleads forgiveness and gets to the point about insurance. Cross the street and stand on the pavement near those bushes. Listen for the sounds of a wounded animal. Sell the car and take the bus.

Morry, who has obeyed Rose without question, now shakes his head. "I'm not taking the bus."

She says it then, what she has been meaning to say for months: "This is the last time I'm getting into a car with you. I'd walk home right now if I could."

He's defiant at first. He mocks her as they stand there on the sidewalk, each trying to catch their breath after the exertion of the inspections and note-leaving. He tells her any driver worth his salt would have done what he did and to go ahead and walk home if she thinks they don't need a car. He's about to launch into a defense of his faculties and how they still function despite his occasional lapses of both long and short-term memory when they hear a sound coming from the bushes. Rose shushes her husband and steels herself for the whimpers of an animal in pain. But it's nothing except a harmless rustling, perhaps caused by a bird or a lizard or simply the wind.

Lucky, lucky, always lucky.

Rose turns to her husband to tell him it's time to go. By the light of the pink sky, she sees the expression on his face with perfect clarity. With her index finger, she catches a singular tear that falls from his eye.

UPON RETURNING TO her apartment from the Center, Rose telephoned Richard's daughter but had to resort to leaving a message—always, this business of young people no longer answering their telephones. She kept it brief: she would be happy to meet for coffee and they should do this soon. She then thought about the girl as she opened the bottommost cabinet in her kitchen. She took out her lone remaining pair of candlesticks and lit them. She looked into the flames and remembered her mother. She could see her mother in their kitchen, passing her a bit of food to taste with her fingers. A weekly Friday morning secret, this sneaking of morsels; this small yet potent exchange of love. Rose wouldn't know how potent until the day she learned she would never see her mother again.

From that same drawer, Rose removed the set of keys. After they fixed up the car at the body shop, she had asked the mechanic if he could just sell the car for her and keep all the profit. The mechanic had happily agreed but at the last minute, Rose asked for the spare set of keys. Something to remember, as if she could ever forget.

Rose held up the keys to the kitchen light and admired them as she would the sparkling of a diamond. There is great beauty, she thought, in the ability to unlock, to secure passage by your own hand from one domain to the next.

Seventeen

NINA HADN'T PLANNED on contacting the rabbi a mere week after her vet excursion with Jon. Upon returning home from the vet, she had been consumed with the cats' recoveries and made immediate mistakes, most notably giving Garfield and Angie free reign of the living room. This, apparently, was a real no-no in stray/feral cat caretaking circles. (Pertinent websites concur: Trap the cat in the trap and let the cat recover from surgery in the trap. Do not let the cat OUT OF THE TRAP for twenty-four hours, even if said cat howls piteously.) Of course, she had not trapped these cats in the first place and so she needed to make her own rules. At any rate, the living room privileges that she had accorded to both felines had gone unappreciated: Garfield hid under the couch for three days and Angie peed on top of it. She then spent the next few days buying every enzyme cleaner on the market and finally capitulating to professional furniture steam-cleaning. Meanwhile, Angie resumed life roaming the great outdoors and eating her meals alfresco with the other not-yet-fixed cats upon the immediate cessation of her twenty-four-hour recovery period. But Garfield, once he emerged from under the couch, ate a bowl of kibble and used the litter box that she had purchased weeks ago. And when she made the alleged mistake of letting him out of her apartment three days after his surgery, he returned some five hours later and rubbed against her legs before eating his dinner.

During this time, her friend Allison gave birth to her daughter Paige via an emergency C-section. Nina had visited them in the hospital, where she consoled Allison, a huge proponent of natural childbirth. "You did what you needed to do to keep you and Paige safe," she said. And when Allison handed Paige to her, she had cradled the infant against her chest with wonderment and happiness for her friend but nothing more.

Also: Serena had called her into her office after her Thursday class for another chat. She wanted Nina to know that her existing classes were no longer in jeopardy plus the Friday night slot at six had just opened. It was hers if she wanted it. Apparently, the studio had received some angry emails and comment cards from students who had been loyal to her Monday/Wednesday evening class.

You mean I still have a following even though I'm not a social media superstar? Nina had swallowed the sarcasm, thanked Serena for the good news, said she'd think about teaching the Friday night class, and understood that she only enjoyed a temporary reprieve. The recession had showed no signs of ebbing and she knew that Serena was only one of millions preaching the gospel of personal branding, promotional authenticity—whatever the fuck that meant—and all things social media as a means of economic and personal salvation. One trend would outlast another but one thing Nina knew for sure: no matter what form they took or the tools they used, the marketers stood to inherit the earth and she did not count herself among them.

And yet: for the first time in months, Nina did not want to cry because something nice had happened to her. She had left Cat/Cow that day, intending to go home, take a bath, drink herbal tea, and read a book. But when she arrived home and went to pee, she saw the blood. No longer was she some three weeks late. A long shot, she thought as she flushed the toilet. You're free, she thought as she washed her hands. That was so not the way, she thought as she turned on the water for a shower instead of a bath. You're not that old, she thought as she looked at herself in the mirror. Maybe you really do want a child, she thought as she crouched to the floor. Maybe you don't but a loss is still a loss, she thought as she buried her face into her hands. Time heals all wounds, she thought as she unearthed what appeared to be a burial pile of silent screams.

She had called the rabbi the next day and made an appointment for the following Monday morning.

THE RABBI HAD a second floor office on Washington Boulevard, a block away from the beach and above a restaurant famous for its Latin-fusion brunches and bottomless mimosa specials. Nina walked up a narrow, white-painted staircase and marveled at the rabbi's ability to procure such prime real estate at the Venice-Marina Del Rey border. Fortunately, the rabbi, who had a going-rate that explained the prime real estate, charged on a sliding scale, which included professional discounts to fellow clergy, therapists, and yoga teachers.

The rabbi had left her office door open, and Nina stood at the entrance, observing that the office resembled a yoga studio. It was a bare, spacious room with hardwood floors, large windows that faced Washington Boulevard, a wooden desk flanked by two beige-colored plush office chairs, and a very low wooden coffee table surrounded by lavender cushions. A light green ceramic vase housing a lone orchid in fragile bloom had been placed in the center of the table.

The rabbi stood next to her desk massaging her neck. She was a small woman with shoulder-length thick red hair, pale freckled skin, and large blue eyes. She looked to be about Nina's age and her outfit of jeans, a dark blue tank top, and sparkly-blue flip flops seemed distinctly un-rabbinical. But what was a young, female rabbi supposed to look like anyway? Like the white-bearded rabbi who led Bubbe Essie's congregation during much of her childhood or the black-hatted men who had whizzed by her when she walked through Haredi Jerusalem neighborhoods as a Hebrew U student?

It took about a minute for the rabbi to stop massaging her neck and notice her. She welcomed Nina and asked whether she preferred to sit at the desk or on the cushions.

Nina chose the cushions and only after seating herself in a cross-legged position did anxiety replace her temporary feeling of ease. The last time she had sought out a fellow human for spiritual advice and existential guidance in the non-yoga world was more than sixteen years ago, right before her junior year in Israel. Then, she had consulted a fortune-teller on the Venice Boardwalk who shuffled a deck of tarot cards and told her: *You are at the beginning of a very long process.*

Honestly, had anything changed?

The rabbi sat facing Nina in a similar cross-legged position. She seemed to be waiting for Nina to speak. So, Nina said, "I don't know where to begin."

"It's not necessary to begin," the rabbi said. "You can continue with whatever is currently on your mind."

"There's a lot of things on my mind. That's part of the problem."

At the rabbi's suggestion, Nina closed her eyes, took a few deep breaths, and with each exhale, tried to empty her mind. *Let go of who you were before you walked into the studio. Let go of who you think you will be when you leave.* She often facilitated such exercises for her students at the beginning of her classes. And sometimes, she joined her students in their collective attempt to render their minds into blank canvases. Sometimes, she succeeded.

But as she sat and breathed in the rabbi's office, Nina watched her blank canvas morph into a black and white image of her at the wheel in Laz's rental car. She could still feel his hand on her thigh. Or wait, was that her hand on his thigh? *This is the end. My only friend, the end. Can you see her, the youngish but no longer young woman sitting in the driver's seat of a green PT Cruiser rental? She's doing about ninety in the left hand lane of the 15, about a half hour north of Barstow. In the midst of a Doors sing-a-long, she pretends that they are forever young. And so when he grabs her hand, which rests on his thigh, and brings it to his lips, she can overlook the message embedded in his kiss. Hey baby. Be a good little girl and I'll let you come along for the ride.*

"Do you want to talk about it?" The rabbi's voice punctured her image, gentle yet insistent.

Nina opened her eyes. She looked at the rabbi and then stared at the hardwood floor. She pretended that she sat in her apartment, communing with Rose's possessions and petting Garfield, who would decide that her skin was in more urgent need of grooming than his fur, and start lapping away at her hands. Her apartment, when she conjured it up in her mind, had started to feel safe again. It was a start.

She talked for what seemed like much longer than a half hour. She explained what had happened with Jeff and Laz, how she had come to know Rose, and why things had grown difficult between them since the day they visited the senior center. She tried to summarize her Jewish background, pointing to the influence of Bubbe Essie, her piecemeal Jewish education, and Laz's ex-Orthodox psyche. She mentioned her recent experiences teaching yoga, how fragments of Hebrew prayers and phrases would infiltrate her mind as she communicated or chanted something in Sanskrit.

"I've never turned to Judaism like this before," she said, as if she had reached a conclusion. "It's not like I'm trying to reconnect with a past that I left . . . like my . . ." *Like you can label him now.* She flashed back to her year in Israel, where Laz lay on her narrow Jerusalem dorm room bed, trying to teach her the art of yeshiva thumbs. She had not understood it then, the extent of his suffering born from his desire to escape without becoming completely untethered.

The rabbi stood up and stretched her arms over her head. "Feel free to stand whenever you need to. And actually, it sounds to me that you are very much trying to connect with your past."

"I don't understand."

"Let me put it this way. Your Jewish role models include your grandmother who fully embraced Judaism and a boyfriend who tried really hard to reject Judaism. This is part of your inheritance."

Inheritance. If only she could invite the rabbi into her living room. What would she make of all the knickknacks and personal heirlooms that did not originate from her own biological family?

"Every human being has to contend with some kind of inheritance. That can mean something collective or personal. If it's collective, you might say that the Holocaust would be a prime example of what we as Jews have inherited. And if it's personal, it's the genes our parents gave us or the behaviors they couldn't stop perpetuating that we, in turn, absorbed like sponges. Sometimes, we inherit cultural or religious ideas that may or may not have relevance in our generation. But they still belong to us. Whatever it is, I strongly believe that everyone has the responsibility to examine what came before them and how it might be affecting their lives."

"A responsibility?" Nina felt a jolt of new anxiety.

The rabbi smiled and re-joined Nina on the cushions. "These things have a way of creeping up on you."

"I guess they do."

They continued to sit in silence for at least five minutes while the rabbi closed her eyes and appeared to go into a sudden and deep meditative state. Nina watched the rabbi closely, willing to suspend judgment. When the rabbi opened her eyes, she told Nina the following: "Astrologically, you and Jeff were not compatible. You did not bring out the best in him, nor he in you." And: "You believe that the rape was your fault." And: "Rose has surprised you because she's not really like your grandmother and yet you feel a deep connection to her life.

It's not too late to repair the misunderstanding you had with her." And: "You can be both a yogi and a Jew. Your ex-boyfriend probably learned that he wasn't allowed to pick and choose his Judaism but I believe you can integrate the parts of Judaism that are meaningful to you so that you can be a complete person."

And: "When Jeff died, did you say kaddish for him?"

Nina nodded. "I was at his funeral."

The rabbi shook her head. "That's different. Have you personally said kaddish for him?"

Nina shook her head.

"It sounds like you haven't been able to fully mourn this loss. There's a reason why many Jewish people who haven't led particularly Jewish lives observe the Jewish mourning rituals when they lose a loved one. When we return our loved ones to the earth, we seek structure and meaning and often, this forces us to reckon with how we've lived and how we are living."

Nina thought of her mother, apologizing to her as they sat shiva for Bubbe Essie. Seated on the rabbi's cushions, she had to concede that this memory of her mother felt a little softer.

By the end of their allotted hour, the rabbi had prescribed the following: When she felt ready, she should visit Jeff's grave at the cemetery and say kaddish. She should explain herself to Rose and afterward, do what her heart told her to do. Finally, Nina needed to tell Laz what he had done to her and how it had made her feel. The rabbi emphasized that she would never casually recommend that someone confront her rapist, but in her case, an encounter with him seemed necessary. For inspiration, the rabbi recommended that she perform a Google search for "restorative justice," in particular the process of victims confronting and demanding accountability from their perpetrators. From all this, a tikkun, a true healing, will emerge, the rabbi said with confidence.

"A tikkun?" Nina remembered afternoons in Hebrew school, where her teachers would make these bland and vague pronouncements about the necessity of tikkun olam, of repairing the world. As Jews, we are obligated to perform tikkun olam, they would say, or they would learn a song filled with platitudes about healing the world, but Nina could never grasp the specifics of what this meant.

"A personal tikkun," the rabbi said, as if she had read Nina's mind. "In the meantime, do what you're doing and continue to teach your classes. We can still bring light to others even when we find ourselves struggling to emerge from the dark."

THREE DAYS LATER: Nina called Rose with a proposition of her own. Could they please meet in person? Perhaps, they could take a stroll along the boardwalk toward that grassy lawn area by the sculpture that marks the epicenter of Venice Beach. Didn't she like that part of the boardwalk? Then, if Rose felt up to it, they could do a little movement.

Rose had emitted a noise that sounded like a cross between chuckling and choking. "I'm lucky if I can walk a few steps without everything hurting."

"But you told me once that you can still move in your mind. That you mind-dance."

"I don't do this so much anymore."

A dark and weighty pause had descended upon their conversation and Nina felt derailed, unsure as to her next step. Perhaps she should have suggested something more familiar, the Fig Tree or a shopping trip. Or perhaps she should have finally invited Rose over to her apartment for a meal, which would have forced her to figure out how to assimilate Rose's possessions into her home. Perhaps this was nothing but selfishness on her part, wanting to make amends this way because to do so through movement only served her own therapeutic needs.

"I miss you," Nina finally said. "So please, can we meet?"

Another pause descended on their conversation and Nina didn't know what to do. But then Rose cleared her throat and told Nina to come over tomorrow at two in the afternoon. She promised to wear her most comfortable pair of shoes.

Eighteen

THERE THEY ARE, the younger woman and the older woman taking slow, deliberate steps on the Venice Boardwalk. They're easy to miss, even on a Tuesday at four in the afternoon before the peak summer season. The boardwalk has attracted a seasonally appropriate crowd today. Couples and families speaking foreign languages walk side by side eating French fries and soft-serve ice cream. Mr. Turban weaves among them, swaddled in clean, white fabrics, doing S-curves in his rollerblades, and regaling those he has chosen to be his listeners with Jim songs, either Morrison or Hendrix. Groups of pre-teen and teenage boys practice skateboarding tricks and take breaks to ogle groups of teenage girls sashaying along the boardwalk barefoot in short shorts and bikini tops. The girls pretend to ignore the male attention but they move almost as slowly as the two women.

The younger woman holds the elbow of the older woman who insisted that she didn't need her walker, only her cane. For this reason, the going is especially slow. It's a dance that the younger woman didn't choreograph for the occasion. Rather, they are improvising. Two steps forward then pause, then perhaps a mutual deep breath or three. Four steps forward, then pause, then a small groan from the older woman, then an un-assuming "are you okay?" expressed by the younger woman in a give-her-space kind of voice. Then a dismissive nod from the older woman, who clutches the younger woman's forearm as if she might lose her balance. The younger woman holds the older woman's elbow as firmly as she can, thinking: *not on my watch.*

They proceed in this fashion down the boardwalk, toward the grassy area where the older woman had gotten lucky with her stakeout of the younger woman. For the younger woman, the passage of time feels like hours, possibly days. For the older woman, the time simply feels like the time, but she senses that the younger woman now has a visceral inkling of what it might feel like to grow old.

"Shall we keep going?" the younger woman asks periodically in that give-her-space kind of voice.

Well, if you must know, I'm doing this for you. The older woman knows there's a time for speaking and a time for silence, especially when she needs to concentrate on taking one step forward. And then another step. And then another.

Finally, they arrive at the grassy area and the older woman gestures with her cane to a nearby bench halfway between the sculpture and the police substation.

They face each other for the duet of sitting down: One hooks the cane to the bench and grabs the other's elbows; the other holds on to the other's forearms and begins the process of bending her knees and lowering her center of gravity onto the bench. For one minute, maybe two, one woman sits and the other stands. One tries to catch her breath and the other asks herself why she thought this was a good idea. One thinks: *I should tell her everything anyway.* The other thinks: *maybe we can do modified Sun Salutations.*

The younger woman sits next to the older woman and tries to remember why she thought this was a good idea. Did they not share a love for movement? Did they not possess bodies that brimmed with unsaid things? Could they, by moving their bodies, communicate and release what had so far been impossible to say?

The older woman sits next to the younger woman, wondering whether or not to reiterate that these days she no longer derives pleasure from mind-dancing. It's not that she believes she's unqualified to derive such pleasure; rather, she has simply lost the drive. This tells her something about the passage of time and that she has made the correct decision.

You are not me. This is what the older woman wants to tell the younger woman. *You have time.* And: *Sometimes I imagine that you are my granddaughter or even, my daughter.*

"I'm sorry," the younger woman finally says. "I didn't mean to exhaust you."

The older woman holds up her hand. "You are not the cause of my exhaustion."

The younger woman nods and it's unclear as to whether she grasps the multiple meanings of the older woman's response. They sit in silence for a few minutes and then the younger woman says, "That day, when we went to your Center, you were right. I wasn't myself. That other man I had told you about? I was having a hard time understanding that he had raped me. He had come to my house one night and . . . and yes. That's what happened."

Here, the younger woman pauses, unable to look at the older woman but allowing herself to be seen. She has finally abdicated the role that she always played with her Bubbe Essie, that of editor-par-excellence, intent on eradicating all her lesser selves. *What you see is what you get.* It's a thought that both liberates and terrifies.

The older woman places her hand on the younger woman's elbow. "Dear," she says, thinking how good it feels to reclaim "dear" in their dialogue. "That's terrible. Did you call the police?"

The younger woman shakes her head and the older woman swiftly decides that she has asked a useless question. Sometimes, people don't want to call the police, she thinks. Sometimes, there is only one good question. "Are you all right?"

"I hope to be. But that's why . . . maybe not completely why but . . . I guess I thought I couldn't be . . . I mean, I was so wrapped up in my own—"

The older woman holds up her hand. She doesn't mean to interrupt but she desperately needs the younger woman to know that she finally understands. The younger woman seems to grasp this and they allow the moisture in the younger woman's eyes to evaporate without comment.

After maybe a minute of silence and mutual staring at the ocean, the younger woman asks, "Do you want to try a little yoga?"

The older woman gives a single nod and says, "Show me."

The younger woman raises her arms above her head until her hands touch. Then she bends her elbows and lowers her hands past her face until they rest in a prayer position at her heart. She does the movement again, with an inhale and an exhale. She repeats the movements as the older woman joins in. The older woman cannot raise her arms above her head but she holds her hands up toward her eyes, as if she's about to bless the Sabbath candles. Then, she too, moves her hands into a prayer position near her heart.

One woman chants the first few words of the kaddish in her head, unsure as to who she's saying it for; only that she needs to say it, no matter that she only knows the first few words of the prayer by heart. The other woman resolves to keep breathing for just a little while longer. In this way, they move separately yet also together.

Nineteen

IT WAS ROSE'S turn for confession and she refused to budge on her choice of venue. But how wonderful, that they could resume their rituals for just a little longer. The girl pulling up at the curb in front of Rose's apartment building between three to five minutes late; the getting in and out of the car; the folding up of the shopping cart; the locking of doors and fastening of seatbelts; the negotiation of venues. Didn't Rose want to shop at the nice Ralph's in the Marina instead of the 99 Cent Store?

"No thank you." Rose merely desired a few canned items such as tuna and corn, a new pair of slippers, dishwashing liquid, and the opportunity to present the complete picture in a beloved setting.

"How are you?" The girl turned off her hazard lights and pulled away from the curb.

"Getting along all right." Rose felt seized with a peculiar impatience as she answered the question. Had she ever answered otherwise, particularly when she wasn't getting along all right? Had she ever responded: I feel terrible and on my deathbed but thank you for asking, for example? Who spoke like that in Los Angeles, where the sun ruled the question "how are you?"

"How are you, dear?" Rose decided to change the subject. It did feel a tad manipulative on her part, to work some shopping into the real reason for today's outing. Perhaps, she should have suggested that the girl teach her some more of that yoga. In the end, she had enjoyed the simple practice that the girl had introduced to her. That she could still press her hands together in a prayer position. Now this was something.

The girl hesitated. "I'm okay."

For both their sakes, Rose opted for nosiness. "Are you feeling better?"

The girl shrugged. "I've been meaning to tell you that I wear your coat whenever it's cold enough at night. I'm always getting compliments. People want to know where I bought it."

"Is that right?" Rose proceeded to experience delight from a distance, as if she perched on a cloud with a bird's eye view of the girl schlepping around Los Angeles in her coat.

"It's a wonderful gift. I can't thank you enough."

"It's you who did me the favor, dear."

They pulled into the half-empty parking lot. Enormous, exclamation point-studded, black and red signs in the windows of the Big Lots and the pharmacy advertised final, closing-out sales. Whole Foods was still moving in but the 99 Cent Store had been saved, thanks to a grassroots effort by a significant number of Venetians who believed that gentrification in their neighborhood had gone too far.

The girl drove toward the 99 Cent in search of the perfect parking space. "I heard they're not tearing it down. You must be thrilled."

"Yes. It's absolutely marvelous." Rose tried to express an opinion that the girl would expect. But the truth was this: her happiness for the 99 Cent felt the same as hearing about the girl's success with her coat. "But I read in the paper that this Google company may be moving into the neighborhood and people are concerned."

The girl scoffed. "That's the rumor."

They passed an old woman outside the Laundromat who slouched against a cart nearly her height and piled high with dark clothing. She looked close to Rose's age and wore a gray scarf over her head. She had cut her brown pantyhose at the ankles, which bulged over her shoes like bread rising from a shallow pan. She appeared to be catching her breath.

"A shame," Rose said. "A woman like that, having to do her laundry this way."

The girl nodded and parked. Rose could tell she wanted to say something on the subject but opted instead for good manners. Or were they good manners? Why shouldn't the girl just say it, that it must feel terrible to grow old and how could Rose stand it? That even if you were lucky enough to avoid the dreadful diseases of the mind and body, you still wound up shrunken and limited, dependent on your family or the kindness of strangers. This is what absolutely everyone in the world could look forward to provided they didn't die young. And if you had no family or there were no kind strangers, then you washed your clothes alone, that is, if you had the strength to do so.

ROSE WAITED UNTIL they finished perusing the grocery section and had firmly ensconced themselves in the aisle with all the cleaning products. She knew from previous trips that the girl despised this particular aisle. She always trailed Rose through the canned foods and perishables with a mask of neutrality, as if she were a UN envoy performing impartiality at the scene of a war zone. But whenever Rose led her to the cleaning products so she could select the cheapest scouring powder or disinfectant, the girl's mask cracked open into a grimace and she would start singing the praises of chemical-free alternatives available for purchase in more expensive stores.

Rose figured that today would be no different, hence bringing the girl here to break the news. She didn't want to sway the girl's decision by asking for the favor in a more pleasing and festive section, such as the aisle with all the party decorations.

Rose reached for a bottle of window cleaner and waited for the girl to make her pitch, which happened three seconds later.

"It's really no trouble for me to get you some natural cleaning products. They're much better for you and the environment and I could—"

Rose gave a dismissive hand wave. "Thank you, dear, but everything I need is in this store."

"I was just going to say that you can find much better cleaning products for almost the same price. Like at Target. I could take you to Target, if you want. Target's great. You can even find organic brands there sometimes at the store on—"

"Dear . . ." Rose hesitated, as she was tempted to first tell the girl that she didn't want to hear another word on the subject of organic anything and that she had never eaten an organic strawberry in her life and that people today worshipped longevity without understanding that there was nothing to understand. Only that some people got lucky and others did not. That it was neither art nor science but an alchemical process all its own.

Nu Rose? Are you ready? The Man from Television winked at Rose from a nearby bottle of furniture polish. For so long, he had waited to reveal his physical appearance, which, in truth, was nothing special. He had dark curly hair, small, glittering black eyes, pale skin, and a thin, impish face. He was no Mr. Clean.

"Rose?"

Only Rose just stood there watching the Man from Television vanish completely. She tried to hear him in her mind but it was true. She didn't need him anymore to tell her what she did not want to hear.

"Rose, are you okay?"

"There is something I've been meaning to ask you."

The girl folded her arms and narrowed her eyes. She reached into Rose's cart, extracted the window cleaner, and placed it back on the shelf. "These products are toxic. They're completely unnecessary for housecleaning. I'm going to get you something you'll like, I promise."

"I have some plans and I don't know if you'll like them, but I could really use your help."

The girl re-folded her arms and waited. Rose took a deep breath.

WHAT A BEAUTIFUL sunny morning for taking a stand. Nothing like a little perfect weather to help one stick to difficult principles. So thinks Rose as she sits at their dining room table watching Morry search for his keys.

Minutes pass as Rose stirs her cold cup of coffee while Morry looks in the usual places. The dining room table. The living room coffee table. The pockets of his winter coat. The end table in the living room next to his favorite chair.

"Rose? Have you seen my keys?"

Rose shakes her head and sips her cold coffee for added effect. "Might as well let them stay lost. Maybe it's a sign." She keeps her voice light and casual.

Only Morry says, "A drive a day keeps the doctor away."

Rose appraises the husband who stands in front of her. He's feeling fit today, she thinks, and so the game must be played accordingly.

"No," she says. "A car is not an apple."

"Come on my beautiful Rose-in-bloom. Help me find them. I'll take you shopping afterward. Buy whatever your heart desires."

They both know he's not taking her shopping but nonetheless, Rose opts for diplomacy. "My heart desires nothing except keeping you alive."

"Driving keeps me alive."

It hovers between them, the subtext of their clashing opinions. Yet Rose continues to sit, cradling her cup of coffee as if it were a cherished family heirloom. She feels morally obligated to answer yet whispers so softly in the hopes that he will not hear her. "I can't help you. Not that way. Not anymore."

He makes a huge production of ransacking the apartment, breaking a glass in the process. He overturns drawers, unmakes the bed, and hurls books to the floor after poring through their pages. Rose can understand that from his perspective, the drama is warranted. Yet, she feels morally obligated to reason with him, especially when he starts abusing their book collection.

"Why don't you give it a few days? If you're still feeling like this and you're in good shape, then fine. We'll find a way to replace them. But maybe, you'll discover that not having them doesn't make much of a difference."

Morry, about to hurl a biography of Modigliani to the floor, pauses to catch his breath. Rose attempts to remain calm as she watches the inevitable suspicion dawn on his face.

"Rose, where are my keys?"

"How should I know?"

"You know."

"What are you talking about?"

Rose picks up her coffee cup and toast plate and walks into the kitchen. She puts the dishes in the sink and is about to turn on the water when Morry claps her on the shoulder. She turns to face him and encounters an expression she has never seen before. There's a vacancy sign flashing on his face, different from the ones of the recent past. His eyes look through her, as if she's nothing but empty space. Suddenly, she can't breathe.

Morry reaches behind him, toward the countertop that separates the kitchen from the living room/dining area. He picks up the framed photograph of them standing in front of the Tel Aviv Sheraton in 1973 with Morry's two second cousins and holds it over Rose's head. He starts to laugh. "Did this ever exist? Did we ever exist?"

Morry hurls the photograph into the living room and Rose hears it collide with a thunk against their couch. She backs up against the refrigerator and wishes the appliance was a warmer place with a lock on its door. More than anything, she yearns for solitary refuge, to insert herself into a bubble of frozen time.

"Give them back."

She doesn't want to admit the truth; that she's never been this frightened by his behavior. Instead, she begs. "What do you need them for? Jewish Family Service has a wonderful ride share program. We can sign up."

He grabs her by the arm and digs his nails into her flesh. "Give them back. Now."

"Don't speak to me this way."

"Now!" He starts shaking her arm.

"Stop it! You're hurting me."

Does it occur to Morry that Rose has never spoken these words before in their forty-two years of marriage? Rose doesn't know as she covers her face with her hands and waits for the blow that never comes. She takes her time peeling her hands off her face and when she's finished, Morry still stands before her but now as a shrunken, terrified version of himself. He's not only sorry, he's more than sorry, he tells her. In fact, he's the sorriest he's ever been. And then he says, "It's true. Sometimes, I don't recognize myself."

Quite frankly, Rose is having trouble recognizing both of them. Who were they exactly after forty-two years of marriage? And was it just two days ago that Morry couldn't remember either of their names? Rose can't remember.

Morry takes her hand and kisses it. "Will you ever forgive me?" And Rose remembers. How it took fifteen minutes for Morry to cast off the blank canvas that had draped itself over his soul uninvited. How her name burst forth from his lips with the most conviction she had ever heard from another human being. And how she wanted to photograph the relief and victory on his face. It was a sight comparable to the first time Rose laid eyes on the actual land of Israel from her window seat on the El Al plane. She had been weeping along with the other passengers while "Jerusalem the Golden" played on the plane's PA system, fully copping to the musical manipulation. But when she looked out her window as the plane touched down at Ben Gurion airport, she understood that she hadn't needed the music to bring her to tears. And it wasn't that she was seeing anything in particular in the brownish-greenish, flat landscape. It was simply in the air, the most indomitable manifestation of the will to prevail.

"Wait here," she says and leaves the kitchen for their bedroom, where she opens the bottom drawer in her dresser. She extracts her cosmetics bag and rummages through the lipsticks, eye shadows, and facial powders. Predictably, they have sunk to the bottom. They are intact, however, though somewhat smudged with pink and purple dust due to remnants of makeup spills of years past. Rose always tries to keep her cosmetic bags for as long as possible, as she does clothing, furniture, and husbands.

She finds her husband still standing in the kitchen. She decides they need a border for now and so she stands on the living room side of the bisecting countertop. She dangles the keys because she feels like it. "For this you should get so worked up? They are hardly anything."

She has never seen her husband look so sad. Or maybe she has. Rose only knows she needs to sit down. She moves to the living room couch and clutches the keys in her hand with as much vigilance as she can muster. After several minutes, Morry joins her on the couch. They don't speak for what feels like hours. Every time Rose tries to speak, it shames her that she doesn't quite understand what she's feeling and so she keeps quiet.

Morry finally breaks the silence. "In a nursing home, there are no locks on the doors. Or maybe there are, it's just that people don't have any keys."

Rose turns to look at her husband. She notices his slumping shoulders, his thin arms, his trembling hands, his refusal to meet her eyes.

She puts a hand on his shoulder. "Please. Look at me."

He does.

Was he the man she had married?

Careful Rose. Careful of the spaces between people.

"What's my name?"

"Rose. My beautiful Rose."

"Who's the president of the United States?"

"George W. Bush."

"Where were you born?"

"Warsaw. Emigrated when I was four years old."

"How many fingers am I holding up?"

"None."

"Good. What about now?" Rose holds up eight fingers.

"Eight."

"What did you do for a living?"

"I was an art history professor, specializing in early twentieth-century European and American art."

"How long have we been married?"

"Forty-two wonderful years."

"When I was sick in the hospital, how old was I?"

"Seventy-five."

"What did I have?"

"Pneumonia."

"What were you doing when I was sick?"

"I never left your side."

"You were different afterward."

"No, I wasn't."

"Yes, you were."

They fade into a minutes-long silence. And then Morry says, "Watching you in that bed, I couldn't bear the thought of you going first. As terrible as it was to imagine you having to bury me, this was something even worse. I'm sorry, Rose, I'm a weak man. All these years, I guess I wanted to . . ."

She shakes her head. "No."

"For three days I kept praying. Please God, anything but that. Please don't let her go first."

She whispers, "Take them."

He doesn't at first. But then he does. Rose remains on the couch while he uses the bathroom and puts on his winter coat. He has no trouble finding his wallet. He pauses before her on the couch and promises to be careful. She nods and they kiss each other goodbye. Afterward, he reaches out his hand as if to pat her on the leg or shoulder but he doesn't. He only says, "Thank you Rose. I love you."

Rose remains sitting on the couch, regretting her silence. Why doesn't she tell Morry that she loves him back? Of course he knows, but still.

She sits there, waiting. Time passes, at least until the police officers knock on her door.

IT FELT LIKE hours, this business of Rose waiting for the girl to respond.

"I'm sorry if I upset you," Rose said.

Still nothing.

"I understand if you're angry with me. I shouldn't have waited so long to tell you."

Still nothing.

"The truth is, I was concerned that I wouldn't be able to manage it on my own. But I will so if you can't help, I understand."

Still nothing.

"Listen, dear. I want to apologize if I made your house feel too cluttered. If you want, I can call up the Goodwill and have them take care of it. Or maybe the National Council of Jewish Women. They have that nice thrift store over on Venice Boulevard."

Still nothing.

"You should know that I'm not crazy. I thought I might be headed that way but not yet. I'm not even the depressive type, not in the way you read about in the papers at least. I just know when enough is enough. I knew when to stop dancing and I knew when to stop driving and I have to say that I was never one for overeating. I've always known when to push away a perfectly good bowl of spaghetti."

Still nothing.

"I never thought I'd watch so many people wear out their welcome. Year after year, I've watched. Either they start harming themselves or cause harm to others. Everyone suffers and the lucky ones become sheep. So many years of being human and suddenly you're a sheep."

Still nothing.

"My dear friend Lillian. She's now a sheep. That was Morry's greatest fear, that he would become one. He preferred to die. He and I were alike in this way but I have tried to learn from his . . . from our mistakes."

Still nothing.

"Okay, dear. You'll find me in the slipper aisle."

Rose had already chosen a pair of bright blue, terrycloth slippers when the girl caught up with her.

"I thought we were friends," the girl said.

"We are."

"So you could recruit me for this?"

"No. You were already my friend when I thought of it. But I had to be sure of things."

"You could have told me sooner."

"Well . . . sometimes you can't say something right away, even if you want to."

Rose watched the girl wince and look away. Message received. They were honest-to-God friends, weren't they? She felt this now with conviction, which produced a sadness she could not name.

"I just want to understand. You're not in the hospital hooked up to a million tubes."

"Not yet dear."

"You're still living in your own apartment."

"I've been a lucky woman."

"You can walk."

"For now, dear. For now."

"So why not live for now?"

"Because there's tomorrow. And when you're my age—"

"I could never . . ."

"I would never ask you for that. I just want the company, someone who can be there and afterward, remember things. Like how my mother was a wonderful cook. She used to bake her own challah every Friday. If I had grandchildren, I would have told them this, so that they could tell their grandchildren."

"You really wanted children?" she asked.

"I suppose I did. But it wasn't in the cards."

She nodded. "Sometimes, I don't think I want children."

"It's okay if you don't."

Was it? Rose thought of the photograph in Yad Vashem. This photograph she would take to her grave. Other photographs she would leave behind and perhaps the girl would want them.

"But it makes me feel ashamed."

"Why?"

"I don't know yet."

Rose nodded.

"It's just . . . I've never known anyone who would do this."

"Dear? Have you ever visited a nursing home?"

"Yes."

"Have your eyes hurt so much that you couldn't even sleep because it hurt too much to close them?"

"Yes."

"Have you ever woken up in the morning unable to remember your own name?"

"No."

"Would you want to live like that?"

"You're not living like that. Are you?"

"Some days are better than others."

"What does that mean?"

Rose locked eyes with the girl and proceeded to conduct the most exhausting of staring contests. It took some doing, but finally, the girl looked away. For Rose, this felt like the most Pyrrhic of victories. This business of their ages dueling for the upper hand, it was like an elephant defending itself from a mouse.

Twenty

BEFORE NINA CALLED him, she followed the rabbi's advice and googled restorative justice. The rabbi had correctly intuited that she would be interested in this idea of survivors and perpetrators meeting each other face-to-face. But it seemed that the goal of these encounters within the restorative justice model was to achieve restitution for the survivor and rehabilitation for the perpetrator. Was this what she ultimately wanted from another encounter with him? Why did she need to see him again, exactly?

She finally called him on a Sunday evening around eight, conscious that it was on a Sunday evening around eight when she had received his hey-Nina-I'm-in-LA email. She knew it was both logically and cosmically erroneous to think of it as the email that *set everything in motion* but she couldn't help herself.

He picked up on the first ring and she said, "hey," forcing herself to stop there. It was so automatic, asking him, or really anyone, the question "how are you?"

"Nina." *Neeeee-naaaaah.*

She flinched. "I think it's time we met in person."

He suggested the bar in her neighborhood of their initial Los Angeles reunion and she decided not to hold this calculation against him.

"That's nice that you'll drive my way," she said.

"Of course." As if he had spent his entire adult life dedicated to her greater convenience. "I'm really looking forward to seeing you."

Even now, she could close her eyes and feel the reciprocation of the sentiment bubbling within her as she pictured his face. Even now, she could not fully obliterate all the previous versions of him. But she only said, "See you then."

She hung up, considered opening a bottle of wine, and decided to take a hot shower instead. She went to bed early that night and woke up a few hours later drenched in sweat. It had taken her so long to have this kind of nightmare. In the dream, she was at the scene of the accident, ripping up her clothes to stanch the blood flowing from all parts of Jeff's body. Jeff murmurs words she can't understand. As his body grows stiff and his eyes become glass, she looks up at the car, its windshield glinting in the sunlight and smeared with blood. The car door opens. Laz walks out. He points at her and opens his mouth but she wakes up before she can hear what he's saying.

AS USUAL, SHE arrived at the bar a few minutes early. The bouncer waved her in without checking her ID. He was the same bouncer who worked the door the first time they had met here, and she appreciated that he too, had recognized her. Tonight, she hadn't dressed up in glitzy and/or seductive bar clothing, though she had chosen her outfit with great care: old jeans ripped in the knees and a black T-shirt emblazoned with a golden image of a dove carrying a flame-lit arrow in its beak. She chose the T-shirt for its literalism; because it seemed to say: *I come in peace.* But also: *Don't fuck with me.*

She took a seat at the bar and ordered a glass of Pinot Noir from the Santa Ynez Valley. As she sipped her wine and waited, she kept her eyes glued to the myriad bottles of varietals that filled the wine racks nailed to the wall that comprised the back of the bar. *What an excellent example of functional décor.* She would do whatever it took to distract herself, but even so, she couldn't help but steal a glance in the direction of the cave-like room.

Once upon a time, there was a cave-like room attached to a neighborhood bar and a woman who longed to sit in it. "It suggests things," she once told a man she thought she loved with all her heart, but he didn't understand. So, one day, the woman sat in the cave-like room with someone who did.

He walked inside, this time only around five minutes late. He told the bartender he wanted whatever she was having and asked if she wouldn't mind sitting on one of the booths that faced the street as opposed to sitting at the bar.

"Sure," she said, trying to simply accept the pounding of her heart and the sudden clamminess of her palms.

She shook her head when he gestured for her to sit next to him on the booth and sat on the chair opposite him.

"It's so good to see you." Laz reached out for her spare hand, the one not clutching her glass of wine as if it gripped a rope held out to her in an act of rescue.

It's not that he has to die. It's that you have to live. Do you see the difference now?

She retracted her spare hand and rested it on her lap. "You are . . ." Again and again, she had no words for what he was to her. All these years and she still could not name him.

"Nina . . ."

She looked down at her lap, understanding that this encounter was going to be even harder than what she had anticipated.

"Can you just explain to me why you wouldn't return my calls? I honestly don't understand what happened to us that night, why you would cut me off that way." Laz spoke to her in a soft, soothing voice, the way she sometimes addressed Garfield when he seemed spooked by a behavior that she clearly committed but could not pinpoint as the source of the cat's fear.

She forced herself to look at him, to try and see the man sitting in front of her, sipping his Pinot. *That's him now, not in 1993 or 1999 or 2001 or 2005 or two months ago when he lay on top of you and wouldn't stop when you said no.*

"I said no that night," she said, finally syncing her speech with her thoughts. "I said no and you didn't stop."

Was that genuine bewilderment on Laz's face? Nina couldn't tell.

"I honestly didn't hear you," he said without breaking eye contact. "I mean, I know you said 'no' at the beginning but that's how you are sometimes—"

"That time, I really meant no."

She noted the slight shift in Laz's expression, how something seemed to illuminate then obfuscate the eye contact that he continued to maintain with her. "Well, I guess it wasn't clear to me that night what you wanted but I swear to you I never would have—"

"But you did," she said. "I said no and you did it anyway. What is that called?"

Silence. Then more silence. And still more silence. Surely, this was the longest silence in the history of THEM and Nina resolved that she wouldn't be the one to break it.

"Can you forgive me?" he finally asked.

The sound that came out of her mouth sounded suspiciously like a laugh. "It's complicated, don't you think?"

He stared at her, and she stared back, making sure to take a healthy gulp of wine. In the span of that stare, she believed she could detect the minutia of his calculations. *She doesn't really think it's rape so all I have to do is remind her of what we have, what we have always had, only now I'm ready to pursue this. And if things go well, I'll thank her for waiting.*

Really, it wasn't that difficult, even now, to walk in his shoes.

"Nina?"

"What?"

"How can I make this up to you?"

"You can leave me alone," she said.

"Is that really what you want?"

"I get it, you know. How many times have I told you never to contact me again? But the thing is . . . it is, until it isn't. You know what I mean?"

"You have to believe me, what happened that night was unintentional, and if I hurt you, then I am deeply sorry. And yes, I understand that I did some schmucky things to you over the years. But I was young. We were young."

She scanned the face that she had etched years ago deep into the cracks and crevices of her mind: the large green eyes which now started to shimmer with an old and familiar fear; the olive skin; the dimple on the left side of his face; the full lips that kissed and whispered and told a thousand stories she would always remember as long as she had a memory; the smile on his face that made her feel so alive. But she could not see the old man within. There would be no his or her rocking chairs on some beachfront porch purchased by joint retirement money where they could watch sunsets in the exalted state of quiet contentment. Not that she had ever really wanted that from him anyway.

"Yeah," she said. "We're older now."

She could tell that it was starting to dawn on him, that the woman who sat across from him didn't sound the way she always had. She watched him eye their now empty wine glasses. How comforting it would be to drink another glass, to sink into an alcoholic haze, to stare into his eyes and only remember the good parts, even now.

But she declined his offer to buy them another round. She found herself thinking of Rose, who surely had plenty to say on the subject of growing old with someone. She had not spoken to Rose since their conversation at the 99 Cent Store and she definitely owed her a phone call. *Whatever you decide dear is fine with me. I had just wanted you to know.*

"Nina," he said in his soft, don't-spook-the-cat voice. "I've always loved you."

"You always had such a hard time saying that."

"But I don't anymore. People change."

She felt it again, the urge to laugh. "I never told you about Rose. She's the widow of the man who hit Jeff. She's ninety-three years old. We became friends and I never thought I'd be good friends with someone so much older, but we are. Last week she told me she's ready to die. She says she's not sick or even depressed. She's just done."

"Nina." He said her name in a new way, the vowels sounding sharp and crisp, like biting into a fresh apple.

"One thing I've learned from Rose is that it's important for people to respect when other people are done."

He stared at her with an expression that she couldn't read as she stood up and grabbed her purse. On the way out, she saw the bouncer stare at her with a different kind of recognition, as if he could now catalog her with the thousand other individuals that had fled this bar, in dire need of a different destination.

She walked out the door and headed south on Abbot Kinney. She had covered maybe half a block when she felt his hand on her shoulder.

"Don't do this," he whispered.

She turned to face him, this time determined not to look too deeply into his eyes. "It's over."

He grabbed her wrist. "You don't mean that."

The sensation of his hand on her wrist: it took her everywhere. Her mind became a mish-mash of split screens, just like on that old TV show *Hollywood Squares*. There she lay on a trampoline in a Jerusalem park, feeling his eyes pinning her down. There she stood, sandwiched between him and a dark and deserted wall, and also at the entrance to her apartment in New York, slamming the door in his face. And there she sat clutching herself on her bathroom floor, zoning into the black cracks of space between the door and the floor.

"Let go of me," she said.

But he wouldn't. He tightened his grip on her wrist. "Please calm down."

Really? Did she sound angry? *Careful, Nina. No one likes an angry woman. An angry woman is a lonely woman. Just think of all the men who stopped you on the street, especially when you were in your twenties, and told you to smile. And on the occasions that you decided to reward them with a fake, fuck you kind of smile instead of just ignoring them, they would say: See? You're so much prettier now.*

"I'm not angry," she said. "I just need you to let go of my wrist."

She forced herself to look at him then and realized with something close to shock and awe that she wasn't angry. Rather, she was exhausted and ultimately, humbled. Because here she stood on the street with a person she thought she knew so well when in truth, he surprised her. All these years and she had mistaken his peripatetic presence in her life for a kind of thoughtlessness or carelessness. But now, his grip on her wrist communicated something else: that she had meant something to him in that he could reliably expect that her resistance to him would inevitably dissolve. But now, she could resist him and he would not accept this.

"Hey. Everything okay here?" The bouncer now stood to her left and she noticed details about him that she hadn't before: He was a tall, muscular Latino man with a shaved head, a neatly trimmed goatee, and a tattoo of two crosses on his right forearm. She could picture him in some other life, as a priest hearing confessions. This made her think of the rabbi and what she had learned about restorative justice, about the importance of mediators to facilitate encounters between survivors and perpetrators.

"Yeah, we're cool." Laz let go of her wrist and said nothing as the bouncer positioned himself so that he formed a barrier that she could stand behind.

The bouncer turned toward her. "You want him to leave?"

She nodded.

"She wants you to leave."

It felt both so fast and so slow; the several seconds of limbo where she watched Laz ponder his next move before emitting a sonic mix of a sigh and a "huh." He held up a hand. "It's cool." He stepped off the curb and paused to look at her. She heard his voice, soft yet audible. "We're not finished yet."

She thanked the bouncer as they watched Laz jaywalk across the street.

"I've seen it before," the bouncer said, and she did not ask him to elaborate. The bouncer told her to "stay safe" and returned to his post just outside the bar's entrance.

Meanwhile, she watched Laz get into his car, noting that the lucky bastard had found a prime parking spot on hard-to-park Abbot Kinney. She waited until he drove away, until she couldn't see his car anymore. Only then did she tell herself that she could stop waiting; that the time had come for her to do something else.

BETTER LATE THAN never. So thought Nina as she unlocked the door to her apartment and ushered in Rose, who seemed especially reliant on her walker today. But Rose's eyes still seemed to work just fine as she scrutinized Nina's living room with genuine interest.

"Is that my vase?" She pointed to Nina's coffee table. "It looks lovely there."

Nina nodded in the direction of the large blue vase whose shape reminded her of a harp. From the moment she had gotten off the phone with Rose four days ago to invite her over for lunch, she had spent most of her free time cleaning, organizing, and decorating her apartment. And while she hadn't fully completed the task, at least Rose's possessions no longer experienced their Diaspora as a refugee camp. At least now, the possessions lived in more permanent quarters, even though she had wound up settling many of them inside her two storage closets.

"I love the painting you gave me," she said, pointing at the Miro reproduction that now hung prominently on the wall against where she had formerly stacked all the possessions. The painting was a reproduction of the artist's 1942 *Woman, bird, stars* and she had loved it upon first sight. It was a classic Miro painting in terms of its abstract whimsicality, but one could clearly see the woman, the bird, and the stars. To Nina, it suggested a world of multiple possibilities. From the vantage point of her living room couch, she could stare at the woman with the stalk-like neck, upon which hung a heart-shaped head, and feel a sense of identification but also of space and freedom.

Rose inched over to the painting and marveled at it, as if she had never seen this particular piece of art before. "Morry loved Miro. He and I once visited the museum in Barcelona. That was a wonderful trip."

"I bet it was."

"Have you been to Barcelona?"

She shook her head. She hadn't traveled all that much since the year she spent in Israel. But maybe that would change. In the meantime, she had been thinking about going to Burning Man. She had even contacted Jon for advice but he had yet to return her call. He had only sent her a text, telling her that he got her message and would call soon.

She led the way to the kitchen, where she seated Rose at her Ikea table. She had already prepared their lunch: tuna fish sandwiches with lettuce and tomatoes on whole wheat bread and a wild rice salad with shredded cabbage, carrots, and scallions. This morning, she had also taken Rose's candlesticks out of her top kitchen drawer and placed them in the center of her kitchen table. At first she thought: overkill. But then she reconsidered. She honestly liked the way that the candlesticks occupied the space on the table, as if they had always lived there.

She served the sandwiches and salad and noticed that Rose did smile at the sight of the candlesticks as she struggled to sit upright at the table. "Did I tell you that I bought them because they reminded me of my mother?"

"They're great candlesticks." Nina took the seat across from Rose and urged her to eat. This was the first time she had heard Rose question her memory of what she had and hadn't told her and she would not be the one to point this out.

Rose smiled again. "You're very kind, dear." She took a bite of her sandwich.

They each took a few bites in silence, and Nina squelched an urge to debate her friend's assessment. *No, I'm not just being kind. It's not like I loved everything you gave me.*

She saw then how Rose's hands trembled whenever she picked up her sandwich or held the fork to scoop up some rice salad. She remembered how Spartan Rose's apartment had seemed when she saw it after their last expedition to the 99 Cent Store. The living room walls no longer had any paintings and the kitchen table had, for its lone centerpiece, an array of medications housed in dull white bottles.

Nina wiped her hands on her napkin. "I can do it. I had to think about it but I did. And I can."

Rose did not react other than a more pronounced slumping of her shoulders.

"Are you sure?" she asked in a soft voice.

Nina reached across the table and clasped Rose's hand. These last four days, she had tried her best to walk in Rose's shoes and had come to the conclusion that she wouldn't know what it was like to be ninety-three until she got there herself.

"Yes," she said. "I'm sure."

They sat like that for a few moments, not moving or speaking or even attempting eye contact. They only stayed connected through their hands and Nina learned something new: that sometimes, it was better to leave things unsaid.

Twenty-One

ROSE WOKE UP the morning of the fire, remembering her dream. It was about toast. Whole wheat toast, thoroughly buttered and lovingly smeared with strawberry jam. This was Morry's breakfast for over forty years, along with a glass of orange juice, a small bowl of raisin bran for the fiber, and a cup of instant coffee. Sometimes, Rose ate this exact same breakfast but she also liked to mix things up a bit. Eggs, for example, or oatmeal or even the occasional waffle. Such culinary possibilities, if not endless, made Rose's kitchen that much more of a complex and interesting world.

But sometimes, Rose and her husband ate the exact same breakfast in the exact same order at the exact same time. First the orange juice, then the cereal and finally, the toast with coffee. They both liked to read the newspaper at breakfast so the apartment was always silent, except for the sounds of their crunching. Sometimes, they crunched at the exact same moment and continued to do so for several subsequent seconds. And sometimes, the moment in the course of the same breakfast repeated itself to perfection.

Crunch, crunch, crunch. Silence. Crunch, crunch, crunch. Silence.

Some people had a song. Rose and Morry had their breakfast.

THE SMELL OF toast inspired Rose to lie in bed for a few moments longer than usual so she could bask in the luxurious anticipation of breakfast in bed. Had Morry ever served her breakfast in bed? Rose couldn't remember.

Rose got out of bed. She washed her face and brushed her teeth. As she rinsed off her toothbrush, she remembered: her husband did not like eating in bed, though in general, he wasn't opposed to picnics.

She got dressed and felt embarrassed. How could she forget a thing like that? She didn't realize her larger error until she finished the increasingly brief task of smoothing down her hair. Good gracious. She put the kettle on for instant coffee and asked herself a few questions. Had she actually expected her husband to materialize from the depths of her refrigerator or the stovetop flame or from the recesses of her coffee cup? Would he be dressed in gauzy fabrics and turbaned headwear, waving and winking at her from absolutely everywhere, like the genie character in that silly TV program she used to love?

Rose stood there, paralyzed in her kitchen and feeling both the expected terror and unexpected liberation. Was this all it was? So, what then? Did she not still possess the essence of her husband? What did his real-world status matter, as long as she still knew how to find him?

The smell of toast permeated every corner of Rose's kitchen. Burnt toast, to be precise, infused with the scent of roasted nuts. It was a smell that triggered memory and promoted confusion. Was it common to descend into olfactory hallucinations when losing one's mind? Rose wondered.

But then Rose proceeded to have the most brilliant thought thus far in her day: maybe she wasn't losing her mind at all. Maybe, all she had to do was look outside her window.

So, Rose looked. The sky was orange. The sight was a tremendous relief, until she remembered the suffering of others.

Rose turned off the kettle and decided to go downstairs for more information. The smell told her that the fire must be close. Having lived almost seven decades in Los Angeles, Rose knew from fires. Several dear friends over the years, in fact, had lost their homes to fire and Rose had always thanked her lucky stars she lived in Venice, where human-engineered disasters generally superseded natural ones. Back in the days when she heard gunshots right outside her apartment on a weekly basis, well-meaning friends and acquaintances from Malibu, Topanga Canyon, the Hollywood Hills, and other rugged, brush-ridden neighborhoods would wring their hands on her behalf and wonder how on earth a person could live surrounded by gang violence. It was pointless to argue with these people and so Rose had never asked them how they could live in a fire zone. Personally, she preferred Venetian crime. It was an ancestrally familiar hardship, closely related to the pogrom.

She left her apartment, taking her walker with her. At the coffee shop next door, she recognized the man behind the register as the one who always offered her free coffee. Also, he had helped her out that day with the skateboarder. When was that? Rose couldn't remember.

They said hello and Rose asked, "Where is it?"

The man pointed toward the ocean. "Malibu. You can see it from here."

Rose promised the man that she would return to make a purchase. After a few starts and stops, she walked to the end of her street and stood where it merged with the boardwalk. She looked to her right. The curving, mountainous coastline appeared the way it usually did on a clear day from this vantage point but with one exception. Billowing smoke obscured the farthermost portion of visible coastline, which normally resembled an alligator's snout or a gigantic ladyfinger cookie dipping itself into the ocean. The smoke transformed it into a funeral shroud.

Rose stared at the smoke. She thought of her husband, becoming one with the earth yet clad eternally in a white linen shroud. This made her recall something she once read about people wearing white to funerals in some countries, only she couldn't remember which countries. But then Rose remembered something else, a certain article that Morry insisted she read. *Now that's the way to do it.* Had he actually said this and when was that? Around the time he started to refuse to see his doctor?

Rose remembered that she didn't want to read the article, that she only did it so she and Morry could stop fighting. The article had something to do with elderly people living in certain Japanese villages, where it was an accepted custom to decide when enough is enough. There was something about asking their children to take them to the nearest mountain that they will ascend alone to wait out their final moments of time. They choose this because there's nothing left to do. They've already said goodbye to their children, who may or may not know that dying works differently in most other places, though there's certainly Varanasi, another destination where Morry had wanted to travel once upon a time. He had once shown her amazing photographs of this city, where people kneel on the banks of the Ganges and at the feet of the crematoriums, ready and waiting. After their trip to Israel, Morry loved to pore over photographs in his beloved *National Geographics* and scout out the alternative and parallel Jerusalems. Only Rose had preferred that they keep closer to home.

Rose released the smallest of chuckles, astounded and not astounded by this triggering of memory through spectacle. If anything, she felt relieved. Timing was everything and because of the ravaged coastline, she now knew what to do. No longer would she feel compelled to survey the medicine bottle collection arranged with care on her kitchen table with fear, longing, and resentment. The Man from Television had reappeared to take up permanent residence within the parameters of this collection and made his voice known every time the girl called to check up on her. But now that Rose knew who he was, she didn't mind his presence.

Nu Rose? What are you waiting for?

And truth be told, Rose never had a good answer. She only knew that some people could and some people couldn't.

Nu Rose? You think only the goyim do this? Didn't you see the Masada *TV mini-series in 1981? Surely you remember me, one of nine hundred Jewish zealot extras on the set? I know what you and all the other Jewish women were doing, glued to your televisions and dreaming in treif, i.e. dying to shtup the great Peter O' Toole. Maybe you missed the point about offing yourself in the spirit of principled conviction, not to mention avoiding an even more miserable death? Well bubbeleh, I'll be happy to set you straight. You're not the first Jew who believed there was a choice.*

Rose returned to the coffee shop, where she purchased a small cup of regular coffee and a blueberry Danish. She handed over $4.75 to the man at the register. "I normally don't eat such things."

The man nodded, as if he believed her and all the other women of Los Angeles who provided him with unsolicited reports on their eating habits. "It's good to live a little. But it's probably best to stay inside today. The air and all."

Rose nodded and tried to respond like a responsible person concerned for her own welfare. "Yes. Best also to keep the windows closed."

The man told her to "stay safe," which she tried to obey as she left the coffee shop. She returned to her apartment and took her time eating breakfast. As she bit into the Danish, she stopped craving toast. She savored every bite and decided to write the girl a note but not because that's what people usually did. She wanted the girl to understand her broken promise to pick up the phone when the time came.

So, Rose wrote a note. She tried to think of everything and used both sides of two pages of stationary, which she folded in half. Then she leaned it against her remaining vase in the center of the kitchen table. She simply could not part with this vase, which Morry had received from a colleague as a retirement gift. It was a white, earthenware vase from Portugal and Rose had always loved it because she could go places simply by appreciating its foreign elegance.

She spent the next hour touring through her bedroom closet, befuddled by the question of what to wear. In the end, she chose the lavender dress that she bought to celebrate her fortieth wedding anniversary. Her last purchased special occasion garment, found in the petite section of Macy's. Rose had known immediately. The dress, ninety percent silk, fit her like a glove, a sartorial rarity ever since she turned eighty. It reached midway between her knees and ankles and showed off a slight curve in her waist. The sleeves ended properly, right at the juncture of wrist bone and hand. Even the teenaged salesgirl helping her out had been impressed.

"I hope I look like you when I'm older," she had said.

Rose put on the lavender dress and looked into her full-length mirror. *I used to be a dancer.* She did her best to solicit the old and heavy sadness that afflicted her during the years she still danced for the stage but verged on retirement. This particular sadness loved to visit Rose directly after performances, when she sat in front of dressing room mirrors removing her make up. It would descend upon her reflection, adding years to her appearance. Into her ear, it screamed the future. Then it would disappear, leaving Rose to rub her blistered and aching feet alone. She had resisted this sadness as hard as she could until one day, when she felt nothing.

Rose looked at herself in the mirror for a long time. She needed to be sure, a hundred percent sure, to be precise. But the sadness did not return.

She decided to apply a moderate amount of makeup, nothing too garish or overdone. Just a little lavender eye shadow, matching lipstick, and a hint of blush. She also contemplated taking some food and water since she didn't know how long she might be waiting but decided against this. She only took some bread for feeding the birds, just in case.

What else? Rose wanted to make sure she remembered everything. To buy time, she switched on the television for an update and on channel four, a very tan man with thick blond hair and milk white teeth warned people throughout

Southern California to stay indoors. Other fires had erupted in Santa Clarita, Big Bear, northern sections of San Diego County, and even on Catalina Island.

Rose admired the man's teeth as he stood in front of a satellite map of Southern California and pointed at various, red, pin-pricked locations. Not so long ago, she would have been envious of such beautiful, large white teeth, as hers had seemed to shrink in size over the years and had long turned yellow and even, brown. Of course, Rose still had most of her teeth, which was no small accomplishment. But now, as she listened to his advisories for the very young, the very old, and all people with respiratory conditions, she simply admired the color of his teeth like she would a cloud or newly fallen snow. The prettiness merely passed through her, like images in a 3-D movie.

Rose, however, knew the weatherman told the truth. Her lungs were simply not what they used to be. To think that she used to smoke cigarettes. And what about the pneumonia she contracted just a few days past her seventy-fifth birthday? She had stayed in the hospital for three days and Morry never left her bedside. He had been the one to eventually tell her how she had hovered between life and death and how the doctors had their doubts.

Watching you in that bed, I couldn't bear the thought of you going first.

Finally, Rose felt 99.9 percent ready. The remaining percent of it, she figured, would materialize once she went outside. She proceeded to turn off the television and thank the weatherman and his beautiful teeth for the advice. She shut off all the lights, brushed a few remaining crumbs off the kitchen table, and made sure three times that the stove and oven were in the off position. She checked that no water leaked from either the kitchen or bathroom faucet. Only one loose end remained: a book—mystery, large print—due at the library in four days, so Rose decided to place it on the kitchen table next to the note, wedding photograph, and keys. She had left the girl instructions about the photograph and keys in her note but figured the library book was sufficiently self-explanatory.

For a few moments, Rose stood at her front door. Briefly, she contemplated taking one of her remaining photographs or a piece of well-worn jewelry or even the Portuguese vase, but this didn't feel right. It reminded her of customs practiced by the ancient Egyptians, Vikings, and other civilizations where people expected to be surrounded by all their worldly possessions. At the end of the day, she was a Jew. Plus, she had given most of her esteemed possessions to the girl.

She continued to stand by her front door and tried to survey the apartment as if she had never lived there. But this was impossible. She had lived there for far too long.

In the end, the telephone came to the rescue. Just as Rose grabbed her cane and opened the door, it started to ring. Rose started to laugh. Such timing! She stopped laughing when she realized she had no desire to answer it, though it was probably the girl or possibly, Richard's daughter. Who else called her these days?

She closed the door and left it unlocked. As she made her way to the elevator, she could hear the phone ringing and ringing. It rang and rang, until it didn't.

THERE'S ROSE, SITTING on her favorite bench at the end of Windward Avenue next to the police substation. She's wearing a lavender dress and has extra breadcrumbs to spare. Her cane sprawls across her lap like a substitute cat. She's easy to miss but at the same time, she stands out. This is primarily because she has the boardwalk to herself. Everyone else is at home, watching the orange sky on their computers, televisions, and even, through their windows. Plus, she's coughing and easy to hear in the intervals between the siren songs of the fire engines.

Rose watches the sunset. It's terrible that the sunset should be so beautiful, she thinks. The setting sun reminds her of one of those cheerful, bouncy beach balls, beloved by children playing in the water. It is perfectly round, fat, and a color both orange and red. It hovers very close to the ocean while the surrounding sky presents itself as fields and slashes of delightful colors: vibrant reds, deep oranges, dramatic violets. Staring into the eyes of a sky like this makes it difficult for Rose to see anything besides promise and possibility. How can such beauty rise from utter destruction? It's a question that assaults Rose with the briefest of second thoughts.

Rose? Is this really how you want to finish up? At long last, Rose hears her unfiltered self speaking to her unfiltered self. *So much for reposing on the summit of a pristine Japanese mountain, where you can just sit like you do in the synagogue until the conclusion of services.*

Rose shrugs off the second thoughts. So what if she doesn't have the luxury of a pristine Japanese mountain? A person has to work with what's available. Plus, all this had been home.

Rose starts to cough. She takes a Kleenex from her purse and holds it to her lips. She tries to make out the mountainous coastline, now thoroughly obscured by smoke and brownish haze. She stares straight ahead at the ocean, still complete in its blue-green expansive visibility. She watches ash fall like snow and how it dots her lavender dress with a decoration all its own. And finally, she returns her attention to the sunset. At least this, she thinks. Okay by her if that's all there is.

"ROSE? CAN YOU hear me?"

Rose discovers she can't open her eyes, which at first, confuses her. Is she in the midst of one of those dreams where you just sit there, helpless as a piece of furniture while terrible things happen? Or has she in fact passed over?

Rose tries as hard as she can to open her eyes. This time, she succeeds. It's dark but she sees the girl looming over her, tall as a basketball player. An even taller man in a uniform stands next to her. The man looks familiar but Rose can't place him.

"Rose?"

The girl sounds far away and fuzzy, as if they're speaking on the phone with a bad connection. Rose wants to tell the girl she's perfectly all right, that the boardwalk pavement is actually more comfortable than the bench. More room to stretch out. She opens her mouth to say exactly these things but no words come out.

"Rose? An ambulance is on its way."

Rose closes her eyes and tries to remember what she told the girl about what to say on the appointed day. Instead, she sees her husband. He's looking well, not a day over eight-five and with his white hair still relatively thick on his head. He's wearing a dark blue suit and matching tie and it's unclear as to whether he's attending a wedding or a funeral.

"I didn't mean to hit that boy," he tells her. "That part was an accident."

Rose asks Morry to swear on his grave if indeed this is true.

Morry gives her a smile both happy and sad. "There are no graves, my beautiful Rose. You'll see."

Her husband disappears as quickly as he arrived. Rose knows she must hurry. She opens her eyes and sees the girl talking to the man in the uniform. The girl notices that she has opened her eyes and kneels down to take her hand. What a warm hand. And Rose remembers their first handshake: the tropics versus Siberia.

The girl squeezes her hand. "I won't leave you alone."

Rose opens her mouth only there's no sound. She even tries screaming but no luck. She needs to tell the girl what Morry just told her. She wants her to know about the children in Japan. She hopes the girl will forgive her about the keys. She wishes she wrote more about them and other things in her note.

The girl continues to hold her hand. Into her other hand, her mother presses some photos, dated on their backsides with smeared black ink.

Until we come. Something you'll have. So you'll remember.

"Dear . . ." She knows it's her last chance to speak. It amazes her really, that she suddenly knows everything. Nobody told her that's how it would be but of course she understands why.

"Rose?"

Rose can still feel the girl squeezing her hand. What a warm hand. And then she thinks she sees something new. Is the girl wearing her coat? Rose doesn't know. The air is growing colder, despite so much fire. Or maybe it isn't. Since when does a fire bring about colder temperatures?

Rose's sister strokes her forehead. She sings to Rose in her beautiful voice.

The candlesticks I gave you. They remind me of my mother.

Rose can't ask the girl if she's wearing her coat. She can only hope.

And so, for a few seconds, Rose hopes.

Shlof zhe yidele.

Shlof.

Twenty-Two

ONE BY ONE, Nina watched the women lower themselves into the three rows of folding chairs that had been set up for the funeral service. Once seated, some of the women made small talk while others either stared at her with curiosity or stayed focused on the rabbi. As a collective, they conveyed the message: *We've been here before and no doubt we'll be here again.*

Nina smiled at the women who stared at her, feeling grateful to everyone in attendance today. How nice of them to endure the cross-town trip, this largely octogenarian/nonagenarian crowd from the boardwalk senior center and all but three of them requiring canes, walkers, or wheelchairs. Fortunately, she had been able to secure group transportation to the cemetery, thanks to the helpful senior center director, who arranged for a van and driver.

Nina waited for the last woman to take a seat before signaling to the rabbi. Rose had wanted the rabbi from the synagogue where she attended High Holiday services to conduct the funeral. *I wasn't so much the synagogue-going type,* she had written in her note, *but I do want to be buried as a Jew.*

Rose had left concise yet detailed instructions. She was to be buried next to her husband at Mount Sinai's Hollywood Hills cemetery and she didn't want a big fuss, i.e. no blinkered caravan snaking along the streets from the synagogue to the cemetery. She personally had never endorsed lifecycle events spanning multiple locations and freeways. *It should be short and simple,* she had written of her request for a brief graveside service. *Keep the driving to a minimum.*

The rabbi nodded back at Nina and stepped up to the gravesite. He thanked everyone for coming and began the service by reciting the prayer Kel Moleh Rachamim. The rabbi then spoke about Rose's life, a narrative which relied heavily on what Nina had told him on the night of the Malibu fire. Which was this: Rose danced with several local ballet companies and retired from performing in her late thirties. For many years, she operated and taught at a local dance studio. She was twice married, forty-two years to her second husband. She loved her second husband very much. She knew how to live gracefully on a fixed income. She took a trip to Israel in 1973 and visited Spain sometime in the 1980s. She loved the 99 Cent Store because it always surprised her. She was a very generous woman who always listened without judging. She always made tea for her guests using two bags per cup. To the end, she was loyal to the people she loved and tried to do what her conscience told her to do.

As the rabbi spoke, Nina tried to prepare herself. She had limited experience with eulogies and for a few seconds, she traveled back to Jeff's funeral, where she didn't say a word. She had merely sat there in the second row of synagogue pews, silent as a different rabbi listed the names of loved ones Jeff had left behind.

And now, at Rose's funeral, the rabbi gestured for her to stand. It was time for her to speak. So she stood on the grassy knoll and faced the assembled congregation. On this slight incline, she could view the cemetery landscape in its entirety: the expanse of freshly mowed grass and the planters filled with brightly colored pink, purple, and blue flowers that created a sense of demarcation between the grass and the bordering sidewalks. She could see row upon row of square, gray plaques that suggested large, rarely brushed teeth frozen somewhere between a smile and a grimace. Jeff had been buried in a cemetery near the airport that possessed a similarly homogenous, manicured perfection. *So this is what passes for tombstones these days.* She had thought this during Jeff's burial and how her storybook perception of cemeteries as wild, overgrown venues crammed with tombstones of different shapes and sizes did not resemble in the slightest the reality that unfolded in front of her.

Nina swallowed several times, trying to moisten her suddenly parched mouth. She scanned the group of women, many sitting there with their arms folded protectively over their chests. Some looked impatient and others simply seemed exhausted. She didn't recognize any of them from her visit to the senior center with the exception of the woman who worked as the cashier. The woman whose voice she could still hear in her mind was not in attendance. *Well, if you want to have children, then don't you think you better get started immediately?*

She glanced briefly at the notes that she clutched in her right hand and took the plunge. "Most of you don't know me but Rose was my friend. For months, she was the only friend I wanted to see, because we had both lost people we loved. I could talk to Rose about anything and she never judged me. She reminded me of my grandmother, probably the only person I ever knew who loved me unconditionally. When my grandmother died, I thought I would never meet someone like her again. But I was wrong.

"I didn't know Rose for most of her life. But I do know she was someone from a generation that has mostly died out. She came from Eastern Europe, a Yiddish-speaking Jew who mastered English, ballet, and how to find the best pizza slice on the Venice Boardwalk. She remained self-sufficient to the end, from taking the bus to the 99 Cent Store for groceries and to buying clothes in the beachfront stores where tourists flocked. She never stopped trying to live her life on her own terms."

Nina paused and blushed, suddenly unsure of what it was she meant to say to this group of women who looked like they had better things to do than listen to her. In her notes, she had tried to elevate the personal into something historical and sociological with observations such as: you don't really meet people like Rose anymore since the world where she came from no longer exists. Or how Rose's passing represents the end of an era and how in a few more years, you will only be able to find Rose and her generation in museum exhibits, where you can study black and white photographs and obsolete household kitchen tools used for the preparation of gefilte fish and yellowed posters from the Yiddish Theater and think to yourself, that's how they lived. Or how you might perk up when you see an actress playing an old Jewish woman on TV, but you will probably cringe hearing her overdoing it on the "oy veys" and the emasculation of her sons. And how you might say to your children watching TV with you that their great-grandmother was sort of like that, feeling slightly guilty for trafficking in such cliché but knowing you can't do any better.

Is that what these women need to hear right now?

Nina looked away from the piece of paper still tethered to her hand and refocused her gaze on the cashier. Was her name Denise? Nina wasn't sure. All she knew was that the woman had treated Rose with respect on a day when others had tormented and abandoned her. *But you didn't abandon her.* She stared at the cashier and saw that her eyes were filled with tears.

Nina closed her eyes and tried to see Rose from the beginning. But she couldn't see her this way since she had only been her friend at the end. It would have to do.

"I think Rose had a gift for understanding what others needed. When we met, I had moved into an apartment that was empty and she gave me things to fill the space, her candlesticks, jewelry, clothing, and beautiful paintings. She wanted to help me and she also hoped I would remember her. I hope she knew that I would have remembered her anyway."

Nina nodded at the rabbi. The time had come to cover the coffin with dirt and she figured that she and the rabbi would do most of the shoveling.

AFTERWARD, TWO WOMEN lingered at the gravesite to speak with her: the cashier and a woman who gripped a cane in one hand and the cashier's elbow in another. The woman took her hand off the cashier's elbow to grip Nina's hand. The woman's hand was dry and ice cold and Nina did her best not to react.

"It's so good to finally see you." The woman smiled at her. "They finally let me go outside. Regards to Morry. We haven't seen him in a while."

Nina smiled back at the woman, trying to see the person who stood in front of her. She was a tiny woman, even smaller than Rose, with matted blond hair that must have been a wig. Her smile was the kind that looked permanently plastered on, as if it was the only means for preventing her face from collapsing into a boneless heap.

And then the cashier stuck out her hand. "Denise. From the Center."

They shook hands. "Yes, of course. Thank you for coming."

"Lillian, that's not Rose. Rose has passed away. We're at her funeral." Denise put her arm around Lillian's shoulder. "This is Lillian Rabinowitz," she said to Nina. "She was very close to Rose."

"A funeral?" Lillian stopped smiling and when her face did not collapse, Nina silently cheered this small victory. But then she saw the confusion and fear in Lillian's eyes.

"It's so nice to finally meet you, Lillian. Rose always talked about you."

Lillian re-grasped Nina's hand. "Rose never told me about her daughter. You look just like her."

"Rose didn't have a daughter." She tried to break the news as gently as she could, as if this woman had staked her entire life on the opposite being true.

Denise looked at her and shook her head. "She had us. She had you."

AFTER THE FUNERAL, Nina didn't have a moment to herself until sunset. The Center women had decided to gather at Rose's apartment, feeling they should do something since Rose had no family to sit shiva for her. And thanks to Rose's landlord, who had given Nina until next week to clear out her belongings, they could sit shiva at the apartment. Nina had bought takeout from the bagel store on Main Street and covered the mirrors with old newspapers, just so Rose's home could feel the way it should.

The rabbi made a brief appearance at the apartment. He wanted to know if he should recruit someone from the synagogue to say kaddish for Rose on a daily basis during the next twelve months, since she had no family members to say it. Nina didn't know what to tell him, as Rose hadn't expressed any opinions about the kaddish in her note.

"It was important to Rose that her life be remembered," she finally said. "But she wasn't religious like that."

Carla and Jon also stopped by and took it upon themselves to eat bagels. Following Rose's instructions, Nina had called them and though both had scheduling conflicts with the funeral, they promised to pay a proper shiva call. When they arrived at the apartment, Nina immediately retrieved the wedding photo, which she pressed into Carla's hand. *So she'll remember.* This is what Rose had written.

"Your dad was really handsome," she said.

Then the three of them spent about five awkward minutes together, where Carla tried to thank her but kept tearing up and muttering "fuck" under her breath. Finally, she told Nina that Rose had met her for coffee about three weeks before she died. "We had a nice time but she still wouldn't talk about my dad. She would only say, 'he had his good points.'" As she and Carla spoke, Jon tried to communicate a wordless message that she did not understand and so he verbally promised to get in touch soon so that they could properly catch up.

Finally, several hours later, after saying goodbye to the last visitor, Nina sat at the kitchen table with Rose's note in front of her. In her left hand, she clutched the car keys that Rose had also left on the table. *I had made a terrible mistake with these keys dear and I hope that one day you will forgive me. Please do with them as you see fit. It's the last thing I'd like to leave with you just in case it helps you get on with your life. You should know dear that I'm sorry I won't be there to see it, you, getting on with your life.*

For several minutes, Nina stared hard at Rose's handwriting, the letters small, thin, and spidery yet complete and legible. Then she folded the note and picked up the keys, jangling them in her hand. They felt like any other pair of keys, the metal cool and sharp against her skin. What should she do with them?

Nina put her hands on the kitchen table and pushed herself to a standing position. She stretched her arms above her head and decided to finish packing up Rose's apartment tonight. There would be furniture to donate to the National Council of Jewish Women thrift store or to put out on the street. There were still boxes to label either for donation or recycling or trash. And then she would sweep and mop. Finally, when there was nothing left to do other than turn off the lights and leave, she would only take with her the note, the keys, and the yellow, tattered prayer book that she had found the day before, buried at the back of one of Rose's bookshelves. The discovery of the ancient siddur had surprised her and she wondered whether Rose had deliberately left it behind or simply forgot about it as she handpicked her possessions to bequeath.

From Rose's living room window, Nina watched the dull red ball of a sun disappear into the ocean. She opened the window, smelled the salt air, and listened to the sounds of the crashing surf. How lucky for Rose, that she lived so close to the ocean for so many years. Or did Rose think so? Nina closed the window, resolved to get back to work. It was impossible to know everything about another person, she thought as she headed for the bedroom to assemble more packing boxes. But you could love them anyway, or maybe, that's why you could love them.

THERE'S NINA, STANDING in front of Jeff's grave at the cemetery near the airport. She's standing under what she thinks is a willow tree because of its drooping branches but she's always been terrible at identifying vegetation. The tree however, large and majestic, provides her with plenty of shade and she feels somewhat cocooned standing under it.

Considering its proximity to LAX, the cemetery seems especially quiet. Nina can only hear the sounds of birds and the faint rumblings of lawnmowers. No doubt, gardeners are at work somewhere on the premises. If Nina has learned anything about the modern cemetery, it's that the landscaping is always exquisite.

There is a tombstone now on Jeff's grave, which means that his family already held the unveiling ceremony. *It's okay.* So Nina thinks about not receiving an invitation to this particular event, that according to Jewish tradition, must take place within a year of the person's death. After all, she had only met his parents twice during the two and a half years of their relationship. She had spent more time with his sister Frances but they had drifted from each other after the funeral. Perhaps they only invited those related to Jeff by blood or marriage. And if there was another reason for exclusion, she no longer needed to know.

Nina searches the ground for spare rocks to place on top of Jeff's grave. She finds two small white ones and after positioning them accordingly, she remains in a yogic squat pose and touches the tombstone. It feels just like the rocks she had found: hard, smooth, and absent of anything pulsating within. As long as she touches the tombstone, it's difficult for her to conjure up the living, breathing Jeff and so temporarily, she derails off the path of her chosen task. *Now you know what death feels like.*

Nina disengages from the tombstone and stands up. From her handbag, she pulls out the yellow, ancient siddur that she found in Rose's apartment. Having prepared for the occasion, she immediately locates the desired page.

Yisgadal.

I'm sorry for hurting you.

V'yiskadash.

I loved you as much as I possibly could.

Sh'mei rabbah.

I came here to honor your memory and remember what we shared while we were both alive, both the good and the bad. We were human beings making human mistakes but we tried.

Didn't we?

She recites the rest of the Mourner's Kaddish without further liturgical embellishments. When she closes the siddur, she kisses it in the way that her Bubbe Essie used to do after using a prayer book for any given duration of time. Then she stands there for a few more minutes, allowing the Hebrew words of the prayer to evaporate from her mind. Finally, in English, Nina says Jeff's name aloud, as inscribed on his tombstone, and attempts to say goodbye.

Twenty-Three

THE FIREWORKS FINALLY set The Man on fire and Nina can't take her eyes off the effigy on top of a sixty-foot obelisk engraved with flags from around the world. She's standing on the Playa with thousands of other Burners, witnessing a multi-colored display of pyrotechnics and also waiting for whatever else will happen. All week, she has interacted with art installations that riffed on this year's theme, "American Dream," with the knowledge that most of these monuments will be destroyed by the end of the festival. So now, she watches The Man burn with a developed sense of awe at the phenomenon of human beings creating purely for the sake of creation, purposefully detached from humanity's other yearnings for fame, profit, power, legacy, or even, survival.

The watching and waiting pay off: one of The Man's arms falls off and Nina screams, her voice joining with the thousands of other voices in primal acknowledgment of what this really means. Then, a few minutes later, The Man's other arm falls to the ground in a fiery heap and for a second, Nina plugs her ears to shield herself from the roar of the crowd. Then she looks at Jon, who grasps her signal: Time to wander.

Nina taps her new friend Esmeralda on the shoulder. She met Esmeralda five days ago and still doesn't know her real name, even though she knows other things, such as the fact that her new friend lost her mother about a year ago. Two years ago at Burning Man, Esmeralda had a fling with Jon, which ultimately resulted in an off-Playa friendship. Does she want to join them in their wandering at this present moment? Esmeralda flicks her dust-covered dreadlocks to the side in substitution of a nod.

She links arms with Esmeralda and Jon and they start wading through the crowd. Everywhere in Black Rock City there is drumming, singing, yelling, chanting, flames, smoke, ash, and people of all creeds and costumes. Some conduct their own private ceremonies as they march around the perimeter of The Man. Others are dancing: some with poi, hoops, torches, and other fire toys, some in interlocking groups resembling multi-limbed and rainbow-colored mythical beasts, and some gyrating on nearby art cars, those dancers lost in private meditative trances and/or consciously busting out their best moves for the benefit of anyone who cares to watch. The sounds of the drummers duel with the collective boom, boom, boom of the bass from the art cars. People hug, kiss, wrestle, tango, and move on. All around them, the lights of the Playa are blinking and traveling. Illumination is precious yet everywhere: from flashlights, bike lights, art cars, the environmentally frowned upon glow sticks, L-wire, and the many art installations scattered throughout the desert. The lights produce blobby, iridescent after-glows because of the smoke. From time to time, Nina looks down at her costume of a red wizard's robe entwined with purple L-wire and she too, shimmers with color.

For the last two days, Nina has possessed an unusually acute sensitivity toward color. Jon thinks it's the residual effects of the mushroom-laced chocolate they had consumed and perhaps he's right. But she has never before felt so inspired by the flashes of color that she has witnessed in this desert, especially at night. In the early hours of the morning, when she finally closes her eyes in her snug one-person tent, pixilated dots of reds, greens, pinks, blues, and purples swarm then swim across her consciousness, gradually forming recognizable images of towers, flowers, and faces. Sometimes, the faces are ugly and distorted but this only reminds Nina of how she felt after consuming the chocolate; how she felt less afraid of all the things, both inside and outside herself, that have always frightened her.

Nina briefly locks eyes with Jon as they wade through the crowd. He had finally called her several days after she had finished settling Rose's affairs with news of his own. He and Carla were "taking a break" and he was moving into his own apartment. As for Burning Man, he would be joining a camp on the other side of the city from where Carla would be. At Carla's camp, there was a human car wash. At his new camp, visitors would get to sample various "American Dream" cocktails that came with "American Dream" fortunes. The camp needed help with writing more fortunes. Did Nina want to participate? She could also teach yoga, if she wanted.

She only had to think about it for a few seconds before telling Jon she would commence the search for a cat sitter ASAP. Jon had immediately texted her a packing list, which precipitated a flurry of activity. She arranged for her friend Allison to feed the now domesticated Garfield and his still feral brethren and for subs to teach her classes. She also made multiple shopping trips to buy goggles, baby wipes, a tent, a headlamp, and costumes. During this period of preparation, she received a "that's so cool you're going" from Serena, and a phone call from Carla which got straight to the point. "Not that you need it but I wanted you to know that you still have my blessing."

He's a good guy. This, Nina thinks as she continues to lock eyes with Jon. For now, that's all she needs to know.

And then Jon screams, "Are you having a good burn?"

Nina gives Jon a thumbs-up. Earlier, people in her camp and complete strangers had wished her "a good burn" and she couldn't put her finger on why the exchange felt so familiar. But now, she could. This was just like Yom Kippur, where people wished each other an "easy fast." On the other hand, this was absolutely nothing like Yom Kippur.

She looks away from Jon, distracted by the oncoming sight: a cluster of five drummers creating their own special groove; a man on stilts in a pink tuxedo and top hat wielding a horse's whip; and a woman wearing the bottom half of a gorilla suit with a purple sequined harem-style tank top and a bright green pirate's hat. They follow the man and the woman to an art car constructed like a covered wagon, where women in corsets and hoopskirts dispense fluorescent pink and orange cocktails from large wooden buckets. The stilt-man and the gorilla woman immediately start to dance.

"Wait," Jon says. "Let's dance with them."

They do. For a few minutes, Nina connects completely with the DJ's musical choices. She appreciates how this DJ is mixing standard techno beats with Middle Eastern and Balkan melodies and she can feel the fluidity of her dancing body. She'll never need drugs to dance, she thinks of her decision to remain sober on her last night at Burning Man.

After a few minutes, Nina retreats to the outer circle of the dancing group and watches her friends in mid-roll, their MDMA-drenched brains guiding them to stay lost in the music. It's suddenly clear to her that she doesn't need to attend the temple burn ceremony tomorrow. Jon had left the decision up to her. If they left at sunrise, they had a much better chance of avoiding the leaving-Burning-Man-bottleneck and getting stuck in a six-hour traffic jam just to get out of Black Rock City. On the other hand, the temple burn was a powerful event, something perhaps not to be missed by a first-time Burner.

Yesterday, Nina had visited the temple, created out of recycled trash and in homage to Gaudí's Sagrada Familia in Barcelona. *Have you been to Barcelona? No Rose, I haven't. But I've now been to Burning Man to see this and I don't know, it's different than, let's say, visiting the Eiffel Tower in Las Vegas.* She had walked both the perimeter and the interior of the temple, stopping to read the notes that people had inscribed on the structure itself or tacked onto a post or railing. The notes reminded her of the Western Wall, as did the temple's general atmosphere, where people sat silently to meditate or grieve or remember.

In the end, she had climbed a steep and narrow staircase and left the keys on the temple's second-floor balcony. Then, she leaned against the railing of the structure, bowed her head, and allowed herself to feel both the collective grief emanating from her fellow temple-goers and the kind that still lived inside her. Would it always be there, residing deep within yet forever tender to the touch, especially when visiting a holy place? Or would it one day become nothing more than a kind of abstract, educational memory that she would then try to impart to her own children? *Learn from my mistakes.*

That is, if she decided to have children.

At least now, she could sometimes contemplate the subject without a racing heart or the burning sensation of shame. She could close her eyes and see Rose and thank her for helping her feel less afraid.

Afterward, she had ridden her bike to Center Camp to buy coffee and she thought she saw him. He looked familiar, this man who stood at the front of the coffee line, shirtless and wearing gauzy, sea-green, Thai-style pants with a turban in matching fabric. She couldn't see his face but certainly, she could remedy that by stepping out of the line to investigate.

She had wondered if he would go, the way he always talked about it. He had a group of ex-Orthodox Jewish friends who formed a camp here and considered the festival a must-experience destination in their series of pilgrimages to re-fortify the selves that made them leave the fold in the first place. She could easily picture him here, having the time of his life. And she could still picture herself dancing with him, at least until the high wore off.

She watched the man ascend to the very front of the line to buy his coffee, one of two items sold for money at Burning Man—the other being ice. And then she averted her eyes. It didn't matter who that man was or wasn't. He would buy his coffee and eventually exit Center Camp for some other destination. And she would do the same.

"Come back." Jon stands next to her, grinning and pointing to the center of the dancing crowd, where Esmeralda performs a series of hip gyrations while on her knees.

"I will."

She looks at Jon and he looks at her. Their faces are so close, almost within kissing distance. Nina thinks how easy it would be to move just a little closer. Only she doesn't and neither does he. She's certain now, that it's time for her to return to what Burning Man calls the default world because after all, that's where she lives. She can feel it, this gentle yet insistent fluttering in her stomach at the prospect of the journey home.

"Actually, I think I might go on a walk. I'll see you guys back at camp at some point. Oh, and we can leave at sunrise."

Jon stares at her for another second and then nods. She clasps his hand and squeezes it and he squeezes back. Then, he retreats back into the sea of dancers.

Nina starts walking, marveling at the crowds of people she passes, both elaborately costumed and stripped down to their essential selves. Five days later and it still fills her with wonder, this place where people exhibit art and give each other gifts and play drums and dance all day and fall in love. In this place, she doesn't need to ask herself what is love. She only has to look to her left and to her right and the question dissolves.

Acknowledgements

I am indebted to Barbara Myerhoff's landmark 1978 ethnography *Number Our Days*. I read this book shortly after moving to Venice, California in 2005 and it provided the initial inspiration for this novel. It's worth noting that some of the characters in Myerhoff's book reminded me of my beloved, Yiddish-speaking grandparents Hyman and Minnie Katz, who told me stories of the world they came from and tried to keep alive the memories and heirlooms that mattered most to them. Thank you also to my uncle Manny Katz, who moved to Venice in the early 1970s, and my aunt Cheri Katz, both of whom I credit for instilling me with a lifelong fascination for our neighborhood.

I am enormously grateful to C.A. Casey, Liz Gibson, and the entire staff of Bedazzled Ink for making the hard work of publication possible. I want to thank Michelle Caplan and Molly Zakoor for reading earlier drafts of this novel and providing invaluable editorial feedback, and to Sharon Goldman and Julie Gruenbaum Fax for trading writing with me over the years and offering essential creative and emotional support. I also don't think I could have written about a yoga teacher had I not studied with a variety of amazing practitioners for almost twenty years and particularly want to thank Tracy Krosnoff for all the conversations we used to have about the yoga world.

I want to give a shout-out to Bam Bam, a feral orange tabby turned house cat extraordinaire and my top feline muse. And to Igor and Marina Fineman, for all the discussions and connections to people and experiences that have undoubtedly sparked my creative process. Finally, I must thank my husband Mitch Duitz for absolutely everything.

Susan Josephs is a Los Angeles-based writer with a background in theater, dance, and journalism. She spent eight years writing about dance for the *Los Angeles Times* and her articles, essays, and short fiction have appeared in over a dozen publications including *Salon, LA Weekly, Lilith, The Forward*, and *ARTnews*. As a playwright, she has written five plays that have either received full productions or staged readings in New York and Los Angeles. Susan has collaborated with choreographers and performance artists as a dramaturge and spent eight years working as a domestic violence crisis counselor/advocate. She recently received a master's degree in counseling psychology at California State University, Long Beach and looks forward to writing more fiction.

Visit Susan's website at https://www.susanjosephs.com.